catchpenny
by sarah wathen

Catchpenny

ISBN-13: 978-1-942938-11-8

Cover art by Sarah Wathen
Edited by Racquel Henry
Interior design by Sarah Wathen

www.sarahwathen.com

Give feedback on the book at:
layercakeproductionsllc@gmail.com

Twitter: @SWathen_Author

First Edition
Printed in the U.S.A

catchpenny

sarah wathen

For Maxine.

part one:
wicked lover

chapter one

I stepped off the school bus, my brain still foggy and my eyes still sleepy. But when I saw the janitor re-painting my locker again, my early morning funk was slapped right off my face. Someone must have used spray paint that time, or maybe a permanent marker—not so easily cleaned as lipstick or a simple splatter of oozing garbage. My eyes scanned the lockers on either side, all faded and chipped orange paint, while mine was a bright beacon of fresh lacquer. I wondered what graffiti Henry had seen that morning on his 5 a.m. arrival to campus. Maybe just a word: "slut." Maybe something more creative, like the enormous penis, complete with pubic hair and a little squirt coming from the tip, that had been drawn on my locker door a few weeks ago. Luckily, most sharpie-wielding dipshits at my high school weren't so clever. Clever was remembered better.

It looked like Henry was almost finished covering whatever new allusion to my reputation had been left for me to find. I didn't need to guess whether or not anyone else saw the graffiti before it had been painted over—darting eyes and stifled giggles nearby told me they had. Thankful that I already had the book I needed, I changed direction, and headed for my first period class instead of my locker.

How did people even get into the school at night? I walked to class with my gaze focused straight ahead and my face expressionless. Who had I newly pissed off—and how? Whose boyfriend had been caught with his eyes glued to my ass as I passed? Or, maybe a jealous underclassman brat hadn't developed quite as well as me yet? I had been the first girl to grow breasts in grade school, years ago, and it hadn't escaped anyone's notice, no matter how baggy the shirt I wore was. Those babies just kept growing over the years, while the rest of me stretched out tall and lean. Most guys can't help but stare, and most girls hate me for it.

But I don't wear baggy shirts anymore. I pushed my shoulders back and straightened my spine, the shock and embarrassment of morning graffiti already wearing off. It never took long to remember who I was, and shrug off the ridicule of who people thought I was. Who they needed me to be. I readjusted my backpack and fluffed my hair. Screw them.

A pair of eyes locked onto mine. Tristan Jameson, Andrew Jackson's star quarterback, was walking down the hallway in my direction, staring at me. He was holding the strap of his backpack over one shoulder, the other hand in the pocket of his jeans, strolling. A half-smile played on his lips.

"Hi," he said in a low voice as he passed, so close we almost bumped shoulders.

"Hi." I glanced behind. He was looking back at me.

"Watch it!"

"Oh, sorry." I stopped short just before slamming into the oncoming student traffic. Several girls were walking together; a wall of bodies, chatting and laughing. I shot my elbows in front of me for protection, and accidentally toppled the books from one of the girl's hands.

"Why don't you look where you're going?" She stooped down to gather her things, tugging the hem of her miniskirt down and muttering under her breath.

"Here. Sorry." She snatched the book I held out for her and pushed past me with a scowl, running to catch up with the herd.

"Why don't you get a backpack?" I mumbled, watching her bustle away in the direction Tristan had been headed. He was already gone.

♠

I sat on my favorite table in the outdoor courtyard, my feet propped on the back of a conjoined concrete bench. The yard was all brick and concrete, a square space open to the sky where four school buildings met and a lone tree sprang up from a hole in the center. The tables were mostly empty, with only a few guys loitering by the doors to the cafeteria. The cafeteria was where the bulk of the student body preferred to eat. I prefer solitude. I leaned back on my hands and closed my eyes, knowing that extending my tan was hopeless so late in the season. I let the sun warm my shoulders and face, soaking it in with greed. It was the last of the summer heat, the days already shortening and the shadows lengthening into autumn.

A burst of laughter erupted nearby as a group of girls swarmed around one of the empty tables, flinging their purses and book bags on top, and my moment of peace vanished. I opened up Tolstoy's *Anna Karenina*, the pages blue after letting my closed eyes bake in the sun. I had been slogging through the book for days, and I thought once again about seeing the movie before I finished. I hate that seeing a movie changes the way a character looks in my mind, but I detest how much a movie stinks after I've already read the book. I thumbed a few pages forward to see where the chapter ended, not really in the mood for reading, but always more comfortable to have a book in hand at lunchtime.

"Meg?"

He was standing just behind me, his head cocked to one side, looking over my shoulder at the Tolstoy. I gasped—I couldn't help it.

"Hi, I'm Tristan."

He was squinting into the sun, and it was hard to tell if he was smiling or frowning.

"Yeah, I know who you are."

He shaded his eyes and laughed. Didn't everyone know who he was? He was on the billboard in front of the football field, for god's sake, his arm cocked back to throw a winning pass. *Go Bobcatts!*

"What are you reading?" His voice was soft and curious, with the hint of a Southern drawl that you didn't hear in my neighborhood. High-class molasses. He squinted to read the pages I held open in my lap.

"Uh…" I faltered. The sun shone through his light irises like glass, shocking against his dark hair. His black polo shirt was gathered loosely around one hip, the hand in his pocket pushing it up casually over the waistband of his jeans. A slice of flesh was made visible. He stood in perfect contrapposto, bookbag slung over his shoulder like Michelangelo's David holding the slingshot. I closed my book and tossed it onto the table, pretending not to notice how his jeans hung, low and delicious on slender hips. "Just something for English Lit."

"Man, that's a fat book. We never have to read stuff like that in my class."

"Aren't you a senior, too?"

"Yeah. What English class are *you* in?"

"AP," I shrugged.

"AP. What's that mean?"

"Advanced Placement."

He furrowed his brow.

"Based on college reading lists." I held up my "fat" book in illustration. "You take a test at the end and get college credits, depending on how well you do."

"Oh, wow."

I could tell he was surprised I had a brain. Most guys were. I wasn't sure what to say next, so I held his gaze, challenging him to ask me more about books.

"How can you read out here? It's so bright."

Because I'd rather read a book than sit alone with no one talking to me. "I heard that people with light eyes have a harder time adjusting to bright light."

"Really?"

He stepped closer to me, shifting his weight and putting his back to the sunlight. The color of his eyes reminded me of Halls Mentho-Lyptus cough drops after I'd sucked on one for a while and the zing got too strong to keep it in my mouth—icy blue and transparent.

"I don't want to bother you or anything," he said, dropping his voice lower, since we were face to face then. He smelled like soap and clean laundry, with something gritty underneath. Something undeniably male.

"No, I—" I cleared my throat. He was even better looking up close. "I'm not busy."

He glanced back over his shoulder and the group of girls who had been watching suddenly picked up their conversation again, all of them talking at once and fumbling with their lunches. I was waiting with as much anticipation as they had been—why on earth was he talking to me?

"I'll let you get back to your book, but I just wanted to ask you something."

"Sure. What's up?" *Those eyes.*

"Would you be my date for Homecoming this weekend?"

"Cough drop—" I spluttered.

"Huh?"

I slapped my chest and choked out a cough. "I mean…uh, the dance?"

"Yeah, the dance."

"In five days?" It was Tuesday and the dance was Saturday. I hadn't planned on going, for many reasons.

"Four. Depending on how you count it," he said, a blinding smile spreading across his face. "Today's halfway through."

"I guess it is."

"And Saturday would only be a half-day, since the dance is that night." He was daring me to accept the challenge. I could never refuse a dare, especially one with such an irresistible smile attached.

"Wait. Don't you have a girlfriend?" I wasn't exactly buddies with anyone in the popular crowd at Andrew Jackson, nowhere close. But everyone knew that the star quarterback and the head cheerleader had been together since freshman year. Sugary sweet.

"No. I don't have a girlfriend." That smile again, but with an undercurrent in his voice.

The neighboring table had gone silent once more, the bombshell news of Tristan's single status freezing them all mid-prattle.

"Absolutely." I grinned over his shoulder—a present for our shocked audience.

"Absolutely, you'll go with me?"

Did he really think I would say no? The curiosity itself was enough for me to agree.

"Sure. Why not?" I shrugged, like it was nothing to me. Yeah, right.

"Great. Okay, lemme just get your number..." He handed me his phone and I punched my number in, wondering what kind of psychedelic rabbit hole I had accidentally wandered through. Had somebody drugged my orange juice that morning? He took his phone back and saved, whispering, "Meg...Shannon," as he typed. "I'll call you, so you'll have mine."

"I don't have a cellphone. That's the number at my house."

"Oh."

I felt my cheeks getting hot, and nothing to do with the sun. Was I the only person at school without a cellphone or something?

"Okay. Well, I'll see you around, then?"

"Yeah, see ya." I resisted the urge to bite down on my knuckles.

He winked at me and waved over his shoulder as he turned back to the courtyard entrance. His jeans looked even nicer from behind, snug around his well-shaped glutes and muscular thighs. "Bye, Meg."

"Bye."

I picked my book up again, refusing to gaze at his retreating form in concert with the other females. A wink, though. What did that mean? Maybe it was just the bright light on his Mentho-Lyptus eyes. I opened *Anna Karenina* again and pretended to concentrate for the rest of lunch. But I couldn't read another word.

chapter two

I checked the clock as I rushed through the bedroom. Shit, it was already 5:45. I picked up dirty underwear and odd socks with my toes, transferring them to my hands like a monkey, before flinging them into the laundry hamper. If I let stuff lay around for more than a few hours, my tiny, overpopulated home was likely to explode into chaos that was hard to recover from. And I planned to be gone for a while that night.

I wondered if Tristan was a punctual kind of guy, and how much longer I had to obsess over household chores. My stomach was in knots; he said he'd pick me up at 6:00, though the dance didn't start until 7:00 and my place was only a few minutes from campus. That was worrisome. Either he wanted to arrive early to the dance (while I definitely preferred to show up late and leave early for most social functions) or he had a pre-dance plan. He also told me not to eat dinner, but the only restaurant in town was Big Joe's, and I hoped to god he wasn't planning to take me there in a Homecoming dress.

I paused in my frantic tidying to picture the scene: Big Joe's is your classic mountain log-cabin, Southern-country-grub-with-all-the-fixin's kind of place, and I was good friends with several people who worked in the kitchens. They had known me in cutoffs and tank tops, with dirty feet and unwashed hair, for most of my life, just like extended family. If Tristan brought me there, they would take one look at me and laugh their asses off, then ask where the real Meg Shannon was hiding. But, Big Joe's was the likeliest candidate for a pre-dance dinner date—hell, the only candidate. And anyone else Homecoming-bound, who wanted to eat out, would be there, too. Gross.

"Meg! Piper said I can only have two fish sticks and I need three," my youngest sister, Tessa, yelled from another room.

I threw down a broken toy truck totally unconcerned anymore whether filth attracted more filth. Let someone trip over it. I stomped past the living room and glared at Piper in our cramped, galley-style kitchen.

"You guys made *fish sticks?*" My nose crinkled at the rising aroma. I imagined microscopic fishy particles, detaching from the fried finger food and wafting through the air, clinging to my hair and skin. "Great. Now it's gonna smell like fish when he shows up, Piper."

She shrugged, but her shoulders were tense. She banged another tin tray into the oven. "That's all we had. You need to go grocery shopping."

"I will on mom's next payday. Just make a buttload of french fries."

"What do you think I'm doing?" she said, then in an undertone, "Thank you very much, Piper."

I wanted to strangle her, but repeated, "Thank you very much, Piper. I really appreciate you taking over today. You're amazing."

My lips pursed in forced gratitude. Like I hadn't done my share of baby-sitting, ever since I was practically a baby myself. But, I needed Piper's compliance that night, and why not let her soak up the accolades for once? I had spent most of the day in Tenakho Falls at Cassie's salon, getting the freebie cousin special. As soon as I got home I had to shower—hair pinned up, careful not to ruin my painstakingly made-up face and fresh manicure—and change into my dress. I was about to take off for the whole night and Piper would have to corral the beasts without my help. Or mom's help, of course. She was working a double shift again. Of course.

"Well. You look awesome," Piper offered, softening just a little. Her cheeks were still flushed from the heat of the kitchen and the irritation of whining siblings, but she returned my smile. I was proud of her for restraining her jealousy; Piper loved to dress up and she would have killed to go to the dance, but no one had asked her and she wasn't the type to go stag. "I can't believe Cassie got your hair to do that."

She motioned to my ringlet curls, as shocked as I was by how well my hair was behaving. I had earned the nickname "Afro" at a young age because of my normally bushy, unruly mane. I usually just tried to keep it out of my face in a ponytail, or tamed into a thick braid, but Cassie works miracles. Smooth locks cascaded over my shoulders in artful spirals. When I left the salon, she shoved two bottles into my hands—a "curl enhancer" and a "frizz eliminator"—and made me promise to use them every day. Like I wanted my hair to be a big poof ball? Of course I would use the stuff, now that I knew what it could do. The right haircut helped, too. Thank god for generous, salon-owning cousins.

A soft knock.

"Oh no." I looked towards the front door, anxious and elated. "He's early."

"Why are you wringing your hands? You look ready," said Piper.

"I am."

"Don't worry, I got this. Get outta here."

"Thanks." I swooped in for a hug, suddenly overcome with affection for my sister. She did have it, I could trust her. Piper squeezed into the embrace and I shoved away. "Don't get all mushy on me. Cassie will kill me if I wreck her make-up job."

Piper wiped a tear and I almost killed her. I gave her a warning look, before twirling away in the other direction to retrieve my purse from the bathroom.

"Well, you're graduating soon. I'll miss you, is all," she called after me.

I had almost a whole year before I graduated, and for me it seemed like an eternity. I stuffed my lipstick and compact into the glittery handbag and hurried back through the house. My little brother scurried underfoot and I nearly went sprawling. "Charlie, watch out."

"Meg, wait."

"What? I'm in a hurry, sweetie." I heard the whine in my tone with a measure of shame. I hate whiners.

"I just wanted to tell you that you look like a princess."

Seeing his honest, innocent face, I stopped in my tracks and squatted down so that my face was on his level. "Thank you, Charlie Brown. Piper, what kind of princess movies have you been showing him?"

My sister walked into the living room with a knowing smile, wiping her hands on a kitchen towel. "The Great Gatsby. He thinks all the pretty ladies at the big parties are princesses."

I snorted in surprise, nearly blowing snot from my nose at the irony. I was even further away from being a chick in the Great Gatsby than I was from being a princess. "Those are just rich people, Brownie." I ruffled his hair as I stood up and swooshed my arms in front of me in an everybody-out-of-my-way gesture.

"I love you, Meg," said my littlest sister, Tessa, appearing waist-side.

But I didn't have time for any more touchy-feelies. I nodded and held my finger to my lips as I neared the front door.

Tessa whispered, "I know. We're not here."

I mouthed, "Good girl," then I cracked open the door, slipped out, and shut it behind me in an instant, hoping to leave the fishy smell behind.

"Hello, Tristan."

He was facing away from the door with his hands locked behind his back, one of them holding a plastic box. I tried to get a look at what was inside it, but he turned around when he heard my voice, in a tailored black tuxedo with a dark red vest and tie. His eyebrows shot up over those bright blue eyes when he saw me, and he scanned me from head to toe.

He chuckled softly, but said nothing.

I put a hand on my hip and let him take it all in; I knew I looked hot and I was never shy about that kind of attention. My brother was actually closer than I gave him credit for when he compared me to a Gatsby girl. I had acquired a smashing hand-me-down from my cousin, Debra; a blood-red, slinky flapper dress from the 1920's. I wasn't an expert on antique apparel, but it looked authentic to me and had obviously been handed down a dozen times. Judging by the amount of original fabric it had left, the dress also been altered almost as often, but it was nothing I couldn't handle touching up again. I started sewing as soon as I was old enough to be embarrassed by my shabby thrift store wardrobe. My clothes may be old and used, but I know how to freshen something up so it fits like a glove. The flapper dress was a pretty tight glove, I knew. I'm taller and bustier than Debra, and so the finished effect of my most recent alterations made a shorter, more revealing shift than most flapper girls would have been comfortable wearing.

Tristan still hadn't said anything.

Okay, so my tits were kinda pouring out, I had to confess, following his eyes with a smirk. Oh well, I like mesmerizing guys. Especially guys that looked like Tristan Jameson.

"You look…" he started.

"Don't act so surprised or you might start to hurt my feelings." My feelings were in no danger of being hurt; I had figured out soon enough why he asked me to the dance. It wasn't hard to catch snippets of gossip in a small town, especially when people purposely talked loud enough for me to hear. In the few days I had to prepare for the dance—in a frenzy of sewing and calling in favors from family members—I also had ample opportunity to prepare for my supposed role. Word in the halls and bathroom stalls: the quarterback was dying to get laid and his girlfriend wasn't putting out. But, I was already used to the "Meg Shannon's a sure thing," rumors.

"I'm sorry." He snapped out of his momentary daze. "Beautiful just didn't seem to be a good enough word."

"Oh. Er…"

He just kept staring at me.

"Stunning?" I offered.

"Well, yeah. I guess that's better," he admitted, regaining composure and flashing me a smile. "You are stunning."

"Thanks." My laugh sounded tinny and thin.

"Don't thank *me*." He stepped through the comfort zone, close enough that our noses could've touched if I leaned in, and so suddenly intimate that

I felt my cheeks grow hot. I hadn't noticed how white his teeth were—they almost rivaled the brightness of his eyes. It was my turn to feel stunned as he curled one of my ringlets around his finger.

Oh…

A grin split his face, inches from mine, my discomposure obvious. He was showing me up. I guess I had sort of baited him. He ran a knuckle over my beaded antique headband (which Cassie insisted completed the Roaring '20's look), then leaned in and gave me a soft peck on the forehead.

"Lovely would work, too," he whispered.

I narrowed my eyes. He knew how gorgeous he was and he knew what he did to girls, without a doubt. I felt like an idiot and out of my league, suddenly unsure of whether I was up to the challenge after all.

"So." He straightened up and glanced over my shoulder at the front door, and I knew that the polite move would be to invite him inside.

I wasn't going to do that, etiquette be damned. "So?"

"Doesn't your mom want to take pictures, Meg?"

Pictures.

I hadn't thought about pictures. Was he serious? Would his mom be expecting to share snapshots with my mom? The thought was ludicrous. My mother wasn't into stuff like that, especially with the likes of Stephanie Jameson, PTA president and Bobcatt enthusiast.

"She's at work."

"Oh. Where does she work?" A polite question.

"The hotel."

"By the interstate? What does she do there?" He cocked his head to the side, as if he really wanted to know.

"She's a maid," I said flatly. Were we done with polite, yet? I let the uncomfortable moment linger.

His eyes darted to my shoulder. "Is that chocolate?"

"Huh?" His hand shot up to wipe a brown smear from my skin with one finger. I felt the blood drain from my face, mortified. "Damn it, Charlie. I'm sorry, let me get you something to clean that off with…"

"Forget it." He popped his finger into his mouth. "Hazelnut."

I stared at him, remembering my brother's grubby, chocolate-coated fingers. Did he have any idea where those fingers roam all day long? "That doesn't gross you out?"

He shrugged, "I have a little sister who loves chocolate, too."

"Oh." It was kind of disgusting, but I loved it. That was the last thing I would have expected from a guy like Tristan. But really, I had no idea what he was like at all. Intriguing.

"This is for you," he said, unaware of the impression his humble chocolate scavenging had made. He opened the little plastic box; it held a corsage of deep red roses. "I don't think I can pin it anywhere…"

"Um, yeah it's…enormous."

We both laughed, as he made a show of searching for a wide enough stretch of fabric on the bust-line of my dress, ducking low to inspect all sides and shaking his head, helpless. The corsage was huge, the fabric of my dress tiny. I took the roses and placed them right on top of my breasts, which were high enough in a push-up bra to be a nice table for them. "Are you trying to cover me up?"

"That would be a crime." He stepped back and appraised me in illustration. "Although I think maybe my mom had that in mind, now that I see it on you."

"Maybe…" I left out the obvious. His mom probably hadn't been happy that her golden boy was taking me to the dance, rather than his reportedly prim and proper ex-girlfriend. The rumors had probably reached Mom, and she may have suspected I'd wear something skimpy. I *had,* so I couldn't really take offense to that. More likely, though, she thought I'd need some dressing up. Now that was offensive.

"My mom, jeez. She's a little too into this stuff."

"I'll show her."

I pulled one of the buds from its nest of greenery and baby's breath and snapped my teeth around the stem, determined to make a joke of it. I did my best at a bobcat growl.

"Or, we can prune it down a little, and there'd still be plenty left," I said.

Another rose went into the band at my temple.

"Don't mess up your hair." His brows knitted and his smile gone, he took the rose from my headband, then smoothed my locks back into place.

We got quiet.

My eyes found his boutonniere, already inserted into his lapel expertly. So, his mother had supplied *his* roses, too. How was she such a part of our date when she wasn't even there? I wasn't sure whether to feel creeped out or thankful.

"I forgot to get you a boutonniere anyway." I motioned to his immaculate tux, aware that I hadn't yet complimented him. "You look very nice, by the way."

"Thank you."

He ran fingers through his dark hair, almost as black as his jacket, then flashed me the famous billboard smile. That reminded me how far he was out of my league, and I told the butterflies in my stomach to calm down. *Do not fall for the god damn star quarterback, you idiot insects.*

"And look," he said, taking the corsage from me and bringing my hand to his lips in one fluid motion. He slipped the flowers over my hand and stroked the inside of my wrist with his thumb.

"Oh." I looked down at our intertwined hands. "A bracelet band. How ingenious." At least he knew what to do—knew it like he'd read the manual. The whole corsage thing was foreign to me, but of course he'd given out more than a few.

He half-turned and offered me his elbow, "Shall we?"

A loud wail sounded from inside, followed by a sharp smack, and then Piper's muffled warning. The "we're not here" charade had met its end. I put my flower-free hand in his arm and urged him away from the front door before anything more embarrassing happened. "Definitely. Let's go."

chapter three

As soon as we rounded the corner of the Shannon Family trailer, a stretch limousine came into view. I marveled at the juxtaposition.

"Nice ride."

"Just borrowing it," he said with a wink.

There was that wink again. What did it mean and why did I feel it in my thighs?

A shirtless old man sat on his stoop next door, glaring at us, with a lit cigarette dangling from his lips. I waved. His pit bull growled next to him on a chain. I tried to seem nonchalant and keep my stiletto heels from plunging into the dirt. A hulking driver stood by the limo like a bodyguard, and he opened the door as we approached.

"Barney, I told you I wanted to do that," Tristan said under his breath, as the big man bent a little at the waist in my direction.

I was impressed that this Barney was professional enough to keep his eyes off my chest, but I noticed the stifled humor at the corners of his mouth. Tristan sighed, irritated, and then softened his expression for me as he held out his hand to help me into the cab.

The inside was cool when I stepped in. It was spacious, all cream-colored leather and chrome, with couch-style seats lining most of the walls under heavily tinted, panoramic windows. The open central area was carpeted in luxurious charcoal gray, with a small sideboard across from the door that looked like it served as a bar and storage cabinet. There was a remote control on the table, and music playing quietly in surround speakers. Country music. I'd have to fix that; there's nothing grosser, musically speaking. Living in a small Appalachian town where it was ubiquitous was tough on the ears. I flopped down on the comfy leather seat next to the sideboard and was messing with the remote before Tristan closed the doors.

"Satellite radio, awesome." It was a rare luxury for me. Cassie had one at the salon, but she wouldn't let me tamper with it during shop-open hours. She kept it on some kind of pop hits station to please the average customer until the doors were locked. Forgetting my gorgeous date for a second, I flipped through dozens of stations. Lots looked interesting but inappropriate. Alternative Rock? A country music boy probably wouldn't like that. A comedy station wasn't the right fit. Howard Stern, no. NPR, nope. "Ah, this is good."

Vivaldi tinkled through the cabin and I smiled to myself about my brother's earlier princess remark. Princesses probably listened to Celtic Lutes or Gregorian monks chanting in the fairy tales, but Vivaldi set the scene just fine.

Tristan was dubious. "Classical?"

"Classical is better for the occasion, don't you think?" I motioned to our wardrobes and our lush surroundings, then waved my hand in front of me as if I was holding an imaginary lace handkerchief or some other dainty nonsense. He caught my mocking fingers and pressed his lips to the top of my hand. Soft and warm. I had been wondering how those full lips would feel, but I didn't think I'd find out so quickly. I batted my eyelids like it was a joke. Except it wasn't.

"Whatever you like," he said, settling onto the seat next to me. "You seriously like this stuff, though?"

"Hell yeah. You can check out tons of classical CD's at the library, and they never have any scratches since no one ever listens to them. Plus, Mozart's good for studying."

He cocked his head. "Is it?"

"The best."

The two hours I get every school night to study goes much more smoothly if I can block out all the household melodrama with noise-canceling headphones—which I also borrow from the library. My mom never even graduated from high school, and she says she wants more for her oldest daughter. She knows she can't really give me much but a rigorous work ethic. But, hey work ethic is great for studying. She insists that my chance in life lay in my intellect and she's always strictly enforced study time. That rule works fine for me, since I've been saddled with mothering four younger siblings since before Kindergarten. It's the only chance I get to be blissfully unencumbered at home.

"Oh, speak of the devil—this one's Mozart," I said, as the next tune swelled into *Symphony 35*.

"Why is Mozart good for studying?"

"Helps you concentrate." I closed my eyes to illustrate. After the song was half-over, I opened my eyes and saw him watching me. "What?"

"You look…peaceful."

"Do I?" Funny. Peaceful wasn't how I felt at that moment at all.

"I think I like Mozart now, too."

I closed my eyes again and smiled inside. He was admiring me. I could almost feel his gaze. The violins rose and fell, trilling and swooping. Soaring. I tried to keep my breathing as steady as the deep cello base notes, but my pulse quickened with the crescendo, knowing he was watching me. I could hear Tristan's hushed breathing next to me, and I felt him sink further into the cushions, his shoulder rubbing against mine.

"Does it work?" he asked, once the symphony came to a close.

"Work?" I had been trying not to think; trying to sit there and look pretty, and not think about how much I liked him watching me like that.

"For studying."

"Seems to work for me." I sat up, feeling a little…dreamy. Guys never ask me about my grades. What should I say? "My grades are pretty good, I guess." I was almost straight-A.

He groaned. "Mine aren't."

"I can help you with your homework, if you want," I smirked.

"Really?"

"Oh yeah, I have some pretty good study techniques I can share with you." It was hard to hold in my laughter. The irony of him being my study buddy was too much.

"Thanks," he said, frowning.

He wasn't getting the joke. "And S.A.T.'s are coming up. I already took it for practice last year, so I can give you a few tips."

"I haven't even thought about the S.A.T.'s yet."

"Well, you're in trouble," I sang, shaking my head and looking down at my hands.

"So, you already took it?"

"Yeah. I did okay, but I want a better score, so I'm gonna re-test." I watched his face turn down in worry and I patted his thigh, "Don't worry, we'll get you through it."

"Good, thanks."

He was honestly asking me to study with him. He seemed so genuine. I had left my hand on his thigh, perplexed, and he covered it with his own. Then he leaned in.

"Homework later. First…" His face was so close to mine that I could smell his skin. Aftershave, something spicy and crisp. My eyelids closed and I felt my lips parting like they had a will of their own. I was more than ready to taste him, too. But he moved past my lips and whispered in my ear, "Champagne."

I blinked. Genuine, indeed. *Bah!*

He winked at me—the jerk—as he rose, crouching low in the cabin to kneel by the side table. He opened a hidden cabinet beneath and pulled out first a bag of ice, which he emptied into an ice bucket set into the table, then a bottle of bubbly.

"Where'd you get that?" I looked behind me to check that the window through to Barney was closed. "That window mirror's not one-way is it?"

"Like he can see us, but we can't see him? Nah," he shook his head, returning with the bottle and two red plastic cups. "I already checked."

"Okay, well if you're sure..."

"I'm sure." He popped the cork and poured slowly, letting the fizz settle, while I peered through the side windows around us. We were on a pretty lonely road, not hard to find in Shirley. But Shirley was a dry county, added to the fact that we were underage. I wondered whether drinking in a limo was considered against an "open container" law. Yet, since alcohol was more illegal on so many other points at that moment, it didn't seem to matter. Did the fact that Tristan's father was the town sheriff make it easier or harder for him to break the rules? Was he being dangerous to impress me, or would his dad simply lose any paperwork that happened to cross his desk about his son? Having never been on the other side of the law before, I had no idea. But I liked the thrill and I'd never tasted champagne.

"Sorry, the plastic cups aren't so romantic," he said, handing mine over.

"Actually...I think it's very romantic." I shrugged, feeling shy. I wasn't used to that kind of treatment from guys. Champagne, wow.

He clinked his cup against mine, the plastic sounding more like a dull tap. "To a promising night, full of new possibilities."

I felt my eyes widen and my eyebrows raise, as I took a sip. "And where'd you get *that?*"

He laughed. "The toast?"

"The champagne and the toast."

"My older sister came home from college for the Homecoming weekend. She set me up."

"That was very nice of her..." I left my comment open, hoping he'd continue with some kind of explanation to our odd date.

"She just wants the night to go smoothly."

I waited. Then, couldn't resist, "Why?"

Tristan shrugged and looked out the window. "It's a celebration. Ashley's no good for me, and Liza—my sister—she's the one who helped me see that."

Well, it was good to get that out of the way. But I wasn't sure what to say. Tristan took in a huge breath and let it out. "Huh. That felt good to admit." He looked at me, perplexed.

"So. That's all fine and good, but I have to say I was surprised when you asked *me*."

His face split into an ironic grin, but his eyes were serious. "You're the most interesting girl at school."

"Interesting?" I folded my arms and raised an eyebrow, hoping my look would force him to the truth. I was trying to bait him, make him admit that he had asked me to the dance so that I would sleep with him afterward.

"A lot more interesting than Ashley, I can tell already." He exhaled loudly and leaned forward with his elbows on his knees. He shook his head and scrubbed his scalp with his fingers, like frustration was mounting just thinking of her.

Whoa. A change of subject was in immediate order. I didn't want to discuss exes either and the bubbly was heating up my knees. "Well anyway, you told me not to eat dinner. Did you just want to get me drunk, Tristan?"

He smiled and let his shoulders fall. "No. I have a surprise for you."

"Another one?"

He went to the magic cupboard again, saying, "We don't have many fine dining options around here—"

"Many?"

"I mean, no fine dining options. So I thought we could eat here."

"Here?"

"Yep." He brought out a picnic-backpack and sat on the carpeted flooring next to my feet, then pulled out plates, utensils, and linen napkins. Next: a small cutting board and a knife. "I wasn't sure what you'd like, so I thought variety would be good."

"Liza thought," I corrected.

"Yeah."

"I like this sister of yours." I watched him dig out cheeses, meats, spreads, and pre-sliced fruit in little containers, placing them around himself on the floor and leather seat. He was just the cutest, sniffing the items as he brought them out, probably as unsure of what awaited us as I was. He dropped one of the containers and a grape escaped and rolled against my shoe. He apologized and wiped my high heal with his napkin. How could someone look so clumsy and so gorgeous at the same time?

"You know, you're very different than what I expected."

"What do you mean?" He paused in his mobile fine dining operation to look up at me.

"You just always seemed like such an asshole when I saw you from a distance," I blurted. "But you're a really nice guy."

"An asshole?"

"I mean, before I really met you."

He looked at me, his pretty face scrunched confusion but the corner of his mouth turned up in a smile. He returned to his task. "Maybe you shouldn't judge people before you meet them."

He said it without a hint of resentment; it was probably just something he'd heard repeated all his life. But it felt like a slap in the face to me, however gentle. Why should I think his personality sucked, just because he was beautiful? I had always thought of myself as open-minded and accepting, the least judgmental person I knew. How wrong I was about Tristan, and maybe myself, too.

He had started slicing pepperoni on the cutting board and my mouth began to water. I was so ready to let down my guard. "This looks like the best celebration feast I've ever seen. Gimme some, I'm starving."

While he sliced off pieces of cheese and hard sausage, buttered fresh buns, and placed them on the plate in my lap, we chatted about nothing in particular and commented on Liza's taste in food. We agreed that one of the cheeses was too stinky and the liver-mousse-thing was just nasty. Tristan chucked both out the window. The prosciutto stuff was mouth-watering and the grapes were so sweet that we fought over the last one. Barney meandered through the back mountain roads. Shirley County bordered a National Forest to the south, and we wandered in and out of it, along tranquil, deserted roads. Tristan asked about what was playing on the classical station now and again, and I supplied information where I could, but there was way too much material for me to recognize it all.

"A harvest moon," I gasped, when I glanced out the window through a clearing in the trees. Were we already that late into autumn? I crawled across the seats to the front of the cabin and rapped on the divider window. "Barney, stop for a minute."

"What's up?" Tristan slammed the rest of his champagne and motioned to mine. He tucked the empty bottle into the backpack as I felt the limo slow and pull onto the gravel shoulder.

"Shit, I didn't think about the champagne. Sorry." My words slurred and my tongue already felt thick; I knew I couldn't drink the rest of mine in one gulp, so I handed it to him and he hid it in the cabinet.

"S'okay, what's goin' on?"

I grabbed his arm, craning my neck for a better view. "The moon. I have to see it—it's huge."

chapter four

As soon as I pushed the door open I recognized where we had stopped: my old stomping grounds from when I was grubby-footed, tangle-haired kid. It was a perfect outlook, where the road bordered a sheer cliff face. The slice of sky was sublime, the view of Shirley Valley below breathtaking.

"Beautiful," I murmured, heading towards the edge, magnetized to the moon as surely as the tides. I felt my heels sink into the dirt and I was done with those shoes. I slipped both of them off and threw them back into the cab, narrowly missing Tristan as he got out.

"Good arm," he said, and whistled in appreciation.

"Thanks," I called back over my shoulder, momentarily free. My toes had been pinched in those things for over an hour and the dirt felt good between my toes.

Tristan picked up his pace behind me. "Careful, you're really close to the edge."

I shot him a look full of arrogance. Valley boys visited the mountains, but they never played there. "Please."

A narrow column of rock jutted up from the valley, separated from the main cliff by about two feet. We had always called it the exclamation point (or just "the point" for short) when I was a kid, because that's exactly what it looked like. It was the first and smallest of the buttes, as the valley below met the canyons, and the mountains on either side squeezed the land into a bottleneck, with violent rapids rushing below. The point was wide enough for a couple people to sit on, maybe four people to stand on carefully. I hopped out onto the column of stone, my bare toes gripping the stone when I landed, steady and sure. I'd done it a million times. I focused on the moon; it looked as big as a planet about to crash right into the earth. A yellow sphere of Swiss cheese, in planetary proportions.

"The wolves will be out in force tonight," I said, then threw my head back in a long howl. A prompt response echoed in the distance, the owner of which was more likely a hound dog hunting with his master than a roaming wolf. I laughed and looked back to see my date turning green behind me. "Don't worry, I've got good balance—my mom says I've always been a mountain goat."

He shook his head, sizing me up from the rear. "More like a mountain lion. Please come back, though."

He held out his hand, obviously closer to the rim than he was comfortable with, but I ignored it. I turned back to the moon. "It's not full yet."

"Looks pretty full to me."

"No, it's still waxing. It'll be full tomorrow."

"Want to bet?" He stuck his hand out further, daring me to accept a shake on it.

"Okay. I know I'm right."

The instant my hand made contact with his, his grip turned to iron and he yanked me towards himself, off the point and across the chasm. I crashed into his chest and he moved backwards with me—solid, not stumbling. His arms wrapped around my shoulders like steel girders, his body immovable and his face unflinching.

"You're dangerous," he mumbled, eyes blazing.

I tried to say, "You should talk," but I'd somehow lost my voice.

"Away from the sheer drop."

"Okay." I nodded, glad to finally produce a sound with my startled vocal chords. I let him thread his fingers through mine, and he led me back to the car.

In the safety of the limo, he lounged back onto the seat, his eyes smoldering as he watched me. I settled myself opposite, arranging the beads of my cocktail dress and fluffing my curls, not really sure what had just occurred between us. Maybe he was angry with me; he sure looked it. I said, as innocently as I could manage, "Are you afraid of heights?"

"Afraid of having to dive off a cliff to catch you, maybe."

I snorted. "Right."

"Reckless," he sighed, shaking his head.

"Sorry…"

"Sorry? You're not like any girl I've ever met, Meg. It's a lot to take in, but there's no reason to be sorry."

I fumbled with my beads a little more, unsure of how to proceed. I felt the car start to roll and I looked up in reaction, to see a door in the ceiling just over Tristan's head. I had an idea. "Hey, we can get a perfect view of the moon from in here. That's a sunroof, right?"

He looked above his head and his expression cooled. "Actually, I've been wanting to try that ever since I first got in."

"You mean...ejector seat?" I met his spreading grin and he nodded, then reached over to push a button by his armrest. The window in the ceiling slid open and Tristan grabbed my hand, pulling me over to crouch with him on the seat below the skylight.

"Ejector seat!" we yelled together, springing up through the open roof, him laughing and me cheering like a five-year-old. The sky spread over us like velvet lavender, a blanket of winking stars around the glowing lunar orb. It felt so close I wanted to reach up and touch it—moments like that are the closest I ever get to church.

We watched the sky together in silence. I slid my eyes in Tristan's direction and saw his own closed, his face content. The air was getting cooler, twilight fading into night, and I shivered as Barney picked up speed. My hair started to whip around my face and I grabbed as much of it as I could in one hand to save the ringlets, gripping the roof with the other. I wondered if my "frizz eliminator" would hold up to such abuse, and I squeezed eyelids shut against the wind and frenzy of escaping curls. Strong fingers encircled my wrist, pulling it down and trapping it behind my waist. My eyes snapped open and found him so close I could feel the tickle of his cheek against mine. My hair whirled around us like a tornado.

His voice was deep and urgent in my ear. "Don't put your hair back."

"It'll be an afro in a minute."

"I like it wild. I like *you* wild."

I turned a fraction and my lips brushed against his. His eyes watched my mouth. "Kiss me, Tristan."

He cupped my face with his hands, so large and warm I felt my cool cheeks blaze instantly, but so gentle he was barely touching me. He looked at me and hesitated, holding my gaze as if he were about to say something first, his face close enough I swear I could feel a spark between our lips. I couldn't wait another second. I found the heat of his mouth and slid my hands inside his jacket and around his waist. He answered me, caution forgotten along with the moon. Was that him who moaned in relief or me? I couldn't tell, melted together as we were. As one.

Both our knees gave way and I felt myself collapsing onto the seat below, then toppling to the floor. His arms were around my shoulders and under my thighs, catching our fall in an expert roll. He landed on top, hovering over me and devouring my neck while I locked my ankles around his back. His lips were as soft as his body was hard, and I felt an electric zing at every point where we connected. All thoughts of preserving my pristine Homecoming costume faded into the smell of his skin, the taste of his mouth, and the hills and valleys of his body. I blended into the texture of him.

"Meg, you're doing it again," a little naggy voice reminded me in my head. I was losing myself, losing control. Again. *"What kind of girl gives it up in a limo on the way to the dance? I mean, you haven't even finished the date yet, dummy."*

"I don't care."

"Don't care about what," Tristan said between kisses, his voice husky.

I'd said that out loud? I sat back in a daze, trying to catch my breath and focus. How was I suddenly on top? I looked down and saw the glare of streetlights on Tristan's face and realized we were heading back into town. Towards school. Towards the dance. My dress was pushed up around my hips, silk panties dark red against black tuxedo pants. At least he had controlled himself; his pants were still zipped.

Wait a minute. I did care what I looked like at that damned dance. I did want to retain the carefully crafted princess veneer that Cassie summoned like magic, and that my little brother adored. And I wanted to look beautiful on Tristan's arm.

I looked out the window and tried to regain my bearings. "I think we're almost there."

"Oh…okay," he panted. "Alright, I'm sorry."

"What are you sorry about? I was the one acting like an animal," I chuckled, sort of embarrassed. I spotted the Bobcatts billboard with Tristan as the model, that classic smile pasted on his perfect face. Then I looked down at him, still pinned under my satiny crotch, and saw that face twisted in frustration.

"Poor guy, I'll help you with that." I know a few tricks to relieve a boy's frustration in two minutes flat, and Tristan deserved it that night already. I smiled, thinking of it as an appetizer. I stretched across the seat and reached my arm up to knock on the divider window. "Barney, once around, please."

Tristan gasped when I unzipped his fly, and I listened for more—I love when boys make fun sounds. Afterwards, I straightened up and patted his pretty cheek affectionately. As I tamed my hair and considered that applying more lipstick would be a good idea, I caught the glazed-over look on Tristan's face. He lay like a puddle of Jell-O, staring at the ceiling and not bothering to fix his pants.

"Come on, Tristan. Don't tell me that was your first BJ?"

"Are you kidding?" His voice was hoarse. "Ashley made me get down on my knees with her and pray for forgiveness, after what her dad called heavy petting."

He must've been be joking. I laughed, but he didn't. Oh, god. He wasn't joking. "Er…how humiliating."

"Yeah." He didn't seem embarrassed, though—more like enlightened.

Praying after a little boob squeeze. Was that really what other girls did? Surely Ashley was an exception. I didn't know what to say. I wasn't religious, but I didn't care if someone else was, as long as they didn't involve me. Was Tristan religious? I tested the spiritual climate, "Forcing someone to pray is kinda sick."

"That's what Liza said." His breath was coming fast, like he'd been gifted with an epiphany. He sat up, tucking his shirt in and straightening his tuxedo vest. "She said Ashley's been controlling my heart through my… dick." He paused, looking abashed at the word. I smoothed away my smile with an effort. "Like I'm her puppet. Or something."

I resisted the urge to shake my head in disgust. How long had they dated? Since Freshman year, until right before he asked me to the dance. So, four years. That sucked. Fourteen through eighteen, if Tristan already had a birthday that year (I had already turned eighteen). He had all those hormones raging just as mine were, and I was hard-pressed to resist them. The idea that guys are more into sex than girls is a myth.

I didn't understand girls like Ashley, pretending to have no passion of their own and always fending the boys off. Chicks like her made it harder for honest, sexually liberated young women like me to be myself. The logic made no sense: in our culture, boys are allowed—no, *expected*—to be "virile" and "hot-blooded." But who the hell are they supposed to sow their wild oats with? Not nice girls. Girls who had sex with boys were "sluts."

Like me, according to the rumor. One of my favorites was the joke that, "Meg Shannon will sleep with anyone, just to spend the night in a house other than her own." I'd been called much worse than "slut," too. I had gotten used to the nickname but I'd never own it. I like sex as much as any guy I've ever met, maybe more. Why should I be ashamed of that, just because I'm female? Hasn't our society moved past such medieval thinking? Not in Shirley County. It was like everyone was playing some game that I didn't understand the rules to. It made me want to scream and beat at my head like Rainman. No, beat nice girls' heads.

But I didn't say any of that aloud, like a catty nice girl might. I sighed and glanced at my date, all buttoned and zipped back together and sitting quietly, bemused. I remembered how anguished he had looked minutes before. Tristan had obviously been administered more than his share of the crazy, too, only in a different kind of dose. Maybe he wasn't playing the game, either.

"What's wrong with feeling good, and making someone else feel good at the same time?" I finally asked.

His eyes locked on mine, and for a second I sensed something else there. Sadness? No, resentment. "I don't know."

"I'm glad you listened to your sister," I said. "She seems pretty smart."

"She is, yeah. Well, smarter since she went to college," he said, smiling easily again. "Oh. We're here."

chapter five

My heart fell just a little; he was right, we were parked. I was so absorbed in my thoughts (and I guessed Tristan was too) that I hadn't noticed Barney's hulking shadow against the glass.

My palms started sweating, thinking about what was in store for me inside. Sometimes people were aggressive and sometimes they left me alone. Mostly, they just shit on me behind my back. Would things be better or worse for me, with Tristan by my side? My steadily growing desire to have Tristan "by my side" was making me uneasy, too.

I sighed, resigned. "Let's do this."

He pulled the handle and stepped outside, blocking Barney with his body and offering me his hand. Barney nodded at us and chuckled in a deep baritone, "Good luck, kid."

I bit my lip to keep from smiling at Tristan's sour puss after that remark, but he regained his swagger in seconds. He took my hand and tucked it into the crook of his arm, knowing I was nervous. But it was one more day at the gym for him, one more easy social event where he was widely adored. We fell in with several other pairs of dates making their way to the doors of the gymnasium, and my eyes darted all around—jittery as a squirrel—trying to recognize anyone friendly. The crowd thickened as we got closer, and I peered ahead and saw the reason for delay; the double doors were decked out with dozens of balloons and partially blocked by a welcome board on an ornate brass tripod. I couldn't really see what was on the tripod, but everyone slowed down to rubberneck as they passed it. Tristan greeted friends or acquaintances here or there as we slowly made our way to the doors. Everyone wanted to be close to him. His fingers started twitching on top of my hand as bodies moved aside and my line of vision cleared. It was my turn to rubberneck.

There in front of me was a poster-size photo of Tristan and Ashley, standing together on a makeshift stage, the football field peeking through on either side. Ashley wore a sparkling tiara and held an armful of red roses over her cheerleading uniform. She was grinning and sobbing at the same time, wiping a tear and gazing up at Tristan. He was staring straight ahead, stone-faced. Still in his football gear, he had two smears of eye black on his cheeks and a sheen of sweat on his brow, under a silver, jewell-studded crown.

My eyes shot to his. "You're the freaking Homecoming King, Tristan?" I hissed.

His gaze was wary. "I should have told you."

"Oh, you think?"

"Does that bother you?" He winced as he said it. "It just happened last night, at half-time. You didn't go to the game, I guess."

"Nope," I said, trying to pull my hand from his arm, but he held onto my fingers in a vice grip.

"Come on, it's just a plastic crown," he murmured in my ear, shifting my hand so that he held me more firmly by his side.

"It's so much more than that."

"No it's not."

We moved through the doors and the vestibule roared into my consciousness, friends talking at high volume, music echoing out of the main gymnasium, and a flash from the professional photographer who was set up right beside the front doors. I blinked hard, momentarily blinded by the glare. There was a couple standing arm in arm, posing next to a column supporting a "2014" foam cutout, painted in glitter.

"Hey, Pretty-Boy!"

"See, I told you. Tristan's always on time."

I swiveled around to see a massive linebacker, Will Bartlett, bustling through the crowd with a petite blonde hanging on.

"Hey, Meg," he said as they drew nearer, and I saw the blonde elbow him in the ribs with a sneer. He turned to her, confused. "What?"

Oh, not allowed to talk to me anymore, huh? I looked at them both, impassive. There was no reason to start a fight. Of course, Will would be receiving no more help from me on his anatomy labs. We had been lab partners since the beginning of the year and he leaned on my superior skills with a scalpel and my ability to read instructions to get him passing grades. I didn't mind, since he was always nice to me—nice to everyone, probably. But, who would expect him to stand against that prissy trophy girlfriend he had on his arm? Nope, he would let her corral him to the dark side, I was sure of it.

"On time for what?" asked Tristan, oblivious to the exchange.

"For the first dance with Ashley, of course," said the blonde, her fist on her hip. "They're waiting to announce you guys—she's already backstage, come on."

"There's nothing to announce, Shelly," he groaned. "Why would I dance with her?"

"Because you're Bobcatt King and Queen, *Tristan*," Shelly said with a scowl. "It's just one dance."

Will looked back and forth between them, keeping silent and avoiding my eyes.

"I don't care. I'm here with Meg. Ashley and I broke up—you know that."

"Don't be an asshole, Tri—"

"Hey." I couldn't help myself. He was only mine for the night, sure, but nobody was going to verbally abuse my date. I grabbed his arm and hauled him off to the side, ignoring Shelly's glare. "Look, it's no big deal. I don't mind. Just come and find me afterwards, okay?"

He closed his eyes and gritted his teeth. I wondered what he was thinking, as emotions played over his face. My stomach tightened at the thought of him dancing with someone else and I reminded myself to get a grip. "It's just a formality. Get it over with and it's done," I said, then watched Shelly over Tristan's shoulder as I rested my hand against his cheek. Her frown deepened and my hand twitched with an urge to slap the hate off her cute little face. "Right?"

"Right," he said, his voice even again. He opened his eyes and smiled. "Thank you, you're right."

"See? Deep breaths." I laughed.

"You're sure you don't mind?" His fingers grazed my wrist, found my elbow. "I'm *your* date tonight."

I dropped my hand back down to my side. The touch was so...tender. It was unnerving with everyone watching.

"I'm sure." It was only a tiny fib, and a necessary one—I hated seeing that torment on such a beautiful face.

He blew out a breath. "Okay."

"Bye for now." I kissed his cheek and backed away, wishing I were as good at winking as he was. I turned and headed toward the gymnasium entrance, and away from that bitch Shelly. Good riddance.

He called after me, "Where will you be?"

"Around." I waved at him over my head, not bothering to look back. I knew what he was looking at—I had tailored my dress to fit just so around my hips, the delicate strings of beads swinging around the tops of my thighs.

"Okay, don't go too far."

I smirked to myself as his voice faded behind me, the noise of the makeshift ballroom drowning him out. Inside, it was gloomy in the corners and twinkling with light from a rotating disco ball over the central court, the abiding smell of sweaty gym socks and leather balls seeping from adjoining locker rooms and equipment closets. Orange and white streamers clung to the corners of the wooden bleachers, which were collapsed along the walls for the party, cascading in bulk in an attempt to dress them up. I wondered how much Tristan's mother had been involved in the decorations. She just loved sprucing up the shabby.

And *someone* must have had to rush to get that photo from yesterday's game ready in time for the dance. Thanks, lady.

I wandered through the crowd, scanning it for anything helpful. I wasn't sure what. Something to occupy me for a few minutes until Tristan was done with "the first dance." Kids clustered around the edges of the basketball court, milling around folding tables with plates of food and cups of punch. They chatted explosively in groups, people packed tightly together to deliver and receive the freshest gossip.

"Like suckling piglets around mama's teats," I muttered to no one.

Unchained Melody started playing, and I wrinkled my nose in distaste. How cheesy. At least the deejay was kind of interesting, though the dance floor remained empty.

"*Interesting…*"

I thought of Tristan's earlier assessment that I was "the most interesting girl in school," and felt confused instead of suspicious. In hindsight, I thought he was being sincere instead of snarky, but I had no idea how he got the idea that I was interesting, or when. I had never seen him even glance in my direction at school. I usually keep to myself on campus, too, and forget about socializing after school. I supposed there were probably weekend functions and the odd party when parents were out of town, but I never showed up at that stuff. How did he even know enough about me to think about me at all?

Two girls dangerously close to my eardrums burst into excited screaming and ran into the bathroom giggling. A tangle of friends trailed behind, forcing me to stop in my tracks and halt my reflections.

You Spin Me Round, by Dead Or Alive, was pulsing out of the portable loudspeakers.

Man, the guy was really trying hard. "First, we get the oldest love song in the world for all the star-eyed couples, and now 80's British dance-pop." I remembered the latter from a Jazzercise class Cassie had made me go to once. Looked like his effort was all for naught, though; the wallflowers stood firmly planted along the outskirts, everyone waiting until someone else went first.

"And that would be Tristan and Ashley." I decided I just couldn't watch. I picked up my pace and headed for the back doors.

"Meg Shannon, I want to talk to you." Shelly appeared at my shoulder. I slowed and gazed down at her imperiously; I knew her little legs would have a hard time keeping up with mine.

"Ugh. What do *you* want?"

"I don't know what you think is going on with you and Tristan, but you should show some respect for Ashley," the venomous troll squeaked.

My lips curled over a sneer. "And why should I respect some chick I don't even know?"

"She's not just 'some chick.' She and Tristan are in love and they're meant to be together."

"I think Tristan feels a little differently…" I said, turning away from her pinched little face.

"You better not be planning to do what I think you are tonight." She grabbed my arm and yanked me back. The shrimpy thing was stronger than she looked.

"Excuse me," I glared down at her hand.

"Ashley's been waiting a long time, and they're supposed to lose that together."

"Lose *that?*" I laughed. Nice girls were so prissy, and I wanted her to say the word.

"You know what I mean, their first time," Shelly said, her face going red. "With her, not with you." Her eyes were black shiny buttons in her scrunched face. She looked me over from head to toe with distaste.

And then I was mad.

I leaned down close, to make sure she could hear, and said in a low snarl, "Get. Your. Hand. Off. Me."

She had the sense to let go of my arm.

I straightened to my full height. "Tristan has the right to do whatever he likes with his own body, in his own bedroom. And as for what I do with mine—that's none of your damn business," I said, lacing my tone with as much ice as I could summon, then stalked away.

Dead Or Alive faded out and a microphone screeched in painful feedback on stage.

"The moment we've all been waiting for, everyone…"

I winced as I finally reached the gymnasium exit and pushed through.

"I give you our newest Bobcatt King and Queen. Give it up ya'll, for Tristan Jameson and Ashley Da—"

I let the door slam behind me.

"Ugh!"

How did I get talked into coming to such a nightmare?

I leaned up against the brick wall outside, panting. I took in a slow, steadying breath, glad the night was turning cold. Crisp air filled my lungs with a cleansing tingle. The music inside rose again—was that a Justin Timberlake love song? I put my ear against the metal door and could just make out the lyrics, *"I don't wanna lose you now. I'm lookin' right at the other half of me..."*

On second thought, I hated the deejay. I pictured Tristan and Ashley spinning in a circle, her arms wrapped around his neck, adoring his Mentho-Lyptus eyes. I thought I might hurl, and I pushed myself away from the door determined to walk it off.

I hadn't gone two steps before a burst of incoherent hooting and jeering erupted from close by, then quickly died away. I stood still and listened, straining my eyes in the darkness. After a few muttered words and a moment of silence, the noise flared up again, just around the corner where light spilled around the side of the building. I crept towards it.

"Pay up, you bastard," I heard someone say once I was close enough to make out the words.

"Is that what I think it is?" I chirped, rounding the corner with glee.

When I popped my head around, half a dozen stunned faces were staring at me with eyes as wide as saucers, their owners frozen in the act of doing something illicit.

"Shit, you scared me."

"Hey, Meg."

The guys all relaxed, most of them squatting back down to haggle over bets and resume shooting dice against the sidewalk curb.

"Hey, you want in?" said my friend Chris.

He lived a few doors down from me—he was scrawny, but always sweet and often smelly. That night was no different. Apparently, not everyone shines up like a new penny. I looked around at the group, wondering what guys like that were doing at the Homecoming Dance; I counted at least two drop-outs. Well, there wasn't much better to do in Shirley, I guessed, and three counties fed into Andrew Jackson's school district.

I shook my head at Chris, "Don't have any cash." I'd spent every spare penny I had getting ready for the dance, not that I frequently had many spare pennies.

"I can spot ya," he said. "I been bleedin' these fellas dry all night."

"I couldn't pay you back, if I don't win."

"You can work it off with me, sweet tits," said a boy I didn't recognize, eyeballing those sweet body parts. He was promptly smacked in the back of the head.

"Dude!"

"Shut up, man."

I was one on the guys whenever I gambled with them, and making a remark that reminded anyone of my femaleness was strictly forbidden. The newbie blushed at his faux-pas and moved aside to let me accept a fiver from Chris.

"Alright, what are we playin', boys?" I mimed rolling up my sleeves and took my place around the pit.

A little dice would be fun, and the perfect panacea for wounded pride and blooming jealousy. I settled on my haunches and took a drag from Chris's cigarette.

"Nice flowers," he snickered.

The corsage went to my elbow and my fist went to his shoulder, hard. "Shut up."

I love street craps. It goes fast and the bets are small, so a player can stay in the game for hours with a little luck, even without winning big. As it happened, Fortuna was smiling down on me that night, and I hadn't lost once after at least half an hour. Chris's five had already turned into thirty-three, and I never mess with a winning streak. I keep betting while the dice are hot.

I was up to roll again. I had kicked off my heels and was squatting down barefoot, holding my dress closed with one hand and clicking the dice together in my other.

"Here we go—eight the hard way, y'all. Eighter from Decatur. Who's in?" I blew the dice a kiss, and it was like a fog horn in the unusual silence that had suddenly fallen.

I glanced up. The guys had gone quiet, most of them looking past me and over my head.

"What?" I said, my spine prickling already.

"Hi," said a deep voice behind me.

I knew that voice in my bones, and my skin went flush from head to toe in response. I twisted around and turned my face up towards him, smiling broadly.

"You in?" I displayed the dice in my hand and chewed my lower lip.

Several of the guys straightened up and shuffled their feet. I wondered if I should introduce my date. It wasn't exactly his crowd.

Chris stuck out his hand for Tristan to shake. "Hey, good game last night, man."

Grunts of agreement sounded all around.

Tristan kept his eyes on me. "Thanks."

I rolled the dice in my palm. Quirked an eyebrow.

"Yeah, I'm in." Tristan pulled out his wallet and threw in some cash to manly sounds of approval.

"Alright, man."

"Come on, Meg. Roll the freakin' dice already."

"No, you take 'em." I tossed the dice to one of the boys and squeezed Tristan in next to me, searching his eyes with curiosity as he crouched down on my level.

As the racket picked up around us again, he leaned close to whisper in my ear, "What are we playing?"

I chuckled softly and shook my head, "I knew it. Craps. Just follow my lead."

He paid close attention while I gave him silent clues—slight nods and smiles or the tiniest shake of my head. He kept his hand on my back and tapped out the number he thought he should bet on. I told him the right number by pressing my fingers into his thigh, if I thought he needed help. So much intimacy is involved, when teaching someone a game on the sly.

We sat so close together, I barely had to raise my voice. "How did you find me, anyway?"

"Were you hiding?" he murmured.

"No. But I'm glad you came to find me." I smiled, looking down at his sculptured lips in anticipation. When could we get out of there? "Why'd you look out here?"

"I watched you walk out, door slammer." His lips spread wide, white teeth brilliant in a teasing smile.

I felt my face turn hot and snapped my gaze back to the dice pit. He saw that, great.

"You know, Meg, you're an enigma—Yes!" He stood abruptly, and punched the sky. They all traded masculine banter over a big win.

I blinked. Enigma? What did he mean by that? Maybe I could glean more insight on my "interesting" qualities with that line of conversation. When he settled back next to me, I hoped he hadn't forgotten his last comment, because I was dying to know what he meant. But I felt too shy to ask. I settled for a questioning look. He replaced his hand on my back once more, though he was getting the hang of the game and no longer needed my instruction.

"By day you walk to classes with nerds and work in the library," he started, then wormed his fingers over to my side to tickle a rib.

"Hey! Being in advanced classes does not make you a nerd." I giggled and shoved his fingers away, hoping they'd find their way back.

They did.

"By night you gamble behind the gym in a cocktail dress."

My cheeks were aching I was smiling so hard. "Well, the cocktail dress is a rarity."

"I can't wait to see what else you can do," he said.

My heart thudded against my ribs, remembering our limo delights. His breath tickled my ear and I drank in the smell of him. A sharp tweet interrupted us, and Tristan pulled out his phone to check a text message. I read it out of the corner of my eye.

"picture time where r you? get ur ass over here!"

He grunted an expletive and dropped his face between his knees, then looked up, massaging his temples, "We gotta go in, come on."

"Now?"

"Yes, I'm sorry." He grabbed my hand to help me stand with him.

"I was on a winning streak, though."

"I'll make it up to you," he said, his smile not reaching his eyes. He ran a hand through his hair and looked towards the entrance to the gym with a frown.

Maybe it wasn't the best time to argue. I shrugged, "Alright, I guess."

I returned Chris's spot, we said bye to the guys, then headed back to the door. I shuffled through my winnings, stopping short at a bothersome thought and crumpling several bills aside. Tristan had lost all his money in the end, so I separated the wad, with about fifty bucks for each of us. "Here, take it."

"What? No." He shoved my hands away, appalled. "That's yours."

"No, it's yours."

"No."

"Come on, Tristan. I know you're cleaned out. I saw your wallet."

He shook his head resolutely and sidestepped me, "I lost, you won."

"And that's not exactly cool, since I was teaching you how to play."

I lunged forward and stuffed the money into his outside jacket pocket, cramming down his red silk handkerchief, then ran away with my hands overhead. I refused to take it back—my cost for being such a shitty instructor. It was only fair.

He caught up to me. "That's big of you, but I'll just spend it on you later." A quick, familiar kiss found my lips. A boyfriend peck.

Would there be a "later," after tonight? I was too hopeful for my own comfort and I wanted to pinch myself. I cleared my throat, "So, why were you subpoenaed?"

"Oh yeah, I forgot to tell you. They want pictures with all the Homecoming Court."

"You and Ashley," I nodded, my high spirits plummeting.

"No. No more of that, I made sure of it. They want us with our dates." He brought my hand up to his lips, then kept hold of it as he opened the door back inside. "We were subpoenaed together."

♣

He didn't let go of my hand throughout the whole argumentative photo-shoot. I was suspicious that I was being employed as a safe buffer from the venomous troll, Shelly, since she gave me a wide berth. Me and Tristan lingered on the edges of the shoot together. I held his eyes most of the time, while the other girls whined about who should stand where according to rank and height. I was surprised and pleased that no one produced the crowns, and I noticed Tristan had fallen in rank because of his loyalty to his date. The snubs were hard not to notice—a fact that sent us both into barely stifled fits of laughter and drove us further to the outskirts of the royal court ensemble.

Another couple, who seemed as disinterested in pictures as we were, drifted in our direction. Tristan introduced the guy as a junior, named John. I figured he was on the football team, too. They launched into shop talk and I looked to John's date, who seemed about as comfortable as I was. I noticed John wasn't holding her hand like Tristan was mine; she was wringing her fingers, tugging at her dress and readjusting the bodice.

I leaned over and raised my voice above the music still playing on the other side of the stage, "I'm sorry, I didn't catch your name. It's so loud in here."

"Oh. Erica. Nice to meet you."

She held out her hand, and when I tried to release Tristan's to accept the shake, he squeezed tighter. I pursed my lips and squeezed back, hard. His eyes creased at the corners when they found mine for a second. I looked pointedly at our conjoined hands, but he turned back to John and kept talking. I offered Erica an apologetic look and my left hand. She fumbled with her clutch purse as my face blazed, finally getting it under her arm and glancing at Tristan with adoration. Then at John in frustration.

"Hi," I said, pumping her hand firmly.

"Hi."

"I'm Meg. Nice to meet you, too."

She pushed imaginary glasses up on her nose, probably out of life-long habit. "That's such a cool dress. Is it a real flapper dress, like real vintage?"

"I think so." I raised my arms and scanned my figure. "It's been altered a few times, so the fit isn't really authentic."

She shook her head emphatically, "Who cares, it fits you like a glove. I love vintage stuff."

"Thank you." I couldn't remember the last time another female was so nice to me, outside of family members. "Your dress is absolutely gorgeous," I said, feeling like a gushy girlie-girl. "And you look awesome in it."

It was true. Erica's dress was a floor length, strapless satin sheath gown, and she had the body to hold it up. It looked expensive. I could tell she felt awkward in it—sort of like the ugly duckling that found her reflection in the pond and saw she was a swan, but didn't really believe it yet. I guessed this event was her first Homecoming Dance, like mine. I secreted a looked at her date, who was almost as attractive as Tristan, and I wondered what the deal was. Friends?

"Your hair looks so cool. That headband, wow."

"Oh, my cousin gave it to me." I touched my flapper version of a crown. "Yours, too. It's so elegant up like that."

Erica couldn't find the words to accept my return compliment, and merely blushed and bobbed her head instead. I shifted my weight in my high heels, wishing I had thought to clean my feet off before putting my shoes back on. They were starting to sweat, just like my hand clutched in Tristan's. I heard the music change out on the dance floor and sucked in my breath. I yanked on Tristan's hand, "Hey..."

He looked at me, his forehead furrowed in concern. "What's wrong?"

"Nothing's *wrong*. Disco!"

"Huh?"

"I have to dance to this song, Tristan. Are we done here?" I pleaded desperately.

His eyes softened. "Yeah, we're done." He signaled to one of his buddies, then let me haul him away.

"Erica, come with us," I said, waving her over to join my tiny entourage.

Erica's smile was brilliant. She grabbed John's hand, and he followed with a matching grin. I imagined myself as Cupid, loosing a golden love arrow.

"We're not done over here you guys." Shelly.

"Yeah we are," Tristan called back, jogging next to me as the four of us rounded the stage, headed for the main gym. As we all met the dance floor, he wrapped an arm around my waist and his lips met my neck, just below my ear. "You've been more than patient. Thank you."

"Screw patience. I want to dance," I yelled over the music. My fingers intertwined with his and we lunged onto the miraculously crowded basketball court.

"Good," he mouthed, letting his gaze slide over me as I started to whirl, ecstasy surely plastered on my face.

I love to dance. Rarely ever do I feel so free, so uninhibited. I let my head fall back and closed my eyes against the glittering light from the temporary disco ball, on another planet for all I cared of my surroundings. Relaxing shoulders and hips, I smiled to myself and felt my body move with the beat like it was compelled. My arms swung out around me—a trick I use to shoo away other dancers and give myself some room to move. I prefer to dance solo, since a partner just knocks me off rhythm, but boys always want to try. I sneaked a peek and saw Tristan moving around me like a satellite, blocking access and glowering at lusty-eyed rivals.

"That's sweet," I said, but the music was too loud for him to hear me. He didn't see me either, on patrol as he was.

I'd never felt so unencumbered on a dance floor and I wanted to thank him. I moved around to face him, caught his eye, and beamed him my gratitude before spinning away. The music changed and I spread my arms wide, my torso undulating with the natural current of the song, the electricity of the dance mix racing across the surface of my skin like a blue flame over spilled kerosene. Tristan caught my fingers in mid-swing and whipped me around to face him. I remembered where I had seen that blue flame before. In his eyes.

I could feel the urgency in his grip—he wanted to play, too.

"Yay!" I shot both hands in the air, gleeful.

He held onto my waist with a quizzical expression.

"Time to dance you, pretty boy," I sang, accepting his embrace.

Guys are shit dancers, for the most part. Usually when they say, "Wanna dance?" what they mean is, "Wanna grind?" But, if a boy is limber enough and we have the right points of bodily contact, I can usually get him at least moving to the same beat with me. I call it "dancing the boys." Tristan had been an excellent date so far, and I certainly didn't mind multiple points of bodily contact with him.

I locked my shape with his; hands, shoulders, hips, and thighs. But he wasn't used to being physically overpowered. He reeled me in and held the small of my back with authority, his fingers stretched wide enough to wrap around the sides of my waist and move me where he wanted me. I twisted my arms around his neck and held on. He was dancing *me*. With my four-inch heals, we were almost the same height, and his lips were less than an inch away from mine. As a slow song began to drift into my ears, I felt my hips roll easily with his.

Whoa. He was actually a good dancer. "Years of athletic training must help you to gracefully react against opposing force," I thought out loud. That was stupid. How did he rattle my mind so fast?

"Huh?"

"Just. You know, most guys don't. I don't know..."

"What are you talking about?" He leaned in so close I could feel his breath on my ear. "Just dance with me."

I nodded, incapable of speech. Yes. Just dance.

We pressed together in gentle friction and I forgot place and time. How did I finally find someone I could move so perfectly with? It was like we'd taken dancing lessons together for years. Erotic dancing lessons. I felt him stiffen against my pelvis and I pushed into it, grabbing his hips. Not even hearing the song anymore, my body took on a more carnal rhythm of its own.

"Meg," Tristan said, his voice rumbling deep within his chest, vibrating against mine. "Let's get outta here."

I nodded eagerly and let him lead me off the dance floor. I barely registered faces flashing in the strobe light, bodies ebbing and flowing past me in more casual celebration. Tristan shoved through the outer doors. My face was so flushed that the cold air felt like a slap on my cheeks. But, I've never really listened to warnings like that.

chapter six

He let Barney open the door without complaint, supporting me and patiently stalling my groping hands until we were in the privacy of the cabin. Before I heard the click of the door lock, we tumbled onto the floor in a tangle of limbs. My crazy afro of ringlets was everywhere, but I didn't care. I plunged my hands between us, my fingers fumbling desperately for buttons and zippers, but Tristan took them in a firm grip.

"Wait," he said in a ragged voice. He sat up. "Just wait."

Blowing out a long, slow breath, he closed his eyes and brought outstretched hands towards his lap, palms down in a calming gesture. I rose from the floor and propped myself on my elbow, confused. He just sat there breathing, lips pursed, while I watched him, barely daring to breathe.

Finally, he opened his eyes and smiled. "Okay."

The limo started rolling and I grasped the carpet to avoid toppling over. The sound of my own throat clearing crackled through the cabin. We pulled out of the school parking lot and turned onto the state road, and Tristan turned to watch the countryside flow past outside through the panoramic window. What the hell did I do? I thought "the benefits" were the reason he asked me to the damn dance in the first place. I clenched my fists in the carpet to stop myself from throwing them in the air, then I put them in my lap, feigning demure. Demure my ass. I wanted to attack him and he was done with me, apparently.

He smiled down at my hands twisted together, pried them apart, and pulled me up to sit with him on the seat. A shoulder squeeze and a forehead kiss, then he reached over to switch on the radio. I looked out the window on my side, hoping to hide the horror on my face.

What the hell just happened? What changed his mind? I closed my eyes and let my thoughts race, trying to recall the last few minutes where things must have gone wrong. Everything seemed to be going okay before we started dancing together, then…I sort of lost control. Our exodus was abrupt. He said he liked me wild, but maybe that was too wild. I pictured the scene, imagining how I must've looked, clinging to him like a stripper on a dancer's pole. Dancing always makes me lose myself. I blinked at the streetlights zooming past, wondering who he saw watching us dance that had embarrassed him so much.

"I'm sorry I got carried away back there," I whispered, miserable.

"Are you kidding? I was the one having to count to ten."

My head snapped around. "What?"

"I'm glad you can't read my thoughts," he said, raising his eyebrows and chuckling quietly. "They might've scared you."

"I doubt it."

"Trust me," he snorted. "Girls never know the half of what guys are thinking."

I gaped at him. He shook his head and looked back outside at the passing landscape.

"I don't get it," I said, finally alert enough to my surroundings to recognize where we were. We were driving northwards into the valley, not south to the mountain cove where I lived. "Wait. Aren't you taking me home?"

"Do you want me to?"

"No. I just thought…where are we going?"

"To my house. Didn't I tell you? I thought everyone knew my mom and dad went out of town this weekend, to leave the place to me and Amanda. Sorry, I should have asked if that was cool with you."

"So, you're having a party or something?"

He shook his head like he was dislodging an uncomfortable memory. "No. That's why everyone's so pissed off at me. Or, one of the reasons. I don't know, I think my sister's having a couple friends spend the night. They're just sophomores, though. They won't bother us."

"Oh."

Ooooh…

"Should I tell Barney to turn around—"

"No!" I grabbed his arm before I could stop myself. Seconds before, I was dreading the night I thought lay ahead of me: lying alone in my bed all night, sleep impossible. I would've sorted through every detail of my fantasy date with Tristan, over and over, sifting for clues as to what had gone wrong. I may have murdered Piper in her sleep, to silence her habitual, incessant snoring in the next room. "I mean, are you asking me to spend the night with you?"

"Well, yeah. Is that wrong to ask?"

I looked at him in the dark cabin, the music flowing around us drifting into my consciousness. Our classical station was playing Pachelbel's *Canon in D,* the famous, ultra-romantic string composition so popular at weddings. It was an odd moment. What could've been considered a lewd invitation—a crude assumption—was made sweet and romantic. Tristan's shy smile helped.

"No, it's not wrong. I'd love to. Thank you."

"Good." He leaned over with a lingering kiss, then settled back onto the seat beside me. "I'd love to have you."

Butterflies again. I couldn't remember the last guy who had riled up those tiny rainbow-winged beasts so much. I tried to relax and sort my thoughts, watching the valley roll past. The fact was, falling for a guy like Tristan Jameson was the dumbest thing a girl like me could do. I preferred not to feel anything for guys—it was the only way to avoid being hurt by them—and Tristan was in a totally different social strata than my own. I wanted to have fun that night, but I just had to keep my head together and not let my heart take over. That's what I tried to tell myself. But it felt too good to have him look at me like that, with those, blue, blue eyes.

Before long, a walled subdivision came into view. Tristan pressed a button, and the window dividing us from Barney slid down. "Heard anything from my sister yet?"

"Not a word since I dropped her and her friends at the high school after you."

"Nice. I hope she stays at the dance for a while. My mom made us split the limo tonight," Tristan explained in an aside to me. "You're a bargain, right Barney? Driving all over the valley for Jameson & Co."

Barney lifted a shoulder, "Ain't been no trouble."

"I'm sure you know where to go, after two trips there already."

"Yes, sir. No problem."

Sir. I smiled at Tristan and he returned a goofy grin. We left the window open while Barney drove through the twisting streets, lined with old-fashioned iron street lamps, scattered picket fences, and low hedges. We pulled up in the Jameson driveway and as the car rolled to a stop, Tristan reached through the window clapped Barney on the shoulder, with a crisp bill between two fingers. "Been a pleasure."

So, there was a secret pocket in that wallet. Sneaky.

"Aw, Mrs. Jameson took care of that already, sir."

"That's extra. So you might drive extra slow on the way home with my sister. And so you'll let me open the door for my own date?"

Barney laughed. "I'll take your sister for ice cream, how's that?"

"Perfect." Tristan shook his hand before sliding off the seat and opening our door. He waited in the street for me, his hair fallen over his eyes and his smile mischievous. I scooted towards the exit, retrieving my heels and slipping them on before accepting his help out.

I looked back at the limo as we walked up the driveway. "Is he just gonna to sit there?"

Barney had moved out to the street and was clearly parked for the duration. He turned off the engine and cranked his seat back, the blue glow of a miniature flat screen display already lighting up his face and the sound of a sports announcer floating out of his cracked window.

"Until Amanda needs him to pick her up, probably. The limo company is based in Tenakho Falls, over an hour from here."

"Kinda nice to have a massive bodyguard stationed outside your house."

"I guess." Tristan shrugged as he pulled a lanyard of keys from under his shirt.

I felt a warm whoosh of air when he pulled the door open, and the smell of cinnamon and fresh bread swept over me. Someone had been baking recently. A lot. "You're sure no one is here? What if they decided to come back early?"

His mother was so present with those happy homemaker smells, that it was hard to believe she wasn't sitting in the dark somewhere, waiting to catch us. I felt naughty.

"Don't worry, they're making a weekend of it. They won't be back until tomorrow night. Late."

I stepped inside the foyer, still a little unsure, and looked around in the dimness. I've never been comfortable meeting parents and generally feel unwelcome in boys' homes, especially with their mothers around. The place did seem empty, though—silent, except for the slow tick-tock of a grandfather clock directly across from the front door.

"So…this is it," said Tristan, a little too loudly.

The peculiar note in his voice snapped me out of my timidity, and I turned to him in wonder. "So it is."

He was fidgeting with his keys and rocking from his heels to the balls of his feet, all wooden and shy.

Aw. He was nervous. How cute. "And now what?" I felt compelled to ask.

"Are you hungry or thirsty? You want something to eat?" He motioned towards the kitchen, then scratched the back of his neck. "Like a sandwich or something. I think there's cake—my mom made one for the Pumpkin Festival this weekend and one for us to keep. It's pretty good."

"I'm hungry alright. Not for food."

He blushed and I caught my breath; Tristan Jameson just got hotter. I glanced past the kitchen, where I had no intention of going, and into a long, dark hallway. Where was his room? I was starting to worry that he might chicken out, and I thought we better get this after-party started before he did. How could I move things in a better direction than his mother's cake?

I reached out and ran my finger along the bottom edge of his tuxedo vest. "How long are you gonna make me wait, you big tease?"

He let out the breath that he had been holding and flashed me a smile that made my knees weak. "Yeah, pretty long night."

He was still rooted to the welcome mat.

"Give me a tour?" I offered.

"Sure." He took my hand; it was sweaty, but at least he was touching me and not jingling his keys from hand to hand anymore. We both knew neither of us had any intention of touring, but I was surprised when he led me away from the long hallway and towards another wing of the house. I stopped short when we ended up in front of a door to what was obviously the master bedroom.

"Your parents' room?"

"My sister's room is right next to mine. I don't want her bothering us." He rolled his eyes, then added, "Plus, my room isn't nice enough." He turned the handle and pushed the door open.

I frowned, unsure. But the idea of deflowering the quarterback in his mother's bed gave me a perverse thrill, especially since I had been expressly forbidden to do so. I followed him inside with a private smirk.

The room was huge—almost like a separate suite all to itself, with a seating area around a TV and a door that opened onto a private bathroom. Someone had left a light on by the commode, and I could tell the bathroom was bigger than my living room. The bedroom itself was dimly lit by a small table lamp next to the bed. And when my eyes roamed past the lamp...

"Oh my god."

The bed was covered in rose petals. I swiveled on my heels to gape at him, then at the bed, speechless.

"Do you like roses? My mom has about a million of them in our back-yard. I didn't think she'd notice if a few were stolen."

"A few? Looks more like a few dozen." The entire king size bed was covered with them—red, pink, white, yellow.

"It's October. They needed pruning anyway."

"Just part of your yard work chores?"

"No," he said softly.

I was being rude, I realized, and I felt like a jerk. "They're beautiful. I love roses." Actually, I wasn't too familiar with them before that night.

While he searched a night stand drawer under the lamp, I noticed the candles. Lighter in hand, Tristan moved around the room, igniting each one, until the whole suite was aglow in warm, dancing, incandescent light. It was magical.

"Ouch." My fingernails bit into the flesh at the back of my own arm. He turned and smiled at me, and went to put the lighter away.

I didn't understand. Why all the effort? All the wining and dining and romance. It really wasn't necessary, and I almost said so. But, he was approaching me with a crooked smile. An innocent smile. Then everything made sense. The limo, the champagne, his sister wanting to help, the bed full of roses, him not letting things go too far in the car on the way to his house. That stupid twit Shelly's infuriating demands.

All this wasn't for me, it was for him. This was a special night for him and he'd been waiting a long time, too. How many times had Ashley turned him down? No matter how gorgeous he was, being rejected hurt. Prolonged, constant rejection by someone who supposedly loved you must have been unbearable. Years as the acting mother for all my younger siblings had honed my nurturing urges, and I felt like cradling Tristan's head against my chest, stroking his face like I would with Charlie when he'd had a nightmare or skinned a knee.

That wasn't going to help, though.

My heart ached for him. He looked so unsure. If he'd had pockets in his tuxedo pants, he probably would've stuffed his hands deep inside them. I looked around the room, searching for something, but I wasn't sure what. There was a glimmer in the darkness outside, just past the sliding glass doors. The view was partially blocked by vertical blinds, but I caught the unmistakable flash of a slice of moon reflected in water. "Is that a swimming pool out there?"

"Oh yeah," he said, brightening. He reached past me and flicked a switch on the wall. The pool materialized in blue-green brilliance. "Want to swim?"

"It's probably too cold, isn't it?"

"It's heated. My dad keeps it open until November usually—after Halloween, when the jack-o'-lanterns have all rotted. That's his signal to close it up for the winter. We'll probably carve Pumpkins next week, actually. It know it's weird but we still have a jack-o'-lantern contest, even though my youngest sister is already in high school. Very fierce family competition. The pool's salt water, too, so we won't reek of chlorine after we swim."

Nervous rambling again. I had to act fast. "I'd love to swim."

"Okay, cool. I'll go get us some towels."

I watched him leave.

Since I didn't have a suit, skinny-dipping was obvious, and I have never known a guy to resist for long after seeing me naked. No more over-thinking. I eased off my flapper headband, laid it on the bureau, and grabbed a pencil I saw there. My zipper went down and my straps went to the brink of my shoulders. Facing the glass doors, I made sure they were unlocked, and when I heard Tristan's footsteps returning, I let the heavy beaded thing drop straight down to my ankles. I sighed in relief. Then I stepped out, one foot at a time, bending over slowly to remove first one shoe, then the next. Satin panties dropped and I kicked them aside. Without turning to acknowledge Tristan, I eased open the sliding door and stepped outside.

Shit, it was cold. But, I strolled around the edge of the pool until I was facing him on the other side, pretending to ignore his presence. Goose bumps were rising on my arms, but I took my time twisting my hair up and fixing it with the pencil. I stepped into the warm water and tiptoed down the steps. Once I was submerged up to my waist, I looked up to see Tristan slipping outside, already naked himself. He closed the door behind him and set the towels on a lawn chair in a hurry, not bothering to pretend he wasn't. The beauty of his body was astonishing, the glow from the pool illuminating every curve from below as he strode across the patio. He was a present unwrapped. All night I had wanted to get him out of that tuxedo—to see that long, lean, muscular body, built for the speed and precision he was known for on the field. But in the flesh, it was almost too much. Every inch of him was perfection, as if chiseled into marble. He slid into the water like a demigod from a Greek poem.

Suddenly I was the one feeling like a fumbling, awkward virgin—until our bodies found each other in the fevered heat of the pool. Within minutes, we were racing across the patio back to the bedroom, laughing and shivering, hastily drying off before plunging under the down comforter. Rose petals flew in the air.

"My roses," I gasped, almost serious.

He pushed the petals away, his voice rasping, "I'll get you some more."

What happened to my shy schoolboy? He had vanished, replaced by tender lips and sure hands. Soft kisses followed my clavicle and made their way down my chest. He traced the line of my waist with his fingertips and sent goose bumps prickling up to my breasts. Then he kissed those, too. His skin was already warmed, his whole body radiating heat, the weight of him delicious as I clung to him.

Gentle and demanding at once, it was like he had a map of my body and my mind. "How do you know exactly how to touch me?"

He smoothed my hair back from my face and nudged my nose with his. "I've been thinking about this for a long time."

It was all so overwhelming I was panting. "With me?"

"With you."

I threaded my fingers into his hair and shook my head, confused. "I don't understand."

"You're so different from everyone else." He brushed his lips over my mouth, my cheeks, and I closed my eyes. "You don't hide who you are." He kissed my eyelids, one by one. "So beautiful. Deep down." A warm hand rested on my chest, over my heart. "I can see the real you."

The real me. The real me. I breathed him in all around me and hugged his chest to mine.

"I want to know you, Meg. Every inch of you." It was barely a whisper.

He gathered my hair behind my neck and twisted my face to his, insistent and almost desperate, his lips suddenly hard and his hands rough. I felt my knee pressed into my shoulder, his erection hot against my thigh. In a daze, I heard him digging in the night stand, a condom in place so fast I barely registered what he was doing until it was done. I was shocked and thrilled and I could hardly get my words out right, "I want to know you. Tristan, I do."

chapter seven

I watched him sleeping.

Sigh.

I almost said it out loud, I felt so foolish: "Great job, Meg. Just go ahead and sleep with him right away, just like everyone said you would. Don't leave anything to the imagination, just let him have it all."

I rolled over onto my back, angry at my own trepidation bubbling up inside my gut.

"Stop it, you dork," I admonished myself silently. I don't need to fall in love with someone in order to have sex, and I never have. Rules like that were for brainwashed lemmings who would follow the crowd off a cliff rather than think an original thought.

Plus, love is even more dangerous than sex.

I let my head loll to the side for another look at Sleeping Beauty. He was so peaceful. I had never seen anyone look so gorgeously relaxed, in deep, blissful slumber. His lips were slightly parted, irises darting under their lids in a dream state. The lines of tension in his forehead I had noticed off and on all night were completely smoothed away.

Yes, he was a delicious sight. But it wasn't love.

I flounced onto my back and watched the ceiling for a few minutes.

And damn it, I didn't want it to be love. Right?

I scowled at his adorable, cupid's bow mouth. There was no way I could keep still enough not to disturb him, so I eased out from under the covers, trying to feel annoyed at his sleeping face rather than enamored. How could he just pass out like that? Sure, he said some nice things—guys would say anything to reach the holy grail—but he was gone as soon as he got what he wanted. I myself was still zinging head to toe, nowhere near sleep.

And starving.

I wandered the room, focused on procuring food instead of the tightness in my chest. Errant doubts invaded my head, relentless. I had to concentrate on eating, not the amazing male specimen lying naked in bed. Although the thought of that pumpkin cake he mentioned earlier set my stomach growling instantly, I didn't want to go into the kitchen without him in case his sister came home to find a stranger rummaging through the fridge. My mind finally settled on the image of a miniature cheesecake at the bottom of the picnic bag. I had to have it. It would still be in the limo; we'd been too distracted when we got out, and I didn't remember grabbing that bag or my purse. I remembered focusing on Tristan's eyes.

"Brilliant, Meg. Just brilliant," said that naggy little voice.

Hoping Barney was still waiting in the car, I found my dress puddled by the sliding glass door and slipped it on as quietly as I could. I looked back at Tristan, still dead to the world. It was probably safer to go out through the front, since the cold air from the patio might wake up my suddenly inattentive date. Shivering, I plucked Tristan's tuxedo jacket off the floor, then padded out of the master bedroom barefooted. I slunk down the hallway and peeked through the leaded glass window by the front door.

The limo was still parked outside. "Yes!"

Barney let me into the main cab to grab the cheesecake and my purse, then begrudgingly obliged as I climbed into the front to listen to the comedy channel with him. I didn't give him much choice. We munched cheesecake together, him chuckling intermittently at some comedian I'd never heard of and me winding myself up into a frenzy of second-guessing.

Would Tristan even talk to me at school on Monday? He never talked to me before…

God, why did I go all the way?

Wait. I don't say things like, "go all the way."

I slapped my knee in irritation, provoking a curious look from Barney. I grinned and he shook his head, then looked away.

"Go all the way" sounded as archaic as "heavy petting." That kind of thinking was not what I was about. I had sex with him because I wanted to have sex with him, damn it.

Barney's laugh turned into a roar at some joke the comedian cracked; his broad shoulders shook and tears streamed from the corners of his eyes. I couldn't help but join in, even though I had no idea what had just been said.

I felt better after the endorphin rush. Tristan really did seem to like me, too. I remembered him holding my hand during the photo shoot, and the look in his eyes when he said I was beautiful, deep down. I chewed on a strand of my hair. Maybe he really did mean the stuff he said. I flicked a cheesecake crumb off my knee. Would it be that strange, the two of us together?

A look out the window, in the direction of the master bedroom, reminded me how far apart our worlds were. Such a beautiful house.

"It *would* be strange. It was one date, Meg," I had to remind myself privately. "Don't lose your head."

I thought of him inside, dreaming, with rose petals all around him. Those were the first roses a guy had ever given me—no, the second. The second in one night, counting the corsage.

"Fine. I'm just gonna roll with it," I said aloud.

"Pardon me?" Barney's pitch ticked up in surprise.

Yes, I *did* want to cuddle up with Tristan again in those roses. But not yet. I wanted to do something crazy first, something that didn't involve falling for the freaking quarterback. I had to reclaim myself, before all was lost. The clock on the dashboard said it was almost midnight. Was it possible to still get in a hand or two?

"Barney, do you play poker?"

He frowned at me, suspicious. "On occasion...sure."

"Want to take me to a game, not too far from here? You know where After Dark is? It's a little entertainment spot in the hills."

"A bar?" He looked me over, not bothering to hide his disapproval.

"Now Barney, this is a dry county. No alcohol allowed," I said, with what I hoped was a seductive smile.

"You're outta your mind, girl." He shook his head and looked out the driver-side window.

"Come on, it's almost midnight. I know you're off the clock soon."

"So?"

"What do I have to do to get you to take me? Come on."

"Show me your tits," he snorted. I reached to pull the straps of my dress over my shoulders. "That was a joke—pull those back up!" His pitch hit the roof and he looked around wildly to make sure no one had seen. "What's wrong with you?"

"If you don't take me, I'll just have to walk." I gathered up the cheesecake trash and made to get out of the car.

He started up the engine and glared at me sideways, "Alright, Jesus."

"Whatever happened to Amanda anyway?" I settled into my seat happily, making conversation.

"I have no idea," he muttered, then looked at me out of the corner of his eye again. I detected a smile. "I'm off the clock remember. Ain't no baby-sitter."

"Ain't indeed." I rubbed my hands together; that fifty bucks would get me in, and I knew I could run it up. In a much better mood, I found a good rock station and cranked it up. "I love this song." I cheered and sang along as Barney drove out of the valley and up into the trashier parts of Shirley County.

♥

Barney decided to accompany me inside once we arrived, though he said he couldn't get involved in a poker game. I could tell he was nervous to simply drop me off when he got a good look at After Dark, and as it turned out, I was glad to be on his arm as we walked in. More than one set of bloodshot eyes fixed first on my dress, then on my chest, then on my bare feet. When the gazes finally roamed to the hugely muscled man towering over me, each guy quickly found something more wholesome—pool cue, television, or empty tumbler—to occupy his attention. I usually came to the place in jeans and a T-shirt, and looking down at my beaded dress, I saw how shortsighted I had been not to have thought of that. I pulled Tristan's tuxedo jacket closed, buttoning myself in as best as I could. It hung on me like a sack, a protective barrier.

"Meg! What are you doing here?"

I turned to the familiar voice in relief. Larry. He used to date my mom back in the day and was sort of an uncle figure to me and my siblings. "Hi, Larry. Not too late for me to get in a hand or two, is it?"

"Nah, come on back. Love to have you, sweet thang," he said, motioning to the bartender with authority.

Barney lifted an eyebrow in question and I nodded. "Thanks for the ride, I've got friends in the back." I extended my arms as far as they would go to give him a hug around his wide shoulders. "See you around," I said, knowing I'd likely never see him again.

"I'll stay for a while," he said loudly, offering the look of a bouncer all around. He claimed a bar stool and folded his arms across his chest.

"Thanks," I smiled, touched. In a way, Barney had been a big part of my magical night. I made my way to the back, hoping that magic was still in effect.

Cards are one of my favorite pastimes, especially poker. But I rarely had enough cash to play at After Dark, even though I was finally old enough to play there. The buy-in was fifty dollars, usually too steep for me. That night, if I borrowed a little from Tristan, I'd have enough to hang for a while.

"Thanks, Tristan. You don't mind, do you?" I said, patting the front pocket of his jacket. I knew he wouldn't, and I'd split the winnings with him to make up for it. If I didn't win…well, he said he would only spend it on me later anyway. He was buying me a good time, even passed out as he was. It was his fault I had to have fun without him, and I felt luckier with his involvement by monetary contribution. It was weird, but I had been feeling a lucky streak all that day. Things had just fallen into place, and the feeling only intensified when Tristan came to pick me up. The Tristan Effect. I mused over my new lucky charm as I walked into the card room, and—one more fortunate detail—my cousin Zach was there, with an empty seat next to him.

I rounded the table practically skipping. "Zach, did you finally get some big boy pants?"

"You should talk." He squeezed me in a bear hug. Already tight enough to be painful, he constricted my chest further to force a squeak from my lungs, like I was a baby toy. He loves to do that. We're less than two months apart in age, and I had towered over him for most of our childhood. It was only in the past three years that I stopped getting taller and Zach hit a colossal growth spurt. Plenty of time in a weight room helped to enhance the effect. He rubbed it in and abused his strength whenever possible.

"You'll pay for that, junior," I said as he set me down. Since I was technically his superior in age, I never let him forget it.

"Can't wait to see you try, kitten." Of course, he would always have the upper hand at poker tables in Shirley County, him being a guy and Shirley being totally sexist. I scowled at him and he chuckled, "I win."

"For now." He had no idea how my day was going, But, I thought it wise to keep my secret Tristan Jameson weapon private.

I placed my money on the table, already nicely broken up from dice wagering. Those guys rarely used chips, and it pissed them off if you didn't bring enough for change. I nodded to the other fellas, some of whom I knew pretty well, before sitting down next to my cousin. I smiled at Ricky; he was in me and Zach's class at Andrew Jackson, and one of my best friends. Well, one of my only friends. Terry Finley was a guy who lived in my neighborhood—kind of a scumbag. One of the old cowboys I'd seen at Coleman Ranch had stiffened when I pulled out my chair, but Sean McBride gave him a thumbs up in my honor, and the man nodded curtly. Sean was my first boyfriend when I was in middle school. He had been a senior in high school at the time, and he could've gotten in a lot of trouble messing around with someone so young. But I've kept my mouth shut to this day, and he damn well better give me the A-okay.

"Hey, Ricky. Hey, Sean," I said. Terry Finley squinted across the table. Did he expect a hello, too, gross old lech? I always thought he looked like a wife beater.

I recognized another face and smiled as its owner tipped his baseball hat to me and started to stand, but stopped himself, embarrassed. Mal was so old-fashioned. Everyone knew him and liked him. He had been the mail carrier for the southern half of Shirley County for decades, almost a permanent fixture in the neighborhood. He had even consented to play penny cards with me and my friends once or twice on this or that doorstop, and he'd revealed many poker secrets to our hungry young ears.

"What are we playing?" I asked, trying to sound as nonchalant as possible, though I was nervous as shit. Real poker at After Dark, here we go.

"Seven-Card Stud," said Zach.

I plastered on my poker face. My favorite—could this night get any better? "Hi-lo?"

"High."

"Wild cards?"

"Nope."

"Pot limit?"

Ricky broke in, "Of course not. Shit, Meg. Why don't you get here on time next game?"

"Just trying to get my bearings, keep your shirt on." I knew anytime I arrived was fine with Ricky. He'd had a crush on me since elementary school. "I had to be somewhere," I said, motioning to my strange costume of red dress, tent-like tuxedo jacket, and bare feet. "Why didn't *you* go?"

"Cuz you never came to pick me up. I was waitin' all night," said Ricky.

Sean cleared his throat.

"Please," agreed an older gentleman I didn't recognize. He looked like a banker from out of town.

That was as far as romantic allusion went at the card table. I glared at Ricky, willing him to be quiet and not ruin my cool. He grinned and goosed my knee under the table. I jerked away, but couldn't stop a tiny giggle from escaping. Infuriating.

"So, speaking of time…" said the banker, pointing to his wrist.

"Just waitin' on Larry."

"Yo, Larry!"

"I gotta take a piss, then."

"Come on, man."

Jesus, like a bunch of old ladies. I was feeling much more confident listening to them all bicker and whine. It's funny how reality is never as good as the imagination. Well, almost never. I pushed a memory of Tristan's perfect, chiseled abdomen out of my mind. I had to concentrate, and not on that.

Larry came back with a lidded tray that he put by his feet. A few seconds later, a shot of whiskey appeared by my elbow. So the secret shooter tradition was true. It was one of the things Zach, Ricky, and I had found so fascinating about the famed, illicit After Hours poker game as adolescents. I knocked it back in one gulp, keeping my face as neutral as I could—but god was it nasty—and sat it upside down on the floor. Everyone else did the same, the ritual so firmly established as to be practically law.

"Youngest scrounges," reminded Larry.

"Oh, Zachary angel. I think that's you," said Ricky.

I tried not to smile but Zach saw it anyway and flipped me off.

But law was law, and Zach got down under the table, retrieved everyone's glasses, and snapped the top back over the tray. Larry slid it towards the door with his foot. Even there, the Shirley County prohibition on alcohol loomed large, and no one would risk a night in the sheriff's drunk tank by being sloppy.

The sheriff...

Sheriff Jameson—that was Tristan's dad. Heat rose in my cheeks and it had nothing to do with the whiskey. I thought of what awaited me, naked and sleeping in the sheriff's own bed, and I was antsy to get the game started.

"And without further ado..." Larry, the unofficial leader of the poker club, finally called, "Ante up, boys. Five buckaroos."

I resisted the urge to rub my hands together and let out an evil chortle. Eat your heart out Ashley Freakin' Davis. She was probably decked out in hoodie-footie pajamas at a slumber party with that bitch Shelly. Old Maid or Go Fish?

Everyone threw in but Ricky, who was still underage, poor lamb. Larry was adamant about the age restriction—absolutely no players under eighteen. He hadn't been in on the shots, either. Larry upheld his own laws faithfully. He shuffled, let the cowboy split the deck, then shuffled again. He burned the first card, then slid each player their first hole card in turn. I noticed that no one else peeked at that one, so I waited, too. One more down, then one card facing up. My heart fell when I saw mine: two of hearts. I glanced around the table. A couple more low cards were scattered around, but Sean had the ace of diamonds and the banker had the king of spades.

Damn it.

Ricky sent me silent sympathy with his eyes and patted my thigh under the table. I pinched the top of his hand as hard as I could, nails extended.

I finally reached for my hole cards to have a look. Another two, that one in diamonds. Things were looking up. At least I had a pair, though a low one. I turned up a corner of my second blind: the seven of spades. Well.

I knew it was cheesy to feel a tremor of excitement run through me, because everyone's lucky number is seven. And I'm not a superstitious person, except when it comes to cards. Two of hearts may not have seemed fortuitous at first, but there with the lucky seven of spades? Spades represented the sword of a knight, and what was my Tristan if not some strange high school Homecoming knight in shining armor?

"Meg, you got the low card. What are you waitin' for?"

"Oh, sorry. What's the bring-in?"

"Twenty," the wife beater snapped in irritation. I could almost hear him thinking "dumb bitch" underneath.

All the better. I decided to play the bimbo role—my personal riff on the poker face. Zach would know what I was doing, but he had a low card showing, too, and he sighed when he looked at his blinds.

"Okay. I guess I'm in?" I tossed in my money.

Larry, who was to my left and next in the betting round, gave me a fatherly look as if to say, "You sure, sweet thang?"

I ignored him.

"Alright…call that," he said with a shrug and shoved a twenty toward the pile.

"Call," said the wife beater.

"Fold," said Mal, and handed Larry his cards. I saw that he had at least one spade, as Larry flipped them over next to his arm.

The banker was next. He had a five card showing. Another spade. "I fold."

Wimps. Come on, let's run this up some more.

The rancher tossed in a twenty and made a hand gesture. I took mental notes.

Sean nodded and added his money to the pot.

I could tell Zach was unsure, but then he pulled a couple bills from his wad, too. "Yeah, call."

Larry passed around our next card, face-up.

Mine was a seven of clubs, to my delight. Two pair then. With the way my night was going, I wasn't afraid to hope for a full house. I smiled inside and snuggled into Tristan's jacket, his cologne wafting up, spicy and warm. I heard Ricky chuckle beside me (my hand showing didn't look promising), and I punched him on the shoulder, making sure to display an embarrassed pout while I cased my competition.

Larry handed Sean another ace.

Crap.

He flipped over another jack for himself—that was a pair of jacks for him.

Double crap.

Sean had the high hand showing, so it was his choice to check or bet. I knew Sean pretty well and he was notoriously macho. I knew he'd keep it rolling. He grunted something incomprehensible and threw in another twenty dollar bill.

Zach's eyes darted around to the other players, his fingers thrumming the table. "Fuck." He crammed his cards together and handed them to Larry.

I was next.

I was sweating. After I made a move, they'd know I had something. It was all in or all out. I didn't want anyone to fold too fast, though—the pot wasn't heavy enough. "I'll raise your bet, Mr. McBride," I said, trying to sound dumb and chipper as I tossed in a twenty and a ten. I saw Zach narrow his eyes. He was onto me, but he was already out of the game. Ricky elbowed him under his arm and grinned at me. Stop it, Ricky, you ass.

Larry shrugged and met my raise; he had tons of money and he liked to keep the game running.

The wife beater folded in disgust and I felt the chill in his gaze down to my toes.

The cowboy had gained the four of spades to go with his king. He met the raise without hesitation.

Shit, was he working on a flush? That would totally beat what I had so far.

Sean threw in another ten for my raise, then Larry looked to each of us in silent question. The bet went around the table again and everyone simply stayed, then we were ready for our fifth card, face up.

"Alright, y'all," said Larry, as he flipped over another spade right in front of the cowboy.

Oh no.

The cowboy had three spades showing, but he needed five for a flush. What were his blind cards? My mind raced, trying to remember how many spades I had already seen that game.

Damn that whiskey.

Sean smiled and pulled a third ace next to his other two.

Then, I almost lost it when I saw Larry flipped over a seven of hearts in front of me. I had a full house! That beat everything showing around the table. Hallelujah and thank you, my sweet good luck charm. In my mind, I nuzzled Tristan's sleepy face with my cheek. He'd be so warm and cozy right about then.

But, Sean still had the high hand showing, with three aces. He threw in forty bucks and smirked at me. A big raise. He knew my game by then, and he was trying to intimidate me. Four of a kind would beat my full house, but there was no way he had another ace in his blind. The odds were like four-thousand to one. I looked at the cowboy. He could be going for a flush—I doubted it, with all those spades I'd seen flying—but now that I had a full house, he didn't stand a chance anyway.

I added up all my bets. I would be gratuitously dipping into Tristan's cash.

If I stalled more than a few seconds, I was done.

The cowboy fiddled with his hands, and I knew he was waiting for the game to pass to him so he could fold. Larry had nothing, the game was over for him; he glanced towards the door, probably wondering how long he'd have to wait before heading back to the bar. I fingered the bills in my pocket. Tristan's pocket. The decision was made.

"I'll see your raise," I added forty bucks to the pot. "And raise another twenty." My skin felt singed when I let go of those last bills.

"I'm done," said Larry, scooping his cards together and marrying them to the discard.

The cowboy's face contorted like he was constipated. "Fold," he finally produced.

Sean held my gaze and nodded to Larry.

One more card up.

Nothing on either side.

"Check," said Sean.

"Check," I agreed, relieved. At least I wouldn't have to add more money to stay in. I was out of cash. Maybe Sean was, too.

The last card was blind. I hardly dared to peek. I stared at Sean hard, until he finally broke away to look under his last card. He was faltering—he couldn't beat me and he knew it. But he was such an asshole. He still had the highest hand showing, so the bet went to him. If he decided to bet or raise, I couldn't meet it. I was cleaned out.

Damn it, I was so close! What was I gonna say to Tristan, if I lost it all?

A lit cigarette butt sailed into the room through the open doorway, and landed on the card table.

chapter eight

"Hey!" Larry was on his feet with an immediate violent reaction, like most of the guys. "What do you think this is, your goddamn toilet?"

"Sombitch…" was the garbled expletive, just outside the door—some drunk fool probably on his way to the bathroom, tossing his finished smoke before stumbling past to take a piss. A split second later, a glass mug exploded on the door next to Larry's head.

"You gone be sorry for that, you piece-a-trash." The cowboy had the thick end of half a pool cue in his fist and he was already across the room, holding it cocked back like a baseball bat over his shoulder.

Sean said, "Show me," rolling up his sleeves, his glare focused past me. I flipped my cards over and he glanced at the table.

"Nice hand. Take it before somebody else does." He jerked his head towards the pile of money and bustled past me into the billiard hall. Sean was a jerk, but at least he was honest. I turned over his cards, just to see.

"Nothin'," I smiled. I'd won fair and square.

Shouting erupted just outside our safe little enclave. It was time to disappear.

I grabbed my cousin's arm, "Zach, you got your bike outside?" He was already on his feet, fury darkening his features and the thrill of the fight pumping in his veins. I could hear the dispute escalating in the main room, and I knew that an accident could easily turn into a bar brawl on any given night at After Dark. The last thing I needed was to be floating in a sea of testosterone, with an enticing display of flesh barely concealed. Not to mention broken glass under my shoeless feet. "Can you get me out of here?"

Zach tried to yank his arm away, annoyed. He loved the fray. But I clung on and he sensed my desperation; the fog cleared from his eyes as he looked down at me. When I held open Tristan's jacket to let him see how scantily clad I was underneath, he stepped back, his eyebrows shooting up.

"Yeah, you don't need to be here. Come on."

He helped me stuff my winnings into the little beaded handbag I had bought for the dance, and I winced as I heard a seam pop in the lining. Zach pushed me out the back door, just as Terry Finley hollered from deeper inside the bar, "Hey! We ain't finished playin'—you can't just sit in one hand."

"Yes, I can."

The back slit of my dress tore up to the zipper as I hopped onto the motorcycle behind Zach. He didn't have helmets, so I took Tristan's red silk handkerchief and wound it into a rope to tie up my hair. I held on tight to my cousin, the engine already roaring to life. Thank god, too. The wife beater looked mad. He was scowling in the doorway and his rage washed over me like a cold shower.

Just then, a fist met the back of Terry Finley's head and I didn't care if it was wrong to leave or not. "Go, Zach, go!"

We tore through the gravel parking lot, and I saw the melee was already spilling out onto the front porch. I gripped Zach's torso tighter, craving the safe, warm bed where Tristan was snuggled more than ever. My pulse was thundering, louder than the motorcycle in my veins, as we raced down the road.

When we were clear, Zach slowed and asked, "Where to? Home?"

"Um. No. You'll never guess."

He rolled to a stop and twisted in his seat to look at me. "I think I might."

I felt my cheeks burn. Who in our high school hadn't heard about my scandalous Homecoming date? "You know where the Jameson house is?" I asked, attempting nonchalance.

"The *sheriff's* house? Uh, yeah. What delinquent doesn't?"

I wondered how many times that house had been toilet-papered over the years. I looked away, not really wanting Zach's opinion.

"You sure, Meg?"

"I was invited, and very welcome to stay tonight."

"Alright, alright," he shook his head, chuckling, and he put the bike in gear. "Let's go."

We reached the valley floor and picked up speed, hurdling down the highway in a tunnel of roaring wind. I cheered him on and squeezed him with my knees to urge him faster and the engine roared louder in answer. My stomach lurched and a thrill zinged up my spine. I thought about the wad in my purse—I hadn't counted it, but I knew it was a lot. And Sleeping Beauty was waiting for me. I didn't think I'd ever felt that good.

I wasn't sure if Tristan and I would still be alone, so I had Zach drop me down the street. Sure enough, as I walked up to the house, I saw an illuminated window in the opposite corner from the master bedroom.

At least his sister had finally come home. As annoying as that was, I was glad she was safe, for Tristan's sake. I crept around the back of the house to look for an opening in the fence. The gate screeched when I eased it open, so I slid through the narrow crack and left it ajar. Neat white stepping stones lined a path around to the back, where I imagined led to the patio and swimming pool. My heart picked up its pace in anticipation, while I tried to slow my steps. I couldn't wait to cuddle in. But, as I rounded the corner, my heart slammed into my throat and my toes nearly tripped me.

No!

The undulating blue light of a TV glowed through the curtained windows of the master bedroom. He was awake. The blood drained from my face, realization dawning. My poker game hardly seemed so fun anymore. How stupid—why did I leave while he was sleeping? What did he think when he woke up to find me gone?

The glare from the pool light reflected against the glass doors, so I couldn't see what waited for me inside. I hesitated, not sure I wanted to see. Hooking a finger in the handle, I held my breath and slid the door open, relieved it was still unlocked for me.

"Please don't be too mad," I prayed silently, my eyes shut tight. I opened them and scanned the dimness, looking everywhere but where I figured he must be. The light and noise from the TV blended reality into an eerie multiverse microcosm.

He snapped it off and the remote control clattered onto the coffee table.

Silence loomed so large my ears rang.

Looking at my feet, I finally managed to say, "Hi," in a small voice.

After a grueling pause: "You know, I really didn't think you were coming back. But then I saw you left your shoes…"

I finally looked at him. He was sitting in an armchair with his legs crossed and a blanket across his lap. His hands were busy shredding a rose petal (one of many, lying tortured in front of him), his eyes were focused on my feet, and one corner of his mouth was turned up in a rueful smile. I tucked my toes in; my feet were as dirty as if I'd been playing in a schoolyard all afternoon.

"Of course I was coming back, Tristan. How long have you been awake?"

"Since right after you left." He ran a hand through his hair, then waved it in the direction of the street. "I saw you drive off with Barney in the limo."

"Oh." I pictured him sitting there awake the whole time I was gone, while I'd been imagining him blissfully unaware, curled up in cozy covers.

Jake's earlier remark about deviants knowing this house was a bitter re-crimination. So that was my crowd. "I'm so sorry I didn't take you with me, but I didn't want to wake you up and I couldn't sleep——"

"Take me with you." His tone was suddenly harsh. "Is that a joke? Take me where?"

"To the poker game, where Barney drove me."

He stared at me.

I flinched; his gaze was blue fire.

Without warning, his face split into a breathtaking smile and he collapsed back into his chair. "She went to a poker game," he said to the ceiling, then clapped his hands over his face and laughed softly.

"Why is that so funny?"

"I thought you left *with* Barney," he said into his hands, his voice muffled. He shook his head wearily and scrubbed his knuckles against his scalp.

"*With* Barney?" Oh. My face went up in flames with the knowledge of what he thought I'd been doing all that time. Not playing poker. "Are you kidding? No," I bristled. Was my reputation really that shitty? "Like I would ever do something like that. My god."

"Now I'm the one who's sorry," he said quickly, sitting up and reaching a hand towards me. "I'm not trying to insult you. I just get weird ideas when I'm jealous."

Jealous. I looked again at the torn flowers in his lap.

"You're hard to predict, you know that? Where did you find a poker game?" he asked, amazed.

"After Dark," I said with a shrug. "They always have one on Sat——"

"After Dark, the bar?" He'd stopped smiling.

"Yeah."

"You went to that shithole in the hollows, dressed like that?" His face warped into a mask of fury. "Do you have any idea how dangerous that place is? You should hear what my dad's seen there."

"Come on." I rolled my eyes and found my cuticles to be extremely fascinating.

"How could you do something that crazy?" He kept from raising his voice, but I could tell it was an effort. "And when I was supposed to be taking care of you tonight."

He rose abruptly, spilling the blanket and rose petals to the floor. As tense as a bow ready to be loosed, he paced the room in front of me. Naked limbs—perfect, tempting naked limbs—stalked past and I wished more than anything that I could just go back and erase whatever I had done to screw up our previously enchanted evening.

He stopped and rounded on me, his jaw clenched and his voice deceptively quiet. "That was on *my* watch, Meg. What would I do, if something happened to you?"

"I..."

"Huh?"

"I'm sorry," I mumbled. My chin started to tremble. I wasn't used to anyone caring what the hell happened to me. I shrank back from him, watching his chest rise and fall with his rapid breath, his eyes molten.

"Just taking off!" His volume was rising. "Didn't you think I would worry when you split?"

"I...I don't know..." Concern was foreign to me. He was right; the bar was dangerous and I knew it. But, no one ever worried whether or not I was safe. Tears sprang to my eyes and I wiped them away, totally freaked. I never cry.

Tristan softened immediately, his taught shoulders relaxing and his fists unclenching. "I made you cry?"

I stared at him, wide-eyed and silent (besides the embarrassing snuffling sounds), and then looked at my feet again. He moved close enough that I could feel the heat of his anger. It was fading, tension melting. I wanted to throw myself on him, but I what if he pushed me away?

"That's the last thing I wanted." He reached a hand up to touch my face but let it hover, tentative. A tear rolled down my cheek and he caught it with his thumb, then turned his hand to brush my jaw with his knuckles. "Please don't cry."

Then the waterworks really started.

He grabbed my shoulders and crushed me to his chest, strong arms enfolding and soft voice shushing. He stroked my hair and kissed my head and I don't know how long we stood together like that. It was long enough for me to calm down, probably longer than I'd be proud to admit.

"Well, how much did you win?" he finally asked, his voice muffled against my hair.

"Uh." Hiccup. "I don't know. Lots. The buy-in was steep, so I'm sorry but I stole your dice money," I admitted, rambling like an idiot. "But I think I doubled or even tripled it."

His chest rumbled in a laugh. "I told you that was yours."

"Well, I better get it all out now." I separated from him just enough to look him in the face. "Me and Barney polished off that cheesecake."

The corners of his lips raised, but his eyes darkened. His shoulders recommenced rigidity. "Look, Meg. I don't know what you think is going on between us." He averted his gaze.

Shit. "What do you mean?"

"I don't know." His eyes were wary.

"What did I say wrong now?"

"Not wrong, just," he shrugged and looked at the floor.

I shuffled my dirty feet. "Please, tell me."

He looked at me point blank.

Oh no, what?

"I can't have you with anyone else," he let out in a rush.

I stopped breathing. Pure pleasure, with a dose of fear, flitted through me.

"That came out wrong," he sighed, looking away into the darkness over my head. "I just mean. *I* don't want to be with anyone else. This is all really. Just. Fast. I know. Do you?"

"Do I?" Could this be real?

"Want...to be with anyone else?" He almost winced.

I had already started shaking my head before he stammered out the words. "I'm yours, Tristan."

Blatant, heart-wrenching vulnerability was etched into his features, before relief washed it away. I grabbed his face in my hands and smothered him with kisses. Someone so beautiful, so perfect, and yet so uncertain. I forgot that we all feel the same pain.

"Every girl I don't want has chased me down all my life," he said between our mouths. "But when I finally find you, you run for the hills."

"I wasn't running. That's just who I am."

"I don't understand it." He grabbed the hair at the back of my neck and balled it into a fist. He pulled me back to look at me, zeroing in so close I was dizzy. "I really don't."

"I'm sorry—"

"No. I like who you are."

And I was covered once again with his mouth, his hands, his hair, enfolded in him. I was suddenly so exhausted I could hardly keep upright any longer. Did this glorious human being just tell me...wait, what did he actually tell me? I decided I didn't care about details. I leaned towards the soft, warm bed that I had been craving since I left it.

I got tripped up in the blanket he had knocked to the floor, but he caught me easily and scooped me into both arms. "Tired out?"

My head lolled back against his shoulder. "Mmmm..."

"Yeah, I bet," he snorted. "You'll have to tell me about it sometime."

"Uh huh," I managed through a yawn.

"But not tonight."

"No, please." Please, let's forget about my devious ways tonight.

Tristan lay me down gently and helped me pull the covers up to my chin. Heavenly. He slid in behind me, all silky warm skin and firm muscles.

I felt entirely too dressed, my beaded gown scratching against soft cotton and softer skin. I sighed when I felt him unzipping the back and I almost sobbed in relief when I wriggled out of my clothes, so eager to feel him without any hindrance.

"Oh, that's too perfect," I said when our limbs were blissfully entwined again, smiling up at him.

He drew back, curious. "What's Meg short for anyway? Meghan?"

"No, Mekaela. My little sisters could only say 'Meg,' and it just stuck I guess."

"Mekaela," he said, testing my name on his lips. "Pretty."

"Yeah, whatever…"

"Like you."

"Oh. Thanks."

"I mean it."

I blushed. Why did that simple word, pretty, mean so much to me? It was so sweet, so delicate, so shy. If he would have said "gorgeous" or "sexy" I probably wouldn't have noticed. But pretty was something else.

"Do you mind if I call you that?" he whispered, resting his palm on my chest.

Could he feel my heart pounding? Hear it hammering? I think that thought made it beat even faster.

He looked at his hand, covering my heart, and smiled. "I like you, too, Mekaela. A lot."

Holy crap, he did feel it.

He leaned down and kissed the spot right over my heart.

Oh, just roll with it, *Mekaela*. No, I didn't mind one bit.

chapter ten

I climbed the steps into the school bus behind a couple of sullen guys with my head down, dreading the snarky remarks and whispers I knew were due. If there was one thing I knew well about living in a small town, it was that its citizens weren't allowed to climb up the rickety social ladders without being kicked down a rung or two in the effort.

I should have hitched a ride on Zach's bike.

But I didn't want to mess up my hair.

Silly girl.

Too late; by that time, the hated yellow school bus was my only option. As if Mondays didn't suck enough. I wrinkled my nose at the familiar smells of worn vinyl, dusty floors, morning breath, and various brands of cheap shampoo. The driver ignored me as usual and lurched the bus back along its route. I had to grab the top of a seat to keep my balance, then kept my eyes on an empty bench towards the back until I tossed my book bag in front of me and slumped in. My gaze stayed fixed outside the window. After the bus pulled out of the Southern Cove Mobile Park, I braved a look around.

Everyone was still asleep. Quiet heads bobbed in front of me with the motion of the bus. One kid nodded off, his forehead thudding against the glass window. At least that was something good about Mondays: zombies.

I leaned back, shifting to the side when a spring poked me in the kidney, and closed my eyes. I hadn't heard from Tristan since he dropped me home on Sunday, but why should I have? He brought me breakfast in bed after sleeping late (neither of us too keen on an audience with his sister and her friends), and I didn't kiss him goodbye outside my place until almost noon. That was only yesterday. And what would he have needed to call me for? All our teachers had held off on homework over the Homecoming weekend, so it wasn't like he would have called me to study or anything.

That was ridiculous anyway, he wasn't going to do homework with me—he was just pretending to be interested to be polite.

Guys simply don't call me to study.

I sighed and fingered my curls. Still damp.

I got up early that morning, before anyone else was up, to go for a jog and try calming my nerves. It hadn't worked. While I was running, the thought kept popping into my head that it had all been just a dream. Then, I'd feel like someone kicked me in the stomach and I'd have to slow down to catch my breath, my heart racing so hard it hurt. A shower hadn't soothed much either, but at least the hair product Cassie gave me worked. My ringlets behaved under my own hands, just like they had for Cassie, and they were nice and bouncy.

Unfortunately, the morning was chillier than usual and wet hair didn't help. I repressed a shiver, wrapping my arms around my shoulders and glancing down to see that my nipples were poking right through my thin tan sweater like bullets. Nice. That de-simplified the simple shirt I chose to go with plain blue jeans, in an attempt to avoid undue scrutiny that day. I smoothed the front of my sweater with my forearms, willing my breasts to simmer down. Once again, I yearned for my jean jacket; I saw it in my mind, flung to the floor in frustration when I felt the crusty dried grape jelly on its sleeve. There was no time to find anything else before I rushed out the door.

I let my head bounce against the seat—just another zombie—for the rest of the drive. I closed my eyes and tried to block my brain from the delicious details of my night and morning with Tristan. Sunday had been daydreamed away, and that only made me feel more urgent and frantic Sunday night. I'd hardly slept at all, actual dreams out of reach.

"And tired eyes are so attractive," said the nag.

Did it even matter? Would I even see Tristan or talk to him? God, I didn't have any idea what to expect.

The bus wound through several neighboring housing developments higher in the mountains, before heading down past the narrow piedmont and into the valley. Way too soon, I felt the driver turn off the main valley highway and into the parking lot of Andrew Jackson High, and my gut rolled with panic.

I thought might actually throw up.

I scanned the crowd as the cheese wagon passed parked cars, and I quickly found Tristan's forest green Jeep Cherokee. He was leaning back against the hood with his feet crossed in front of him carelessly—hair still wet, but cozy in a leather, bomber-style letterman jacket—laughing at something a friend was saying. Several of his buddies were ribbing each other and shaking their heads. One of them arched backwards to howl at a particularly funny comment.

Shit.

Shame bloomed instantly and my stomach flipped, wondering what they were laughing about. I imagined the classic jokes, "Some conquest, dude. No need to beg Meg!"

As soon as we stopped, I threw my book bag onto my back and stomped down the aisle, hopping down the steps in pairs, and then heading towards the school entrance posthaste. I trudged up the sidewalk, berating myself. What was I thinking? Me and Tristan Jameson, give me a freaking break. Just another thing I'll have to live down.

Just get to home room, just get to home—

"Mekaela!"

I nearly had a coronary.

I turned, barely daring to hope.

He was jogging towards me, mouth turned down in confusion and that little furrow in his brow—above those blue, blue eyes. I looked past him and saw his friends moving away, apparently uninterested.

"Hi," I said, my blood rushing in my ears. I was unprepared for what it would feel like to see him in the flesh again; he was even more beautiful than I remembered.

"Hey," he said with the hint of a question, then kissed my cheek. "You're freezing—your face is like ice. Where's your jacket?" Accusatory, now.

"Uh. I. Um." God, stop stuttering, Meg. "I didn't realize it was so cold when I left," I lied.

"Here." He plucked my backpack from my shoulders, took off his letterman jacket, and held it open for me. "Wear mine."

Really? Asking seemed pathetic, but I couldn't mentally assimilate this new paradigm. I managed a quiet, "Thanks."

His jacket was worn-in and toasty with wool lining, the smell of leather and Tristan rising up from inside as I snuggled into it. I held my hand out for him to return my bag, but he slung it over his shoulder, against his own backpack.

He frowned at me, reproachful. "Why'd you take the bus? I came to pick you up."

"You did? I'm sorry, you didn't have to do that."

"My girlfriend's not riding the bus, wait for me tomorrow." He slipped an arm around my waist and steered me toward the front doors. It was good someone was steering. I was adrift on a sea of screaming hormones.

Girlfriend?

"You really need to get a cell phone. Your house phone has been busy since yesterday."

"It has?"

"Yeah, I've been trying to call you."

"Oh." How thoughtless not to check; Charlie always hung up the phone wrong so the receiver stayed just off the hook.

We reached the front of the building and Tristan leaned forward to pull the handle first, stepping aside for me like the perfect gentleman.

"After you," he said when I hesitated.

As I walked through, several plump little faces crumpled in dismay, gawking openly at me and Tristan, who were obviously a pair. The girls turned to stare as we walked past. I met their gazes and grinned. I knew it was childish and catty, but I couldn't help it. Then, I turned back around to catch unbelievable hatred seething in another pair of eyes, just inside the foyer. Ashley.

Tristan ignored her.

I gulped. Holy shit. How was this gonna play out?

I was used to glares, of course. I could already feel whispers tickling up the back of my neck. But I knew Tristan wasn't used to anything like that. How would he react to it? I retreated further into his jacket like a scared turtle.

"You *want* me to pick you up, right?"

"Huh?" Was he really oblivious to the brewing melodrama all around us?

"For school," he said, a crooked smile playing on his lips. "In the mornings."

Jesus, he looked so worried. How could he not see how crazy I was about him?

"Tristan, please," I laughed, reaching up to smooth the worry line in his forehead that I was already getting used to. I smothered him with a kiss, reveling in the gasp of another passerby. I deepened the kiss and ran my hand through his hair. After I heard a grunt of disapproval from someone who could've been a teacher, I leaned back to look at his beautiful face.

His swollen lips raised in a little smile. "That was nice."

"And does that answer your question?"

His eyes were still closed in pleasure, tuning out everything but me. "Yeah."

"Okay, then. No more doubts."

He came out of his daze, gave me a lustful grin. "No."

My fingers threaded in his, I towed him towards my locker first, wanting to relieve the poor guy of dual book bag duty as soon as possible. But, I felt his hand clench when we rounded the corner, his breath catching as he came to a halt in the middle of the hallway.

"What's wrong?"

His eyes were burning with rage, fixed ahead of us. Right at my locker. "What the hell is that?"

"Oh. Great."

Someone had written "TRAMP" in dark red lipstick across the door of my locker. It was the exact hue of the dress I had worn Saturday night. Nice girls always paid attention to such details. My ears prickled with heat, but I continued on to my locker. I was instantly wide awake; humiliation is better than a cup o' Joe on a Monday morning.

I squeezed his hand, begging him to follow me, and murmured, "I'm surprised Henry didn't already catch it. He's usually faster than that."

"Someone is going to pay for that," Tristan said through clenched teeth, stalking closer, glaring at the lipstick.

"Probably won't ever find out who did it," I shrugged. My eyes slid over to him as I fumbled with the combination on my lock. At least he hadn't run yet.

"Yeah, well." He dropped my hand.

No.

Without another word, Tristan dumped my book bag at my feet and was gone. My guts went liquid. My nose tingled and I begged myself not to cry. Why was I suddenly crying all the time now, for fuck's sake? And why should he have to share in my shame anyway? Last thing I wanted to do was taint somebody so perfect.

"Crap," I choked. I couldn't let them see me cry.

I kept my eyes off the new commentary on my character, stone-faced, as my lock clicked open and I pushed the door aside. Henry would clean it later. I could do this. Just had to get through the day. I reached down for the zipper on my bag.

Oh. He left both our bags.

"Let me get that off first, Mekaela."

Tristan appeared next to me with paper towels.

"*I'm* gonna find out who did it." He slammed my locker door shut and smeared the red lipstick in a bloody gash across the door. Throwing the dirty one down, he resumed wiping with another paper towel, with about the same effect. I twisted my fingers together, not daring to look around and hoping he had brought enough supplies from the bathroom.

"You don't deserve this," he fumed, his breath starting to come fast with the effort.

"I know," I mumbled. If only he could clean away all that the graffiti meant, and the enmity behind it, too. "Can't let it bother you, I guess."

"Yes. You can."

I sighed, desperate for the chore to end.

"There. Ridiculous." Finally finished, Tristan balled the paper towels together and sent the wad soaring past several surprised freshmen. They scurried like surprised pigeons as it slammed against the inside of a trash can, echoing out of the hollow cylinder.

"Thank you," I said in the answering silence.

He turned back to me, warmth and understanding in his eyes. "No problem, darlin'."

My heart skipped a beat. High-class molasses.

I felt a smile spreading into my cheeks, but Tristan remained severe. He stood next to me, offering a scorching look of suspicion for everyone who passed by, as I opened my locker again and found the books for first period.

"I'll walk you to class," he said, taking my bag from me as soon as I zipped it up.

"Okay." I accepted his hand greedily, more relieved than I wanted to let on. The halls seemed pretty empty all of a sudden, though. No wonder.

But when I risked a glance at Tristan's face, his features were serene. His smile was easy again, the swagger replaced in his stride. He winked and I grinned—would I ever get used to how that little gesture affected me? Soaking up his confidence like a sponge, I squared my shoulders and straightened my spine. Hands clasped, we made our way through the bare corridor.

Together.

part two:
battle ax

chapter eleven

As soon as I walked through the doorway to the courtyard, I could see the group gathering in one corner—mostly guys, packed together to hide the fight from the Andrew Jackson faculty long enough to see some action.

"Shut your mouth or I'll knock the rest of your teeth out."

Oh, shit. I recognized that voice like it was my own, and the fury that laced it twisted my stomach into knots.

Another voice, higher pitched, cackled, "Let's go, Pretty-Boy."

I climbed onto a bench for a better view and saw the misleadingly scrawny Shark Powell, aptly named for his dangerous arrangement of front teeth and his habit of circling prey in a fight. He was circling Tristan. The assembled crowd was starting to roil with angst, egging on the combatants and watching the doors for threat of adult interference.

I pleaded under my breath, "Watch out, Tristan."

I wouldn't have been surprised if that creep had a knife hidden in his combat boots. I craned my neck to see inside the building, hoping for sign of some teacher bustling through the doors. "Come on come on come on!"

Scum of the earth shouted, "Alright, let's go," and, "Do it, you pussy."

I grabbed my hair and pulled hard. I turned back to the fight, cramming my fingers to my lips, but my mangled nails had already been chewed to the quick. Shark lunged and I caught my breath. But Tristan was nothing if not fast, and he ducked away easily. Then they were both circling.

I sucked in a lungful. "Crap, here we go."

Another look at the doors showed no teachers alerted yet, just more students spilling outside. I wasn't sure whether I should go get someone or not—I didn't want to leave him out there. Like that.

"—uck!"

My head snapped back to Tristan. His shouted expletive was muffled under his shirt; Shark had pulled it over his head, effectively blinding him, and then twisted it down so that Tristan was forced to hunch over.

Dirty trick. *Oh please, oh please, don't break his beautiful nose.*

I saw Shark's knee rising to Tristan's face.

"No!"

Tristan wrenched free and threw a solid uppercut on his way up. I heard his fist make impact with something bony.

"Alright, break it up. Break it up, darn it."

"Oh thank god," I breathed as Mr. Davis brushed past, shoving spectators out of the way.

Relief flooded through me, but I shook all over. I got a glimpse of Tristan's face as the guidance counselor hustled him towards the office. He was scanning the crowd, looking for me.

"I'm here," I called in a trembling voice, waving my hand high.

He flashed me his home run smile just before ducking inside the building, and then was gone. I blew out my breath in both gratefulness and disappointment—he didn't seem hurt, but I'd be eating alone. The dispersing crowd offered more than a few dirty looks in my direction. The ones who hadn't heard what started the fight were being filled in via whisper network. I wondered what nasty comments had been made about my supposedly loose nature to set Tristan off this time. I swallowed hard, my throat lined in sand, and looked down at my lonely lunch bag.

"Think I'll get some extra studying done instead," I sighed, trying to sound perky, as if I could fool myself into believing exile to the library was my own choice. The library was my constant haunt lately. Maybe if I whistled "Zippity Do Dah," it would help. I thought of the scowls *that* would elicit smiled. The smile flickered out and I kept my head down as I left the courtyard.

chapter twelve

I was still in the library when the final bell rang; my last class was study hall. I also worked there after school three days a week, so it was an easy transition from school to job. On the days I worked, I needn't muster any courage to brave the riotous after-school hallways where spitballs flew and clicks re-glued. Usually, Tristan would meet me in my hushed, book-lined safe haven, but an hour after the bell, I still hadn't seen any sign of him.

I pushed the cart through rows of musty books, shelved floor to ceiling, wondering what his punishment had been. I was never sure whether his dad's role as the town sheriff helped or hurt when it came to school discipline. The fact that our guidance counselor, Mr. Davis, was Tristan's ex-girlfriend's father only further complicated the issue. On the one hand, Mr. Davis might have been bitter about his daughter's dismissal by Andrew Jackson High's once beloved quarterback. However, too harsh a sentence could be viewed as revenge, so maybe the man went easier on Tristan than he normally would have. I knew he kept a paddle hanging on the wall over his desk as a threat, and I heard he'd actually used it, though surely not on Tristan? He would probably trust Sheriff Jameson to mete out fair punitive behavior at home, but as far as I'd seen, Mrs. Jameson was the disciplinarian in the family.

"And she's worse than a paddle any day," I grumbled, peeking around the side of the aisle to see who had walked into the library. Just a couple freshmen.

I slid "Harry Potter and The Sorcerer's Stone" into its proper slot and sighed. The black eye was almost completely gone now, really.

I remembered when Tiger Mom had gotten a load of that one…

Tristan got out of the car with flowers in front of his face.

"What are you doing?" I asked suspiciously.

As soon as he'd shut off the engine, he looked away from the driver side window, gathered the wildflower stems off the passenger seat, and held them up to cover his eye. He wasn't fooling anyone.

"Is it that bad?"

"Depends on what you mean by bad," he said, one perfect, uninjured eye peeking around the side of yellow daises. "I think it's kinda cool."

"Even with a black eye, your face is better than flowers." I'd been worried ever since I got his text that morning. I wrapped my fingers around the haphazard bouquet and pushed down gently. "Thank you, though."

"I know you love flowers."

He handed them over and I gasped.

"Is that why you were in the nurse's room all day?" I asked softly, wincing at the angry welt surrounding his left eye. Eggplant-violet was creeping from the corners of his eyelid. I touched the puffy lower lid as gently as I could. "Oh, Tristan…"

"Nurse Myers had someone bring me all my work from each class." He shrugged and murmured, "She kept me in an ice cycle."

"What's an ice cycle?"

"Nothing, come here." He snuck a hand around my waist and with a firm tug, I was much closer to his eye. Then I couldn't see a thing as his lips found mine and I forgot about bruises for a minute.

Which I was sure was his intent.

I leaned back so I could look him in the face. The vicious injury was all the more obscene compared to the bright blue irises gazing at me, happy and carefree. "So what did they say this time?"

"Say?"

"Whoever pissed you off. What did they say about me?"

He smiled like he was playing a guessing game with a small child. "They is two or more."

"He, then?"

He focused on my lips. "That's none of your concern, you."

"Of course it is—" But he smothered my objection with another kiss. He loved to act like I was some innocent, wide-eyed schoolgirl—of the gentler sex—and he was hard to resist physically. It was actually kind of scary to realize how easily he could overpower me if he wanted to. His lean, muscled arms bulged under his T-shirt and I broke away with a firm hand against taught pecs, "Okay, okay. But, I'd feel better if we went inside, so you could rest."

He sighed hard. "I've been resting all day."

But he let me lead him down the steps to the Coffee Stop, one of our favorite places to hang out after school on the days I didn't have to work at the library. The stairs were notoriously treacherous, scaling the steep hill that marked the edge of Shirley County's tiny downtown, and I held onto his bicep like I was guiding my little brother Charlie to the bathroom after he'd awoken in the middle of the night.

"Be careful. Can you see okay?"

"It's just a bruise, Mekaela. My vision is fine."

"Well, it's still slippery with the ice melting."

We'd had a bad sleet storm as soon as school resumed after the Christmas Break and it was freezing, even in the afternoons, so not much ice had melted. Earlier that morning, the sun finally broke through the clouds and everything was thawing, though.

The good weather set all kinds of spirits free and the evidence all over my boyfriend's eye. Tristan insisted on defending my honor whenever he felt it was breached and unfortunately, that happened all too frequently, especially to his standards for respectfulness. It was ludicrous; I had only messed around with a handful of guys that even still attended Jackson, and most of them had remained quiet. It was the ones I refused who were the problem, seeking vengeance for my rebuffs. Rotten little liars.

"Hold onto the handrail, there's puddles everywhere."

"I can handle a little water." He sounded irritated. I knew he liked the attention, though. He loved to be macho, but he loved the soft touch, too.

"Let me help, Tristan. It's the least I can do."

He rubbed my knuckles with his thumb in gratitude and followed me inside the shop, which was cafe, ice-cream parlor, game room, and cozy make-out hole, all in one.

"Okay, let me just see if I can get an ice pack," I said, depositing him on a beanbag in the corner, next to a bookshelf full of joke books, cross-words, and the odd poetry tome. A wide hutch separated the cozy nook from the rest of the store, and it was stuffed with almost any kind of game you could imagine. We had probably played them all.

"It's freezing outside, I don't need ice."

"It's warm in here. Come on, it'll keep the swelling down."

"Ugh. Fine." He played the doubtful patient and laid his head back on the beanbag while I went to find supplies. When I came back with an ice bag and an ice cream, I could tell he was feeling just fine. He was sitting on the floor and he peered up my skirt as I approached, even though I was wearing thick wool tights.

"It might feel better if you kissed it," he said, now playing up the injury.

I knelt down next to the beanbag and leaned close to deliver a chaste kiss to his sore eyelid. "Here?"

"My rib still hurts, too. On this side." He lifted his shirt to show me a bruise-free abdomen.

"That was weeks ago." Of course, I didn't mind kissing it anyway. Tristan had the best six-pack I had ever seen in real life, my favorite muscle right over the hips nice and defined. I think it's called the external oblique, but me and my cousin Cassie always call it "the this," with lewd hand motions indicating that perfect diagonal that some guys own at the bottom of their abs. I bent lower to kiss him there.

"And it hurts here, too."

"Shut up, no one kicked you in the balls," I said, straightening up to see his lascivious smile.

"Your ice-cream's melting."

"Oh, shit." I tossed the ice pack in his lap and licked the sticky drip off my wrist, just before it trickled into my sleeve. "This is yours, actually. Injured boys get brownie fudge ice-cream, with dark chocolate chips."

"My favorite."

"I know."

He didn't take the cone, preferring instead to wrap an arm around my bum, "Come here, I'm not gonna break." He pulled me onto the beanbag with him, so I fell against his chest, and then plucked the ice cream out of my hand just as I lost my balance, "Share it with me."

We snuggled together, trading licks and talking about nothing in particular. I had to keep slapping his roaming hand, spring fever definitely having set in, until I finally threaded my fingers in his and pinned his hand against my stomach.

The sugar cone was almost gone and Tristan was nuzzling into my hair, saying, "Mmm, love dark chocolate," when the door banged open. The bell flew up and cracked against the molding.

"Tristan Jameson, I have been looking all over for you," said a shrill voice from the front of the cafe. I looked up to see Tiger Mom, all in a dither, stalking towards us with her fists on her hips. "What the Sam Hill are you doing here?"

"What? We always come here after school on Tuesdays," he said, cowering behind my bushy mane.

"Not today you don't. You are in big trouble, young man. Fighting again—" She gasped, her eyes wide with horror, when he sat up straight with his black eye in full view. "Oh my god."

She dropped her purse and a heavy tote on the floor and ran to him. I moved out of the way before I was bulldozed, catching a bookshelf to steady myself.

Her voice broke when she whined, "Tristan, your eye."

Was she crying? I glanced sideways at them under my lashes, and the scene was so intimate I blushed.

"Your sweet baby blues..." Her fingers flitted around his face without actually touching it, brushing his hair out of his eyes. He was looking down at his hands, submissive.

Yikes, this is weird.

A couple apples had rolled out of her tote and I picked them up and repacked the bag, glad of something to do. When I looked back, he caught my gaze and pushed his mother's hand away.

"I'm fine, Mom."

"No, you're not. Keep this ice on it. Here." He accepted the ice pack I had given him earlier with a petulant groan. "We're going home right now, Tristan."

"What? Why?" He sat up straighter and glared at her, but his complaint didn't offer much resistance. He knew he was already defeated by mother love. He looked at me, the apology already written on his face, then stood up, a giant standing over her frantic, petite form.

"Excuse us, Meg," she said, finally acknowledging my presence, but not bothering to look me in the eye.

She scooped up her things and held onto Tristan's arm, hauling him to the door like he was an overgrown five-year-old. He mouthed something to me over his shoulder and held his cellphone up behind his back in illustration.

"You just wait until your father gets home…"

Jesus, were we in an episode of Leave It to Beaver or what?

"…and sees that eye," she was saying, a constant stream of muttering as she pushed Tristan through the door.

"Dad'll be proud of me."

"Don't you smart talk me, young man."

Their voices died away. I let my knees crumple under me and slouched into the beanbag in relief.

…yep, the black eye episode sure didn't win me any points with Mom.

I shuddered at the memory and pushed another library book into place. I was lost in my thoughts, everything comfortably muffled by row upon row of books stacked around me. When two stealthy arms circled my waist from behind, I jumped and dropped the leather-bound journal I'd been holding.

"God, Tristan—you scared the crap out of me."

He caught the book as it left my hands, chuckling over my shoulder. "I'll say. You just let out a sound like one of Tessa's 'squeakie plushies'."

I pressed my lips together in silent complaint. "So what happened this time? You didn't get suspended, did you?"

"Detention."

"That's not so bad." I twisted around in his arms to look at his face, always surprised by the beauty of his smile, spread ear to ear at the sight of my own. His expression changed. "Why the I-just-got-my-lollipop-taken-away face, then?"

A lopsided smile and averted gaze. "Because…"

"What?"

He winced. "My mom came to the office, too. She was on campus."

"Oh."

"Grounded."

"On Friday night?" I snorted and crossed my arms over my chest. Of course his mother would be more than happy to keep us apart on the weekend. "That's freakin' childish, isn't it?"

Tristan pinched the bridge of his nose with one hand and I felt him stiffen, tense.

Right. Best not to insult one's mother out loud. I cleared my throat and softened my tone, "So...how long are you grounded?"

"Just tonight." His smile crept back as he traced the edge of my face with a finger. "I'm gonna miss you tonight, though. Lollipop."

I blushed. "Watch out or maybe I *will* take it away."

He just chuckled, knowing that would never happen, then leaned down to kiss my neck. The head librarian strode past our aisle, muttering.

"Sorry, Mrs. Yates," I called in a hushed voice, pushing Tristan's face away with a warning look. Mrs. Yates was his aunt and one of Tiger Mom's best buddies; she would report any impropriety with glee.

He sighed, "You'll be at the game tomorrow?"

"Of course."

"See ya there." He swooped in for a kiss anyway, and he was rarely satisfied with a quick peck.

"Tristan, seriously. You're gonna get me in trouble," I hissed, my grin belying my stern admonishment.

He winked and gave my butt a soft pinch before sauntering away, careless of gossipy ladies. "Don't be late tomorrow."

"I'll see what I can do," I muttered, watching my favorite view moving away.

Tristan turned back and caught my lecherous gaze, let his eyes linger over my own form, then turned away shaking his head. He offered a thousand megawatt smile as he strode past my boss. "Bye, Aunt Meghan."

chapter thirteen

I checked my watch and cursed the time. I was always late to baseball games. I bumped through the impromptu parking lot trying to find an opening. Cars were parked in a rough approximation of lines, stretching back from the baseball diamond to the border of a wooded park, so it didn't matter much where I stopped, as long as I didn't block anyone in. The ancient Volkswagen Rabbit chugged and coughed, and I stomped on the clutch, picking a spot and rolling in just as the car shuddered in a death rattle.

"I hate this thing."

I pounded the steering wheel, reprimanded by an off-tune beep of protest.

"You're right," I frowned, not sure whether to feel thankful or martyred. "Well, at least I have a car today."

I had bribed my sister, Jo, into letting me borrow the beat-up vintage thing by taking an extra baby sitting shift again. I'd been doing that at least twice a week lately, and was starting to get better at the stick shift. But the Rabbit was such a dinosaur that it grew cranky easily—not that it was a fun drive in the best of moods, with shoddy power steering and the air-conditioning long ago pooped.

I wiped my forehead and it came away wet.

"Sweaty already," I growled and fished around in my purse for a compact. "In the morning. In March. Wonderful."

When I hopped out and slammed the door behind me, cheering erupted from the field.

"Now that's a warm welcome," I said, sucking in the fresh, cool air—a stark contrast to that within the musty Rabbit. "Sorry, Black Beauty. I love vintage, but not in automobiles."

I felt better with every step I took away from it, my sneakers squishing in the dewy grass. It was a beautiful morning, with a clear, limitless blue sky, and my Tristan was in the near vicinity. I felt the electricity I always did when I knew I was about to see him. I love baseball, and I felt more comfortable at those games than I ever had at football games, where there was always a mob of students, hollering parents, the marching band, the drill team, and…oh yes, the cheerleaders. I had refused to attend even one football game since Tristan and I got together. To say I might suffer a few evil glares would've been an understatement, so we just met after the games and I listened to Tristan recall the highlights. But baseball games were more low-key. There was never much of a fan turn out, and the fans that did come were mostly my kind of people.

"Hmm…wonder what's up." As I neared the field, I noticed Tristan wasn't pitching. I hoped to god he wasn't getting a hard time from those guys now, too. Recognizing the kid running a hotdog cart by the entrance to the bandstand, I decided to get the skinny before venturing further.

"Hey, Doug."

"Hey, Meg, how you?"

I lifted a shoulder. Can't complain. "Something wrong with my man? He usually pitches first."

Doug spit into the dirt on the opposite side of the cart from where I stood. I smiled. That was as polite as you got with most guys from the hollows. "This un's an easy win—the Falcons from up north. Think coach wants to train up Davey Watts a lil' more. Ain't gonna have Jameson 'round next year."

I nodded agreement and continued towards the dugout with a wave.

"Sure as shit won't," I said under my breath when I got out of earshot. "Only a couple more months."

I was counting down the days until graduation and I had a feeling Tristan was, too. I hugged myself, imagining those gaudy orange mortarboards flying into the air. Seventy-two days left to go. I peered into the dugout from a distance. Where was that tight little ass?

I changed direction to skirt the bleachers and headed back past the cars, towards the woods where I knew Tristan liked to cool off in the shade between pitches. I slowed down when I got closer to his usual spot and my ears prickled with the sound of hushed, urgent voices. I recognized Tiger Mom's voice and bit my lip, then hung back to eavesdrop behind a clot of overgrown azalea bushes.

"But you and Ashley were so perfect together, Tristan…"

Oh this was just getting ridiculous. My temper blazed. They broke up like five months ago—fuck!

"…and don't you know the heartache this is causing our families. Family. We're practically one family."

"Yeah, and that's creepy, Mom. Ashley's like my sister. My neurotic, annoying, religious zealot sister."

A pause. Then a sigh.

"The Davises are a little on the devout side, I'll admit."

"Uh, yeah."

"But, there's nothing wrong with strong values—"

"Mom, I don't want to be with her anymore. I don't know if I ever did. Live with it."

"I thought she made you happy."

A snorted chuckle. "Really? Did I really seem *happy* with her?"

Silence.

"Well, all couples go through rough spots."

A strangled groan. "Mom, we're not a couple anymore. That's it."

"Okay."

"Okay."

"So…so, just take a break. Like you are…"

Damn, the woman was relentless. I heard a few words uttered so low that I couldn't make them out, then sounds of someone stuffing things into a bag.

"Why does it have to be *her* then, Tristan?" Anguished now.

I leaned in closer. They obviously weren't talking about Ashley anymore.

"Her? Her name is Mekaela. What is your problem with *her* anyway, mom? At least she doesn't keep my balls in a candy jar—" A shocked gasp. "Plugging your ears. Nice. You're ridiculous." He raised his voice almost to a shout, "Just as ridiculous as Ashley and her 'chastity'."

I bit my knuckle to keep quiet—I could almost hear the air quotes he used, his voice was so filled with sarcasm. I hated to laugh. Poor Tristan. Was his mom humming *Mary Had A Little Lamb*, too?

She stopped, sighed.

The silence lingered and I held my breath.

"Well, you should just stay unattached for a while then, son. Just stay single—"

"I love her, Mom." With finality.

I gasped before I could help myself. We had never used the "L" word before. "I love your hair," or "I love your smile," sure. But never like that, never as in "I love you, Mekaela." At least not out loud. It felt good to think it and to hear it. My heart hammered dangerously fast and my breath came hard. It felt like a dream.

Thankfully, Tiger Mom's pained groan covered up my noisy surprise.

"Well, you had better be using condoms is all I can say—" Her lecture was interrupted by barely stifled annoyance from her son. "Well, I don't want her getting in trouble or something and ruining your future, Tristan."

How dare she.

"In trouble? Mom, this isn't 1950."

"Pregnant, then."

"Why, because that's what happened to you?"

Another pause.

"That was a very rude thing to say, young man. But, yes. Exactly."

Oh...

"Mom. Have you ever thought that something like that would ruin her life a lot more than it would mine? She's already been accepted to at least three colleges. With scholarships."

"Well. Good for her then. I'm glad she has other plans."

"Other plans than me, you mean?" A bitter laugh. "Trust me. She's not hanging her future on me. Like Ashley would have, by the way—"

"That's not a nice thing to say."

"—she's doing a finance track. And she's gonna be really good at it, too. She's really smart."

My chest swelled with pride.

"Well, you should let her concentrate on her studies, then. If you really love her, like you say you do. Leave her be, so she—"

"I can't leave her be." Stated as fact.

My pulse raced in the dead silence that followed, thundering in my ears for what seemed like an eternity. I finally heard Tiger Mom grumble once again, and then stomp through the trees in the direction of the baseball field. I waited for a few minutes to hear his footsteps, too, but by the sounds of intermittent scraping and occasional grunting, Tristan seemed to be warming up. I took a deep breath, stepped away from the bushes, and then lost it again when I caught sight of him. His long leg was propped high against a knot in a tree, his head turned away as he leaned into the stretch. Those pesky butterflies soared nearly out of my throat, as they always did when I saw him again, after we were separated for too long.

Even after only one night apart. I smiled to myself, knowing I was being a dopey romantic. I was getting used to the butterflies. I stepped loudly as I approached, shuffling leaves and looking around innocently. "Tristan? You out here?"

Undisguised delight: "Mekaela."

He loves me. Tristan loves me. "Sorry I'm late. But I guess you're not starting today anyway, huh?"

"Nah." He met me halfway, reaching for my waist when I was still several paces away. He gathered me in hungrily, like he hadn't seen me in weeks either. "I'm up next, though. Gotta head over soon."

"Always time for a hello kiss, though?"

He held my chin and brushed his thumb across my lips, "Always," he said, before meeting them with his. "Plus, I got you something."

"You and all the presents." He always had some little trinket or picked flower or some sweetling for me.

He smiled mysteriously and let go of me.

"What is it? I love your presents." My suspense mounted, watching him root around in his duffel bag.

"Here." He snapped a ball cap on my head and I took it off immediately to study it. It was a crisp new Andrew Jackson Bobcatts baseball hat, in orange and white, with the growling mascot on the front.

And on the back…"You had '27' embroidered on it? Is that like marking your territory with your jersey number or something?"

"Yeah," he said, his eyes gleaming.

I pulled my ponytail through the whole over the adjustable Velcro strip and tugged the bill down nice and snug. "I love it, thanks."

"You look pretty in a cap." He thumbed his nose as he studied my face, then watched me for a beat before saying, "I'm sorry you had to hear all that. My mom can be sort of…opinionated."

"Hear what?" I asked, playing dumb. And unwounded. It was tough to listen to.

"Come on, you know I can read your face like a book." He wrapped his arms around me and crushed me against his chest, so that we were eye to eye. I turned my face and looked down, but he wriggled around to find me again. "And I know you love books."

I met his gaze. We were saying "love" a lot. Did he know that I'd heard that, too?

I love her, Mom.

His eyes were as clear as the sea in a Caribbean paradise, his gaze as scorching as the sand. Was I supposed to say it, too? But, he hadn't actually said it to me. I'd been eavesdropping on a very private conversation and I was suddenly unsure of how to react. Love. That was major.

"She really hates me, doesn't she?" I said and looked away. Coward.

His shoulders relaxed, in either relief or acquiescence.

"No." He shook his head doggedly. "She just doesn't know you. Yet."

"Doesn't want to…"

He pulled my chin up with one finger to look at me again. "She'll come around. Don't worry about her."

I noticed he didn't say, "Who cares what she thinks?" or, "Oh, screw her." He and his mother. I reflected on the old saying that the way a man treats his mother is similar to how he'll treat his wife.

Wife? Please. I had to get my head out of the Jane Austin novels.

I felt my pout hardening into a scowl. "Oh no, I won't worry about her. I'll have too much to worry about, keeping enough condoms on hand."

He loosed a startled guffaw and pulled the bill of my hat down further. "That's a tough task, it's true," he snickered, turning away to finish the last of his stretches.

"I'm sure the idea keeps her up late at night."

He shrugged. "My mom's a busy-body, she's got plenty other headaches. Don't think about it too much."

"Hmph." I folded my arms across my chest. I wasn't going to let all that I'd heard out of her painted, prissy little mouth slide that easily. But, I'd keep that to myself.

"She just wants the best for me," he shrugged, leaning over and gathering his duffel bag and his own worn, sweat-stained baseball cap. "She just doesn't realize that the best for me, is you."

"Uh-huh."

He winked and turned to walk towards the field, then stopped short and snapped his fingers. "Hey, I just remembered. I got an email from my sister this morning."

"Liza?" I asked hopefully. I'd never forget the help she gave Tristan on our first date. I often wondered if we would've even hooked up without it.

"Yeah, Liza." He laughed and kissed me on the cheek. It was no secret that his little sister, Amanda, made me uncomfortable. Maybe even more than his mother. "She invited us up to the university for some big party. My mom thinks it's a friend's birthday party—she has no idea what college is like."

"Oh yeah, when?"

"April 25th."

"In Nashville?"

"Wanna go?"

"Prom weekend," I said flatly, to his knowing smile. We'd be out of town for the whole damn thing? Sign me up. I was beginning to think of Liza as my guardian angel. "Heck yes—that's perfect."

"I know."

"I can't wait to meet Liza."

"She can't wait to meet you." He tweaked my nose and strutted ahead of me, clearly pleased with himself.

And why not? I wondered how someone could look so good in those silly stirrups. I'd seen dozens of flabby butts ill concealed, and enough potbellies hanging over the standard baseball uniform in my life. Tristan's body was made for fitted designs and clinging material, however. I resisted the urge to snap his waistband. *That firm little…*

He turned back to grab my hand and he traced my line of vision. "Later for that, darlin'. I gotta play me some ball first."

My skin prickled all over; I loved it when he called me that, with his deep drawl and honeyed lips. There was something almost condescending about it, in a "me big man, you little lady" kind of way. I don't know why that turned me on, but coming from Tristan it just did.

"I can't wait to watch." I took his hand and matched his stride.

Tristan was fun to watch doing almost anything physical. He was a graceful pitcher, a powerful batter, a sleek runner. I supposed he looked good playing any sport; he was a natural athlete. I frowned, thinking of how I'd missed seeing him do what he was supposedly best at: football. Feeling guilty, I went up on tip-toes in my tennis shoes and planted a kiss on his cheek. "Baseball's the only other thing you look half as good doing. Too bad you can't play in the nude, like the Ancient Greeks."

He smirked and delivered a last, lingering kiss in full view of the bleachers and dugout. "Wait for me after, then," he whispered, then hustled to meet his teammates.

chapter fourteen

I kicked the dirt and let my thoughts wander as I watched him run. Where could we hang out later, after the game? We'd have the whole rest of the day to do whatever we wanted. Too quickly, I reached the entrance to the bleachers and my mind returned to less pleasant details of my liaison with Tristan Jameson. Rounding the bottom riser, I saw his mother, her back ramrod straight in the first row.

Of course.

There was no way to avoid her. I took a deep, steadying breath and walked in her direction.

"Hello there, Meg." She was all business. As if I were no more than another student from the high school, with whom her position as PTA President forced her to entertain pleasantries.

"Hello, Mrs. Jameson," I said, plastering a polite smile on my face. "How are—"

"Alright, Tristan! Let's go, son," the little lady shouted, clipping off the end of my salutation as her pride and joy took up position as the next batter. She proceeded with her usual MO: ignore the slut.

I passed the mini cheering section and climbed the stairs to the back row. There were cheerleaders at baseball games after all. I frowned and plopped down on the metal bench at the top. At least Ashley hadn't shown up again, like at that first game, when Tristan had refused to even speak to her. He'd treated Tiger Mom like a pariah, too, since she'd been the one to invite the ex. He was furious with both of them and hadn't bothered to hide it, so the precedent was thankfully set early.

After the last of the football season following Homecoming, and all of the antagonism that had accompanied that era, I'd been so disappointed to see Miss Bobcatt Queen at a baseball game that I almost cried in frustration. Me and Tristan had both been looking forward to some more neutral territory at the baseball field. I wanted to watch him play, he wanted me to watch, and we were both ready for the melodrama that had accompanied our romance to dissipate. Even though I never saw him until later in the evening, I knew that Tristan had endured at least one fight—petty bickering or all-out testosterone fest—after every football game. Always after. His bro's just snubbed him at school, and they were content to keep such drivel off the field. But, when the girlfriends got involved after the games, trouble would commence.

"Nice girls," I muttered to myself, in my lonely seat at the back.

I remembered Tristan's earlier jab, when his mom had the audacity to assume I'd be stupid enough to get impregnated: *Why, because that's what happened to you?*

That was an interesting piece of news.

So, Mrs. Jameson got into a little trouble herself, did she? I put my feet on the seat-back in front of me and propped my chin in my palms, watching Tristan swing two bats in warm up. "Well, forget it, lady. I've got twice the brainpower you do, and I'm not about to follow in your footsteps."

I glared at her upright back and perfect, curling-ironed ponytail.

But, the problem was simple: Tristan loved his mother, she hated me, and I didn't want to stand between them. Who was I to ever imagine I could? And was I really "good" for him, like he said? I couldn't help question that, in lieu of the constant fights, detentions, and the punitive grounding he'd finally received from his mother the day before.

"Grounding, at eighteen," I muttered, not bothering to hide my disgust, as no one was paying me any mind anyway.

Wait, was he even eighteen yet? For some reason, Tristan had refused to divulge his birthday to me, though I knew it must be close. I watched him chatting with the coach, wondering what the deal was with that.

I folded my arms and frowned. "Whatever. He *does* seem happier than he did before we met. Much happier."

Despite all the social turmoil, he really did. God knows why—I could hardly believe he was so into me, but he was. Part of the reason it had been so hard to see that awful black eye was that his eyes were always smiling when they looked at me. It seemed like he was on cloud nine. I gushed as he blew me a kiss from down below. Tiger Mom's shoulders tightened more (if that were even possible), and I snorted in response, deciding to quit moping and enjoy the game.

"Jeez, let's just roll with it."

Right on cue, Tristan got off a good hit and made it to second base. I had no problem joining in with his personal cheering section in the first row. I knew his mother heard my hoots and whistles behind her, but I never saw her tense up again for the rest of the game. In fact, I almost dared to imagine that her cheering picked up in response to my own. I knew it was crazy, but did I detect a hint of camaraderie in our mutual adoration of Golden Boy? I even met her eye and smiled when she glanced around the stands.

I was immediately sorry for that breach. Stephanie Jameson did not return the sentiment; her backhand inspection was so frigid that I felt I'd been slapped.

"Ouch," I said aloud, forcing a self-conscious laugh, determined not to feel frozen out of my own boyfriend's baseball game.

I tried to concentrate on the field after that, but it wasn't easy. I knew I was keeping my cheering to a minimum—for her sake—and that felt like shit. I tried to pick my spirits back up, but the fact is, baseball is a very slow game. Pulling out a good book from my backpack, I thought of Tristan's comment. He was right; I loved books and I always had one on hand, especially when I needed to bury my head in the sand.

"Okay, Kate Chopin. Gimme a falling through the pages moment."

Over an hour later, I finally looked up when the bleachers burst into whoops and catcalls, the metal risers shuddering with stomping feet. The Bobcatts had won.

"Yay."

I made a split decision to skip the ignominy of Tristan's mother snubbing me again. The stands began to empty and most of the spectators poured onto the field in congratulations. I made my way back to the Rabbit.

My text: *"meet me at the point"*

I slid into the seat and tossed the cell phone he bought me for a late birthday present onto the passenger side. I couldn't afford the service (I didn't say, but he knew), so he had added me to his own plan, saying it was more for him than for me. I sighed and started the engine. The wind would be in my hair before Stephanie Jameson could even be glad I'd left.

♠

I sat perched on the narrow column of rock with my knees pulled in tight to my chest and my hands clasping my elbows. I studied the edges of stone around me, dropping off into thin air, and I thought of strange cylindrical plants that grew in the depths of the ocean. I checked out a DVD once about them from the library, and it was absolutely fascinating. Plants grew along the very bottom of the deepest trenches in the seabed, where not a hint of light reached and pressure from the ocean above was unimaginable. They skirted along the fissures in the Earth's crust that let methane gas escape from below. The plants looked like stacked tubes of flower buds, exquisite and otherworldly. Pink and pretty. They danced incessantly, invisible beneath us.

Beauty for nothing but the sake of beauty existing in the world.

That's how I understood it anyway, since we could never see them or even know they were there, for how long? Millennia? I rocked back and wondered about that. Beauty existed there, because they could feel it, not see it. I watched the billowing clouds above and imagined it was the surf at the skin of the ocean, and I was sitting on one of the undiscovered alien plants. Waiting.

It was only a matter of time until Tristan got there. He would be pissed that I left, but he'd know where to go even if I hadn't texted him. We stopped by the point every time we drove in the area, which was a lot. Ever since Homecoming night, when I'd shocked him into a protective male brain-flood by stepping out over the wide chasm between solid ground and self-possessed euphoria, I'd been on a mission. I was determined that Tristan overcome his fear and join me out there, in the freedom zone. Though he hadn't done it yet, I knew he wanted to. He was close.

I heard the sound of his jeep and smiled. I kept my eyes trained on the clouds and heard the crunch of the gravel shoulder and his engine idling, before he cranked the emergency brake and shut the car off. The door creaked and slammed. His baseball cleats shifted the gravel and then hit soft dirt.

"Sometimes I wonder if that phone helps me find you better or lets you take off easier."

I turned towards him, not bothering to hide my utter failure to know how to deal with our current situation. He could read my face anyway, of course. "Sorry."

"If it makes you feel any better, I blew her off as hard as she probably did you."

"That doesn't make me feel better," I lied.

"I know."

We were both quiet for too long, and I turned back to the open sky.

"That's what will finally make her get it, though," he said. "If she doesn't want you around, I won't be there either. We come together."

I turned to look at him again, taken aback by the passion and commitment in that last comment—a glimmer into his soul. I searched his face. He meant that.

"You gonna do it today?" I asked, looking at the empty space between us pointedly.

"Yeah."

My eyebrows shot towards my hairline. "Really?"

And no shit—Tristan stepped out onto the exclamation point without hesitation. Every sliver of adventure and danger and elation and promise I'd ever hoped for thrilled through me.

"Oh my god. Tristan!"

His face was deadly serious. "We've got to find our own place together, and screw everyone else."

"But, you did it. You conquered your fear." I couldn't let the moment go by without celebrating, and I stood up and grabbed his shoulders, exultant. "I am so proud of you—do you know what this means?"

"I can come play poker with you now?" He grinned, a little unsteady on his feet, his shoulders tense under my fingers.

"The guys are gonna love you," I crooned, hopping back onto solid ground and holding my hand out to him. I could tell he was nervous and there was no reason to make him suffer. He followed, obviously relieved. "I've been priming them and you know how to play now, don't worry. It was your poker face that was missing."

"It was you who was worried," he reminded me. "So, I passed the test? I'm finally cool enough now?"

I detected a hint of irony in his tone, but I let it slide.

"Very." I wrapped my arms around his waist and squeezed as tight as I could. "Onto the Education of Tristan Jameson, phase two."

chapter fifteen

"Get your prom tickets here, kids. Last chance," called a sugary voice among the throng.

Students rushed through the vestibule to the front doors, hasty to get outside and enjoy the remainder of a beautiful April day. With less than a month left of the school year, summer vacation fever had already set in. When the crowd thinned in front of me, I saw what I already knew: Tiger Mom was manning a folding table covered in tinsel and balloons. That woman's voice still felt like razor blades.

She saw me approaching and smiled—not quite engaging, but at least semi-kindly. "Hello, Meg Dear."

"Meg Dear" was how she'd been addressing me lately.

"Good afternoon, Mrs. Jameson," I replied coolly.

My pace didn't slow as I passed her vending table. Tristan had already told her that we didn't plan to attend, and if she was disappointed she was working hard not to show it. Not in public, at least. As soon as I was clear I rolled my eyes and pushed through the exit into the crisp spring light outside, blinking after being inside most of the day.

Actually, Tristan had somehow managed to rouse a mild graciousness out of his mother in the last several weeks. His absence at home had surely worn her down some. Since I felt so unwelcome chez Jameson, I preferred to hang out anywhere else and I took my boyfriend with me. And the two of us together every minute allowable in any given day. I knew her son's rapidly rising test scores had swayed her—though probably grudgingly—in my favor, too. That had been a big turning point for us, I remembered...

The chill was starting to seep in from outside the walls in the back of the jeep, seeking exposed shoulders and toes. I couldn't quite get my hand free to pull the blanket up, so I snuggled deeper under Tristan's arm, my face pressed against his bare chest. He was like a living furnace, the heat radiating from him and making me sweat wherever skin touched skin. He shifted against me and let out a sigh, so I went as still as possible, not wanting to wake him. Heaven was in his embrace.

I had dozed off, hovering between wake and real sleep, so I had no idea how much time had actually passed since we parked. It couldn't be after midnight yet, could it? Time always felt too short when we were together. It was hard to believe his curfew was extended for Saturdays and we were able to hang out as long as we did that night.

Against all odds, Tiger Mom was lightening up. I smelled a rat.

My nose was less than an inch away from Tristan's nipple, his smell gloriously manly and very un-ratlike. I fought with the urge to kiss his chest and lost the battle.

He let out a sweet, sleepy sound.

"You're so easy to turn on," I giggled against him. *I love you.*

I still couldn't say that out loud, and he hadn't brought it up. It was a weird, unspoken game we were playing: he didn't say so, but he knew I'd heard him tell his mother he loved me, and it was turn my next. I did love him. I knew that without a shadow of a doubt. Why was I so scared to tell him?

The alarm on his watch let out a string of beeps and he clicked it off before curling around me again, turning me so that my back was to his front and nuzzling into my neck. We had laid the hind seats flat, pushed the front seats forward as far as they would go, then blew up an air mattress inside. It almost fit. I could lay straight on a diagonal, but Tristan had to keep his knees bent. I found it hard to believe he was comfortable, but he insisted he was and the boy could fall asleep anywhere.

"I'm starving," I whispered.

"Hmmm…"

I wiggled out of my cozy human spoon and reached for the picnic backpack that was crammed into the dashboard. We'd done pretty well stocking it. Liza would be proud. I sifted through empty fruit containers and napkins to get to the bottom, where I knew there was still cheese and pepperoni.

"Its sucks, my man, but time to rise and shine," I said between mouthfuls, shaking his shoulder.

He hissed, "God, your hands are freezing. Don't worry, I'm awake now."

"Sorry."

He smiled up at me, his eyes still closed. "S'okay. Any touch of yours…"

I snorted and took a bite of pepperoni right from the stick. "This was a good idea," I patted the air mattress, "but why not just a sleeping bag or something?"

"Because your sweet ass needs something soft." He'd pulled the blanket over his head and turned his face into our mobile bed, his voice muffled. "And a big fat bed roll in the back of my car woulda been a little obvious."

"Right."

The air mattress folded neatly into the storage compartment under the flooring when it was deflated. I guessed Tiger Mom would have rescinded her generous curfew award if she'd seen that Tristan planned to turn his jeep into a love machine.

That reminded me, "Why the 2:00 a.m. curfew change anyway?"

"I'm acing trig," he said, resurfacing with a look that questioned my mental capacities. "Don't you know what a big deal that is?"

"I told you trigonometry is easy when you take it step by step," I shrugged.

"Mekaela, I think this is the first 'A' I've ever gotten in Math."

"Really?"

"Really." He nodded slowly, waiting for me to catch on. "And it's because of you that I am."

"I love tutoring you," I grinned, tapping him softly on the nose. "You look so sexy with your concentrated face."

"Well anyway..." he sat up and reached for his T-shirt. "My mom's over the moon about it."

I shrugged, modestly uncomfortable. "No big."

He shook his head and left it at that, familiar with my habit of deflecting compliments and gratitude when it came to helping with his schoolwork.

I liked studying—school's always come easy to me—and I loved doing anything with Tristan. Even his mother had managed a "thank you" when she'd run across us pouring over his homework one day in the library. It just wasn't necessary, though. Tristan was more intelligent than people gave him credit for. All he needed was a better work ethic when it came to the books. And it meant all the more time we got to hang out together, doing *approved* activities.

"You want me to take you home like that?" He nodded toward my still nude body as he leaned back against the front seat and arched his hips to pull up his jeans.

"Yeah." I raised an eyebrow. "You can tuck me in. Maybe stay for a while, I bet everyone's already asleep."

"You're crazy. Tessa or Charlie walking in on something like that..."

I felt a little guilty. He was more worried about their virgin eyes than I was. "Something like what?"

He inclined his head to indicate my persistent nudity with a soft laugh. "Anyway. It's gonna be hard enough already getting up for church tomorrow."

"You have to go to church tomorrow?" Of course he did. Family Sunday. So the later curfew came with a punishment. Tricky little lady. "Log a prayer for me, then."

"Think we both need more than one," He scrubbed the back of his neck, looking me over with a spreading smile. "Uh, not that I mind the view and all, Mekaela. But you're still butt-naked and chewing on a sausage. What are you tryin' to do to me?"

"Me?" I looked down at my body with mock-innocence.

"You."

I tossed the sausage into the open backpack.

"One for the road?" It was a good thing he hadn't bothered to button up yet. "You can keep your pants on. Mostly."

...I grinned behind me at the closed doors to the school vestibule and wondered what Stephanie Jameson would do if she knew how we were spending those wonderfully lengthened Saturday nights. Evil mirth rolled through me at the image of her pinched face and clenched fists, as I made my way to the car slow enough that Tristan could catch up.

A shrill voice startled me out of my reverie, "Oh my god, he finally asked you?"

"It's about freakin' time, Stacy," sneered an underclassman, arms akimbo and finger shaking. "You know, you should say 'no' just to prove a point."

"Then I wouldn't have a date. Duh."

I passed another group of girls, squealing about their prom dresses, on my way to the jeep. I had never even considered attending prom, and I wasn't surprised that Tristan agreed. Things were somewhat better at school; there had been no more bodily assaults and he was on speaking terms with most of his buddies again. I still got a fair amount of icy stares from Ashley's friends, however, and me and Tristan still preferred to eat lunch outside, on the fringes of society. I had a feeling the worst kind of whispers remained in circulation, though at least I didn't hear most of them anymore. I did catch one snippet by accident and it made my blood boil. It went something like, "Sure, King Bobcatt wanted to get off with Meg Shannon for a while, but of course he'll still take his queen to the Senior Prom."

My favorite voice rang out behind me.

"Tryin' escape again?" Tristan twined his fingers with mine. "Shoulda never given you a set of keys."

Of course he hadn't. Tristan never let me drive his jeep. "What was the hold up anyway, slow poke?"

He knew I liked to get the hell out of dodge as soon as the bell rang, if I wasn't working.

"Sorry, my mom trapped my ass for a sec."

"Did you explain to her that your ass belongs to me?"

"Yes."

I stopped dead in my tracks. "You did?" The last thing I needed was his mother thinking I was encroaching on her territory. I preferred that she not think of me at all.

"Yeah, I told her I wanted to have 'Mekaela Shannon' tattooed on both butt cheeks," he said, confused innocence radiating from his solemn eyes.

My jaw dropped and my breath caught.

"I'm kidding. God." With a smirk, he lifted my chin with two fingers.

I pressed my lips together. "Butthead." I backhanded his chest and he jumped back laughing.

I trudged up the sidewalk in a huff, but he caught up easily.

"You gotta stop being scared of my mom."

"I'm not scared."

"Whatever you are, then."

"You would be whatever-I-am-then, too, if *I* had a tiger for a mother."

"*Bobcatt*," he grinned, leaning in to nuzzle his nose against mine.

"Tiger," I insisted, sticking out my tongue for emphasis.

He laughed and rested an arm around my hips. "You don't really call her 'tiger' in your head, do you?"

"Tch." I scrunched my face up to indicate the ridiculousness of that question. "No."

chapter sixteen

The remainder of the week was a blur, with most of the Andrew Jackson student body *and* faculty gradually ramping up to frenzy over the impending prom, and Tristan planning and packing for our weekend flight. We would leave directly after school on Friday, and then camp out that night before arriving at Liza's dorm on Saturday evening. I had a feeling that most of the "planning" Tristan was undergoing had to do with convincing his mother that one night camping with The Seductress wasn't going to ruin her darling's life. Liza had finally called to explain that it would be weird having her little brother sleep on the dorm room couch Friday night, because she herself had a date.

"Well, why not just wait until Saturday to drive up, then?" their mom had reportedly whined.

"Mom, I need him here first thing in the morning Friday to help me get things together for the birthday surprise. I need Tristan to move heavy stuff," Liza had lied. "And hang the piñata and everything."

Finally, their dad had bestowed his blessing and shut Tiger Mom up. Whenever that man eventually spoke, she listened. "Hon, Tristan's gonna be leaving for college soon anyway. You better get used to it," or something like that.

Whatever worked for me.

Camping wasn't entirely foreign to me and Tristan—that's what we called it when we drove the jeep out to a secluded spot in the woods and blew up the handy air mattress. For our anti-prom jaunt, however, I could tell he wanted show off his prowess with actual, full-fledged outdoor adventures.

"What is all this stuff?" I watched him load supplies into the back of the jeep from his garage. He had already arranged everything in neat stacks beforehand so we could hit the road before anyone else got home.

"What do you mean?" He flicked his hair out of his eyes, confused, and then set two sleeping bag rolls next to the car. "Guess I'll lay these over the cooler…"

"I mean, I've never actually camped before. It looks kinda intense." I felt lazy letting him do all the work and wandered over to the garage to select something to carry. I picked up a nylon bag that looked harmless, but it was way heavier than I suspected. I dropped it with a grunt, nearly smashing my toe underneath. "Jeez, what's in that bag?"

"You're serious. You've never camped in a tent?" He stopped next to the nylon bag—now obviously a tent—and stooped to grasp the proper handles, then hoisted it over his shoulder.

"Who woulda shown me how to pitch tents, my outstanding father figure?"

"I mean," he tried to shrug under the weight, then turned towards the jeep and swung the cooler inside, "you never did Girl Scouts or… anything…" His voice trailed away, his face suddenly abashed. Flushed and sweaty, he went quiet and focused on sliding the tent into the cab perfectly. I knew he was curious about my father situation, but he was too polite to ask. I wasn't giving any either, not just then.

"Nope. I kinda learned my life skills as I went along. Cooking. Cleaning. Nursing. Studying." I leaned against the frame of the hatch-back, crossing my arms mischievously. "Poker."

He gave me a look that dared to doubt how important a life skill poker playing was.

"I never had much use for camping, though. Not until I met you anyway." I kissed the air in his direction and ended in a toothy grin.

"Well, you're lucky you did, then," he said, punctuating with a real kiss.

In less than a heartbeat he was all serious Boy Scout again. He positioned me away from the door with one arm, before he slammed it closed with the other, an then clicked the garage door remote and moved me around to the passenger side. Time was clearly of an essence. He deposited me in my seat, told me to buckle up, then jogged around to his side and started the engine, just as one shiny silver Honda Accord slid around the corner at the end of the street. Tristan didn't look surprised as he backed out of the driveway and lowered his window to wave at his mother when we passed.

She scowled inside, her last wheedling affirmation in direct contrast. "I love you, Tris—" Her voice was cut off to the whir of the electric motor, and then the cabin was peaceful and numb within the sudden vacuum of sealed glass. I bit my lip but my smile spread anyway, so I faked a cough and covered my mouth with a fist.

"You alright?"

"Huh? Oh…yeah. 'Scuse me, just a little frog in my throat…"

He reached behind his seat and grabbed a bottled water, tossed it my way.

"Anyway, you've been missing out on one of the best things about living so close to the sticks." Tristan shook his head, still marveling. "Well, it's not for every girl, I guess. Amanda hates camping, but Liza's usually game."

"Wonder what type I'll be."

"You? Who's always up for anything? You'll love it."

I watched the manicured lawns and neat houses march by the window. "You know what I love?"

He turned the last two corners, navigating through the winding brick street of his neighborhood, before coming to a slow roll at the stop sign that exited onto the state road. He turned to me, "What do you love?"

"Getting the hell out of here."

Tristan watched me for a beat, his expression teetering between frustration and merriment.

He sort of snort-chuckled. "Right."

Then he gunned the engine and we peeled out of Northern Estates so fast I swore I smelled smoking tires. Unbuckling my seat belt, I rolled down my window and wriggled onto my knees, then leaned outside with my arms spread wide. My hair lashed my face viciously in the wind of our departure. I heard a "YEEEOW!" from the other side of the jeep and I yelled at the top of my lungs, "Kiss my ass, Shirley County!"

A warm, strong hand grabbed that particular body part and squeezed, right on the sweet spot. I tumbled back inside, gasping with emotion and the sudden urge to attack my boyfriend, who was smiling wolfishly at the wheel.

"I made a playlist, get my phone," he said, rolling both windows back up and donning sunglasses. "And put your seatbelt back on."

"You and the seat belts."

"Yeah, they've been known to save lives," he replied, clipping the words.

"Okay, okay," I muttered, clicking the buckle back in place. "So, a playlist, huh. Road trip music?"

"As requested."

I clapped my hands in anticipation. Tristan had a ridiculous iTunes library. "Where is it?"

"Oh sorry, it's still in my pocket," he said, eyebrows flicking over the rim of his shades in a taunt.

"Really? Let me just get that then."

I leaned over, making sure of a choice view down my shirt, and slipped my hands all around his crotch and thighs, pretending to search for a pocket.

"Aw, come on…" he moaned.

"You asked for it."

"You know where my phone is—my back pocket."

"Back here?" I slid one hand through the gap in his jeans and his lower back, my fingers gliding where they would and my palm caressing soft places, before acting as if realization had dawned. "Oh, there's the pocket."

I plucked his phone neatly out of its usual place and thumbed through screens, sitting back in my seat.

"You're gonna kill me one day," Tristan breathed.

"This one looks good—you got those new songs I asked you for, too. You're so sweet."

I found my favorite, "One Republic, sweet," tapped play, and the Bluetooth picked it up. I sat back listening with my eyes closed, waiting for the lyrics to start. I sang softly, unsure of the words at first, but when the chorus started, I really belted it out: "I could lie, could lie, could lie. Everything that kills me makes me feel alive." Finally noticing Tristan wasn't joining in, I opened my eyes to find him watching the road with a strange, almost horrified expression on his face.

"What's wrong, don't you know how to sing?" I teased.

"Uh…" His face was twisted in half a frown and half a grin. "Yes. I do."

He reached over and patted my thigh, then turned up the volume and picked up the song himself. I shrugged, figuring he was nervous to sing in front of other people. There was always some new surprise with Tristan. I decided not to push it; at least he was singing and he actually had a very nice voice. Maybe it was the country music preference. I'd figure it out later, but I just wanted to enjoy the drive. The open road stretched out in front of us, and sweet freedom was within our grasp.

♣

We headed north out of the valley and into the mountains beyond, settling into the serene climate of an afternoon full of promise. The sun dappled through gaps in the forest canopy above like strobe lights along the small winding roads climbing upwards. After a while, the trees cleared and the bright spring sun blasted down on us over the interstate.

We only had about an hour drive from there, and about the time I was getting antsy to just get there, Tristan pulled off the highway down a less traveled offshoot.

"There's the mile marker," he said, after another twenty minutes or so. "Now we look for the path on the left side of the road—there's a huge hemlock tree covered with kudzu right before the turn…"

"That sounds like the entire road." I turned around in my seat to look behind us, and it all seemed the same to me. All we'd seen for miles were huge trees and lots of blanketing vines, thick as walls on either side of the road. "I can't believe you know where you are."

"Been here a few times," he muttered, leaning closer to the windshield for a better view. "There it is."

"That's a path?" There was barely a break in the forest. "So, it's like campgrounds or something?"

"Uh…no," he smiled, turning off the paved road and easing the jeep onto less civilized terrain. "But we've come here so many times it feels like it's ours. It's a nice spot, you'll see."

I kept a panic grip on the handle over my window, my other hand jammed against the dash for balance, while we lurched over what hardly passed for a driving path. Tristan kept the transmission in first gear and didn't seem concerned with the rough travel, making his way slowly over holes and fallen branches, skirting the larger rocks and puddles. Once, we had to get out of the jeep to haul a tree limb out of the way. When we got back in, I turned off the music and rolled down my window, thinking fresh air might settle my roiling tummy. I leaned my head out the window, breathing in the smells of the deep forest, and was smacked in the face by a passing fern.

Tristan chortled, unable to contain his amusement on my behalf, "At least it was a sort of feathery plant."

"Oh yeah, soft as a feather alright." I rubbed my nose and delivered a dirty look over my hand. "You drove closer on purpose, didn't you?"

He patted my thigh in mocking reassurance. "Anything for you, Mekaela."

"Thanks."

We pulled off what I had thought was the last road to the world's end. How far were we going? Just when I was starting to worry my stomach wasn't going to make it, the trees cleared for a sunny meadow dotted with wildflowers, and my mood corrected itself in an instant.

"This is where we stop, right?"

"Right," confirmed Tristan.

Finally, the jeep rolled to a halt and he shifted the transmission into park. Before the engine was even cut, I hopped out and stretched my limbs with a groan. I touched my midsection tenderly. I'd have to remember not to eat anything before we drove out of there; he'd never guess how close I was to losing that beef jerky snack. I yawned in relief. "It's gorgeous, Tristan."

He got out and tossed his keys on the seat through the open window. "Hear that?"

I cocked my head and listened. Rushing water? "Is that a river close by?"

"Waterfall. You put your suit on, right?"

"We're going swimming right now?"

"Why not? While it's still warm out." He pulled his T-shirt over his head, threw it in on top of the car keys, then held out his hand. "Come on."

"Alright, let's get wet." I held onto him for balance while I stripped down to my string bikini.

"Leave your sandals on, though. The rocks are sharp by the water," he said, openly admiring my bare flesh. He shook his head and sighed, "Damn…"

"Not so bad yourself." I gave that yummy six-pack a soft pinch and wrapped my arm around his waist.

chapter seventeen

We picked through the trees on an overgrown walking path and within a few minutes came upon an impressive waterfall cascading from an over-hanging rock about a hundred feet overhead. When the brush cleared completely, I could see that the pool of water below was bigger than I expected; it was about the size of a couple backyard swimming pools put together and it looked deep. Tristan lifted his arm from my shoulders and picked up his pace, then bounded toward the water. At the last second, he grabbed a knotted rope I hadn't noticed and swung out over the water with a whoop, cut off abruptly when he hit the surface and disappeared below.

"Tristan?" Man, the water looked deep.

He came back up in a side-crawl and called, "Water's perfect."

The rope was gently swinging. I judged the distance and terrain.

Wow.

I'd never swung into a lagoon in the wilderness like Tarzan before. Or, Jane, I guess. Something I was bested at in the wild department, for sure.

Tristan's voice echoed of the rocks, "What're you waitin' for?"

"Screw it."

I rushed at the rope.

"Nothin'!"

I leapt for it, the nylon scratchy and gnarled in my grip. I closed my eyes and curled into a cannonball as I flew out over the water and released.

"Geronim—"

I hit the water and my bravado was drowned in an icy grave. I came up spluttering, hoping I had splashed him good.

"Nice jump," said Tristan, shaking his hair.

"W-water's p-perfect..."

He chuckled, easy and confident. "Yeah, it's always pretty cold—it's a system of springs. Feels good after a minute, though, right?"

Actually, it did. My body was already starting to acclimate to the chill, though my teeth were still chattering. The last month in Shirley had been unseasonably hot, and the lack of sufficient air-conditioning in the Shannon Family trailer or the ancient VW Rabbit was stifling. "I didn't think I'd ever get cool again."

"You will tonight. Still gets pretty cold up here when the sun goes down."

"Are we that high up?"

"A lot higher than Shirley Valley," said Tristan, doing a lazy backstroke to the rocky shore. "Come on, I'll show you the view."

"Oooh, are we going to explore the wilderness now?"

Tristan smiled in encouragement, obviously enjoying my lack of wilderness knowledge. "I know it pretty well, I'll be your guide, little darlin'."

"*Little* darlin' now, is it?" Definitely condescending. I splashed him as he hoisted himself out of the water, gleaming wet muscles rippling with the strain.

That sight erased any hint of...well, anything else I had been thinking about. God, he was beautiful. His swim trunks were sagging dangerously low over his hips, and I almost reached up and tugged them down to his ankles before he turned around. But he leaned over to give me a hand up before I had the chance, pointing out the rocks that were the best footholds. We moved around the spring, the walking space between the edge of the water and the surrounding forest narrow enough that we had to go single file, carefully stepping from rock to rock and hanging onto low branches for balance. When we passed under the waterfall, the rock face hollowed into a tiny cave, echoing with the plummeting water and slick with spray. Out of the sunlight, the temperature dropped noticeably and the smell of cold, mildewed stone bloomed

"I love that smell," I whispered to myself, surprised at how my voice was amplified within the cavern.

Tristan looked back in surprise. "Me, too."

"It always reminds me of...of...I don't know, actually," I stammered, completely losing my train of thought in the midst of his intense gaze.

"Uh-huh." His voice was soft, his face wondering.

"I just love it, I don't know."

"Yeah." He pressed his warm lips to my trembling ones and rubbed his palms up and down my arms, smoothing away my goose bumps. "Let's get you warm," he said, then took my hand and led me back into the sunlight and up around the side of the falls.

The climb up was steep and I was quickly out of breath, my shivers completely gone by the time we reached the summit where the chute tumbled over our peaceful lagoon below. I could see the source stream stretching back further into the trees and the climb upwards getting steeper.

Thankfully, Tristan thought we'd gone far enough, though, and he moved behind me, wrapping his arms around my waist and turning me towards a breathtaking view.

"Wow. Is that Shirley Valley?" I breathed.

"It is."

Far in the distance, and from our eagle eye view, Shirley seemed so peaceful and small, its inhabitants harmless and innocent. Bucolic. That must be how most people imagine small towns—people who don't live in them. I knew that assumption was far from true, but it was nice to imagine otherwise, high up in the mountains with Tristan's arms around me.

"Sun's getting low, we better head back and set up camp before it goes down." His voice was soft and deep, his bare chest rumbling against my back.

The moment was perfect. I couldn't stand to let it slip away yet. "Too bad, I bet the sunset is beautiful from here."

"Sunrise is better."

It always is, isn't it? I leaned my head back against his shoulder. "New beginnings, yes."

"I'll wake you up early." He gathered my hair away from my neck. "So we won't miss it," he said, tracing gentle kisses on my shoulder. "We can go back to the tent after and…" I sucked in my breath when he reached the back of my ear, "then we can sleep late."

The rush of memory sent a flood of heat down my torso; we would be spending the whole night together. Alone. "We haven't been able to do that since…"

"Our first night," he whispered, finishing my thought. "I can make you breakfast again."

"Out here?"

"Of course." He ran his thumb down my jaw and turned my face to his.

My fevered brain pictured the pancakes he had made me at his house, and then flicked to a cartoon image of eggs frying on a sunny boulder.

"What would you cook out here?" I asked between kisses.

"You'll see."

Suddenly, I couldn't wait to get back and set up camp—whatever that entailed. Get it done and move on to the fun.

"Look," Tristan whispered, pointing in front of me and down into the spring below.

A deer was leaning over the edge of the water on the far side from the falls, her reflection undulating with the lapping motion of her tongue. I held my breath and stood as still as I could, but the doe spooked after only a few seconds. Her head snapped up, body rigid and eyes watchful, before dashing into the trees in a panic.

"Doe eyes," murmured Tristan, a note of revelation in his voice.

"Hhmm?"

"Doe eyes. The guy says that about the girl he's after—her eyes are like that. In that book you picked from my English Lit reading list? I get it now. Big and dark, round but sort of pointed up at the corners." He turned me around in his arms and studied my own dark brown eyes. "And wary."

I narrowed them in response, "Mine?"

He nodded. "Not scared. On your guard, though."

He studied my face, like he had all the time in the world.

And there it was between us again. He loved me. Tristan loved me, and he wanted to know that I loved him. I did. Oh, I did.

"I thought you said I was reckless."

"You are," he said, searching the sky for the right words. "With your body, but not with your mind. Or your heart."

My heart was racing. "But you can read me like a book, can't you?"

He answered with another kiss. He wasn't going to let me off that easy.

"We better get back." His mood was indecipherable. He took my hand, his voice gentle "Watch out for this stone, it's too loose to step on."

"Wait—" I tugged his hand, edging closer to the side of the cliff and peering down into the pool below. I thought a rush of adrenaline and one more icy splash might erase that little anxious moment away. "Is it deep enough to jump from here?"

Tristan smiled indulgently. "I was wondering when you were gonna ask. Yeah, it is."

"Easier than climbing down, anyway," I shrugged, already backing up and preparing to spring.

"Want me to go first?"

"No thanks."

"Just make sure you clear the rocks," I heard him call after me.

I was already in mid-air, cheering like it was my birthday. I kept my body straight as an arrow for a clean submersion, but the water still stung the curve of my hips on the upward splash and I plunged deeper than I was prepared for. My toes never touched anything solid and I floundered in the watery abyss, struggling to turn my momentum upwards. My ears popped on the way back up. My breath ran short. I flailed my arms and scissor-kicked for all I was worth, watching the light on the surface grow brighter with agonizing slowness. I came up gasping for air and darted to the edge of the pool in a flash, my skin prickling all over from more than the temperature. The knowledge that the unimaginably deep spring was supplied by an even deeper, underground source was terrifying. It was like something I'd read in a horror story: an orifice, to mysterious depths.

Tristan was right behind me, and I clung to him when he reached my side.

"Ready to get out, dare devil?" he asked, deciphering my expression easily.

"Sh-shit. Yes, sir."

chapter eighteen

On the hike back to the jeep, Tristan pointed out examples of good firewood and kindling for me to gather while he unloaded the supplies. When he saw I intended to trek through the woods in my bikini and sandals, he shook his head with a sigh and brought out my overnight bag first. He instructed me to put on jeans, a long-sleeved shirt, and tennis shoes, then advised me to stay between the meadow and the spring—an area with which he thought I should be familiar—but when I started walking in the wrong direction, he showed me the compass app on my phone and gave me more explicit navigational instructions.

"I got it, don't worry," I said, pocketing the phone and starting towards the trees.

"Oh wait." He grabbed my arm, forcing me to stop, and dashed back to the jeep. He returned shaking a can of bug spray, "Blood as sweet as yours'll sing to the bloodsuckers."

Properly dressed and soaked with pesticide, I wandered away to make myself useful.

Tristan called after me, "Keep your phone on and don't go too far!"

I saluted and rolled my eyes.

"Mr. Protective," I mumbled, picking along and scanning the ground for the right kinds of fallen branches, twigs, and sticks. I wondered how much flammable bug spray was being transferred to the stuff and hoped I wouldn't have to actually set up the campfire. I figured Tristan wouldn't trust me with that task, but he was having so much fun bossing me around. He looked pretty hot doing it, too.

"We'll have to go camping more often," I said to my sticks, proud of my selections.

When I got back to the meadow with my first armful of timber, Tristan had already laid out the tent and was halfway through erecting it. After my second trip, he was gone. When I dumped my firewood, it looked like there was a lot more to the pile than when I had left it earlier.

"There you are," Tristan's voice sounded behind me.

He emerged from the forest with an armful of timber at least three times the size of my own.

"This should be enough. Thanks," he said and stooped over to give me a kiss in passing. His smile was genuine as he went about arranging the medium-sized sticks into a little teepee, snapping the longest ones in half by holding them at an angle to the ground and stomping the middle with his hiking boot.

I sidled over to the tent, camouflaged in shades of green and brown, whistling in appreciation. It probably would fit four grown men and was almost as tall as me at the top of the dome. "Oh my gosh, is that a skylight?"

"Yeah," he said, his voice muffled as he bent to stuff the hollow of the teepee with kindling.

I shrugged, feeling like I should be helping more. Understanding dawned, as I unzipped the tent and ducked inside. "Ah ha. He just doesn't want me to mess anything up."

I wondered how many times he had set up a campsite. Our gear was stacked neatly against one side of the tent. My overnight bag and his duffel bag leaned against a clear plastic tote filled with nature-friendly toiletries, an LED lantern sitting on top. Two sleeping bags were already unrolled in the center, zipped together to make one, with the metal zippers arranged on the sides for the comfort of intertwining limbs. I lifted a corner of the double sleeper with one finger and saw a foam mattress underneath—a comfort surely needed by girls only. Who else had he brought camping with him?

"You like it?"

I gasped and dropped the flannel blanketing, twisting around to see Tristan's head poking in through the door.

Hopefully my cheeks weren't as red as they felt. "Er...I love it. This is fabulous, thank you."

"We only bring that when my sisters come," he nodded towards the concealed foam pad, grinning.

I shoved past him to the outside, pretending annoyance. I secretly loved when he treated me like some precious, delicate thing. Nobody else had done that my whole life. "You think I'm the princess and the pea or something, because I'm a girl?"

"I know you are," he said, re-zipping the door. "Trust me, you'll be grateful for it later."

"Will it help me sleep, with my fragile, girly bones?"

"Didn't say anything about sleepin'," he said, and slapped my ass as he brushed past.

"Hey! You caveman."

"Come on, let's start the fire."

Already started, I thought, more than one set of cheeks blazing by then.

♥

To my delight, he did let me start the fire; he rolled a piece of newspaper into a long tube and handed it to me, then pulled a lighter out of his pocket and lit the end of the taper. "Just touch the flame to the stuff inside the cone. It'll take pretty fast, so be ready to toss that in when it does."

I did as instructed and watched the flame grow, immensely pleased with myself. I grinned like I was the caveman, discovering the secret of fire itself, "I just lit a real campfire."

Tristan smiled benevolently—of course, he set everything set up for me. But he let me bask in my glory and looked up at the sky, gauging the approach of twilight.

"Perfect timing, thanks for getting it started," he said with a wink.

"What happens next?" I rubbed my hands together in anticipation. This campfire stuff was more fun than I thought it would be.

"Food."

"Oooh, what's for dinner?" I couldn't imagine, but my boyfriend had proven himself to be rather adept in the kitchen so far. Much more so than me, anyway. I was better with frozen food and a microwave than anything else. "You cooking anything is bound to be amazing."

He watched me for a few moments, amused, before replying, "Let's get the cooler, I'll show you."

I skipped to the jeep, imagining another fancy Liza picnic. But when I grabbed one of the handles of the cooler it was hard to pick up. "Oomph! This feels too light—are you planning to hunt for our dinner?"

"Not tonight, it's a little late."

"I was being facetious, Tristan. It's not light." And then I frowned, "You're not planning on hunting tomorrow either, are you?"

"I don't think you'd be a lot of help with that, no." He glanced sideways at me, impending mirth obvious; I was lugging my side so awkwardly that I waddled like a duck.

"What is *in* this thing?"

"Here, I'll get it…" he said, crouching low and getting underneath the cooler to hoist it up to his chest, "…and I don't think I can handle a 200-pound stag on my own."

My jaw dropped but I snapped it closed, realizing that he probably did hunt with his dad or something. Hunting was just too violent for me, but I kept my opinion to myself. Male bonding, sheesh.

He plunked our dinner down close to the fire and I tore the lid off to investigate, more curious than ever.

"Oh, that's why it felt so light—Tristan, you forgot to pack the cheesecake."

I pulled out a Tupperware of cubed meat, then one of vegetables. There had to be more than that.

"The rest is for breakfast," he said, slapping the lid closed before I could take anything else out.

That's why it was so heavy. Not food, just ice. I eyed the two large bottles in strapped netting he had slung over his shoulder, filled with clear liquid. Water. "Okay, I'm camping with a minimalist mountain man. I can do this."

"The last thing you want out here is a bunch of extra junk food sitting around attracting bears, Mekaela."

"Oh." Bears. I felt the blood drain from my face. Suddenly the idea of French fries and cheeseburgers, wafting their delicious processed aroma through the woods, didn't sound so appealing. "I didn't even think about bears."

"Don't worry. I did," he said over his backpack, digging around and finally finding a wooden box. He opened it to reveal more than a dozen metal skewers. "You'll love it, I promise."

chapter nineteen

I did love dinner, as promised. Not only was it fresh and delicious, the kabobs were super fun to make. They were tiny sculptures on sticks: onion, mushroom, steak, pepper, steak, mushroom. I mixed endless varieties in color and taste and fed them mostly to Tristan. I was too stuffed to even entertain the idea of cheesecake.

"Look, if you spear it through the side and turn the mushroom stem out, it looks like a face. Onion for hair, see?" I pushed a slice of bell pepper under the chin. "There's his bow tie and…here's his body." I skewered a piece of steak next.

"Here's some feet." Tristan broke the stem of a mushroom down the middle, pointed the two halves outward, and added it to the bottom. "Hope he doesn't scream as he roasts on the spit."

"Ew. Yeah, that is a little morbid," I admitted, rearranging the pieces to look less humanoid.

"That's better," he mumbled, his mouth full of my last delivered bite.

"So, you do this kind of stuff all the time? With your family, I mean?" I was still curious as to whether or not the camping thing was a regular dating scenario for him. Four years with the same girl, and not much else to do in Shirley County.

"Mmmm, not so much anymore." He finished his mouthful and wiped the corner of his mouth with his wrist. "Now that Brandon and Liza are both in college—wait, is Brandon still in grad school? I think this is his last year." He screwed up his face trying to remember. Tristan hardly ever mentioned his brother and I had a feeling they weren't close. "Anyway, like I said, Amanda's not into it. My mom's pretty over the hassle, after so many years of herding us four around a campfire, with all the fishing, the swimming, the hiking…"

"The dirty underwear…" I could only imagine what taking care of a bunch of kids out in the woods would be like.

"Yeah," he laughed. "She says it's like being a maid in the sixteenth century or something."

"Sure would be." I fell quiet. I didn't want to out and out ask.

He watched the side of my face, then leaned over and planted a kiss on my cheek. "No, I never brought Ashley here."

Was my expression really that obvious, or could he actually read my mind?

"You're the first, Mekaela," he said, humor in his tone. "Always the first."

Really? Oh. I tried not to grin like an idiot.

He sighed comically, and then reached for the last kabob.

"Are you still hungry? Here, I'll do that." I felt like I was floating above the campsite I was so happy. I slid a mushroom off the skewer and popped it in his mouth.

"Me and my dad still come out here, sometimes with his buddy Ian—his kids are a lot older now, though. With the Vales, too, when Drew and Simon and Max are in town every once in a while. You know George Vale? He owns the gas station."

"Of course—only pump in town. Jo's been working at his garage lately, too. That's how she got the Rabbit." I made a face in honor of the shared car that was both a luxury and a nemesis for me.

"You're kidding. Jo's a mechanic? She's what, sixteen?"

"Fifteen. Technically, she's too young to be driving." I looked at him sideways, town sheriff's son as he was, but Tristan just shrugged. "Well, she's just an assistant, so she's learning with George. That's how he justifies paying her next to nothing."

"Where'd she learn to fix cars?"

"I don't know, ever since she was a scrawny little rat in overalls she ran around helping all the guys in the cove. I mean, there's always half a dozen clunkers on cinder blocks in my neighborhood. You should've seen her—big blue eyes, wide as saucers watching them. She ran around fetching all their tools and offering her little hands to fit in tight spaces." I smiled. Jo had always been more self-sufficient than any of my other siblings.

"Weird," Tristan mused. "Piper is so…"

"Girlie, I know. Piper wears her hair like Rapunzel and acts like a prima donna, always has. They're so different I forget they're twins sometimes."

"Speaking of different," he said, wrapping one of my dark brown curls around his finger and fixing my "doe eyes" with his own. He let the unasked question linger.

"I have a different father, of course," I said, without elaboration.

He held my gaze while he settled back against his backpack.

I was trapped and I knew it. Camping Tristan was so different, so much more…commanding. I felt compelled to dish out the story he probably deserved to hear. Suddenly, I didn't mind at all. I liked dominant Tristan, very much.

"Well," I started, releasing my breath and letting my shoulders fall heavily. "My mom had me when she was just sixteen-years-old. She never talks about the guy, but I think he was a boyfriend that was already out of high school who just split."

"At Jackson?" Tristan asked, his eyes hard.

"No, my mom didn't grow up around here. She's from Iowa."

"Hmm. I always wondered why you didn't have an accent."

"Yeah, I guess. Jo and Piper are kinda picking one up, though." I fiddled with the hem of my jeans, unsure how to proceed. It was an embarrassing story to admit, being fatherless. The fact that I was abandoned before I was even born had always made me feel worth less than the rest of my siblings—less than anyone who's dad actually wanted them.

He watched me, quiet.

I cleared my throat. "Anyway, I don't even know his name, and I'm pretty sure he was already gone before I was born. I've never seen any pictures of him." The angry crease I hadn't seen in weeks started forming between Tristan's eyebrows, and I barreled on in a rush to get it all out. "I mean, I don't care about that guy…" though my boyfriend's glower said that he definitely did. "My 'father' was Jo and Piper's father. I was only two when he met my mom, and he was who I called 'Dad.' He's where my last name comes from, he adopted me. He had the blonde hair and blue eyes like my sisters, of course."

He was thoughtful, playing with one of my ringlets.

"My real dad must have had a curly dark mane, right? Cuz here it is—poof, like magic!" I laughed, motioning to my afro and fluffing it with the flare of a magician's assistant.

"Magical. Yes." Tristan's voice was soft, some of the indignation gone from his face.

I fell silent and gazed into the fire.

"You said he *was* who you called your dad," Tristan prompted.

"Well. He died in a mine collapse when I was seven. Don't you remember that in the news, in the gypsum mine?" Tristan shook his head with an apologetic look. No, he wouldn't remember that. "You would've been seven, too. Probably didn't watch the evening news. I only remember it because of my dad."

"Sorry, Mekaela."

"Don't be. I don't want to sound uncaring or anything, but I honestly barely remember him. I think he was nice to me—I remember that. But I'm not sad. I don't like *miss* him, you know? Except that it's kinda sucked not having a father around sometimes." I looked at my hands; I always wondered if people thought I would've turned out better if I did have a father to discipline me.

Tristan cocked his head, but didn't give his thoughts away. "Yeah, I bet."

"So...obviously Charlie and Tessa come from different stock, too," I continued, determined to finish the uncomfortable conversation and move on. "That guy was a bucket of monkey spunk."

Tristan's face split into a surprised chortle. "Monkey spunk?"

"Yes." That man I did hate. "No! He was the puss, pooped out of the bacteria, that feed on the crust, that forms at the edge of the monkey spunk," I said, delighted to watch the full-fledged belly laugh rolling from Tristan. All traces of humiliation about my sad, motley collection of semi-fathers faded; I made that beautiful boy laugh like that. "I certainly don't miss *that* bastard."

"No," he said, gripping his side. "I guess not..."

"My mom found out he was already married after Tessa was born. Wife, kids, lovely house, everything. He'd told her he was a traveling sales-man—that's why he was always gone. We actually believed that shit, can you imagine? When Mom found out, she went crazy. She wanted to sue him for every penny she could get."

Tristan's face was deadly serious again, all humor lost. "Did she?"

"He disappeared," I shrugged.

"What about his other family?"

"Left them, too."

He was quiet for a minute. Stunned. "Well, somebody should track his ass down and teach him how to take care of his responsibilities," he said, his tone menacing and his eyes furious blue flames.

"We just want to forget he ever existed," I waved it away. I'd always felt so hopeless when it came to disappearing men. "I mean, whatcha gonna do?"

"Something, Mekaela. He can't get away with that."

"Please, let's not talk about it now, okay," I begged. The whine in my voice hurt my own ears, but I was tired of my life being examined. "Please?"

He looked down at my hands, clutching his bicep. I snatched them away, leaving little pink claw marks on his skin, but he caught both hands and held them in one of his. "I just wish things were a little easier for you guys," he said, pushing my hair from my face and brushing his thumb against my cheek. "You know?"

"I don't need things easier."

He frowned in doubt.

I don't. How could I explain it, without sounding like a jerk? Easy is for wimps and people with no character. My life might've been harder than it was for a lot of kids my age, but plenty had it worse, and it was my struggles that have made who I am. I'm proud of who I am. My character was the thing that was going to get me out of Shirley County and into a good college—into a better life, and all on my own. But, I couldn't say that to Tristan, who had lived a charmed life in comparison to mine. Instead, I simply said, "I just want to be happy."

Goose bumps spread up my arms with the intensity of his gaze. "Are you?"

"It's getting chilly, just like you said it would," I said, attempting to divert the conversation from my less than charmed life. The temperature had been dropping steadily, but the weather wasn't what was causing my skin to tingle—it was the way he was looking at me.

"Are you happy, Mekaela?"

I reached up for his hand, which was still against my neck.

"I am now," I assured him.

Gloomy stories of hard-knock childhood out of the way, I wanted to get back to just being with Tristan. I had always felt charmed around him, from the very beginning. I kissed his hand and rubbed the back of it against my face. His gaze hadn't faltered, though, and I knew what he was really asking.

"Mekaela…"

But I wanted to stop being so serious and get back to fun. I wasn't ready to tell him I loved him yet, no matter how much he needed it at that moment. I couldn't explain it, but those words were just too expensive. I'd have to play dirty; I took his middle finger into my mouth and sucked gently.

He let his eyes fall closed.

Bingo.

"Uh…" he started, his voice husky, "…okay, okay." He pulled his hand free and refocused his eyes with a wry smile, relenting for the moment. "We gotta clean up dinner first, though."

"Aye aye, captain," I said, a little too cheerily.

He laughed softly and helped me rise with him.

Tristan resumed his role as commander of the campsite. There's just nothing sexier than a guy who knows what he's doing, and Tristan was in charge of everything. I listened to all his instructions, admiring his adorable face and not even bothering to hide it, since he was focused with perfectionist concentration.

I did have one question, but I wasn't sure how to ask. He looked at me like I was crazy when the potty dance started to take hold.

"Are you…okay?"

"I have to pee, Tristan!"

"You have to go? Why didn't you say?"

"Because I was dreading being educated about how mountain men do that," I said in a rush, blushing from head to toe. "Do I have to use leaves?"

"You know how to avoid poison oak and poison ivy, right?"

I stared at him, dumbstruck. I did have to use leaves.

"Mekaela, I'm kidding. There's toilet paper in the tent. Here, take a flashlight," he said, handing his over and hiding his smile by pretending to scratch his nose. Thoroughly enjoying his joke, he turned back to the fire and said under his breath, "Bury it deep," just as I unzipped the tent.

"I'm supposed to dig a hole? Gross," I muttered, rummaging through a plastic tote. There was a hand shovel next to the toilet paper; he had obviously placed it there so that he didn't need to explain the specifics of taking a crap in the wilderness to me. Thankful I just had to urinate, I decided I'd just cover the paper with some leaves and dirt, and not let Tristan see me with the shovel.

By the time I got back from my bathroom adventure, grumbling about a mosquito biting my bare butt, Tristan had disappeared inside the tent. He probably just peed in a bush nearby, and would say something didactic about a carnivore's urine warding off mountain lions. I had actually read that in a book once. I could see from the shadow the lantern was casting against the nylon siding that he was laying on the ground, already in the sleeping bag, his arms folded behind his head.

"Early bedtime?" I asked, zipping the tent closed behind me.

"Not much to do after dark in the woods."

"Unless you have a banjo in your pocket for campfire songs. Didn't you think of that, Comdr. Campfire?"

He lifted the edge of the covers and peered inside innocently. "I don't have any pockets."

I could see his chest was bare and I thought I knew what the rest of him must look like under there, by the glint in his eye. "You're crazy—it's really getting cold out there. You're naked?"

"Sleeping bags work best when you're naked, trust me."

"Uh huh…"

He watched me toss my shirt into the corner and kick off my jeans, and then he reached for the light. "Come 'ere and let me show you why you need that foam cushion."

I slid into the sleeping bag, the soft flannel warm on my chilled skin and the extra cushion welcome after dinner on a big rock. I was surprised, though, when his overwarm hands turned me to face away from him as soon as our legs intertwined. He stretched my arms flat before me and pinioned my hips with his own, the stubble of his beard scratching between my shoulder blades. Yes, camping Tristan was fun indeed.

chapter twenty

"What took you guys so long?"

A dormitory door exploded open before we had taken two steps down the hallway, and within seconds we were attacked, blonde hair and bare skin all over us.

"Um. Liza," Tristan mumbled against the girl's neck. "This is Mekaela."

"It's so nice to finally meet you," Liza cooed, squeezing me tighter into the compulsory group hug.

"You can call me Meg. Everyone else does but Tristan," I said, feeling shy for some reason and glad my face was hidden on the other side of Liza. I kind of liked that he was the only person to use my proper name.

"Whatever," she pushed back from us both, giving me an extra shove on the shoulder. "You look much more like a Mekaela—I'll follow T's lead."

I tried to hide my disappointment, but Tristan caught my eye, frowning in question.

"Who's been leading who?" I said, to change the subject, and smiled at him.

"Huh?"

"Well…" Tristan began.

"He told me about your help with Homecoming," I supplied. "Thank you, by the way."

"You dummy."

"What?" He put up his hands in defense.

"That wasn't the smoothness I was going for, T."

"And Christmas present," I went on. Tristan had given me a leather-bound volume of American poetry. I was floored when I opened it; no guy in my memory had ever thought much about my love of books, something I'm actually very proud of. And then he actually read me a love poem by Emily Dickinson. It was all so thoughtful and romantic, in fact, that it hinted at female guidance. He admitted to being advised by his sister again, but his involvement in supplying clues for Liza's imagination was obvious. It was the best gift I'd gotten in my life—up to that point anyway. Tristan gave me so many gifts.

"And for convincing Mom to let me spend last night camping with her, most recently," Tristan reminded his sister. "Thanks."

She snorted. "Yeah, what have you and *her* been doing all day, anyway?"

So Tiger Mom's pronoun pet name for me was funny. Good to know.

Liza winked at me—the gesture so like Tristan it was startling—and began walking backwards, beckoning us to follow down the long hallway.

"You know…hiking and stuff…" Tristan thumbed his nose and glanced sideways at me.

"Yeah, the woods are beautiful there," I agreed, clearing my throat and looking away from Liza's piercing gaze. The only hiking we had done was up to watch the sunrise at the outcrop over the spring and back. After that, we lazed around the campsite all day, periodically emerging from the tent to accommodate annoying human requirements for food and nature's call. Tristan said The Complete Kama Sutra: The First Unabridged Modern Translation of the Classic was the best book he had bought me by far. At first I thought it was silly, but that was only until we put it to practical use—his enthusiasm to try new things and his ability to show me more than a few things himself made for an unforgettable afternoon.

"Hiking, sure." Liza shot us both a knowing expression. "Any way I can help, of course. We Middles gotta stick together, right bro?"

"Don't know what I'd do without you."

"Middles?" I asked, as we came to Liza's door and she pushed inside.

I had to muffle my shock—the room was an absolute pigsty, with clothes draped over chairs, dirty laundry piled in corners, and dirty dishes stacked on books, which were stacked on desks.

"I see you're still firmly committed to rebellion, Lize," commented Tristan, stepping around a pair of lacy underwear by the door with distaste. "Doesn't your roommate get pissed?"

"Whatever. Wren's as big a slob as I am." She smirked at the panties and then focused on me, "You see, Mekaela—"

"Meg, really," I interjected, maybe too rudely. I flinched at myself but I couldn't help it, and I don't know why it suddenly meant so much to me.

"Fine." Liza flapped her hand in the air to indicate she really didn't give a shit anyway. "You see, Meg, Tristan and I are The Middles. Middle siblings. We fall in between The Specials. Brandon is the aloof genius and Amanda is the bratty sociopath, but me and T are the model children. We had to be. We've spent our entire lives doing exactly as we were told so we could win brownie points with The Bobcatt Queen—"

"Liza…"

My eyes snapped to Tristan's. His mom was Bobcatt Queen, too, huh? Well, why didn't that surprise me?

"So we could stand out from the middle of the pack," Liza went on, undeterred. "We can do no wrong, right T? Literally. Well, I'm tired of it and I want to do goddamn wrong."

"Liza's been taking Psychology classes since her first semester here," explained Tristan under his hand, but loud enough for his sister to hear.

"I'm teaching Tristan the importance of social unrest," she agreed, tweaking her brother's cheek affectionately.

I looked at him with new eyes. "Hmph. That explains a lot, actually."

He turned a lovely shade of pink before looking away. "So anyway…I see you got your nose pierced after all, huh?"

She admired the sparkly stud in a mirror on the wall. "You like it?"

He shrugged noncommittally, but I had the feeling it wasn't to his taste. I stood back and watched, wanting to interfere as little as possible. Seeing Tristan with his older sister was illuminating; they were obviously close, much more so than he was with Amanda.

"Mom said, absolutely not."

"So you absolutely did," he finished for her. "I'm impressed, that was a big one."

"Thanks."

"She'd probably ask you if you were planning to get dressed before we go out, too. You know, not go out in…that?" Tristan suggested, motioning to his sister's skimpy apparel.

His look was so disapproving that I smothered a giggle. I thought she looked great.

"She probably would. But you wouldn't, would you?" Liza had her middle finger poised. But she relaxed her fist when Tristan shook his head. "One day Mom'll learn that things have changed. She doesn't control me anymore."

Hard to believe she ever did. I felt almost sorry for old Tiger Mom.

"A lot has changed for Mom, don't worry," said Tristan, echoing my thoughts and snaking an arm around my waist.

Liza suddenly gasped. "Dad, too. I've been meaning to ask you about all that Shirley County stuff in the papers with the Sendalee and some kind of Big Joe's property disputes…" She searched her memory for the specifics.

I heard something about that and I tried to remember. The Sendalee owned the Indian reservation that bordered Shirley. I was about to comment when I felt Tristan tense. He was cutting his hand across his throat in a shut-up-now gesture directed at his sister. "That doesn't have anything to do with Dad."

"Well Amanda said something a few months ago about a serial killer—"

"Damn it, Liza," Tristan uttered through a clenched jaw. I looked up at him, but he wouldn't meet my eye. I had never seen him so furious, even when poised for a fist-fight. "If Dad heard you were saying anything like that, he'd freak the fuck out."

"He's not here, is he?"

"Just don't repeat that shit."

"Okay, okay, jeez."

Why was Tristan so pissed? I felt ridiculous not having a better inside scoop within my own hometown. Foggy recollection of disturbing things going on in Shirley bubbled under the surface of my consciousness, but to me, Shirley County was always pretty disturbing. Admittedly, all my energy not consumed by grades, tests, and generally preparing to get the hell out of town for college, went to spending as much time as I could in my boy-friend's arms. Of course he would know more about what Liza was talking about, their dad being sheriff, but he hadn't mentioned much to me. He could probably tell I didn't care, but was that all? He was still avoiding my gaze.

"Well, anyway…" Liza breezed over to a miniature refrigerator and pulled out an ice cube tray. "Who wants a Jell-O shot?"

"I do, a voice called from another room, right before a toilet flushed behind the door. Seconds later, a tall, slender girl with dark skin and bright white hair stepped out in a cloud of air deodorizer.

"Shit, Wren. Literally. I'd rather not wear that as my perfume tonight."

"Soooor-ry," our new addition sang with a wave of her hand.

"My roommate." Liza reached behind her and slammed the bathroom door closed.

After introductions went around once more, Liza explained the correct method for shooting vodka-spiked Jell-O: run your tongue all around the edge to loosen it, then toss it back and let it slide down your throat. Then, she herded us out the door, claiming the party was calling her name. Already buzzing from the shots, I let Liza take my hand and swing it between us as we skipped—I was forced to join in the skipping to keep up—down the hallway and out into the alleyways between dormitories. I sneaked a look back at Tristan, beginning to understand a lot more about his family dynamics. His sister was a force to be reckoned with, and I was lucky to have her on my side. He smiled back in acknowledgement, shaking his head as if to say, "You have no idea."

"Looks like you lost your girlfriend," Wren said as she strode past Tristan and took Liza's free hand.

"How far is this party?" he asked our backs.

We hadn't yet left the university grounds, and although I could see the four-lane highway we had come in on, which bordered the campus in the distance, Liza seemed to know all the back roads.

"It's just up there—that bowling alley," she said over her shoulder.

"We're going to a bowling alley?"

"The place to be on Saturdays," laughed Wren. "You'll see."

As we skirted the side of the building and neared the front entrance, I could hear chaos emanating from within. Several drunk people spilled outside and trouped up the street, arm in arm. Neon lighting from the windows shone down onto the sidewalk in front, heavy base booming inside. Liza put her arm around my shoulder and motioned for Tristan to join in the huddle. "I know someone who'll give me a wristband once we're inside, but you have to be really careful. Meg, I can get a beer and we'll go in the bathroom so we can chug it."

"Okay," I agreed, not sure why since I was already feeling pretty tipsy from the Jell-O shots.

"T, I don't know about you—"

"I'm good, Liza," he said, eying a group of frat boys just inside the doorway. "I think I'll just watch out for you guys, if you don't mind."

"Suit yourself," his sister shrugged, then led the way to the entrance.

There was a line, but it went fast, everyone only required to show an I.D. and get the back of a hand stamped, not pay a cover. Liza licked her thumb and was already rubbing her blue "Under 18" emblem away as we walked through the double doors behind the bouncer. Inside, there was a cacophony of blaring music, crashing pins, and animated chatter mixed with milling bodies, cigarette smoke, and sweaty shoes. The atmosphere was as thick as soup, and I was glad to be feeling numb from the vodka.

"We've got a lane over there," shouted Liza, pointing to where several people were waving at us.

I followed her through the crushing horde of people, Tristan holding my hand close behind. We joined a group that was loosely arranged around two bowling lanes with a common seating area. A pair of ancient computer monitors glowed in the middle, behind the ball rack.

"About time, Blondie," one of the guys said. He might have been attractive, without so many tattoos and facial piercings.

My jaw dropped when Liza smothered him with unabashed wet kisses, a scene straight out of some cheesy romance novel. I felt Tristan's hand flinch in mine, but his expression remained serene.

"Jeff, this is my brother, Tristan. His girlfriend, Meg," said Liza, no longer needing to shout; the lanes were much quieter, away from the other rooms closer to the entrance. Once I could see them from afar they looked like mini dance clubs, one with a flashing strobe light inside and one pitch-black apart from a glowing projector deep within.

Jeff shook hands with Tristan and nodded to me.

The three of us were the last bowlers the group had been waiting on, so Jeff divided us into separate teams: Liza was on his team and I was on the other one, with Tristan.

"I'm not with T?" Liza whined in protest.

"Sorry, babe. We already put all our names into the computer and it's a full house," Jeff said, handing over her shoes and indicating the ball he had already chosen for her.

"Come on, we'll go last." Tristan nodded towards a counter with a wall of bowling shoes tucked in cubbies behind it, and we hustled to get all the necessary equipment before our turn was up.

I groaned and shuffled my feet, wishing I had known that bowling was in my future when I agreed to escape for the weekend. I've only bowled once or twice in my life. It's okay when everyone is just there to have fun, but if there are serious bowlers involved, it sucks. Who knew what Liza's crowd was like? I was sure to roll plenty of gutter balls, and I didn't want anyone irritated with me when I did. I laced up my ugly shoes with trepidation, while Tristan picked out my ball for me. I looked at the clock, thinking about the alternative back in Shirley, mentally cringing at the scene that was unfolding at the school gym at just that time. Bowling couldn't be as bad as prom night.

Tristan brought over several bowling balls, testing my grip and hand strength, before finally settling on the one he thought was perfect. "Ready?"

"Pink?" I frowned at the sparkling fuchsia sphere he held under his arm.

"It feels the best, right?"

"Yours is much cooler looking," I said, motioning to his black ball, with a skull-and-crossbones.

"Mine's too heavy for you," he grinned. The show-off.

"How do you know so much about bowling balls?" I asked suspiciously, putting a hand on one hip and feeling clownish in my clunky, multi-colored bowling shoes. The clown shoes clashed with both my outfit and my pink bowling ball, but Tristan's shoes happened to be black and white, just like his ball. "You an expert or something?"

"I've done some bowling," he admitted, then gestured towards our lane with his chin. "We better get over there."

Liza was waving at us with both arms overhead. I sighed, resigned and more nervous than ever. But when we got back and found a seat amongst our fellow bowlers on the vinyl George Jetson couch (that had seen better days), I could tell by the score boards on the monitors that no one was playing well on either team. Only two or three pins were marked for most of the bowlers in the first round, and more than one person had logged a zero.

I let out my breath in relief. "Good, some fellow gutter-bowlers."

Tristan smiled, but didn't say anything.

The current bowler on our side lobbed her second gutter-ball, right on cue, then swiveled around laughing as the group cheered, regardless of what team they were on. In fact, it was hard to divide the group into two; everyone was all over everyone else, with conversation, smiles, and sometimes hands.

Up next, I gave Tristan a kiss on the forehead before approaching the runway and hoisting my sparkly ball from the rack. I surprised myself by knocking down four pins total by my second try. Immensely pleased with myself, I strolled over to Tristan on my way back to the bench and smacked a wet kiss on his cheek.

He raised his ball out of the bowling rack, "Nice one, darlin'."

I narrowed my eyes. Was that sarcasm or pandering?

He winked at me before heading for the runway with his ball raised to his chest, barely breaking stride when he let his hand fall back to his side. Then he swung his arm in a graceful arch, sliding into a crouch with one leg stretched artfully behind, and released the ball. It hit the wooden floor like it was gliding on oil, momentum rumbling under my feet like a thunderstorm. The skull-and-crossbones crashed with a satisfying crack, every pin slamming and spinning into the pit.

"Aaaaahhhhh…" was the communal reaction, from our group and adjacent lanes.

Every face in the near radius turned towards Tristan Jameson in surprise and admiration.

chapter twenty-one

"You see! That's why you should've put T on our team, Jeff," yelled Liza, slapping her boyfriend in the chest with the back of her hand.

The activity around our two lanes kicked up a notch. The next guys up to bowl rubbed their hands together and shouted challenges across the ball rack.

"Come on, Jason!" cheered a girl waiting her turn, flexing her fingers.

I crossed my arms over my chest and glared at my boyfriend, returning amidst slaps on the back and congratulatory hoots. He stopped in front of me with a sheepish smile.

"Is there any sport you're not good at, Tristan?"

He searched the ceiling with his eyes, pretending to consider my question seriously.

"Ice skating," I prompted.

"I've played a little hockey—"

"Bob-sledding, then?"

"I have cousins in Canada."

I gaped at him and raked my mind for a sport he could possibly suck at. "Olympic swimming?"

"Come on, I grew up with a pool in my backyard."

"What—have you timed yourself and stuff?"

He shrugged apologetically and reached out a hand to take mine, which I promptly put behind my back, willing him to stop dazzling me into a self-conscious nervous wreck.

"Oh, come on."

"You're just so...perfect," I spluttered.

His face lit up and he snapped his fingers with gusto. "Gymnastics. Can't even cartwheel."

"Ah ha! That's something I got you at then," I said, more thrilled than I should've been.

I backed away from the bench and into the relatively uncrowded space between the bowling lanes and the bustling party. I spread my arms and stretched high, then leaned into a perfect cartwheel, rolling an elegant circle before coming back to standing.

I faced my boyfriend with a smirk. "What d'ya think of that?"

"Beautiful," he said, alarm plain on his face. He tugged the hem of my skirt down to my knees. "Maybe not with a skirt on next time, okay?"

"Nice cartwheel," Liza laughed, appearing next to us with a beer in her hand. "Tristan can't even do a somersault he gets dizzy so easy."

"No I don't."

She tickled him in the ribs and he jerked away, barely able to keep his face straight despite his irritation.

"So there's the tickle zone."

"Oh, T's got tons of ticklish spots," said Liza. "Come on Meg, don't you have to pee?"

"As a matter of fact, I think I—"

"Hey, Liza!" Jeff hollered from the front of the lanes.

She swiveled around. "Just a second!"

"You're up next," and he whistled like he was calling a hound.

I fumed inside, but I knew it was none of my business what went on between two people. I chanced a glance at Tristan and his expression was murderous. Oh, how I loved him.

Liza had no objections, though. She blew Jeff a kiss, seeming to enjoy getting under his skin, "I forfeit my turn, you take it."

"Oh, so he takes Meg's turn? No way."

"Come on, Meg," Liza took my arm, ignoring him.

I waggled my fingers at Tristan, and I heard him turn to Jeff with a challenge as Liza and I walked towards the bathrooms.

"Let's go, hip-hop. Scared of a little competition?"

"Alright, T. I'm gonna kick your ass."

I tensed, hoping the friendly pissing contest wasn't escalating into a more serious altercation. Jeff was strutting over to where Tristan stood, his face unreadable.

"Care to make a wager on that?" Tristan put out a hand.

Jeff lifted his chin in tough guy dialect before accepting the shake, then they both ambled back to the lanes together, trading jibes and insults.

"Boys," I shrugged.

Gazing one way and walking the other, I tripped over my own feet. Liza had a firm grip on my hand, though, and she pulled me upright to meet her gaze and held me there.

"What?"

"Nothing," she said, her expression so like her brother's that it gave me the willies.

I wondered if she could read me like a book, too, and made a mental note to guard my feelings around Liza more carefully. She was cool, but I had never trusted chicks, no matter how genuine they seemed.

By the time we got back, Tristan and Jeff had already stood in for two rounds in our absence and the competition was heating up.

"Shit." I steeled myself for the opposite of fun.

"Do I get to bowl at all?" Liza complained, when Jeff stood poised to take her turn at the runway automatically.

He let his ball thud back into the rack and said, "Oh yeah. Of course, babe." He looked at me, with an explicit warning to Tristan.

"Yeah, yeah," I sighed, flipping a hand in the air, hoping I showed how little I cared for my suckiness in bowling. The beer I had recently pounded in the bathroom with Liza helped in my indifference about looking foolish with the sparkly fuchsia ball from hell anyway.

"I'll help," Tristan whispered in my ear, escorting me to the ball rack himself.

In theory, I rolled the next two balls. But in reality, Tristan's body was so glued to mine that I felt like a puppet. With the excuse of "helping with my form," he stood directly behind me, so close it was more like spooning. He guided my hand through the swing somewhere between a caress and an ultimatum, his knees forcing mine to bend with his and his breath tickling my neck, "Now release."

He jumped back and whooped at Jeff in triumph when I rolled a spare, and Jeff was in his face instantly. "Nice move, pony boy. Watch this," he said, pulling Liza back to mimic Tristan's coaching method.

After several rounds of such highly competitive bowling shifts, Liza and I agreed that we might have more fun in one of the side rooms hemorrhaging music across the building from the bowling lanes. I ripped my hideous bowling shoes off a split second after the decision. I couldn't wait to explore. On our visit to the bathroom, I had peeked in to see someone on stage with a microphone under a spotlight, a glowing projection of lyrics behind her.

"I've always wanted to try Karaoke, you should come over when you guys are done," I said, giving Tristan a goodbye kiss.

"Karaoke?" For some reason, I had his undivided attention.

"Yeah, looks fun."

"I can't let you do that."

He was so protective it was cute. I raised up on my toes to kiss his cheek, still holding my sandal high heels in one hand. "Do what?"

"You can't get on stage and sing Karaoke, Mekaela."

"Why not?"

"You're kidding, right? You don't know?" A smile was spreading across his face and I was starting to get pissed.

I frowned, feet planted firmly on the ground again. "What are you talking about, Tristan?"

"Mekaela," he said, gentle and full of compassion. "You're completely tone deaf."

The kindness in his voice was almost painful. I felt my face start to heat up and squeaked, "I am?"

"You can't even hear it." He gazed at me with something like wonderment. "Haven't you ever heard someone sing off tune?"

"I guess so...I sound like that?" And exactly how loud I was singing in the car on the way there finally registered. That explained the look he gave me. "Oh."

Tristan burst out laughing and scooped me into a bear hug, my feet dangling several inches off the ground and my arms pinned to my sides. "And you, loving all that classical music. Finally, I find a flaw."

"Just one?" I said, trying to make a joke to blunt my fresh humiliation.

"Just one." He set me back down and looked at me like I was a new puppy he'd just gotten for Christmas.

Tone deaf. Why hadn't anyone else ever told me that?

"But, I don't know if I can even call it a flaw anyway." He leaned down and pressed his cheek against mine. "It's so cute."

"Alright, alright," I whined and turned away, feeling just as petulant as a newborn puppy.

"Hey, you." He spun me back around and devoured my neck.

"Tristan! Stop it," I giggled hysterically. He definitely knew *my* tickle spots.

"Quit eating each other, I'm gonna vomit," said Liza, suddenly there between us.

Jeff was right behind her, "Hey man, you shoot darts?"

"Do I shoot darts..." Tristan turned towards him, watching the fool with pity.

"Oh, is the game already over? Who won?" I asked.

"Who do you think?" Liza elbowed Jeff in the side, still annoyed about his placement of bowlers. "Well, we're gonna dance. See you guys later."

She towed me along, Tristan and Jeff heading for the dartboards and pool tables. We were weaving through a throng of inert bodies, Tristan slowly ebbing away from me. I heard Jeff ask him if he was up for another wager, and I almost had the urge to warn the poor guy. I had only been in the Jameson rec-room once, but I remembered the dart board I saw in there clearly—scarred by years of frequent use.

A guy in a pink polo shirt with sweaty hair and a beer in each hand intercepted Liza. I looked around for Tristan and saw his back, disappearing into the crowd. I guessed we'd have to deal with the asshole ourselves.

"Hey, Liza," Pink Polo taunted, gyrating his chest and shoulders to make a pair of large, beaded dice hanging around his neck sway and bounce. "Looka what I got."

"You jerk, where did you get those?" Liza demanded, reaching for the dice just as he jumped away with a cackle.

"Traded for 'em," he snickered, immensely pleased with himself.

"What are those?"

"It's a long story," Liza grumbled. "I got them in New Orleans at Mardi Gras this year—and they weren't easy to get, trust me. Then, I lost them in a bet to this creep who keeps trying to make me kiss him to get them back. I woulda done it normally, but he has the worst shit breath..."

I listened, but my mind was racing. How could this girl be from Shirley County? A female that uninhibited, I surely would have heard of her and maybe even been friends with her. But all the family portraits scattered around Tristan's house portrayed Liza as a sweet, almost mousy little girl. I remembered him saying she was incredibly shy in high school. If this was what college did to you, I couldn't wait to get there.

"...I don't know how you got them," Liza finished, stabbing his chest with her forefinger.

"Don't worry, sweetheart," Pink Polo slurred. "I don't want a kiss, just your panties."

Liza looked at him for a beat, suspicious of the bargain, but not for the reason I would've guessed. "You would give me the dice, if I give you my panties. For real?"

"Yep." He took another swig of beer and sniffed, his eyes unfocused.

"Crap, I'm not wearing any panties," she said in an undertone, stomping her foot in frustration.

I considered for a few seconds. Why not? "I am. I'll trade for you."

Liza's face bloomed into an ecstatic smile. "You would? My savior!"

"No big deal," I shrugged, sort of embarrassed by the praise. She had done so much for me before we'd even met.

"Works for me. Your friend's even better looking than you, Blondie," said Pink Polo and Liza punched his arm with her knuckle extended. "Ow. Okay, hand 'em over, sweet tits."

"Alright, but they're just white cotton." I hoped he wasn't expecting anything spectacular.

But, he actually licked his lips as he held out a hand, palm up, "Even better."

I grabbed Liza for balance, glad for the foresight of changing into fresh clothes before we left the campsite. That was an easy decision, since I hadn't been wearing clothes for most of the day in the first place. The Tristan Effect hasn't failed me yet. My pulse quickened just thinking about my sweet good luck charm while I slipped my underwear over my shoe.

I deposited them in Pink Polo's hand as Liza held out her own menacingly. "Dice."

"Here ya go," he said, pulling the necklace over his head and draping it around Liza's neck. I saw him lose his balance and figured one stiff shove would knock the guy to the floor. Liza shooed him away and he grinned.

I prayed in my head, "Please don't sniff my panties. Please don't sniff my panties." But he did, just as he turned to go, leering at me over them. The white cotton was dazzling under a nearby strobe light.

"Yes ma'am," Liza sang, dangling the dice against her chest. "Thank you, Meg—you're the best."

"Sure, no problem."

"Oh my god, I love this song," she thrilled, making an impromptu dance floor on the spot.

I recognized the song playing as one from Tristan's playlist that I had been belting out in the car, and I felt momentarily abashed before deciding to just enjoy the music. I still loved to dance, even if I couldn't sing. Most people around us were kind of grooving along to it, too, but I wanted to really dance and so did Liza. She clutched my arm and we started weaving around people, making our way to one of the club rooms.

"Where's Tristan?" I searched the packed room, just wanting to know where he'd ended up before I felt completely lost from him.

"You guys can't get enough of each other, can you?" Liza shouted through the music, which was growing louder as we neared its source.

"I don't see him by the dartboards—he might be looking for us."

"T's fine, Meg."

"I just want to make sure. Oh, there he is." My eyes finally found him in a clearing by the back door, and it took a moment for me to register a look of pure fury darkening his features. My skin prickled and I shot to attention through my alcohol-induced haze, noticing the dismay in a bystander's face. Everyone around him was staring at the ground. I tugged on Liza's shirt. "Hey, wait."

In a heartbeat, I was grabbing her hand and pulling her in the other direction for a better look.

"Oh shit," she gasped, when we were close enough to recognize Pink

Polo out cold on the floor by her brother's feet. Liza's eyes were wild with panic. "Meg, we've got to get Tristan out of here. Now."

chapter twenty-two

Tristan glanced up at us as we hauled ass to the back door where he stood, his eyes blazing in silent rage.

Liza put her hands on his shoulders and shook him hard. "See those guys over there?" She pointed to a group of oversized jocks on the other side of the bowling lanes. "Those are his fraternity brothers."

While I watched, several of those "brothers" went into red alert, their eyes scanning the building and quickly focusing on the corner where we all stood. They were listening to a girl, who was waving her arms frantically and pointing in our direction.

"Shit. Let's go," I agreed, terror edging my voice.

"Follow me," said Liza, already pushing through the back door. "Meg, wake up Tristan."

"Right." I put my hands on the sides of his face and slapped gently.

He was still in a daze, "Huh?"

Liza clutched his shirt collar and yanked him towards the exit. I shoved him from behind with all my strength.

"This would be a lot easier if you would comply," I grunted against his back, then added, "my love."

It was a dirty trick, but at least he snapped to attention. He looked up and over my shoulder, appropriate alarm sinking in at the image of advancing angry frat boys, and he let himself be towed from the building.

"Thank god, let's move."

Tristan did, but I noticed he didn't take my hand.

"Why are we running?" he finally asked, as Liza lead us back through the network of alleyways. "He deserved it."

"Frat guys are always looking for a fight, T. Please don't make me watch my baby brother get beat half to death by a bunch of drunken glazed hams," said Liza, already out of breath. "It's bad enough that this is my fault."

I heard what sounded like the human equivalent of a pack of riled up pit bulls yammering behind us through the alley, and adrenaline raced straight to my heart. "Frat boys have left the building," I warned.

"If I'm gonna run, we gotta go faster than this. Hop on." He tossed Liza on his back for her to ride piggy-back style. "Just tell me which way."

"What about Meg—"

"She's fast, she can keep up," Tristan said, immediately picking up speed.

I was proud of his vote of confidence, but I was actually hard pressed to keep up with him, even with Liza bouncing over his shoulder pointing this way or that at each junction. "Go that way. Now take a left right up there."

I was gasping for air when we finally reached the jeep.

Tristan was barely winded. "Wait a minute, we're not going to your dorm?"

"What, and hide out until morning, after rumors simmer all night and a bunch of *hung over* drunks wake up at a frat house?"

"She's right, Tristan."

"I don't want to leave you alone, Liza," he said, not even glancing in my direction.

"I'll be fine, as soon as you leave, Tristan. Please, go," she insisted, the worry plain in her eyes.

"Man…I'm sorry, sis." He looked miserable at the thought of abandoning her, cutting the night so dramatically short. But she was right; we didn't have much choice but to go, and fast.

"Get out of here before they see your car. And get theirs."

The thought of some kind of highway chase scene seemed to light a fire under him, thankfully. He kissed Liza on the cheek and unlocked the jeep, without opening my door like he usually did. He headed to the driver side like I wasn't even there. Was he ignoring me? I felt embarrassed, but not entirely sure why I should. A quick hug goodbye and passenger door slammed, I watched Tristan askance as he started the car and pulled away from the curb.

Laughing nervously, I managed, "Wow, that was intense."

Silence from the other side of the car.

After a few awkward minutes, I wondered aloud, "How could Liza think that was her fault, though?"

He tossed something onto my lap without a word. My face went up in flames when I saw my white cotton panties crumpled there. I balled them into a fist and hid my hand on the other side of my seat.

His voice was deceptively calm when he finally spoke, "You cannot fathom how I feel right now, Mekaela."

So, that was why he decked the guy. I gulped. I could feel his rage like a physical thing between us. It was my turn to keep quiet, my mind completely disoriented as I sat next to him, sorting recent memories. He didn't think I had anything else to do with Pink Polo, did he? I wasn't sure whether to feel ashamed of doing something so obviously stupid, or angry that he might be suspecting something worse.

"Those are yours, right?"

"They're mine," I admitted.

"Call me crazy, but maybe you should have kept them on."

The sarcasm in his voice helped me decide for angry. "They're mine, and I'll do what I damn well please with my own underwear, Tristan."

"Thanks a lot."

"What does it have to do with you?"

"Do you even know who that was? You couldn't have picked a worse person to give your fucking panties to. That was Todd Holland, the quarterback last year for Jean Gordon—only Jackson's biggest rival! I hate that guy, and lemme tell you he thought it was hilarious to put me in my place tonight."

"That's not my fault—how could I know that?" I shouted back at him, my ego even more bruised by feeling the fool.

His volume escalated over my own, "He waved them in my face, Mekaela!"

I immediately backed down; I feel like a little knock-kneed girl in training pants when men raise their voices. "Don't yell at me," I said, almost in a whisper.

"Your *panties!*" He wasn't even trying to hold it in anymore.

"Stop the car." It was all I could think to do. Run.

"Stop the car?"

"I want to get out. Stop the car."

Tristan laughed, sounding almost maniacal, "You're crazy. You think I'm gonna to let you wander off down the highway in the dark? Bare-assed, no less."

"Now you're just being mean. Let me out."

"No."

"What, are you kidnapping me?"

"What?"

I knew I was acting childish, but I was dangerously close to tears and starting to panic, resorting to stupid jokes and retorts. "Am I arrested, Sheriff Junior?"

"Arrested?" His pitch rose at the absurdity of the question.

"I feel sick, let me out."

"Nice try."

"Oh what, I'm a liar now, too? A slut *and* a liar?"

He was quiet while my heart skipped a couple beats.

But Tristan was steady and calm again: "I've never called you a slut, Mekaela."

"Isn't that what you were trying to say?"

"No—"

"Yeah. Just some cheap ho who gives away her panties to anybody, right?"

His abrupt silence was deafening. My breath was coming fast and it sounded gratingly loud. Tristan watched the road, his face stricken. My pulse raced, afraid I'd gone too far.

After an eternity, he asked quietly, "Are you trying to convince me?"

Oh, god. Did I? The cab started to spin. "Tristan, I really am going to puke. Pull over." I clutched at the dash with one hand and slapped the other over my mouth.

"Shit. Okay, hold on."

As soon as we slowed, I had the door ajar. I vaulted onto the grass, sweeping my hair out of the way just in time to spew my innards into a ditch. Momentum abating afterwards, I lost my balance and had to grip my knees for support, afro swinging forward again. But I wasn't done yet; acid churned in my gut and my vision rolled, the thought of vomit encrusted hair intensifying my agony.

"Uuuuugh…"

I stayed hunched over, not daring look around lest I see Tristan watching me, disgusted. Or, what if I looked up and he was gone? Maybe he'd just leave me there, after what I'd done. I felt a trickle run down my inner thigh. The force of retching with a full bladder doesn't mix well with giving your panties away.

Bile rose again like a viper. "Oh no."

Then—blessedly—two large, graceful hands came into view and pulled my hair out of my face. The fresh air was heavenly, beads of sweat cool on my forehead. An arm slipped around my waist and held me steady through round two. Tears sprang from my eyes like bullets. That had to be it, there couldn't be anything left in my stomach.

"I love you, Tristan," I blurted between sobs.

He went as still and hard as marble.

"I'm sorry! That wasn't the best way to say that. I mean, not terribly romantic, was it?" Now I was vomiting words. "You're the romantic one. I should take lessons. I'm so sorry."

A humorless laugh. "It's okay."

"You probably don't even love me anymore now—"

"I'm not going to stop loving you because you threw up on my shoes."

I straightened up and swiveled around. "I mean the panties thing. I'm so stupid. I wish I could just erase it, but I can't."

He squeezed his eyes shut. "Let's just forget the panties thing, okay?"

"Yes. Please. We can do that?" Could I love him anymore than I did that moment? I was terrified to death of what would happen now that he knew how I really felt. Now that I'd said those three words. What if all he ever loved about me was the chase? You can't chase someone who stands still for you, and my whole world stood still for him. I held my breath.

It seemed like hours dragged by, my heart hammering and anxiety tearing up my already delicate tummy. But in reality, only a couple seconds passed before relief softened his features.

"Yes. Please," he breathed and pulled me to his chest.

I snuggled in, trying not to get snot on his shirt. Or anything else. I leaned back to look at his face and found his brow troubled. Some kind of joke was in order, immediately. "I didn't really get any puke on your shoes, did I?"

♦

The sound of the highway seams ticking under the tires lulled me to a light doze, but I didn't want to drift off completely. Our new paradigm seemed too fragile to turn my back on. Tristan was pensive and quiet, and it was unnerving.

We made up, we said, "I love you," right. Or, I did. Why did our truce seem so tenuous?

"Where are we going, anyway?" My voice seemed to echo.

Tristan roused himself from whatever private reverie he was mulling over. "I don't know. I'm just driving."

"Can we just go someplace for the night where no one knows either of us?" I offered, hoping I didn't sound as timid as I felt. "I mean, I'd much rather sleep in Grizzly Bear Central than run into anyone else from school."

From our pasts, is what I really meant.

"Black bears."

"Huh?"

"There aren't grizzlies around here."

"Any kind of bear. I just meant...go somewhere, where there's nothing for anyone to live up to. Or live down," I said in a small voice, then reached to hold his hand in mine.

He squeezed my hand in reassurance but didn't respond for a long time.

After a while, he sighed. "Let's just get a room somewhere off the interstate," he said, sounding tired.

He avoided my eyes when I tried to read his expression. He looked thoughtful, but that's all I could tell. I didn't share his gift for mind-reading.

"You should really have your seat belt on," he said quietly.

"Okay." I straightened up and did as he asked, then looked away out the window. The fun weekend was over. As nice as it had been to get out of town, Nashville hadn't been nearly far enough. Not that distance was the only problem. Could Tristan and I could ever forget about the last several months of icy stares, snubbing friends, and fist-fights? That black eye? Lipstick on my locker door? Panties...

"Do you know where you're going to college yet?"

I jumped at the sudden break in the quiet.

"Oh. Florida, I think." A lump rose in my throat when I swallowed. Getting away from Shirley sounded great in theory, but that meant losing Tristan, of course. I wasn't prepared to actually talk about that prospect yet. It felt so final.

"Florida. Really?"

"Yeah. I have a cousin that lives in Delaney Beach. It's close to one of the schools I got into, and she said I can room with her."

"Delaney Beach—where's that?"

"South Florida, on the east coast."

Tristan thought for a minute. "Good baseball team there."

Small talk. He obviously wasn't as troubled by thoughts of us going our separate ways in a few months as I was.

"Is there? I wouldn't really know," I said to the window. I wondered where he was planning to go, but not sure I wanted to ask. Tristan would probably go to the school that offered him the best football scholarship, and that could be as far as California or something. But, I couldn't help it, "Where are you going? Do you know yet?"

"Not yet. I'm working on it, though." He grabbed my hand and kissed it. "Enough talk, I think I'm ready for bed."

"Tired?"

"Oh, not that tired," he said with a wink.

I perked up a little. At least we weren't going straight home. That possibility was a nag in the back of my mind that I hadn't been willing to acknowledge. I forced a smile, trying for alluring, although alluring was far from what I felt. I got my phone from my purse, "Lemme find something close on the GPS."

"Really close." He squeezed my thigh, the top of his fingers slipping just under the hem of my skirt. He raised his eyebrows salaciously, and I knew he was thinking of the fact that I was still going commando.

"Okay," I laughed, totally confused at his abrupt change in mood.

I found a motel, put my phone on the console, and let the GPS guide us. Sitting back, I attempted to gather my splintered brain back together. Tristan switched on the radio and tapped the beat out on the steering wheel. I tried to not feel hurt that he wasn't depressed about the idea of us both going off to college. I didn't really want him depressed, but he didn't even seem affected. He had probably just always known what was in his future, and it wasn't me. I could hear Tiger Mom telling him "the world is your oyster" and all that crap. And it was.

And it's mine, too, I reminded myself.

Tristan was right, I decided. There was no reason to dwell on the inevitable and ruin what little time we had left together. College would come soon enough, and I might as well enjoy him while I could. I knew he'd be enjoying me.

"You have arrived," I heard the GPS announce as we pulled up in front of a roadside motel. A vacancy sign blinked on and off in a darkened office window. Tristan leaned over for a quick peck on the lips, then hopped out and headed for reception. I stayed in my seat, attempting to match his enthusiasm. I did not want to be a drag. He turned to blow me a kiss and I grabbed the air, pretending to tuck the kiss into a pocket against my chest.

"Snap out of it, Meg. What the hell do you want?" I grumbled, watching him disappear inside.

One more night completely alone with Tristan was more than I'd hoped for less than an hour before, so I needed to get a grip and have fun. It should've been enough.

But it wasn't.

My mood settled over me like a fog. I watched "Vacancy" flash hypnotically in red neon, thinking of how ironic the word was for me at that moment. My head and heart were so full. I pasted a smile on my face when I saw him exit the office, jogging back to the car and jingling a set of room keys for me to see. A "No" flickered on in the window behind him. No vacancy indeed. The sign stopped flashing and glowed brighter, steady and fixed.

part three:
cactus heart

chapter twenty-three

"Debra. Howard."

Scattered, polite golf claps.

"Martin. Hughes."

A little more enthusiasm from the crowd.

"Tristan. Jameson."

Hoots and whoops and boisterous clapping from both spectators and fellow graduates. Real applause for a real Bobcatt. Tristan finished mounting the last steps up to the auditorium platform and grinned at me as he approached. He was no stranger to the stage or the applause.

"Congratulations, young man," said Andrew Jackson High's principle, Mr. Warren, shaking the reinstated darling of the varsity club's hand in a tough-guy grip. Tristan's bicep flexed in response, tendons jumping in his neck.

"Thank you, sir." He nodded and accepted a rolled-up diploma, then shook the Valedictorian's hand.

In the honored spot right next to our principle, Miles Evans sniffed regally. He had beat me out for the top spot by only one B in the end, darn it. He made straight A's when I screwed up in Advanced French IV at the last. He knew I took harder classes, the little weasel. Regal indeed.

I was next in line and I tried to keep a straight face while Tristan's eyes bored into mine, looking straight past Miles. "Congratulations, Mr. Jameson." I smiled up at my boyfriend, offering my own hand for him to shake.

"Why, thank you, Miss Shannon." He bulled through the formality, slipped one hand around my waist and cupped my chin with the other, pulling my face towards his. I gasped and glanced sideways at Mr. Warren, and then Tristan's lips were on mine amid whistles and catcalls from the audience. When he released me, I wanted to glare at him. I ended up doing something closer to giggling instead.

Mr. Warren cleared his throat, but offered a magnanimous shake of his head as if to say, "You crazy kids. Go on, seize the day."

Tristan winked and I melted.

"Love you." He tossed his diploma in the air, caught it behind his back, and hopped down the stairs.

I straightened my cap, attempting dignified, and swore to avoid gazing at him adoringly as he made his way back down the aisle. The roster was being called, I had to focus. The Salutatorian should be able to praise each student by name. But I couldn't help it; I peeked in his direction and my eyes locked on of their own accord.

My frown was automatic. He was slapping hands and accepting thumps on the back, as he found his seat within the rows of folding chairs.

In his element.

The return of Tristan's popularity in the past few weeks made me anxious. It was like the prom we missed was the last milestone before the end of our high school careers, and the world had shifted afterwards. I felt it as soon as we got back from our weekend in Nashville. Everyone grew more and more euphoric each day nearer to graduation, the promise of freedom so close at hand. Sleep deprivation from exam cramming led to delirium. When that was mixed with nostalgia, it cast a weird, dreamy spell over the whole campus. People were signing yearbooks of strangers, ditching class for no reason (teachers turning a blind eye), and constantly breaking into sudden tears or spontaneous laughter in the hallways.

It was the longest stretch I could remember where no one really bugged me at school—I hadn't been called a slut once. At least I didn't hear anyone calling me a slut. Tristan assumed his former glory as the much loved Pretty-Boy Jameson, campus stud and billboard model extraordinaire, all slights by friends and foes alike seemingly forgiven.

Why did it all feel so right and so wrong at the same time?

"Tanya. Morris."

The name was a middle finger in my reverie. I narrowed my eyes as a minion of Tristan's ex approached, flicking her side-ponytail forward over a shoulder and sashaying in a bright orange graduation sack. Her hand was a cold wet fish in mine.

"Thanks, whore," she said under her breath.

I plastered a shit-eating grin on my face and looked through her.

"Hmph," she simpered, tossed her hair again and walked away.

"Catherine. Murphy."

I smiled in relief. The pretty, admittedly friendly, class historian's name roused a healthy round of cheers from the crowd. She bopped across the stage to get her diploma and beamed at me when she shook my hand. She was probably the one that took the yearbook photo of me that Tristan loved so much.

Flattering picture aside, yearbook day was hellish. I cringed at the thought...

"You didn't get a yearbook?" Incredulity soured Tristan's beautiful smile.

I plopped my book bag on the ground next to our usual lunch table in the courtyard. "I know what I look like."

"Yeah, but it's like a memento. Don't you want to see all the pictures of...everyone? All the stuff you did in your last year?"

"Eh." He almost said "friends," but caught himself. I looked away, my lips pinched together. Maybe they got a good snapshot of my colorful locker graffiti. I dug for my lunch in my bag, acting casual. "I'm probably not in it much."

"Your senior photo is gorgeous," he said, laying his yearbook out right under my nose and thumbing through the pages.

My stomach turned—I had been dreading the examination of yearbook laurels ever since the order forms were distributed. Prior experience told me there was an index in the back, every student's name catalogued with page numbers for club photos, sport action shots, and candids throughout the year. Names like "Tristan Jameson" would be followed with more than half a column of page references. My only reference was likely the requisite senior photo, which I hadn't even seen. The photo shoot was free, but the smallest package you could buy was expensive. I hadn't even bothered to pick up the proofs.

The fact that Tristan had already seen my diminutive index listing was humiliating. I glanced around the courtyard, feigning disinterest, the smell of fresh print wafting into my face. "Gorgeous. Right."

He found the page he was seeking, "Look, have you seen it?"

I barely dared to peek, but it wasn't like he was giving me much choice. I dropped my gaze and found my face, easy with his finger jammed under it.

"Hmph. Not too bad."

"Are you kidding? It's one of the best in the album, Mekaela. Why can't you see how beautiful you are?"

Irritation edged his voice. I looked at the picture again to avoid looking at him. The yearbook staff had chosen a shot in which I wasn't smiling, my hair pushed back over my shoulders and actually looking pretty tame. It was still wet that morning when I got to the photographer's studio and his assistant had dried it with a diffuser on her blow-drier. In the photo, the look on my face was sort of wistful, instead of the standard toothy grin. The compulsory orange background was complimentary to my coloring, unlike most other students.

"I guess I do look sort of Pre-Raphaelite."

"If that means beautiful."

"In my opinion it does, but——"

"Hi, Tristan. Will you sign my yearbook?" came a sudden nervous request from somewhere behind us.

"Fabulous."

Tristan frowned at me. "Uh...yeah."

I looked back to find a couple of girls, obviously much younger, holding their books over their chests. One had a pen in her fist and she shoved it at Tristan.

"Mine, too?" the other one said, and they both giggled into each other's hair.

"Sure, which page?" Tristan pushed his own book further towards my side of the table and accepted super-fan number one's yearbook. I knew where he would be signing, no need to look. Tiger Mom had bought him a full-page spread, with choice sporty shots, senior photo, and a cheesy quote: *"Shoot for the moon. Even if you miss, you will land among the stars. —Les Brown."* One of the pictures was from a Homecoming Week Intramural thing that I skipped, Tristan faced off against someone after an unfair call was made by the referee. The photo was black and white, very dramatic. Tristan's eyes were smoldering, his jaw clenched, and his whole body flexed. That's the one all the girls wanted him to sign next to.

His elbow bumped mine as he did just that. He did look pretty hot, I had to admit. I thumbed through Tristan's yearbook, busy, discouraging any return signing. My curiosity got the better of me and I flipped to the index to find my name.

Whoa. Five page references. That was a surprise.

I was in the group photo for the Beta Club, I'd totally forgotten. I never went to meetings, but I did the bookkeeping for them during study hall sometimes. Good for my college resume. Also listed were the Honor Society and the French Honor Society—those two were automatic with a good grade point average. The senior photo was another reference, of course. The last one I didn't recognize.

"Hi, Meg. Would you sign my yearbook?"

"Huh? Oh—" I glanced up to see Erica Norman with her yearbook clutched across her chest. Ever since we bonded over the uncomfortable group shots with the Homecoming Court, Erica and I were friendly whenever we crossed paths. "Sure."

"Cool, here." Her finger was already holding the page she wanted and she opened her yearbook on top of Tristan's.

In front of me was a two-page spread for the various service organizations at Jackson, the headline reading, "Let Us Lead by Serving Others." Among candid pictures of kids giving speeches, working at soup kitchens, or organizing clean-up events, there was a picture of me. I looked up at Erica, surprised.

"It's so you."

Heat crept into my cheeks. "I didn't even know they were taking it."

"That one's my favorite," Tristan said so softly it was like a kiss next to my ear. "When you wear your hair like that, all I want is that long neck between my teeth all day."

"Jeez, bedroom voice," I scolded him under my breath, though charmed. I went back to the book. I was leaned over a pile of receipts on a library table, recording numbers into the Beta Club ledger. My hair was in a loose braid over one shoulder and my sweater had fallen off the other, leaving it bare. "When was that?"

"Cathy's pretty good at sneaking around with her camera. It was probably her. I made sure it got in, though," Erica remarked proudly. "I'm assistant editor on the yearbook committee."

I was dumbfounded. "Gosh. Thanks, Erica."

"No problem. Nice to have a little more variety in those pages, if you ask me."

"I'd ask you to sign mine..." I felt Tristan shake his head, preachy. "But, I didn't order one."

"Oh, no big." Erica gathered her book back under her arm. I noticed that she didn't ask Tristan for his signature and smiled to myself. "See you around, Meg."

"Bye."

Tristan watched me, his expression murky.

"What?"

"Nothing," he shrugged. "It's good to see you opening up to people."

I bit my tongue so I wouldn't blurt out, "Screw you." As if my lack of friends was due to my unwillingness to *open up*.

"Hi, Tristan. Would you sign my yearbook?" said a bubbly voice out of nowhere.

I groaned and bit into my sandwich. But the autograph session was welcome that time. Time to think meant a chance to talk myself down from telling my Pretty-Boy off. Was he even mine anymore? The vultures were circling, I could feel them. And vultures only ate dead things. Road kill.

"Well, darlin'," the yearbook whistled under my nose when he snapped it shut, "I gotta head to the locker room."

"Wait. You aren't going to eat with me?" My hand was a claw on his back pocket. "It's not fourth period for twenty minutes."

"I told Coach I'd meet him before P.E. He wants to talk to me about something, I don't know."

"Oh. Okay, see you later then." I tucked in to my sandwich.

Tristan bent to kiss the top of my head, "See ya," then was gone.

I dug a book out of my bag and kept my nose in it until the bell rang.

...and that drifting feeling intensified. Now graduation was here. Do we drift ashore or drift to sea?

"Heather. Zeigler."

I picked my nails under my graduation gown. The stage lights beat down on my ugly orange cap. Almost go time. Mr. Warren was at the end of the list, and Miles and I would be called last. After hearing the wide range of audience response for different graduates, I was worried how my own name would be judged by the crowd. I didn't think anyone would dare to boo me, but I knew whatever reception I got would pale in comparison to Tristan's applause.

One more popularity contest that I would lose.

"Mekaela. Shannon."

Shit, here we go.

"Alright Meg!" my sister Jo yelled from the bleachers. Tristan's ear-splitting whistle joined her cheer and a healthy ovation from the Mendez Family rounded out my ovation. Ricky's family. My heart thundered with gratitude.

I kept my place in line, waiting for the principal to come to me, as rehearsed. "Thank you, Mr. Warren."

"Outstanding work, Miss Shannon. Congratulations."

He handed Miles his diploma next, raised their clasped hands overhead in triumph (Miles forced on tip-toe), then returned to the podium to make his final announcement.

I could hardly make sense of his speech. I was done. Done with Andrew Jackson High. Done with Shirley County. I was soaring.

"...and it's my pleasure to welcome the Class of 2015 into adulthood. I'd like to close with a quote from Edward Koch, *The fireworks begin today. Each diploma is a lighted match. Each one of you is a fuse.*'"

A communal hush settled over the auditorium.

"Congratulations, graduates. And good luck."

Thunderous cheering erupted all around and mortarboards flew into the air.

"I said god damn!" I strangled Miles in a hug.

Suddenly, I didn't want to miss an instant by being up there on the stage, removed from the celebration. I skipped down the stairs and into the throng. Tristan was jogging up the aisle towards me and I vaulted into his arms. We crashed into each other so hard it took my breath away, and he swung me in a circle, lifting me off my feet and high into the air.

"We did it," I breathed, sliding back down to earth against his body.

He held my face against his, and wrapped his other arm around my waist. "You looked beautiful up there, Mekaela."

"Can you believe it's over?"

He chuckled, his chest rumbling against mine. "It's not over yet."

"What do you mean?" I lifted my gaze and saw he wore his smart-girls-can-be-so-silly look.

"Oh, Mekaela. I love you."

I looked back in the direction he nodded, and cringed at the impending onslaught.

chapter twenty-four

Happy faces and insistent hands swamped us from every direction.

"Yay, Meg," said Charlie, tugging at my gown while the twins sandwiched me. I watched over my sisters' heads as Tristan was mobbed himself, moving farther away in a riptide of well-wishers.

"You're awesome, Meg."

"Thanks, Jo."

"Right there on stage, with Mr. Warren. You looked so...so..." Piper stuttered.

"Stuck up?" Jo offered.

"Shut up. Grown up is what I meant."

"Piper, are you crying?" I wasn't surprised. Piper cries at the drop of a hat.

"No," she insisted, wiping the corner of one eye and coughing back an embarrassed laugh.

"Meg. I want to hug Meg," whined my youngest sibling, wriggling in Mom's arms and urging her forward with a kick.

"Aw, come 'ere, Tess." I positioned her on my own hip and let her snuggle into my neck.

My mom didn't want to let Tessa go. She'd said this was my day and I should have absolutely nothing to worry about but reveling in my achievement. I didn't care at that moment, though. Hugs felt pretty nice, no matter how inadvertently suffocating. Mom watched me with her last baby, an adoring look creeping into her eyes.

"Meg, I am so proud of you."

"You're not gonna start crying, too, are you?" I watched her chin tremble, stunned. My mother hadn't shed a tear in as long as I could remember. Come to think of it, I wasn't sure I had ever actually seen her cry.

"She's just bummed she's gonna lose her number one baby sitter."

"Stop it, Josephine." Mom put both her hands on my shoulders and looked me square in the face, past Tessa's squirming body. "Honey, I want you to know..."

"Jeez, lemme put the kid down." I let Tessa slither down my shiny polyester robe.

She was running as soon as she hit the floor. "Char-ee, wait!"

My mom cleared her throat and began again, "I realize things haven't been easy for you around here."

"It's okay, Mom." I felt myself faltering, too, vocal chords quavering. "I don't need easy."

"I know you don't. And I know you're going to make a beautiful life for yourself somewhere."

Hard to hear now that it came right down to it. I swallowed a stony lump. It was true, though. I wasn't sure where I'd end up, but I'd make sure it was far away from Shirley County.

"You're going to make your dreams come true. All by yourself."

"Oh, Mom. It's not like you haven't helped." I folded her in my arms. Her tears were as hard to watch as they were to come by, and I was terrified they might loosen my own floodgates. "You helped make me who I am."

Someone pounded me on the back.

Rescued!

"Hey, chica. Can you believe we're done at this shithole?" Ricky.

My cousin Zach was right behind him. "Come on, Aunt Natalie. I want a squeeze, too," he said, unafraid to force the issue. He grabbed us both at the same time and, sensing too much estrogen in the vicinity, tickled us each in the ribs until we were gasping for air and slapping his iron hands away. He put an arm around my mom, "Some show, right?"

"So, you guys are still coming over for our little fiesta?" Ricky grabbed Piper and twirled her in an impromptu Latin dance move. He learned to dance straight out of the crib. And I knew a *little fiesta* at the Mendez's place would be an all out bash. I couldn't wait.

"God, yes," Jo broke in. "I am so ready for a party—Tessa get back here!"

She ran after our little sister and Charlie gave chase, too. She scrambled under the stage and as Jo tried to tug her out, Tessa's shoe slipped off and Jo toppled backwards on her butt. Charlie squealed with glee.

"Well, that's a slice of humiliation to put things into perspective," I sighed. "New life, here I come."

"Hey, Mekaela. You wanna ride with me?" Tristan was suddenly behind me, his arms encircling my waist.

"What? You know I'm not doing the Project Graduation thing."

Every year, the PTA organized a lock-in in the gymnasium and library. They billed it as the best way to keep graduates safe and away from teenage celebratory urges like booze and parties that were actually fun. I couldn't imagine anything worse than being locked in for my entire graduation night with the good, clean merriment that Stephanie Jameson had planned—foosball and flag football, with a healthy dose of Twister and skit-writing for some amateur talent show. I wouldn't have guessed

Tristan to be interested either, but he could hardly refuse something so important to his mom. He said it was one of her biggest events of the school year.

"No, not that. We're having a cookout at my house before that. My dad invited everyone."

"A cookout? Since when?"

"I thought I told you." He snuggled into my neck, still not letting me see his face.

I grew suspicious immediately, "No. You didn't tell me."

"Sweet Jesus, let's get that party started before I kill somebody." Jo was back, red-faced and hauling a tear-stained Tess behind her. "Meg, are you riding with me?"

Tristan was wounded. "Party?"

"Well, yeah. I was planning to go to Ricky's place for all the after-graduation stuff. I thought you'd be busy with the lock-in." I didn't mention my pique: Tristan would be deserting me for the lock-in, an event he knew I would be uncomfortable attending. I was pissed as shit about it.

"Tristan, you're coming too, right?" Jo asked, just as Tessa stomped on her foot and darted through the mingling crowd. Jo let out a howl and charged after her again.

"I wasn't invited," Tristan answered after she was already gone, watching my eyes.

"I'm sorry." I put my hands on my hips, cornered and defensive. It wasn't fun seeing the hurt on his face, knowing I was the cause. But, he shouldn't have decided to go to the stupid lock-in if he wanted to hang out with me. "I had no idea about your cookout. You never said anything," I shrugged and looked away from my favorite face in the world. "It's not that I didn't invite you to Ricky's—it's not my party."

He gathered me back in, rested his forehead against mine. "No, I know."

"I don't know what to say," I fumbled. Why was I the one feeling like a jerk?

He reached for my hand and positioned it between us, playing with my fingers. "I just thought it would be nice to celebrate with you, before I get locked in all night."

"Well..."

"All night." He let out a long suffering sigh that swirled between our satiny orange chests. His breath smelled like peppermint gum. Those bright blue eyes looked up under long black lashes, and I was done for. "You know what I mean?"

"Ugh. Why do you have to be such a gorgeously sad puppy dog?"

"So you'll come?" He straightened up, his face so hopeful it was heartbreaking.

"Of course I will, Tristan. Like I can ever refuse you when you look at me like that."

"She said she'll come, Mom," he called over my shoulder.

I turned around to find Tiger Mom approaching. Bewildered, I twisted back to Tristan, the traitor in my arms. "Huh?"

"That's wonderful," said his mother, stalking closer and well past our established comfort zone. "Meg Dear, I am so proud of you."

She was going in for a hug. Horrified, I gaped at Tristan, her grinning accomplice.

"How did I not know you were the Salutatorian?" the woman asked, invading my senses with her perfumed crepe blazer and thoroughly hairsprayed up-do.

And then I was embraced. By Stephanie Jameson.

She giggled. "I guess I should have known, shouldn't I? You've made such a difference in Tristan's grades."

"You could've asked, Mom."

"I know, I know." She retreated a few inches, still holding me so close I could see her pink lipstick bleeding into the fine lines around her mouth. "Well, let's just let bygones be bygones, right?"

"Uh. Right." This family barbecue would take place in hell and I'd be on the spit. I cast around for aid, but I wouldn't find it from my boyfriend, obviously in league with the tiger.

"Right. Past is in the past," he replied, then winked at me.

And with that, I was done for. Defeated by my own libido in the wink of an eye. I figured I still had an out, though, if Jo was difficult about letting me take the car. She had finally pawned off the little monsters onto Piper and was hanging around, itching to be gone.

"Hey Jo, can you ride with Mom so I can have the car for a little bit? I'll meet you guys at Ricky's." She'd never go for it.

Jo ignored my pointed look. "Sure, no problem."

"Thanks," I said through my teeth. That was so Jo—almost like a guy, totally missing little clues that a girl should've picked up on in an instant.

"Wonderful," Tiger Mom beamed and clapped her hands, "Tristan Sweetheart, I'll see you at home. I've got to say hello to a few people." She stood on tiptoe to kiss his cheek and ruffle his hair, then gave me a parting squeeze on the arm. "Glad you can join us, Meg Dear."

I rubbed a lipstick smear off Tristan's face as soon as she walked away. He grabbed my hand and kissed it. "So, you want to just follow me to my place?"

"Meg, where have you been?" A flustered Miles pushed through loitering friends and family. Some mousy underclassman wearing enormous glasses was in tow. "We're supposed to do the interview, remember? They want us in the picture together, so it's 'fair' or something."

"Oh, sorry. I forgot about that." I grimaced at Tristan. "I have to go do this interview for the paper. Um…" I motioned to the awkward girl, snapping my fingers.

"June," she supplied.

"Right. June's helping write the article—all about the graduation or whatever—and some kid from the Photography club is taking pictures of us with Mr. Warren."

"Everybody wants a little piece of you today, huh?"

I bristled automatically, "What's that supposed to mean?"

His eyebrows shot up. "Can I talk to you for a minute? Excuse us." Without waiting for agreement, he laced his fingers with mine and guided me off to the edges of the auditorium. Next to the stage, we were partially hidden by the blanketing flags. "Why are you being so edgy today?"

"I'm not being edgy," I said, disengaging my hand and crossing my arms over my chest, the perfect illustration of edginess.

He pursed his lips at the gesture.

I exhaled sharply and transferred my hands to my hips.

"Actually, for like a week now you've been a little..." He cocked his head to the side and reached his hand towards me, but then dropped it, as if unsure I might bite his fingers. "Off."

Great. My brain was like an open-faced sandwich to him. "I have?"

He nodded, then said quietly, "Are you off me?"

"What? No." I pushed back from his chest and he looked down at my hands, his face troubled. That was all wrong. I hugged him close again. "No, no, no. Never. Please don't think that."

I reached for his hand, kissing his knuckles and rubbing them against my cheek. Off of Tristan? If he only knew how opposite my reality was.

"Okay," he said with a nervous laugh and backed away. His hair had gotten so long it was always falling in his eyes, especially when he looked at his feet like he was then. He ran his hand through it and looked out across the cavernous room.

I sighed, "Hey. Let's not be weird, okay?"

"I'm not the one being weird."

"Okay, I admit it. I've probably been feeling uncomfortable with all the...social stuff—all this 'fun' stuff surrounding graduation. You know I'm not good at this kind of thing, I'm sorry."

"Yeah. I know. Let's forget it."

"Let's," I agreed, desperate to lift our dark cloud with a forced laugh.

He zeroed in on that like it was a life preserver and tickled my ribs. "Think I'm funny, do you?"

"Yes."

"I'll show you funny..."

chapter twenty-five

A rush of laughter endorphins cleared the air and we kissed goodbye, all the usual endearments and promises in tact. I got the car keys from Jo and went backstage with Miles and June. The interview and photo shoot took longer than expected, but I was pulling out of the mostly empty parking lot less than an hour behind Tristan. On the drive through the valley to the Jameson place, I had plenty of time to think by myself. Of course I knew why I was acting off and deep down I recognized the kernel of truth lodged in my heart. I had been freaked out ever since I uttered those three vulnerable words, "I love you."

What a sick twist of fate that almost the instant I had told him I loved him, everyone else seemed to remember the same. Everyone loved Tristan, damn it. I had always found strength in my uniqueness, but in this instance I was just another chick in the Tristan Jameson fan club. Not so unique after all.

I gripped the steering wheel and growled, pounded out each syllable with my fist, "Why. Is. Love. So. Damn. Con. Fus. Ing?"

Was I imagining it, or had Tristan grown more relaxed around me since The Declaration? I didn't need him on his toes, standing at attention at the end of my whip. No. But the terrible fear I resisted admitting to myself was that he might be growing bored with me. And boredom wouldn't help me when things ultimately got too difficult between us. We were just so different. His friends hated me. His mother hated me.

His mother.

"Why is *she* acting weird?" I said to the open road. "If anyone's behavior should be examined, it should be hers not mine. He should have warned me."

The memory of our conversation behind the flag poles made me suck in my breath in reaction. It was barely a conversation, and I should have said more. Tristan's imagined rejection—the sadness in his eyes and resignation in his tone—every time the image flashed across my mind my guts twisted another degree. That was a tiny taste of how our breakup would feel, and it was worse than I could've ever imagined. Losing Tristan, saying good-bye. I couldn't do it. I didn't know how I would handle it when we both left for school.

"What am I gonna do?"

I rapped my head with my knuckles.

"Maybe a long-distance relationship could work," I suggested to the windshield, knowing in my bones it could never work. Who would want to be tied down to love letters and phone calls their first semester in college?

I would.

I banged the steering wheel again.

"No. He wouldn't. I'm sure."

I slowed down to turn into Northern Estates, every nerve zinging with trepidation.

I was driving right into the lion's den—no, what do tiger's live in? A lair? I made a mental note to look that up online, knowing full well I was being crazy. I was losing my mind. Over a guy.

"Meg, can you be more cliché?" I wagged a finger at myself in the rear-view mirror. Then sighed. "Oh, but what a beautiful cliché he is…"

I rounded the corner and turned down his street.

"Shit."

There were a gazillion cars, surely all there for the cook-out. The knots in my stomach could have won a Boy Scout award.

"Wonder if Tristan's won an award for that, too," I smiled ruefully, mentally counting the cars lined up on both sides down his street. "So many people…"

But the sad fact was, I couldn't wait to see him again, no matter how nervous I was. I parked well down the block—the closest spot I could find—and cut the engine.

"Well, he did tell me they invited everyone."

I got out of the car, unzipped my graduation gown, and tossed it on the front seat. I checked out the cars as I walked past, recognizing most as belonging to Jackson students, with the odd Bobcatts pendant in the window or a *Class of '14* tassel hanging on the rearview mirror. Nicer cars were parked here and there (parents?), including an immaculate silver Mercedes that I'd never seen.

I whistled as I walked past.

Closer to the house and on the opposite side, two girls in bikini tops and jean shorts skipped up the sidewalk hand in hand, then ran through the front yard and back to the gate. They were more comfortable at my boyfriend's house than I was.

"Tristan might have mentioned it was a pool party," I sniffed.

Jingling my keys in my hand, I strutted up the street in my high heels, trying to look more confident than I felt. At least I was wearing a new dress. The silky fabric clung to my curves and glided across my thighs in what Tristan said was his favorite color on me. Whenever I wore deep, dark red, he commented on my skin and compared my hair to chocolate. On high boredom alert, I was pulling out all the stops.

Reaching the front door, I had a moment of panic when I heard raucous laughter spilling around the house from the backyard. My hand was ready to knock, but I was frozen. I nearly bolted.

Just then, the door opened and a rush of air slipped out.

"Meg, you're finally here. 'Bout time."

My white lips split into a grin so wide it hurt. "Liza."

She threw herself into me so hard I tripped backwards off the top step. "Everyone else here is so boring. You're the only one I can count on to liven things up."

"Really?"

"Duh," she shoved me on the shoulder just as I was regaining my balance.

Tristan appeared in the doorway. "Yeah, you two know how to have a little too much fun together."

I had to remind myself how to breathe when I caught sight of him. He was half naked in nothing but his swim trunks, already soaked and sagging around his hips. His hair was wet and messy and black, and his eyes burned glassy blue underneath.

He pressed his cold soda bottle to Liza's back and she squealed. "Outta the way, Liza. I want some."

"Hey, you're wet," I protested. There was nothing I wanted more than to feel every inch of him. But of course, we had an audience. A big one. He bit my neck with a comic bobcat growl.

Liza slapped him away. "You're a pig, Tristan—you'll ruin her dress."

He didn't offer much resistance, just stepped back to look me over. "Wow, I'm glad I didn't know you were wearing that under your gown all through graduation. That coulda been embarrassing on stage." He grinned and bit his bottom lip.

I squinted at him, perplexed. Rude leering was not normal Tristan behavior, especially around his family. How cocky.

"Tristan, go away. You get to see Meg all the time, it's my turn." Liza grabbed my hand and pulled me into the house.

Relief flooded over me. I hadn't seen her at the ceremony and didn't dare hope for such an ally at the dreaded cookout. I looked back to make sure Tristan hadn't gone away like she'd commanded, and was content to see that he was following with a wolfish smile.

I listened with half an ear, as Liza rattled on about her Spring semester in college. She had broken it off with her boyfriend, she made the worst grades she ever had on record, and oh yeah, that thing with Pink Polo blew over so fast I wouldn't believe it. Turns out that after the alcohol wore off, most of the guys admitted he was an asshole and deserved to be knocked out. Liza wasn't shy about claiming full responsibility for turning a possibly violent episode into a non-issue out of sheer elder wisdom and a keen sensitivity in reading people. I nodded or agreed or questioned when appropriate, smiling at Tristan, who was keeping quiet. And keeping an eye on my behind.

I mostly examined the Jameson digs, which I had never really checked out in the daylight. The living room was massive, with a stone fireplace taking up most of one wall and an enormous flat screen TV almost perpendicular to that. An L-shaped, sectional couch marked off the outside corner with plenty of crawl space and two Barcaloungers in between. I wondered why such a cozy area was empty at a party. What I wouldn't give to be camped out on that fluffy couch for an afternoon. Then I realized it was probably because there wasn't a sport broadcast playing. A glance outside revealed all the males either manning the grill or organizing some kind of flag football game in the yard beyond. The pool looked smaller than I remembered it somehow, maybe because there were so many people crowded around—mostly girls in various states of pool-friendly fashion.

"Liza, I need you to help me with the refreshments," trilled a familiar voice.

I turned around to see Tiger Mom scurrying from the kitchen to snatch her daughter's hand.

"Hello, Meg Dear. Welcome."

"Oh. Thank you. You have a lovely home, Mrs. Jameson."

"You think so? So nice of you to say." She was sweating and glowing. Parties like these were obviously her thing.

"Everyone's fine, Mom. Let people pour their own darn drinks," complained Liza.

"I'm making something special."

"So, why can't *you* make it then?"

"Liza Anne, you have not lifted one finger to help with your brother's graduation party." Her mother straightened to her full height and a storm cloud darkened the glow.

"Ugh. Fine. Mekaela can help, too."

"No. You let those two lovebirds alone."

Lovebirds?

"Mom…"

"You and Amanda are all the help I need. Make yourself at home, Meg Dear."

I hadn't risen to the level of culinary assistant just yet. I smirked as they both disappeared behind a kitchen island stacked high with trays of food, bouquets of flowers, various Tristan trophies, or framed Tristan pictures.

Tristan's hand slid against my bare back, expertly finding the slit in my dress that offered free access.

I stiffened. "Your hands are freezing."

"How are you?" His tone was gentle and honest, all of the weirdness of the past few hours muted.

I kissed his nose and breathed him in. He was the one I loved. We were surrounded by all these people, but it was just the two of us. That soft, intimate question and those intense, concerned eyes were what I knew. What I needed. "I'm good."

"Is this okay?" He nodded to the crowd past the sliding glass doors out to the pool, his question clearly focused on one particular person.

My mood plummeted when I saw her. Ashley was standing with a group of friends. Most of them were in bikini's, but she was still in her graduation dress. Her father stood close by, casting disapproving looks at the quantity of bared teenage skin around him.

"Oh."

Of course she would come—why was I surprised? Tristan told me that the Davises were longtime family friends. The two moms, Stephanie and Kerry, had grown up from toddlerhood together.

"It was unavoidable, with the whole town celebrating. I didn't bring it up, because I didn't want you to not come."

"No, no. I know. It's fine, really," I said, hoping that would someday be true.

"You don't have anything to worry about here. This is my house and anyone that says or even thinks a word against you will get an ass-kicking."

I smiled at him, truly touched even if I didn't believe it. "Even if they *think* it?"

His jaw clinched. "Yes."

"Even a girl? You'd hit a girl?" I knew Tristan would never do that.

"I'll have Liza hit her."

She would, too. Liza was a scrapper, just like her bro. I was aglow. "I love you, Tristan."

He held my gaze, let the moment linger.

"Canonbaaaaaaaaal!"

A sheet of water hit the glass doors and uproarious decent screeched from around the pool perimeter. I couldn't see out the glass yet, but I knew all the nice girls were shaking out their hair and hands, pulling sodden clothes away from their tummies. Wiping dripping mascara from under their eyes.

"You want to swim?" Tristan asked, his eyes alight.

"I didn't bring a suit."

"You can borrow one of Liza's. She has a million."

"Liza's."

"Yeah, she wouldn't care."

"Tristan," I lowered my voice and glanced around to make sure we were still alone. "I can't wear Liza's bathing suit."

"Why not?"

Did he really not get it? The worst thing I could possibly do was traipse out onto the pool deck wearing a bikini that was three sizes too small, my tits pouring out everywhere. Every female at the party would remember she hated me. Every male would remember the juiciest rumors.

"Because Liza's like a freaking A-cup, Tristan." I didn't mean to bite, but sometimes pleading turns out that way.

"Sorry. I've never checked the tags on my sister's bras."

"Whatever," I rolled my eyes, frustrated that he couldn't understand the position I was in.

My gaze landed on a display of picture frames on the upper level of a bookshelf. There were several years of Homecoming photographs, all the siblings included. Only one caught my eye, however: King Tristan and Queen Ashley, in all their fake regalia. The photo *I* posed for was not included. Big surprise. I snapped my gaze to the opposite corner of the house, hoping Tristan hadn't traced my line of vision or seen the fury on my face.

"Look," he said, sounding as strained as I felt. "We have a few minutes before everything gets crazy."

"It's not crazy already?"

He paused, watched the party roll on outside. "I just wanted to talk to you."

Great. What now? "Okay."

"Come on, let's go back to my room."

♠

He led me out of the living room and past the foyer, down a long hallway I'd seen but never inspected. It looked like the wing of the house where the smaller bedrooms lay, quiet and removed from the main gathering space and master bedroom suite. I remembered peering down that way on the first night I'd stepped into the house, almost sure Tristan's room was back there and curious to see it.

That was more than seven months ago.

Our feet padded silently, muffled by thick carpet and closed doors all along the corridor. When he opened one of them, I found myself in a snug, boyishly simple bedroom.

Tidy. And without nauseating pictures, at least.

Tristan closed the door behind us. "You look so beautiful in that dress." His voice was deep and soft in the hushed space. He reached out to finger a curl. "I'm sorry I've been so distracted lately."

"You haven't."

"No, I have. And I understand if that's why you're feeling maybe a little...insecure."

Blood rushed up my neck. He could read me like a tabloid at a news-stand. "I'm fine. Really."

"It's just all this college...whatever. All the details. You know I'm not good at that stuff," His hand found mine, but he was watching the floor. "Just like you're not good at the social stuff? It all comes so fast. Deadlines and shit." He forced a smile.

"Oh yeah?" My heart started hammering. The break-up talk. Already. No. "Do you need help with any, like, paperwork or anything?"

"No, I got it all sorted out—"

Something hard slammed into the wall right by my ear and I nearly jumped out of my silk dress. Tristan dropped my hand and pulled the window curtain aside with a smile. I could hear muffled shouts outside and realized his room must look out onto the backyard.

"Guess there's already a flag football game in progress or something?"

The blue gingham drapery fell back in place. "Nah, not yet. They need their quarterback."

He turned back to me before I could hide my scowl.

"Oh right." My eyes flew to my hands. The room fell still and quiet. I could feel his gaze on my fingers, twisting together. I started gnawing a nail.

"What's wrong?"

"Nothing."

His words were clipped. "Don't you even want to know where I'm going to school?"

I looked up. "Sure. Which one?" I had been afraid to ask. I wasn't ready to hear yet.

"Well," he let out his breath in a rush of annoyance. "You said you're going to Florida. Delaney Beach, right?"

"Don't be so sure."

"Why? What do you mean?"

"The cousin I was planning to live with? She got some modeling gig in Miami, so she's moving there in a couple weeks. Part of the reason I could go was that I could save on cheap rent with her. But now, I don't know." I knew I sounded harsh spitting it out like that, but I had just heard about the big break that morning. I was furious about it, and worse, I felt like the biggest creep on the planet for cursing my cousin's good fortune.

"Oh."

Another bang on the glass, this time directly on the window.

"Nice. Hope you have leaded glass."

"Hurricane windows," he mumbled, ignoring the escalating commotion from the yard.

"Standard procedure?"

Tristan didn't crack a smile at my dumb joke.

"Mekaela…"

He reached for my hand and I almost snatched it away.

"Knock-knock, you two," his mother sang from outside the door. I was actually relieved to see that painted mug appear in the crack, teasing the door open before she got an invitation. "Tristan, no closed doors when you have company. You know that."

"Sorry, Mom. Can you give us another minute, though?"

"Oh," her smile turned down, "sure, sweetheart."

Her face was serious, too!

I imagined them role-playing the break-up talk together. That was the reason she was so perky after the ceremony; she was finally getting what she wanted. Me, out of Tristan Sweetheart's life. Bygones be bygones, my ass.

"You know what? It's okay, Mrs. Jameson. I have to go anyway."

Tristan squeezed my fingers, halted my quick retreat, "You're leaving already, baby?"

Baby?

His mother cleared her throat at the endearment, moving out of sight in a rush. "Let me know when you're through." I could hear her calling loving recriminations and giving polite orders, before she had even entered the living room.

Tristan's hand shot up to massage his temples. "This isn't going the way I planned."

"Through? With what?"

"Just don't leave yet, okay?"

"Why?"

He fell silent, considering.

I put up my hands, "What?"

He smiled.

The way Tristan watched me reminded me of the time I found a crow with a broken wing in our back yard. It was so pathetic and proud, in so much pain and so scared. I wanted to help, but I wasn't sure where to touch without hurting it worse.

"Everyone's waiting for me at Ricky's." Now I was squawking protectively, just like the crow. "My whole family is there. I really shouldn't keep them waiting, you know?"

Tristan started breathing again. Had he been holding his breath, too? "You're right. I guess we can talk later."

I made a break for the door. "Yeah, we have all summer."

"All summer?" He sounded like he disagreed, but his voice was far off behind me, muffled in the carpeted hallway as if in a dream. A bad dream. He caught up to me before I got to the front door. "Wait. Let me walk you to your car at least."

I felt like I was escaping. I felt my hand shaking. I felt my numb lips say, "Thank you."

I squeezed the door handle and I willed myself to pull it together. When I saw Will Bartlett and his bitch girlfriend Shelly walking up the cobblestone path, I felt my self-possession return like a long lost friend. I remembered why I didn't *belong*, with pride.

"Pretty-Boy! Dude, Meg—runner up Val-dick-whatever-thing. Cool," said Will.

"Oh jeez, you make it sound like such an accomplishment when you put it like that, Will," I snapped.

The blonde troll kept quiet and cracked a brittle smile in my direction.

Tristan shoved his buddy hard as we passed, "Didn't know my girlfriend was so smart, huh?"

"Hey, you get your tickets?"

"Oh, yeah." Tristan halted for a minute and turned back to Will, gauging my reaction out of the corner of his eye. "Graduation present."

He ran a hand through his hair and I snapped to attention.

"That's what my mom said. Your parents surprised you with it, right?" Will quaked with the thrill. Shelly bubbled beside him.

"Senior Trip?" I asked, though I didn't need to. The senior class was planning a trip to Mexico, right after graduation. Tristan had been very tight-lipped about it, so I knew he wanted to go. He looked at me like he was bracing for an explosion, but I wouldn't give Shelly the pleasure.

I lifted a shoulder, tossed my curls. "Have fun."

"And what happens in Cancun, stays in Cancun, right?"

"Will, that's Vegas," Shelly said, edging towards the house and holding out her hand like she was offering treats to a puppy.

Will was easy to confuse. "I just meant, like, wild partyin' and stuff."

"We get it, come on." I could almost hear Shelly whistling "here, boy" and I felt a little sorry for Will.

Just a little.

"I'll be right back, just walking Mekaela to her car," Tristan called after them, and then he slung an arm around my shoulders as I headed in the opposite direction. He bent low to whisper in my ear, "Of course the only wild party I care about is right here," and goosed my inner thigh under my dress.

"Hey," I gasped, my composure totally blown. That didn't seem like a break-up move. Something inside me uncurled like a sleeping dragon, warmth seeping through my belly like liquid flame. The look in his eyes told me I had better run, though, and I tried. Of course he was too quick and he snatched the inside of my elbow before I could make a break for it. The threat of tickling made me giggle prematurely, "No, no, no. Don't you dare…"

That only encouraged him and I was off my feet in seconds.

"Tristan, stop!"

"Make me." He pinned me against his chest and carried me the rest of the way to my car, kicking and gyrating, while he put his hands and mouth where he pleased. I squealed and screamed and almost wet my pants.

"What is…with you…today?" I wheezed, when he finally set me on my feet by the Rabbit, breathless and confused—but happy.

Without preamble, he demanded, "Give me something of yours."

"Huh?"

"Something to keep with me tonight." He leaned against my car, a perverse twinkle in his eye.

"Like…" The first thing I thought of was panties, but the last thing I wanted to bring up was the Nashville panties-give-away. Something intimate. I knew by the heat in his gaze. "How about…" I wasn't wearing much jewelry. I leaned over and slid off a shoe, then twisted the silver ring off my pinkie toe.

I set the ring in his palm. Tristan stared at it, dumbstruck.

"Is that too girlie or something? You don't have to wear it." Belatedly, I realized that might've been gross. "My feet are totally clean—I gave myself a pedicure this morning, before the ceremony."

He stood there, the ring in his open hand, looking at me with an expression somewhere between a disbelieving child and a lover ready to take me right there in the street. His other hand found the back of my neck and his lips were suddenly on mine, insistent and almost bruising. I answered his kiss with equal passion, melting in his arms, overwhelmed to have him so suddenly and inarguably mine after such a strained, confusing morning.

"Screw parties and social obligations," I said when he broke the kiss and rested his forehead on mine, his breath rasping.

"Amen," he chuckled.

I rested my hand on his face, "I love you, Tristan."

"Mekaela…if only you knew," he whispered, his brow heavy with some unnamable emotion. His eyes bore into mine, like he was looking for something there. An answer? What was the question?

I waited.

"If only I knew…"

He straightened, features smoothed. He kissed the ring, "It's perfect," before slipping it onto a pinkie finger.

"Okay. If you think so."

"Perfect, like you." Then he gathered me into a companionable hug, so different than our embrace only seconds before. He was relaxed and easy again, burrowing against my neck and nuzzling my hair. Almost joking. "I'm gonna miss you tonight."

I couldn't help it: "Now you're being weird again."

He leaned back against the Rabbit and smiled his famous smile. "Am I?"

"Yes. You are."

"Sorry."

"Don't be sorry, just—" Cheering erupted from his backyard. The flag football game had started without him. My mouth watered when the smell of greasy burgers over an open fire hit my sinuses. "You're missing your party."

"So are you," he said, his eyes wistful. "Have fun tonight. And since you didn't ask, here's something to remember *me* by." He slapped my ass so hard I gasped.

"Hey!"

He loped away, chuckling.

"I love you, too…." I watched him for a few seconds, annoyed that he hadn't returned my earlier declaration, "…you butthead."

He jogged up the path to his front door and ducked inside after a quick wave.

"Bye." I opened my rickety driver side door and flounced into the seat. I begged the car to start without an embarrassing cough or wheeze, even though the street looked empty. She did, and I petted the steering wheel in appreciation. "Thank god for small favors. Later, Northern Estates."

chapter twenty-six

I made it as far as the state road before I turned back. Tristan was my boyfriend. He loved me and I loved him. Forget all the insecurity crap. He was trying to tell me something and I had to hear it. Whatever *it* was. I owed him that and I belittled us both to slink away.

"I'm not a slinker."

My laugh at that stupid comment, to myself, helped my resolve.

The Rabbit sputtered in next to the shiny Mercedes and my feet were on the pavement before I could change my mind. Shades in place, keys in hand, spine straight and proud. I gulped in cleansing breaths as I walked up the street. Self-possession returned with every step.

Until I saw them.

At first, I wasn't sure what I was seeing. Or, I wanted to believe the glaring sunlight and my earlier mental dive into anxious hell was messing with my vision. That couldn't be Tristan, leaned over his ex-girlfriend, one arm braced against the side of his house. Her eyes weren't gazing up into his, wet and longing and shaded by his protective body. That couldn't be the nightmare I was walking into. Certainly not. But when Ashley caught my eye and gasped, and then Tristan looked over his shoulder and his face turned white...well, there was no mistaking it.

I had, in fact, walked into my own hell.

The image of his index finger catching her falling tear was etched on my panicked brain.

I spun on my heel.

"Mekaela. Wait."

I kept walking.

"Let me explain."

I won't run. I won't run.

"Please, stop. Mekaela..."

My car was twenty more paces, tops.

"Will you hold on a minute?"

Fifteen more steps.

"Just wait, alright?"

Ten.

"Stop this."

My head lolled. I shook it. "I always knew I could never have you. Not really."

"Look, you have me alright?"

My mouth was tight. "Not what it looked like to me."

Five steps.

"You got the wrong idea, baby!"

"Don't you dare 'baby' me," I wheeled around so fast I lost my balance. He had the nerve to catch my arm. "And don't you dare touch me."

He threw up his hands. "Why? What did I do?"

"I don't know," I jutted my face into his, didn't care if I spit on him in my rage, "what *did* you do?"

His eyebrows spiked. "Whatever you're thinking, it's wrong."

"Yeah, right." I punctuated that with a hard shove on both his shoulders.

"Do you even know what you saw?"

"Intimacy. That's what I saw, Tristan." I hissed the name.

"So what?" His volume rose to match my own. "I've known her for a long time, Mekaela!"

"Longer than me, you mean?"

"Yes. I have."

"Oh, so you'll always be hers then."

"No. She was upset."

"Poor Ashley. Let's not upset her." I spun towards my car, but he grabbed my arm and flung me back to face him.

"She was crying. *Bawling,* okay?"

"Why?"

He straightened. A belligerent frown constricted his face. "None of your concern."

I winced, "Oh, fuck you…"

"Fuck you. I still care for her, okay?"

I yanked my arm free.

"That's so wrong that I should care? I'm not a monster, Mekaela."

My palms slapped onto the safety of the Rabbit.

"Oh, fine! Leave like this, fine. Great, Mekaela."

I fumbled with the lock. It turned. Rotting leather and motor oil never smelled so good.

"Enjoy your party." His voice was muffled through the window, already dying away.

A glance under my hair saw his back, stalking home. Away from me and towards Ashley.

chapter twenty-seven

By the time I turned down Ricky's street, dusk was settling in.

So was my funk.

"Oh, but it looks like Christmas," I gasped and held my fist to my lips. A Mendez party was just what I needed.

There were tiny lights twinkling in the dimness ahead, down the wide dirt-road lanes of ramshackle bungalows. Several neighbors had strung white Christmas lights from their roofs up to the top of a central telephone pole between their houses, creating a carnival tent of bulbs. My window was rolled down and I could hear the heavy baseline of the music thudding along with my heart.

"They're gonna *make* me have fun." I gritted my teeth, determined to let go of the shittiest of shitty days. "This is what I call a party."

I smiled when I spotted my cousin Zach's motorcycle parked next to a couple of Harleys. I pulled up to the end of a long line of cars, most as modest as my own and half of which I recognized. The Rabbit died in a spot as gloomy as my persistent mood. I looked around to make sure I was in relative isolation in the shadows, then pulled my silky dress over my head and quickly changed into a cotton prairie skirt and a tank top I packed in an overnight bag.

"Crap, I forgot a bra." The dress had one sewn into the lining, but my tank-top didn't provide as much support. "And shoes." I looked at my feet, dismayed, cursed my frazzled mind, and blamed it on my cheating, secretive, asshole of a boyfriend.

Anger didn't work. If Tristan really had cheated on me, I would be devastated. Crushed. Anger was just easier than the depression I would have in store.

"Nope. Not gonna think about this." I shook my head hard, as if I could dislodge the painful memory of two bodies leaning close enough to gather tears.

I opened the door and pointed my toes outside. "Yes, these will just have to do." My high heels were a little dressy, but I decided not to care either way and bounded out of the car, funk held aloft by desperation.

My heels sank into the dirt and I was wishing I had found a closer spot when headlights streamed around the corner. A whistle sounded above the rattling engine of an old red pick-up with a once white hood, its tempo slowing and its rumbling cough deepening as the truck rolled to a crawl next to me.

"Christ Almighty, I must be in heaven."

The truck stopped and I strained to see the faces inside the cab.

"Honey, you lookin' for some fun?"

"No, thank you," I said, picking up my pace.

"Hey, I know you…" That twang, throat like sandpaper, was familiar somehow. "You's that bitch that took off from the poker game."

Terry Finley leaned towards the open window, craning his neck from the passenger side. He was the wife beater who thought I'd cheated him out of winning back the pot, at the poker game on Homecoming night. I hadn't seen him around the neighborhood and I had hoped he'd just moved on, drifter that he was. Or died.

He elbowed the driver, who I felt like I recognized. He was much younger than Finley, but I couldn't quite place his face.

"Think you're hot shit, always riding around with the sheriff's boy, don't you? Thinks she can do anything she pleases, this one," Terry said.

I shouldn't have said anything. I should have ignored him and kept walking. Ricky's place wasn't that far. But I couldn't help it, "That money was mine, fair and square. Ask Sean."

"Yeah, I asked Sean. He told me a lot about you."

My cheeks burned with embarrassment and fury. Yeah, Sean knew a lot about me, and that information coming from a waste of good oxygen like Terry Finley was nauseating.

"Meg, 'bout freakin' time, chica," Ricky hollered from the blazing brightness of the Mendezes' safe haven.

He was ambling my way, oblivious to the menace seeping through the windows of the old red truck. My heart started racing. I did not want Ricky involved in whatever was going on. He was likely to say something stupid and explosive. Blessedly, two more headlights turned the corner and another truck, this one a shiny black Ford F-150, rolled up behind the one still idling next to me.

The window came down and the driver leaned out, "You alright, Meg?"

I let out my breath; it was one of Ricky's very large, very tattooed cousins. He was actually a sweet guy, as I remembered. Not nearly as dangerous as he looked. The old truck pushed on with a stinking rumble and a burning fury. The shiny Ford followed.

"Hey, Ricky." I breathed a shaky sigh of relief, my nerves still on edge.

Ricky walked unsteadily down the lane with two plastic cups. "Who was that?"

When we divided the distance between us, I saw the yellow-green liquid and was sure he carried Margaritas. I was so comforted by the sight that I could've kissed him. The heavenly aroma of deep-fried cinnamon hit me and my stomach groaned in anticipation.

"Your mom made churros?"

"My grandma, still is. Who *was* that?"

"Some creep, don't worry about it." I shrugged off the lingering discomfort. "Sorry it took me a while to get here, I had some stuff to do."

"Whoo-hoo, can't get enough of King Bobcatt, huh?"

Frankly, no. "Oh, whatever. Shut up."

"Here ya go, chica," Ricky said, with a slight slur. He handed me a drink. "Let's celebrate our release."

"Thank you, my dear." Margarita sloshed over the side and I gulped down several mouthfuls. "Come on, you have no idea how ready for a party I am."

As we walked past the parked cars, I couldn't help but notice a white-blonde head facing away from me. The head tried to hide in the shadows about as inconspicuously as a bright yellow beacon.

"Piper?"

"Meg!"

"Oh good, now she can help watch the brats," said a surly male voice on the other side of my sister.

"I'm not watching any kids today," I warned, smirking at Piper's back as I strolled past, then added under my breath, "Especially you two." Piper wasn't a kid, though, and I wasn't her mom. I tried to ignore my concern and rolled my eyes at Ricky. "Anyway...I love this song, who's in charge of the music?"

"My brother brought his whole set-up."

"No shit." I squinted and recognized Tito and several cousins whose names escaped me, huddled around a laptop and some other electronic equipment on a folding table. A turntable? They were near the edge of a canopy, bleeding into the growing darkness beyond the circle of light, Tito's headphones glowing. He nodded to one of the guys about a record he was holding up.

"He's using vinyl?" I asked, shocked.

"You serious? Tito's got tons of vinyl—one of the reasons he got the gig where he spins at in the city."

I looked at the boxes of records by his feet, a wonderland waiting to be explored. "Will he take requests?"

"Of course. 'Specially from you."

"I think I might drool." I slung an arm around his shoulders and we headed to the courtyard between houses, lit like the celebration it should be. "The promise of retro bliss and the smell of churros frying? I love you people—oh my god, guacamole!" I gawked at a table with a brightly colored, striped tablecloth and all of my favorite Mexican finger foods. "Where did your mom get avocados in Shirley?"

"She didn't," Ricky laughed. "Velma brought some with her."

"Velma's here?" I hadn't seen Ricky's sister in ages. Velma was six or seven years older than our little crew, and as a kid I'd always thought of her as extremely sophisticated and elegant. Zach would never admit it, but he's had a serious crush on her from the moment he hit puberty. Velma left town with barely a trace as soon as she graduated from high school, the first person I admired in my generation. Her exodus left an impression.

Comfort people and comfort food.

A tiny caveat tickled my thoughts, *"That's so wrong that I should care? I'm not a monster."*

No, he wasn't. Tristan was only comforting Ashley.

Maybe.

I shoved them both out of my mind once again. "Are those fresh tortillas?"

Ricky stopped in his tracks, his mouth gaping. "Like my mom would ever *buy* tortillas."

I threw my head back and laughed. "I have missed you, Ricky Mendez." It was too long since we'd hung out.

"Don't go gettin' his hopes up." Zach sauntered out of the house wearing a sombrero.

"Are you kidding me?" I doubled over laughing, nearly choking on my drink—big, macho Zach looking so ridiculous was a special treat. "Happy Un-Birthday to me!"

"It's punishment," Ricky chuckled.

I slapped my knees and pointed to the hat, not even bothering to control myself. "Not for me it isn't."

Zach looked me over coolly, "You'll see, when it happens to you."

"Why," I gasped, "would I ever," I wiped my eyes, clutching at the stitch in my side, "let that happen to me?"

"You done?"

I nodded, still catching my breath.

"Here, I'll show ya..." Zach took my hand and led me into the house, past a crowd packed so tightly they couldn't have been comfortable. Ricky's entire family must have come to town for the graduation. Zach hauled me into the kitchen, where there was a little more breathing room. "That 'Rita's a virgin," he said, motioning to my drink. "You gotta earn your tequila here."

So, that was why my heart still ached every time a pair of angry blue eyes flashed through my head. I wondered. And I'd do anything to numb that. "I'm not afraid to earn my reward. What do I have to do?" I noticed row upon row of limes on a cutting board over the sink.

"You have to balance a lime on your nose for three seconds."

"No problem."

"After the shot," Ricky clarified, catching the lime I had placed on my nose as it tumbled down and bounced off my chest.

"Oh."

Of course the game was a lot harder than I first thought. The trick was not letting that involuntary shiver run up your spine right after licking salt, slamming a shot of tequila, and then sucking on a lime wedge. I screwed it up every time.

"Wait, gimme a minute," I wailed after botching my third try.

"No, you gotta balance it while you still have the lime wedge between your teeth."

"That's three. Sombrero time," said Zach, smug. He took the hat off his head and transferred it to mine, pushed it down nice and firm.

"I've never seen a gringo do it," muttered Ricky.

"I like the hat," I insisted. My joints were melted butter. My heart calm. "And I'm gonna show you how to work it, cuz."

Music was pouring inside through the open windows and I couldn't wait to dance. I adjusted the wide velvet brim and played with the furry bobbles hanging around the edges. Ricky's brother was beckoning me outside like a snake charmer, spinning a hip-hop mix of Michael Jackson's 1979 classic "Don't Stop 'Til You Get Enough." The base thudded through my chest, the melody impossible to ignore. My skin was zinging, my body warm and loose from the tequila, and I flowed into the music under the canopy of lights. I let my head fall back and gazed past the lights at the blanket of stars above us.

I imagined Tristan and Ashley dancing away into the sky and I waved at them with a bitter sneer. "Why did I let him go back to her? I'm such an idiot."

"Huh?"

I blinked. Ricky was watching me watch the sky, through velvet bobbles. I laughed, really meaning it for the first time since I'd left Tristan's house.

"Nothing. Let's dance, boys."

Zach was no dancer, but Ricky was happy to partner up. He loved to school me in Latin moves. I giggled every time he bonked his head against the huge sombrero, and I refused to take it off. The hat actually kept Ricky at a safe distance, since he was prone to feely hands when dancing.

During a spin, my fancy punishment flew off and landed near the buffet. "Oh, crap," I grabbed my flattened curls.

Ricky tugged my hand. "Leave it."

"I don't want it to get messed up. Your dad will never trust me with tequila again."

"I don't think the folks have much choice." He nodded to the throng of nearly indistinguishable cousins, siblings, and friends coming and going in and around the Mendez party.

"Guess you're right." Being at one of Ricky's family shindigs was like being in some other country, for all his parents cared about American laws or mainstream customs.

"Anyway, leave the hat." Another tug of my hand and we were nose to nose.

"Hi. Whoa there, Ricky—"

And his mouth was on mine.

The numbness pulled back and so did I, "Wait a minute."

"Come on, Meg. Go easy on me," he whispered, holding our faces close. "You know I've always loved you."

"Ricky, I…"

"Don't make me look like an asshole, here."

"I'm not." But our company loomed in a new light. All of those macho guys watching, and Ricky rejected. "You know I'm with Tristan."

"Tristan ain't here, is he?"

I sighed. "I love him, Ricky. I'm sorry."

He pursed his lips, eyes glued to mine. "Just keep dancing with me. Okay?"

"Yes."

His shoulders loosened and he danced easily again. Just happy to have dodged that uncomfortable situation, I let him spin me and whirl me wherever he would. Octopus arms were tamed and his smile remained shy, but I was determined to shrug off the weirdness.

chapter twenty-eight

We danced for hours. I took plenty of breaks at the buffet table to snack on warm tortillas, cold guacamole, and bubbling hot queso. The only time I ever ate so well growing up was when I was lucky enough to get invited to Ricky's house during mealtime. I savored every morsel that night, especially the crispy sopapillas, hollow doughnuts dripping with honey and chocolate sauce.

"This is one thing about Shirley County that I will definitely miss," I murmured to myself, licking chocolate off my fingers and watching Ricky dance with one of his little cousins. He twirled her around with one arm arched over her head and the other tickling her ribs on each turn. She was beside herself with all the attention, giggling and grinning with two front teeth missing. The sweet thing had worn her best dress and patent leather shoes with lacy socks for the occasion and she gazed at Ricky like he was a god. "Truly Madly Deeply" by Savage Garden was the slow jam playing. My mom used to sing that when I was tiny. Zach was rotating around the dance floor with her, just like she used to with me in our living room.

My eyes stung with tears. "Nice. Tears in my beer, how apropos," I sniffed, setting down my empty Corona bottle. "Time to request something a little less sappy, Tito."

But the old folks were ready for the party to settle down and Tito told me that last song was the finale. Ricky's dad had already dragged out his guitar and was settling into a chair next to his brothers. They were all either tuning their own instruments or kicking their boots up, ready to sing amateur Mariachi.

"Please get me out of here before they start wailin'," said Velma, gripping her purse for a swift evacuation. "There's got to be something else to do on a Saturday night, even in Shirley."

"Think you been away too long, Velms," said Ricky.

My thoughts turned sour again, another Saturday event I happened to know about bright in my mind. How about a nice, old-fashioned lock-in—good, clean fun? I'd have given anything to twirl around the dance floor with Tristan, feeling truly, madly, deeply next to him. I wondered if there was dancing scheduled at Project Graduation. Maybe right that minute, he was dancing with someone. Maybe Ashley.

No.

He would never do that to me, after all we had been through. Consoling a crying friend was one thing, but dancing with her was quite another.

"Actually, there is something going on in Ender's Village tonight. Let's go there," said Piper, keen to spend a little more time with her new male appendage. They had certainly taken advantage of the slow song. I noticed the guy hanging back while we made plans, pretending nonchalance. But he didn't fool me. He gripped Piper's hand like he owned it. I narrowed my eyes at him, but of course he wouldn't meet my gaze. "You know that artsy place across the river?"

"It's an artists' commune," I said dryly. I looked at my watch for no reason at all. Tristan would be locked up all night and Mom had taken off work so I could celebrate, curfew unlimited. Problem was, there was only one place I wanted to be: anywhere with Tristan, our stupid fight long forgotten. There was about zero chance of that happening, though, so I tried to fake good humor. "Should be fun."

Ricky was all up for extending the evening, "Yeah, they're having like an arts and crafts festival, some benefit for that Antonio kid who died."

I sighed, "Oh, well then we have to go."

"I remember that place," said Velma. "Sounds good to me. Ricky, you okay to drive? I'm definitely not, and I don't think I could remember the roads in the dark anyway."

"Little tequila ain't gonna take me down," Ricky said, but a cousin standing behind him just shook his head and raised two fingers, volunteering to be DD for the night.

"Thanks, Manny," said Velma.

Manny, that was his name. He was my savior from earlier with the F-150. I grinned at him and he nodded, then looked away with a forced scowl.

Jo was tramping past us with a group of dirty-haired guys in leather and ripped jeans. She caught the tail end of the conversation and fell back, shrugging into her jacket and giving me a you're-not-gonna-make-me-look-lame-are-you expression. "Meg, you can't ride with me. I'm stowing a bike for Buddy."

"How can you fit a dirt-bike in the car and still drive safe, Jo?"

"I'll put the top down, come on."

"The top still goes down?"

She groaned, exasperated. "Meg..."

"Well, why can't he just ride his bike?"

"It's not running." Her look told me not to be an idiot. "I'm gonna drop it at the shop, don't be a drag. He's already paid me to fix it."

"I thought we were all going to hang out tonight." Having my sisters and friends around me was how I had planned to keep Tristan with-drawal at bay, even before our fight. Jo just watched me, slightly freaked out, as though I were a whining girlfriend who had just said, "But this is my day!" I knew I was being a drag and I let out my breath in a way that was way too close to Mom. "Well, okay. Just meet us after, though? We're going to Ender's Village."

"Okay, cool," she said, already jogging away from me.

"Okay...Drive safe, Jo."

"See ya later." She flicked a hand, not bothering to look back.

I would be riding with the lovebirds, I realized a few minutes later. Ricky was in the seat of honor on the passenger side of his cousin's truck, and although there were three seats in the mid-cab, most of that space was taken up by Tito's deejay gear. Velma was riding on Tito's lap next to the precious equipment. Ricky had offered his lap to me as well, but I declined. Zach would be cruising alongside, but he had already gained a backseat rider on his motorcycle—a pretty blonde who was sure to trump my request if I asked.

Piper and her beau were already nestled together in the truck bed when I climbed in. "No smooching, please. I don't want to vomit on the ride over."

"Soooor-ry," Piper said, disengaging just enough to give me a wither-ing look.

I folded my arms across my chest and sat facing away from them, wet blanket that I was. I reached a hand over and slapped the side of the truck, impatient to get going, "All ready back here."

At least the wind in my hair cleared my head some. I watched the heavens, braiding my hair quickly in a thick, tamed plait. Ricky's place was in the south valley, almost as far down as Southern Cove where I lived, and close to the eastern mountains. We were way on the opposite side of Shirley from Ender's Village, so I had at least thirty minutes of windy peace to think. I roosted against the side of the truck bed, sorely wishing I had remembered to bring a bra.

Yet it was a beautiful night, and an auspicious day. Graduation Day. I had been yearning for this day for so long and now I was sitting right in the thick of it. Time to start enjoying it. I knew there must be a reasonable explanation for the scene I had witnessed between Tristan and Ashley. Of course she was upset that they weren't together anymore. That was reasonable. After all, he had been the one to leave her. He owed her kindness.

"I'm not a monster."

He wasn't. Tristan was one of the nicest guys I'd ever met. But since they'd broken up months ago, did that mean Tristan had been catching her little tears all along? That possibility rankled. Or, was it something else she was upset about?

"None of your concern."

He wouldn't tell me why she was crying. Suspicion bloomed, hot and heavy in my chest.

"Sure King Bobcatt wanted to get off with Meg Shannon for a while, but…"

I wondered where Ashley was going to college. Maybe somewhere near Tristan. The fact that I had no idea where he was going to school suddenly seemed the height of stupidity. He was trying to tell me in his room, but I wouldn't hear it.

I looked at my hands. "Idiot."

No answers were coming while he was at a lock-in, either. Deciding to salvage what I had left and settle into the moment, I closed my eyes, breathed in deeply, and smelled the clay in the soil and the freshly cut grass on a nearby field. The night was still warm, but crisp. Heat rose from the asphalt that had soaked in sunlight all day, but the air blowing around my arms was cool and brought goose bumps to my bare skin. My breasts bounced and rubbed against the cotton weave of my tank top, and my butt-bone jarred against the metal truck bed, the rumbling of the engine vibrating through my whole body. I still tasted tequila on my tongue, but remembered the chocolate and the cinnamon, too. A train whistled, not too far off, and I opened my eyes and looked ahead. Red lights were flashing next to the intersection with the road, the railroad crossing signs not yet descending.

Zach zoomed past the truck and flew over the tracks.

"Oh shit. Better hold on."

Piper pushed her boy toy away. "What's wrong?"

I laughed, "Manny looks like a sweet tattooed teddy bear, but he won't let Zach show him up."

I kicked off my high-heals and rose up on my bare feet as the truck picked up speed. I crouched low in the truck bed, my thighs springy to absorb the shock. The train screamed in admonition. Manny floored it and we crashed over the intersection, the back bouncing high over the rough crossing, the gates narrowly missing my head as we flew past. Piper and her man howled in dismay as she fell back into his lap hard and he hit the metal truck bed even harder.

I crab-walked over and banged on the top of the roof, "You crazy Mexican!"

Manny flashed the headlights in response.

There was another flash from up ahead and I squinted to see the car approaching from the other direction. "Crap, hope that's not a cop."

The thought that it might be Tristan's dad both terrified and thrilled me. Even a tangential connection to Tristan, just an unbidden thought from nowhere, made my belly clench deep inside. The hope turned to annoyance, though, as the oncoming vehicle passed under a streetlight and I recognized that nasty red pick-up with the rusted white roof again. Thoughts of Tristan polluted by Terry Finley.

His mean, pinched up face, mocking me for being taken home by "the sheriff's boy." How dare that scumbag even mention Tristan to me, like it was something dirty, something to feel ashamed of.

"Bastard."

In a heady impulse, I stood and clutched the hem of my skirt. Just as they flew past us, I lifted it, bent over, and pulled my panties down to my knees, my bright white butt high in the air.

"Meg!" Piper screeched.

Her boy cackled and clapped.

I readjusted my underwear and skirt, straightening up with a grin.

"My god, you just mooned those people. Who the heck was that?"

"Get over it, Piper. It's none of your business." I spun around to flick the empty road a bird. My guts turned liquid and my blood ran cold. Terry Finley had slammed on the breaks. "Oh, no."

Piper was on her knees, looking around wildly in the dark. "What? What?"

"Just—" I flapped my hands at her face, "shhhh!"

Sweat prickle along my hairline. I watched the truck grow smaller and smaller, no telltale white reverse lights visible, but my heart raced all the while. Finally, it was out of sight. I collapsed back into the floor of the truck and clenched my trembling hands. I looked over and Piper was already one with the boy again.

♣

When we crossed the Tenakho River, Manny slowed down to a crawl on the narrow bridge. Our only light was starlight and a narrow beam from the headlights, in no man's land. I thought of how Tristan would comment on how close we lived "to the sticks," and smiled. We wound up into the thick woodlands of the western mountains.

Piper's little friend whistled, "Dude, I thought Shirley was the world's end."

I couldn't remember the last time I had been to Ender's Village. Maybe for a school field trip in Elementary School? I said a little prayer of thanks when we finally neared the tiny village center and were greeted with bright streetlights. There was quite a crowd, surprising enough, and there was a roaring bonfire in the middle of it. Velma opened the window to the front cab and made a snide remark about nightlife in Shirley County. We parked in a manned lot, everyone in the front of the cab bickering about artists always having to make a buck, but finally forking over the $5 parking fee.

"Actually a pretty good turn out for a cow town," said Velma when she got out, scanning the full parking lot. "Looks like some outta-town-ers, too."

I recognized the accent Velma picked up when she said "outta-town-ers," hoped one day it would all be so far from me and yet so dear, too.

"Whatever. Where's the booze?"

"Zach at an art show. Pah!" I reached up and ruffled his hair. "It's still Shirley, cuz."

"They always have wine and cheese at art shows. And craft beer," chipped in his new sweetheart, flipping her long blonde braid over a shoulder.

"So that's how she got you to come, huh?" I said to Zach's silent scowl.

The girl shot me a pouty look and lodged herself under his hammy bicep.

A million ways that I could steel her ride home from her flashed through my mind, but I slowed my pace and let the rest of the group roam ahead towards the rows of tents and display tables. I'd never been interested in crafty festivals, but at least I was unlikely to run into any football players or cheerleaders there. I meandered past beaded purses, hand-carved mountain dulcimers, and glass bobbles. One particularly odd tent featured every kind of organ grinder that must have ever existed—tall standing ones, tiny metal ones, painted wooden ones with stuffed monkeys on top.

I looked around, slightly on edge. Monkeys creep me out, especially monkeys playing organ grinders. The wind shifted and I caught the unmistakable smell of horse manure. I wrinkled my nose, guessing who might be working the pony rides. My erstwhile companions having long since deserted me. I decided to let my nose lead me to some sort of familiarity. Before long, the sight of Sean McBride in a makeshift horse paddock came into view.

After a moment of hesitation, I slapped my thighs, defeated. "A comfortable sight on an uncomfortable night. Sue me."

chapter twenty-nine

Sean led a piebald pony around the small enclosure, with a little girl perched on the saddle. She looked about seven-years-old and scared shit-less, but the sweet little thing was holding her own and smiling for the camera. Wooden but needing to please. Her mother snapped pictures with her phone while cheering her daughter on from the edge of the temporary fencing. Sean saw me approach and tipped his hat almost imperceptibly. He listened to the nervous kid chatter away, smiled crookedly and nodded now and then. His boots scuffed the dirt as they plodded around and around. Once the kid's torment time was finally up the family left quickly, the mother promising pretty, shiny rewards for being such a brave girl.

"Hey, you," Sean drawled, removing his hat to reveal dark, sweaty locks, his copper highlights shining in the glare from sparsely spaced floodlights.

"Hiya."

"Dang tourists," he muttered, when his last customers were out of hearing range.

"Get plenty of money from them, right?" I said, raising an eyebrow and daring him to deny it.

He cocked his head and sized me up before responding. "I get paid the same, no matter if I'm sittin' on my ass or listenin' to My Little Pony dreams, honey."

"Sean!" A red-haired girl came running up to the fence, out of breath and frantic. She looked familiar, maybe a friend of Erica's. Another cop-pertop from the enormous McBride clan. "Where's Drew? I thought he was working tonight."

Sean turned towards her, shook his head and took his time before answering, though the girl was obviously at her wits end. "Your worthless brother was supposed to work tonight, yeah. But he got wasted and split."

"What?"

"Again," Sean emphasized, as if it was her fault.

"Where is he now?"

"How should I know—"

"I need a horse, Sean."

Sean picked his nails and ignored the girl's obvious urgency. "Why, Candy?"

"I need to get somewhere fast. Sean, I'm serious," Candy said, her temper rising.

"Why don't you take your little dirt-bike?"

"My bike can't go where I need to go—stop fucking with me, Sean!"

Sean turned his back on her and started unbuckling the pony's saddle, not bothering to address Candy directly, "Seems to me, someone who's been cuttin' out on stable duty for the past two years has no business up and demanding a horse outta the blue." He selected a brush from a hook on the fence and began stroking the pony's mane. "S'not like you even work on the ranch anymore, so I don't see how you even feel you have the right to ride our property."

A horse whinnied on the other side of the paddock, where a small trailer was parked.

"Hey!" Sean spun around in a fury to see his cousin disappearing across the field on a big black horse, her short red hair fluttering behind her in the breeze.

She called over her shoulder as she leaned into the horse, picking up speed, "I'll bring her right back."

"Motherf—-" Sean hissed, then shouted, "You better have your ass back here before I close up!"

I snickered under my hand. Sean was so easy to piss off. It would've been a lot easier if he'd just given her the horse in the first place. But I knew he had a short fuse, so I leaned against the fence and waited for him to cool down. He went back to brushing the pony, leading her to the water trough and talking to her softly, then he moved to the next horse. Routine soothed him after a while.

"I wish I could ride like that," I said. His cousin had looked so amazingly free, racing off on the back of a horse.

"Like Candy? She ain't that good on a horse."

"Well, I can't ride at all, so she looked pretty spectacular to me."

He looked up at me, his eyes shining with sudden understanding. "You haven't ever ridden one, have you?"

I folded my arms over my chest, trying to look tough but actually feeling ashamed. How many times had I been around Sean and horses? I had always subtly avoided riding one, and now he finally got it. "No." Better to just admit it. "Isn't that weird, with all the horses around Shirley?" Horses had always terrified me in an irrational kind of way. They were enormous up close, so skittish and unpredictable. Add to that my absolute equine ignorance.

Sean looked at me like I was an alien, dumbfounded for a beat. Then his mouth twitched up, "Well, you want to go for a ride, sweet thang?"

At least he wasn't laughing, and suddenly, riding a horse sounded fun. I felt like being reckless. That little girl seemed fine on the pony, I could do it.

"I've known her for a long time, Mekaela!" Well, I had known Sean for a long time, too. "Yeah, I do."

But Sean left the ponies munching oats and walked over to the full-sized horses. He selected a huge brown one, and I had no idea whether it was a mare, stallion, or whatever. He shouted towards the trailer, "Hey, Mike—watch the front for me. Be back in a little while."

"Uh...I'm not riding one of the ponies?" I tried not to sound as horrified as I felt.

He led the big one towards me. "This girl's real gentle, don't be afraid."

"I'm not."

He glanced at me doubtfully, then bent to adjust the stirrups. "You're pretty tall," he murmured, his face briefly hidden by the brim of his hat.

I had the chance to wipe my sweaty hands on my skirt. It was all happening so fast.

Before I knew it, Sean was demonstrating how to mount the horse properly, like it was the easiest thing in the world. "Just put your outside foot on the tread here," he ran his finger along the inside of the stirrup, "like this and," he grunted as he hoisted himself, holding onto the knob of the saddle. "Just throw your leg over."

"I shouldn't ride like side-saddle or something, in a skirt?"

"No, you don't ride side-saddle," he chuckled and hopped back down. "That skirt's fine."

I fiddled with it. It did look wide enough, but to throw my leg over like that... "What if I accidentally kick her in the butt? Will she freak out?"

"You won't kick her. Quit stalling and come here." He held out his hand, eyes soft.

"Okay..."

"Her name's Brownie."

I edged toward the mare. One of her dark eyes, shaded by long feathery lashes, rolled towards me. Like doe eyes—dark and wary, Tristan would say. Like mine.

My heart started to race, but the thought of Tristan steeled my resolve. He was certainly having plenty of fun, doing whatever he pleased with whoever he wanted. I put my foot in the stirrup, more determined than ever. Sean made it look much easier than it was, though. When I hopped up the way he had, I found my legs weren't quite strong enough to gain the right height. Instead of leaping over the side, I lost my balance and ended up back on the ground, less nervous and more embarrassed.

"I'll hold your shoes," offered Sean.

Thinking I heard humor in his tone, I looked at him sharply. But he was being sincere, his face impassive and his stance patient.

"Thanks," I muttered, slipping off my shoes and handing them over.

He hooked both of them over one thumb, "Come on, you can do this," and I turned back to Brownie to try again.

I put my bare foot in the stirrup, sucked in a big gulp of air and really sprang for it. Sean aided me with a shove, square in the middle of my behind, and I was up and over. My skirt got caught on the saddle, but he loosed it and guided my thigh around to the other side.

"Whew!" I felt my face split into a ridiculous grin.

"There ya go, see?"

"I did it. Or, we did it," I corrected. There was no way I would've gotten up there without Sean. And I was so high I felt dizzy. I could see the tops of the festival tents and the crepe myrtle trees that lined the Ender's Village town center. "Cool."

"Alright then, let's ride."

Sean hung my high-heels on a leather loop on the back of the saddle, nudged my foot aside with his boot, and stepped into the stirrup. He hoisted himself up behind me, slid an arm around my waist, and snuggled his body up against mine in the close bucket seat of the saddle. Luckily, he couldn't see my scowl from where he sat; that wasn't at all what I had in mind.

I wasn't sure how to protest, or whether objection was even necessary, so I mentally calmed my creeping skin and decided to wait and see. Actually, I felt more comfortable with Sean behind me, doing all the work and guiding the horse. Brownie responded to him like she could read his mind. All I had to do was sit there. We were making our way to the edge of the paddock, and I knew he meant to take us through the fence and beyond, into the pathless mountains. It was exactly where Candy had gone and where I had longed to go just moments before, but I knew I'd never be brave enough to ride a horse in the wilderness by myself, even if Sean was holding the reins. The thought of that was so fantastical that I laughed at myself a little.

The night was just getting stranger and stranger. I looked up at the sky and searched for constellations.

"There you are, Virgo."

"What's that?"

I pointed heavenward, "The Maiden, my patron."

Sean snorted.

Virgo was my favorite May constellation, especially on a clear, dark night when the sky explodes above with so many stars that it looks like a Van Gogh painting. On a work break at the library a couple years back, I read about the over two-thousand intersecting galaxies and star clusters in the Virgo Cluster. One of them has a dark band of absorbing dust in front of the galaxy's bright white center, so it's nicknames is the "Black Eye" or "Evil Eye" galaxy. I've seen it through a telescope and it's a little creepy. Of course, a person can't see most of what's up there in Virgo. There's more to the maiden than meets the eye.

I whispered reverently, "Just absolutely beautiful tonight."

"Mmmmm."

The heavens felt so close on a night like that, almost as if I could reach up and grab a handful of stars from Virgo's belly. Those had to be lucky stars, didn't they? I closed my eyes and drank in the raw night around me. As we headed away from the festival, the sound of the river rose and the cicadas droned. The last sounds of civilization faded. I breathed in the fresh, piney air and wondered what the stars would look like in Florida.

From what I'd read, most of the east coast where I wanted to go to school was heavily populated and light pollution from the cities erased most of the stars from human vision. What a shame. I was still going, though. The fact that I couldn't live with my cousin was a setback, a road-block—not the end of the road. I could take out loans, live in the dorm, and get a job to work my way through school. I had always worked in high school and I was good at balancing a job with school. Everything would turn out fine, I would make sure it did.

I sure would miss the stars, though. My mind returned to the night I slept under those stars with Tristan. We watched them through the skylight in the tent until we both fell asleep.

Wet lips brushed behind my ear and I sat bolt upright, all sense of relaxation vanished.

"You smell so good." Sean's hand brushed my hair away from my neck.

Hell. I knew it. "Sean…"

"Yeah?"

"Come on. I have a boyfriend."

"Gimme a break." He kept one hand on the reins and slid the other up my bare thigh. I pushed it back down right before his fingers reached my underwear, now fully understanding my error in wearing a skirt on a horse. "Don't be a tease."

"I'm not teasing you, Sean." Sean likes to be fought off. Wonderful.

"I know a soft patch of clovers nearby." He twisted the reins around the saddle pommel to free his other hand, then pulled mine away from my legs, locked both my wrists between his thumb and forefinger.

I forgot how strong his hands were. "Look, I'm serious."

"Quit being serious." He rucked my skirt back up. "Quit playin' princess."

"I'm not playing anything, I care about him."

"Shut up." He pushed my panties to the side.

"Stop it, Sean." I pulled his hand away from my crotch. It found a new home against my breasts, pinned my arms in the process.

"No bra. I love that." One boot around my leg and I was ensnared.

"Sean, please."

"I can keep a secret, remember? He won't ever know."

I bit the finger shoved against my lips, drove my elbow back into Sean's ribs as hard as I could.

"Ow—what the fuck, Meg?"

He let go of me and grabbed his rib cage. Momentarily freed, I kicked my leg over the saddle and slid down to the ground, shocks shooting through my soles.

"Gimme my shoes, asshole." I unhooked them without meeting his gaze.

"Are you kidding me? What's your problem?"

I stalked away with my middle finger in the air.

"Where is your King Bobcatt, then?" he called after me, singing the nickname in a taunt. "Huh?"

I wouldn't give him the satisfaction of a response. The ground was brutal under my feet. I winced as I stepped on a sharp pebble, but I was not going to slow down to put my shoes on until I was out of sight.

Sean laughed then. "He ain't here, right?" I felt like clapping my hands over my ears. But I wouldn't. I straightened my back and limped along. "Boyfriend, my ass. Girls like you don't get guys like that."

My ears rang with fury.

"Too good for a romp in the clovers now, huh? Yeah, right."

Did I do that? On the ground? I guess I must have. Had I so little respect for myself back then? My head spun, trying to remember feeling the need to give a guy like Sean whatever he wanted from me.

"Bitch," he finally muttered. "Have fun finding your way back."

His voice changed to notes of sweet reassurance, gentle shushes and clicks for his horse as they moved in the other direction. After a few minutes and many more painful strides away from him, I risked a look backwards. He and Brownie were nowhere to be seen, so I hobbled over to a nearby tree and held onto its trunk while I dusted off my sore feet.

"Well, that was stupid, Meg," I lectured myself, as I slid my shoes on one by one. "What the hell are you gonna do now? Made a new enemy, too. Nice."

The blackness of the night was near complete. Butterflies panicked in my belly, finally registering the danger I was in. The danger I had put myself in. Tristan would kill me. My eyes pricked at the thought.

"Lost in the middle of nowhere." My voice was as loud and high-key as a siren in the quiet woods and I clamped my mouth shut. I scrubbed my hands over my whole body, both to get the sickening feel of Sean's groping hands off me and to quell my creeping nerves.

Why did I get myself into these kinds of messes? I had never thought much about my safety before Tristan. I hopped on that horse to prove something, but prove what? That I was just as untrustworthy as I imagined Tristan was. Anger replaced by fear, my trust was fully restored. Tristan was the only person I had ever trusted.

And look what I did in return.

"Stupid stupid stupid."

I didn't even have the cellphone he gave me—I left my purse in Jo's car when I showed up at Ricky's place, and I was too tipsy to think about grabbing it before we left for Ender's Village.

I wasn't tipsy anymore.

"Alright, alright. Freaking out is going to get me nothing but a missing person's add," I reasoned to myself, cringing at the shake in my voice.

I had to think straight. I stepped out from the tree cover and looked up. Plenty of stars; the night wasn't that black. I heard an owl hoot in the distance; the woods weren't that silent. I stood as still as possible, listening for sounds of life. We couldn't have ridden that far.

Cicadas and crickets droned all around me.

The river was behind me.

Wind rustled the tops of the trees. I took in a deep breath as the air shifted and I smelled...funnel cake.

Bingo.

I started walking again, towards the direction of that fried delicacy. I tried to breathe through my mouth so I wouldn't get used to the smell and lose my lifeline. A whiff every few minutes to make sure the aroma was truly growing stronger. Before long, I smelled hotdogs roasting, too. The sound of a fiddle trilling. The hum of outdoor generators. A burst of laughter from the crowd was the sweetest thing I'd ever heard. Lights came into view through the trees.

"Hallelujah."

I spotted Jo's car parked on the outskirts and picked up my pace, vowed never to curse the Rabbit ever again. The windows were down, and I saw my purse still sitting on the floor of the passenger side when I opened the door.

"That's one good thing about living in a small town, I guess."

I plopped down in relief, smiling at the creek of rusty old springs underneath me, and dug through the contents of my bag. Wallet, phone, house keys—all accounted for. I thumbed to my text messages and saw the first was from Jo.

"going riding w the guys u take the car"

"Oh, Jo." She probably thought of that as a graduation gift. I tipped the driver-side visor down and the car keys slid into my hand. "Good, I'm not really in the mood for partying anymore, as fun as Ender's Village was."

I scrolled to my next message and gasped.

Tristan: *"Escaped the lock-in. You were right, it was lame."*

He was home then. The time stamp on his message read 11:57.

"One-thirty-seven, now." I tapped my phone against my chin, pretending to consider. But, there was really no choice. I had to see him. "Why not?"

chapter thirty

The ignition turned over with little complaint and Ender's Village was behind me. I was so happy I sang to myself as I drove, probably off-tune but at the top of my lungs anyway. The Rabbit didn't have a stereo and I was glad it didn't for once. I was going to see Tristan, and singing was the only way to let loose. All the scary stuff with Sean, all worries about college, all jealousy of the mysteriously intimate scene on the side of the house—all of it faded away.

Tristan, minutes away.

I almost forgot to park down the street, but snapped back to reality just as I neared his house. I rolled past with a quick scan of the perimeter. His jeep and another car I didn't recognize were in the driveway, and god knew what was parked in the garage.

"Hmph. Wonder if Tiger Mom stayed at the lock-in." Somehow, I doubted it. I was going in anyway.

All the inside lights were off, two dim porch lights by the front door the only illumination. I remembered from Homecoming night, after I snuck back to the house when Zach dropped me off, that the Jamesons surprisingly had no security lights. So, I crept through the side yard and flattened my back against the wall with confidence. Sneaking into a house was no extreme job for me. I looked to my right at the long, windowless wall enclosing the garage, running up to the fence.

The fence.

"Damn it, that's right." The gate was on the other side of the house. By the master bedroom.

There was no way I would risk getting caught creeping through a gate by Stephanie Jameson's bedroom window. I'd have to scale the fence. All the horizontal wooden beams were on the inside of the yard. But the walls of the house were brick on the bottom and stucco above, offering me a tiny, shallow ledge to wedge my toe onto. I took off my shoes—the grass was already dewy—and dropped them next to the fence. I gripped the wooden slats with my fingers, then the brick ledge with my toes, and heaved myself over the top.

I caught my breath atop one of the posts. "Good thing I already had some practice tonight with Brownie."

A survey of the backyard told me it was empty. Of course. Barely a trace of the barbecue party left over. All the bedroom windows were dark. My bare feet found easy purchase on the inside fencing, and I hopped down onto the cushy grass. Skulking along the walls, I darted past each window as quick as a thief, before finally coming to the one I thought must be Tristan's by the gingham curtain inside, now grey in the darkness. I crouched close and cupped an ear to the glass, knocked with a wince.

Seconds ticked by.

I raised a hand to knock again, and then let it drop, unsure.

"Maybe everyone got gingham..." Was that blue or purple?

A hand pushed the curtains aside, disembodied in the black room. I glanced around the yard, trying to see the house in a bird's eye view and hoping I hadn't rapped on his little sister's window by mistake. Or Liza's. There was no way Liza could keep quiet.

My pulse raced.

Blinking eyes moved into the light, registered mine, and smiled. I waved and grinned. Tristan shot a cautionary finger in front of his lips, flipped the lock, then raised the window without a creak.

I whispered, "Hurricane glass is pretty easy to breach—"

But he put his palm over my mouth and shook his head.

I shot a glance over my shoulder at the sliding glass doors to the master bedroom, and he gave me a hand to climb inside. My bare feet melted into the fluffy carpet after the punishing woodland trek and a night in three-inch torture shoes. My senses adjusted to the hushed dimness and the smells of Tristan everywhere—the spicy notes of his aftershave mingled with clean laundry, perpetual sporty equipment, and something new. Slept-on linens. His bedroom. Warmth spread low in my belly.

I watched him close the window, dressed in nothing but boxer briefs. My eyes roamed over his beautiful body as he slid the heavy glass panel closed, the graceful contour of his shoulders and torso etched in starlight. The drapes fell and darkness embraced us again. Heat radiated from him. Fingers tickled down my shoulder, to my wrist. Goose bumps rose in their wake.

He found my hand, squeezed. His thumb brushed my knuckles, his voice so deep and low I could barely hear him, "Everyone's home."

The comment sank. Everyone. We were surrounded. Though in a wing of the house separate from Tiger Mom, all three of his siblings were sleeping around us. Even his older brother Brandon, who I'd never met. Of course he would've come to town for the graduation.

I gulped, my throat dry.

Tristan felt me stiffen and chuckled. "It's okay."

He stood watching me with an expression I couldn't name, his eyes hooded. Had he missed me as much I missed him? Was that desire or admonition? He sure was pissed when I left in a huff earlier that day. At least we couldn't talk. Maybe if we never mentioned the tear-catching moment, it would fade away and never hurt either of us ever again.

Before I could think too much, I unzipped my skirt and let it fall to the floor, tugged my tank top over my head in one fluid motion. Urgent hands and gentle lips were everywhere, his body still fever-hot from sleep. I was dizzy and spinning, swooped up and around. The bed was warm and sleep-crumpled. I snuggled in with a sigh. He hovered over me, his weight electric, the mattress pitted and trembling around my head. My toe hooked his boxers, shoved them down to his ankles. He kicked them to the floor and pulled a comforter over us.

"I love you, Tristan."

He shook his head and put a finger over his lips.

chapter thirty-one

I hate Sundays, but that one was worse than usual.

First of all, I was hung over.

Second, the memory of my midnight tryst replayed ad nauseam, a mocking background track loop to the morning. There was so much I needed to say to Tristan the night before that I hadn't been able to—so much that he probably wanted to say to me that I was afraid to hear. I knew he'd be busy with church and family stuff all day, as per the Jameson Sunday routine.

And that left me and the background track.

I decided to let myself mope, and to deep-clean the bathroom as punishment for my stupid secret bedroom stunt. I wasn't sure why I felt so vulnerable in the aftermath, when I was so confident rushing over there the night before. Maybe because Tristan hadn't respond with an "I love you" back. Maybe because the tequila had totally worn off and left a headache and sloshy tummy. Maybe because, in the glaring light of day, I remembered that I hadn't actually been invited to Tristan's bedroom.

"Maybe coffee wasn't the best idea."

I clutched my abdomen and popped another bright pink Pepto-Bismol. I chewed and swallowed, glaring at the toilet.

My just deserts.

I plugged my in earbuds, tucked my phone into the waistband of my sweatpants, and squatted. Urine had pooled and crystallized under the basin (Charlie always blew too far initially, which he called "shotgun pee-pee.") and my cleaning rag was sure to get snagged on the nuts and bolts anchoring the ceramic toilet to the floor.

You look like a princess. Yeah right, Charlie. No Gatsby girl either.

I was down on my knees, sinking into melancholy with depressing music, when Tristan's ring interrupted my playlist.

"What the hell?"

I dropped the rag and peeled off my gloves so fast the fingers got turned inside out. No time to be annoyed at the mistake I would pay for later. I cleared my throat and pressed the answer button on my headphone cable.

"Hello?"

"Hey, watch doin'?"

"Just uh…a little spring cleaning."

"Can I come pick you up?"

His car stereo clicked off in the background.

"Pick me up? When?"

"Now," he said, like it should've been obvious.

Holy crap. I ran a hand through my hair. It was a rat's nest. "Well…I'm kinda busy…"

"Come on, it's my birthday."

I bolted upright, banged my head on the counter. "Ow. What? Your birthday?"

"Yeah." His smile beamed over the airwaves.

"Why didn't you tell me today was your birthday?"

"Be there in ten minutes."

"Well..." I looked at myself in the mirror. My eyes were wide but that didn't make the purple bags any prettier. I hadn't washed my face or brushed my teeth since before the graduation ceremony, and my hair frizzed around my head like I'd spent the night in a mental ward. "Tristan, I need to shower."

My complaint met dead air.

"Fuck!"

I ripped off my clothes and threw them in the hamper, yanked the shower knob. Frigid water hit my back. Shaky hands sought soap and wash cloth blindly. I gasped and choked while the hot water took its time.

"Birthday…" I muttered, pouring shampoo into my palm.

No doubt he had been holding out on the date, just to be able to use it as leverage when he needed it. Not that I minded being whisked away from toilet duty on a crappy Sunday morning, but what the hell was going on? Tiger Mom never let him skip out on Sunday Brunch at Big Joe's. I lathered my body and let the stream wash suds out of my hair. Old anxiety morphed into new perplexity. My mind strained for explanation, but came up blank.

"Must have been a fatality or something." I couldn't help but smile at the image of Stephanie Jameson's shiny silver Accord spinning out of control and over a cliff on her way home from church.

I chuckled to myself, running a razor up my legs. Then a head rush slammed into my brain when I bent low to get my ankles. I stood back up with my hand over my mouth for a few seconds, waiting for the saliva to stop gushing and mentality chanting my new mantra, "Never drink tequila again. Never drink tequila again," until the moment passed.

While brushing my teeth I realized I didn't have a present. "Obviously his goal, but I'll see to that."

I turned the faucet off and listened, grabbed my towel and leaned towards the locked door. The deep rumble of Tristan's voice was palpable in our small house, punctuated periodically by Tessa's excited soprano. Her every sentence ended in a question. I eased the door open, tiptoed out, and peeked down the hallway to see my littlest sister perched on Tristan's knee in the living room. She was blocking his view of me, so I dashed into my room opposite the bathroom. I threw on some jeans and a tank top, still finger-combing the frizz eliminator through my wet hair when I walked out to meet them.

"Tessa, stop crowding him."

"Sorry," she chirped, hopping to the floor and scurrying off in search of some drawing she had just been describing.

Now that I had a better view, I was dismayed to find Tristan wearing charcoal grey slacks, a neatly pressed white oxford, and gleaming black shoes. "You're all dressed up."

"I came straight here after church."

I looked down at my own sloppy apparel, feeling like I hadn't dressed at all. "Well, I need to put something else on, then."

"Okay."

"You didn't need to agree quite so fast." I frowned and rushed back to my room.

"Don't worry, we have time," he called after me.

Worry about what? Time before what? "Where are we going, anyway?" I shouted through my bedroom door.

"Sunday Brunch."

I turned an abrupt pirouette and jammed my little toe against the door-jamb, my shock both tangible and audible.

"What was that? You alright?"

"Uh. Yeah. I just…" I rubbed my toe, trying to ignore the panic seeping in. Sunday Brunch! "Just dropped something. Be out in a sec."

Hangers zinged on the metal pole in my closet. What did one wear to brunch with her lover and his hateful mother? Church clothes, no doubt. What the hell—*heck*—does one wear to church? Something boring and stuffy. Lamenting my self-pity gorge on Doritos and Oreo cookies (and the corresponding bulge in my midsection), I sifted through my more demure skirts and sweaters. Settling on a calf-length khaki skirt and a virginal white

V-neck pullover, I sighed, "This'll have to do."

"But…" I grinned and selected my skimpiest lace bra and thong combo to wear underneath, then ran down to my mom's room to borrow some boring and stuffy tan pumps.

After I was dressed, I raided Mom's jewelry for something delicate and was surprised to find a tiny golden cross drop necklace. "Nah, too much." Instead I chose simple stud earrings, sparkly and probably cubic zirconia.

The churchy crowd would wear make-up on a Sunday. When I checked the mirror, I gasped—I'd forgotten about the bags. My mom's fake-it kit supplied yellow concealer to combat the purple under my eyes. Powder, blush. A soft pink gloss for my lips.

"Here goes nothing," I laughed to myself, returning to the living room tugging things in place and still fiddling with my hair.

Tristan's eyes widened when he looked up. "You look gorgeous," he said, scanning me from head to toe.

"Thanks." I blushed, but for a different reason than usual. The prim and proper Mekaela was as odd for him as it was for me, and those butterflies fluttered like crazy with the way he looked at me. Nice to have them back.

He stood and offered me his elbow, "Ready?"

♥

By the time I finished pleading with Piper to watch Tessa and Charlie, and we were finally in the car and headed into town, curiosity was gnawing a hole in my stomach so big that butterflies were threatening escape.

"I'm either gonna explode or puke." I flicked off my seat belt and turned sideways in my seat to face Tristan, my palms spread in the air and my jaw dropped in exasperation.

"What?" He glanced at me out of the corner of his eye, the side of his mouth quirked up to give him away.

"You know what. Why have you been so secretive lately?"

He grunted, "Secretive…"

"You 'forgot' to tell me about the cook-out yesterday. You spring the fact that it's your birthday on me today—Happy Birthday, by the way."

"Thank you."

"Big one. Eighteen."

"Yep." His chest broadened in satisfaction.

He was so cute, I could never stay mad at him. "And now you suddenly pick me up to take me to the family brunch. Obviously, you had already planned to do so before today…"

He smiled and watched the road, shook his head.

I stared at him. Secrets and Tristan Jameson just didn't mix. He'd give it up in T-minus three, two—

"Alright." His eyes skittered to mine, then back to the road. "I didn't tell you about the cookout yesterday, 'cause if you knew ahead of time, you would've had an excuse ready to not go." He cocked an eyebrow in challenge.

I wouldn't deny it. "That's probably true."

"I didn't tell you it's my birthday today, because I didn't want you to feel like you had to get me a present—"

"That's just insulting, Tristan. I'm not that broke."

"—and Liza a present."

"Liza?"

"Yeah, we were born on the same day, one year apart."

"Are you kidding me? That's so weird."

He shrugged.

"No really, Tristan—how bizarre. I always knew you guys were close, but exactly one year? I'll have to research the time of day and the star constellations for 1996 and 1995 when I get home." Tristan snorted, but I didn't care. I'd always found astrology fascinating, even if a little far-fetched. My thoughts drifted to my minuscule home library, and then to my sisters who were always stealing my books. I remembered how trying it had been for my own mom to have two babies at once, when Piper and Jo were born. A newborn and a one-year-old wouldn't have been much more fun. "Ew, your poor mother."

"Whatever. I didn't want you to feel like you had to get us both gifts. And you would have."

"So?"

"So, it's not necessary."

"Oh, Tristan. Please." He could be so ultra-masculine sometimes. It was actually pretty hot and I loved it. I crossed my arms and tried not to smile. "And the secret brunch?"

He looked sideways at me. "Well…"

"Well what?"

He pressed his lips together, jutted his chin. "Nah, that's still a surprise. You'll find out in a minute."

I settled back into my seat, eyes still on him. "Okay. I like surprises."

"No you don't." He reached over and patting my thigh.

"I don't?"

"Reckless with your body, not your mind. Remember? Put your seat belt back on, by the way." His voice was suddenly stern and he squeezed my thigh with authority. I had a mind to show him my secret arsenal under my frumpy skirt, but I clicked my seat belt buckle in place. "Don't worry, baby. This is a good surprise."

My heart pounded at his new term of endearment. Now that was intimate. I loved it. He moved his hand off my leg and back to the steering wheel, humming absently. He was nervous, too. My stomach resumed rumbling, indigestion mixing and churning with apprehension. I watched the road, alternately reminding myself that I trusted my boyfriend and picturing what lay in wait at Big Joe's.

As Shirley's little downtown came into view, I realized my hands were twitching and I wished I had pockets to stuff them into. I wrung them together instead. They were sweaty. I wiped them off on my skirt. "I hate this skirt. It's so doughty."

Tristan patted my thigh in reassurance. "I love you, Mekaela."

Oh. "I love you, too." I turned to look out the window, to hide my grin.

He blew out his breath, "Here goes nothing."

My eyes snapped to his.

"Now that's a smile." He tweaked my nose, "Here we are," and hopped out of the car, jogged around to my side to open the door. "You alright?"

"Sure, why wouldn't I be?"

He offered his hand, kissed mine before helping me out of the jeep. "Thank you for coming with me."

"Of course."

I was nowhere near alright and I must've looked as pale as I felt, because Tristan held onto me like he was afraid I was going to either bolt or spill through his arms as we walked through the gravel parking lot. We went down the steep stairs that zigzagged the hillside, to the front porch of the restaurant. A group of old men were chewing on pipes or cigars, chests puffed and hands gesticulating. They either complained about their wives or ragged each other as we passed through. One eyed me in appreciation, his tone raising an octave, "Hello there, Missy."

"Nice," I muttered.

"Good morning, sir." Tristan pulled me closer to his side, his arm wrapped possessively around my waist, as he opened the door and we both scooted in together.

I stopped short inside the doorway. "Wow, what a crowd."

"Sunday's are always a madhouse."

"Really? I wouldn't know."

He bent to kiss my cheek in the cramped vestibule, "You do now."

I produced a nervous titter of accord. To find a bustling crowd anywhere in Shirley, aside from organized school or sports events, was rare. I looked around at the diners, some already seated and some chatting, waiting for a table. Every worshipper from thirty miles around must have been starved after a morning of hallelujahs.

"There they are." Tristan had found his family. Tiger Mom's arms were raised above her head, waving us over to join their group in a far corner.

I followed through the throng, close on Tristan's heels. "I can't believe you didn't tell me it was your and Liza's birthday. It's obviously a big deal. Your dad's holding a champagne glass, my god—*gosh*."

"We're in the new dining room, look," Tristan pointed behind his mom, just as she shoved her husband back through a pair of lace-curtained French doors. I'd heard that the new owner of the restaurant made some changes since Big Joe himself kicked the bucket recently, one of them being some secret private room for rent. Apparently, you could drink booze in there and everyone pretended not to know. I was never "in the know" with Shirley County affairs before. How odd. That reminded me that the place wasn't actually called Big Joe's anymore and I was about to ask Tristan what they had renamed it, but when I leaned in to whisper I saw his scowl.

"What's wrong?"

"My dad was supposed to wait for us."

"Well, it's Liza's birthday, too." I couldn't imagine Liza waiting long for anyone.

Tristan shook his head, "That's not what this is about."

He plastered on a smile as soon as his dad was near us. The man had lost his champagne flute, yet would not be restrained by the lilac and cream frilled tiger tagging behind him. I'd always wondered about Sheriff Jameson. He was probably as crooked as senior year was long.

"Meg, darlin'," he growled, nearly squeezing the wind out of me. He had been enjoying the champagne for a while; we'd never formally met.

"Hi," I squeaked, relieved when he finally released me.

"Uh, Dad. This is Mekaela. Mekaela, my dad."

"Ya don't say," he chuckled, red-faced. "Thought she might be the one."

Tristan thumbed his nose. "Dad..."

The one?

"Meg Dear," Tiger Mom crooned, pushing a few people aside, including her husband who was at least a foot taller and maybe a hundred pounds heavier. She swooped in for my second overly-friendly embrace of the week, and kissed my face right next to my ear on either side. "I want you to meet my oldest son, Brandon."

The lipstick heavy on my cheeks, I looked around for a bathroom though I knew I didn't have time to make it to one. Still, it's always smart to know your escape route. I wiped my palms on my skirt again when I realized the whole family was pouring out through the French double doors. I could see Liza hopping up and waving at me from the back of the group, several people I didn't recognize between us.

"Great to finally meet you, Meg," said a tall, dark-haired young man in a pin-striped sport coat. He looked like Tristan, but somehow more feminine, with longish hair curling over his ears and graceful fingers when he shook my hand. "I'm Brandon."

"Hello," I said, suddenly shy. Tristan hardly ever mentioned his brother, and it was weird to be looking into eyes that were so strangely similar to his own.

Liza bounded past her relatives with ease once she got past the bottle-neck. "My turn!" she shouted, pulling me into a hug before Brandon had even released my hand.

"I can't believe I didn't know it was your birthday," I whispered into her hair.

"Oh, that's not what today is about."

"Huh?"

Liza pushed away from me abruptly and I almost lost my footing.

I felt Tristan's strong grip on my elbow and his arm slid back around my waist. "You look a little green," he said out the corner of his mouth.

"I'm good," I said, though I wasn't so sure.

"Okay, give her some air," Tristan raised his voice above the general fuss. He shooed his little sister Amanda, who was loitering close by with an unwilling pout. She flicked him a bird and sulked away.

"Yeah, come on, everybody. We only have this room for another hour," said Tiger Mom, herding the Jamesons back into their private room.

"Jamie's not gonna kick us out, hon. We still gotta eat." Tristan's dad tried to sound authoritative, but he did exactly as she said. Just like every-one else.

Liza was in my ear, "We get sparkling cider, but I have something to make it turbo-cider. We can sneak to the bathroom." She pumped my arm in excitement before skipping away.

I threw up in mouth a little bit and grimaced at her back.

Amanda had overheard. "Think I'll join you guys."

"Forget it, Mandy."

She frowned past me at her brother, "Screw you, Tristan."

His aggravation changed to charm as soon as I glanced back at him. A kiss on my forehead evoked a, "Gross," and Amanda finally wandered off.

"Sorry. I told her to leave you alone today."

I wondered if it would be inappropriate to pop another Pepto-Bismol. Maybe just a cracker. My mouth watered and an embarrassing sound burbled close to the surface. "I'm good," I lied again.

Everyone gradually made their way towards a big, round table. No food. I wondered how long they had all been waiting for us to show up, and why they hadn't just dug in without us. I noticed everyone was standing behind a chair instead of sitting in one. Polite family traditions are so weird. When I neared the last two seats, glad that I would be sitting next to Tristan, I felt him tugging my hand gently. I stopped and turned to face him.

"Mekaela?"

"Yes?"

He dropped one knee to the floor and knelt in front of me.

Oh my god.

One hand held mine and the other held an ornate, antique ring.

Oh my god.

"Mekaela Shannon, will you do me the honor of becoming my wife?"

Oh my god.

I focused on the ring. It looked so old, so thin and delicate that it might be crushed, held between Tristan's thumb and forefinger. The ring stood between us, light catching the diamond facets as Tristan's hand shook the tiniest bit. Or was it me who was shaking? Every face in my near vicinity was focused on me, grinning and waiting. Were they getting closer? I think the whole world was holding its breath.

No, it was just me.

Breathe.

Remember to breathe.

Then, I was the only person breathing. Loudly. Panting. Fast. My heart raced. Beads of sweat prickled from my skin like needles. Black tendrils crept in at the corners. My fingers throbbed. Tristan squeezed my hand. I tried to focus on his eyes.

Clear. Blue. Eyes.

"Hope your reflexes are as good as they say." My knees buckled under me and those beautiful eyes faded from view.

chapter thirty-two

"Here, this will feel good. Are you still dizzy?"

An ice-cold rag slapped against the back of my neck and I jerked back to scowl up at Liza. "Yeah, that feels great."

"Keep your head between your knees 'til it passes," she smirked. "Mrs. Mendez says anyway...you freak."

I propped my head in my hands, my elbows braced against my knees, *not* leaning all the way down as requested. That would surely bring up something unpleasant.

Liza's lime green leather flat tapped a tile next to the toilet. "Like you're in the seventeenth century or something. You dear thing, shall I bring you some smelling salts?"

She had vacillated between bitchy and comforting since The Collapse. It was hard to keep up, but funny was good.

"I know, I'm ridiculous. Fainting."

"How about a cigarette?"

I waved the suggestion away weakly, even though a smoke might have helped clear my head. I hadn't actually fainted. It was more like a panic attack and a melodramatic blackout. Surely the toxins leaving my system, mixed with that atrocious morning coffee, hadn't helped. Whatever it was, it was beyond embarrassing.

"You're not gonna puke, are you? Because if you are, my mom will totally think you're pregnant. That's not why you don't want a cigarette is it?"

I patted my face with the cold towel and sat up. "I'm not pregnant."

Liza leaned against the sink and drummed her fingers on the counter top, confused and concerned. Also mildly hostile.

"Look, Liza. You don't need to feel protective over your brother. I love him as much as you do."

She narrowed her eyes, pushed her tongue in her cheek.

"Different love, yeah. But same, okay?"

"You sound like Mr. Miyagi from Karate Kid."

I blew snot from my nose when I laughed—I hadn't realized I'd been crying. "I do, don't I?"

The room echoed with the sound of me blowing my nose into a wad of toilet paper. Liza watched, her face scrunched. Softening a little, she walked over to stand closer to me and my pathetic scene. I didn't look at her, but I could feel her watching me. Quiet for a minute, she finally sighed and slid down the metal wall to sit on the floor of the huge handicap bathroom stall.

"So what is it, girlfriend? Why'd you get so freaked out?"

I shook my head and claimed the fifth, staring at my mom's ugly shoes. How could I possibly sort out the jumbled circuits in my brain in a way that I could understand, much less in a way Liza could?

"Alright, Meg. I know it must have been a surprise..." she started, gentle.

I looked up and smiled, my chin trembling.

Tiger Mom's harangue escalated in the hallway outside the bathroom again. "...won't have you living in sin, Tristan Jameson. I won't have it."

"Mom, you sound like your buddy Kerry." Tristan's voice. I looked to Liza for clarification.

"Kerry is Ashley's mom," she whispered, watching the door with wide eyes.

"I'm just being a responsible parent, Tristan."

"But that's not who you are—some religious nut," Tristan went on. "Is that really what you think, Mom? Or is that what Kerry thinks?"

"You know what I think—"

"You're pushing her away from me, Mom..."

Their voices died away. I could tell Tristan was pacing outside, the fight with his mother fading in and out for the last ten minutes. I pictured her, hopping alongside him, trying to keep up, and him turning away in irritation again and again.

"He and my mom have always been super close." Liza nodded towards the quiet hallway. "Kinda weird."

"Yeah," I sighed and tried to lean back, but the only thing behind me was a steel pipe and a round flushing disc. I closed my eyes and slumped over instead, wishing I was anywhere else in the world.

"That's what a lot of this is about."

Tender notes. I looked up again and saw Liza frowning at her hands.

"How's it going in there?"

We both jumped; Mrs. Mendez poked her head in through the door. She had been shunting all patrons to the men's bathroom to give us some privacy. I once again thanked my lucky stars that Ricky's mom was working that day, but I knew we couldn't hog the lady's room for much longer.

"I'm feeling better, Mrs. Mendez. Thank you."

"Yes, thank you, ma'am."

"I can give you about ten more minutes, mamita, okay?"

"Yes, I'll be fine."

She offered me a knowing smile before ducking out.

I groaned, "Everyone out there must know what's going on."

Liza rolled her eyes in agreement, with more than a hint of recrimination. "Anyhow…" She checked her watch, then resumed, "When my mom finally understood how Tristan felt about you, I think it made things even harder for her to accept. She had a high school sweetheart herself once. Her true love, the one that got away."

"Not your dad?"

"No." She threw up her hands, started pacing. "Not my dad. I only know this because T told me. He said Mom knew beyond a shadow of doubt that this other guy was the one. He was a year older than she was, though, and when he graduated he did some kind of backpacking through Europe thing. I don't know all the details, but my mom got pissed off about him leaving and she didn't wait for him to come home. She started dating my dad."

Ah, yes. And she *got in trouble*. I remembered from that argument I overheard at Tristan's baseball game. "So, she regrets that?"

"Tristan said she regretted it every day of her life after that."

"My god."

"I know. So anyway, when T found out you might not be able to go to your school in Florida because your living situation fell through…I don't know, they just thought it was the perfect plan."

"What was the perfect plan?"

"That you guys move there together. I don't know who it was that came up with the proposal thing, but they were both pretty into it—they're both so traditional." Liza bugged out her eyes in a way that made it clear how crazy she thought her brother and mother were being.

"I don't get it. Why would that be the perfect plan?" Something wasn't adding up for me. "Did I lose a few brain cells last night or something?"

"Last night?"

"Nevermind."

"What happened last night?"

A headache knocked. "Just—why a perfect plan?"

"Because T had a scout bring him in for that school in Florida. He had a good rank in the draft, and he's totally in. It's a really good baseball school, didn't you know that?"

"What school? Tristan didn't say anything to me."

"Are you kidding? He was so excited. Didn't he say anything?" Liza stood with her hands fisted on her hips, that little crease between her brows so much like her brothers that I almost reached out to smooth it away.

But things were starting to click for me. "No. He didn't. I think he was trying to…" He had been so weird for weeks. And I remembered him pulling me aside to talk several times, disappointed that he couldn't get me alone for long. I slapped my forehead and winced. "Ouch."

"Here, lemme do that for you," Liza laughed.

I hushed her, trying to think. I had assumed Tristan was trying to gently start the break up talk, when he was trying to tell me he wanted to move to Florida? With me? That's why he was being so strange. He was nervous. And probably frustrated that I wouldn't stop for one damn second and listen to him. My head spun with the colossal paradigm shift taking place. I felt the urge to peek behind all the bathroom stall doors to find out who was playing the joke.

"Wait." I stood and smoothed down my skirt, my butt cheeks numb from sitting on a toilet seat for so long. "No, it just doesn't happen like this, Liza."

"Huh? I mean, I know you guys are pretty young…"

I moved to the mirror to splash some water on my face.

"I know you're not the traditional type, Meg, but think of it like this: nobody gets married at eighteen anymore, so you would actually be kind of retro-cool."

"I'm not worried about looking cool." I dried off my face on a paper towel, tossed it in the trash can, headed for the door.

"Well, what's your fucking problem, then?" Liza grabbed my arm and yanked me back to face her. "I thought you loved Tristan but you're making a fool out of him!"

"I would never—"

"What? Not good enough for you? Think you can do better?" Her shrill dismay echoed off the bathroom tiles. "Because I know I couldn't. If I was lucky enough to have someone like Tristan fall madly in love with me like that, it would be my fairy tale."

"I don't live in a fairy tale, Liza!" I wrenched my arm free and bent to match her yell, right in her face, "And I'm not a goddamn queen, no matter how perfect the king!"

I stood panting. My whole body throbbed.

Liza's eyes slid over me like I was an alien, her face crumpled in confusion. She finally broke the silence, "What the hell are you talking about?"

Maybe I *was* an alien. Or maybe I just spoke Martian. I wasn't even sure I understood me. "Oh, you wouldn't get it."

I flung my purse at the wall, harder than I meant to. My compact and lipstick flew out and rebounded off the wall, spinning and clinking at our feet. We watched them until they slowly came to rest, the lipstick against Liza's pretty shoes.

She bent over, picked it up and handed it to me, "Why can't you believe you're worth it?"

"*Worth* it?"

"Worth him." Liza crossed her arms over her chest and looked me square in the face.

"How dare you insinuate…"

A gentle knock sounded at the door to the restaurant.

"Mekaela, are you okay?" Tristan.

I cleared my throat. "Yes."

"I've gotta get out of here," he said, strained. I looked at Liza and she glared at me hard. "I bet you do, too, huh?"

I tried to produce a natural sound, but it came out maniacal. "Yeah."

"I'm goin' for a walk by the river."

"Okay." It was all I could do not to fling the door open and race after him, but the look on his sister's face, wavering between condemnation and hope, let me remember that I did not want an audience.

Tristan's footsteps faded away.

"He sounds terrible, I'm gonna go talk to him," said Liza, reaching for the handle.

"No." I slammed my body against the door. "Let me do this."

"Fine. But whatever you're gonna do, do it fast. You're breaking *my* heart now."

"Just give me a minute, okay?"

She jerked her head, narrowed her eyes. "I'll go keep my mom busy while you leave." I moved away from the door to let her slip through, but she stopped on her way out, her face downcast as she addressed me, "You know, it was just a stupid Homecoming tradition. Tristan didn't even ask to be voted as the king. Most people admire him for it, but you judge him for it." Then she was gone.

I stood still. It was as though Liza had slapped me in the face. Was that who I really was? But I had to get out of that place, first and foremost. I put my ear to the wood for sounds of ensuing drama, but all I could hear was noise from the nearby kitchen. The swinging doors whooshed back and forth every few seconds to emit clanks and bangs and shouts from deep within the galley. Taking a deep breath to steady my nerves, I eased the bathroom door open and peered outside.

The hallway was empty. I crept to the end. The doors to the private dining room Tristan's family were likely still occupying stood open, but I couldn't see anyone except for Tiger Mom and Liza from my vantage point. They were arguing just inside the lacy doors, but Liza was blocking her mom's view of the bathroom with her body.

"Thank you, Liza..."

I'd have to traverse the main dining room to leave by the front, and that was too risky. I knew a better way out—Ricky had worked at Big Joe's (or whatever it was called under new management) since he was old enough to sweep a broom, and I used to hang out with him on his breaks. I back-tracked along the hallway and opened the door to the cellar, hoping Ricky wasn't down there stocking or getting supplies.

He wasn't.

I bounded down the steps and squeezed past sacks of flour and rice and beans, making for the doors outside before anyone could interrupt my exodus. As soon as I opened the trap doors and pushed up into the open air, I exhaled with relief. I vaulted up the last steps and let the doors slam behind me.

"Tristan?" It was a vain hope. I knew he'd get the hell out of dodge.

But where? The Riverwalk was a popular place for strolling—I wasn't sure if that was what he meant by "taking a walk by the river," since he probably wanted to be alone. But that was the best place to start. I could hear the brunch crowd overhead as I passed under and around the patio, like a soft rumble of barking dogs mixed with the occasional quacking duck. There was no reason to hide, but I would've rather not been found. So, I oscillated between pride, stealth, and safety as I scrambled across the rocks between the river and the restaurant. I reached the paved walkway with a measure of shame, knowing Tristan had probably strutted right out the patio door and down the steps.

I had time to sort through my thoughts as I walked, but I didn't give a crap anymore. I was over it. The whole king and queen crap—had I actually said that out loud to Liza? Enough of the self-loathing, pretending I didn't care. Enough of trying to be something I wasn't. I was proud of who I was, and it was time to set the record straight, once and for all.

"I'm done with all the stupid fairy tale bullshit," I muttered, grinning at an old woman who glared at my foul mouth as I passed.

I climbed steadily uphill, not sure where I was going except up, and loving the burn of thin air in my lungs. Every step and every breath gave me momentum. The crowd was thinning, most Sunday revelers unwilling to make the steep trek to the apex of the Riverwalk.

I smirked, "Valley folk."

When I reached the top, I put my hands on my hips and surveyed the hill. A cool breeze dried the sweat on my forehead and neck. The rapids were especially fierce around a crook in the river just at the point below where I was standing, the western mountains closing in on the other side at the tightest, most violent point in the rapids. Movement down by the river's edge caught my eye: Tristan skipping stones.

"My love."

He was crouched on a boulder that was separated from the mainland by a fast current. Rapids swelled around him. He had taken off his dress shirt and shoes, a quarrelsome schoolboy with his white undershirt, deep frown, and messy hair. His tricep tightened and he chucked another rock with expert precision, the perfect angle and speed to skim the rapids effortlessly. He was no boy.

I climbed down the mossy hillside from the paved walk as quietly as I could. "You must have been bluffing," I said as I approached, slightly winded.

My clumsy entrance was not a surprise. He glanced at me sulk intact, arms dangling lazily on his knees, then returned his attention to the water. "Bluffing?"

"You were scared to go out on the point, up there in my mountains. But, you're fine on the edge of certain death here in the valley."

He repositioned his bare feet on the rock. "Certain death..."

"Class V rapids."

He was quiet and certain, still not looking at me. "I know you can swim, Mekaela."

"I know I can't swim those rapids, Tristan."

"I didn't ask you to."

"I was never worried you would."

"I was never scared."

No. Tristan never seemed scared, black-eyes and drunken frat boys notwithstanding. "Oh, and I'm supposed to trust you now, right?"

He rubbed his jaw and chuckled softly. His thoughts were so loud they echoed against the cliffs beyond, screamed above the sound of the rapids. "I've lived next to this river all my life. Fished in every offshoot for miles around since I could hold a rod. What would scare me about a little water?"

I threaded my fingers together so tight I was glad I hadn't worn any rings that day. Rings. We weren't really talking about water. "The unknown."

Tristan stood and shoved his hands in his pockets. He peered into the woodland clinging to the cliffs on the other side of the river, blind to all of it.

I picked my way to the shoreline, right where the earth ended and the water thundered past. "Have you ever tried this with your eyes closed, though?"

"Only you would be crazy enough to do that," he said, finally turning towards me. He held out a hand to help me over to his boulder.

"Maybe it is crazy," I said, closing my eyes as I dipped my toe over the rim of the last rock. I ignored Tristan's outstretched hand. "But that's exactly what I'm going to do." All dizziness of the day and uncertainty of the last month disappeared. I hopped across the abyss and met him face to face. He clenched my biceps to steady me.

I opened my eyes to look up into his intense blue gaze. "You kill me, you know that?"

"Is that why she was crying? Ashley? She saw the ring."

"That toe ring you handed me," he let his head fall back, shook his head at the sky. "The ring I wanted to give *you* was burnin' a hole in my pocket. I took it out for just a second to look at it."

"You're the crazy one—that ring in your *swim shorts?*"

"Any shorts for like two weeks, Mekaela," he laughed.

I didn't.

"Marriage, Tristan?"

"Just try it on."

♦

Tristan slammed his door, the jeep rocking with his weight.

"So, what time do we have to be back?"

"Be back?" The engine roared to life. "Mekaela, I'm a grown man now. I don't have a curfew."

"Grown man, huh? Your family's weird. Yesterday it was a criminal offense to be out late with me, but now that you're officially eighteen, they don't care what the hell happens to you?" I left out the obvious: his mother probably assumed we would be engaged by now.

"And you're complaining?"

"No. I just can't believe Ti—your mom is being so lenient." Crap, I'd almost said "Tiger Mom" out loud. If this woman could be my mother-in-law, I had better erase that nickname from my brain. I pinched the underside of my arm for a reminder. I still couldn't help teasing him, though. "What about Tristan Sweetheart's virtue?"

He leered at me as we pulled away from Shirley's tiny downtown, squeezed my thigh under my skirt. "Well, I'm sure she knows that's long gone."

"Oh, I still have it. Don't worry."

"Besides, sex would be a sacrament if we were married. No one would mind from now on, not even my mom."

"A Sacrament?" The idea was hilarious, after all the sneaking around we had done for months. But a few words in front of a priest, a little piece of paper filed at the county courthouse, and sex was ordained by the god with a capital "G."

"Darn straight."

"You know, that sweet ass of yours was always a piece of the holy for me," I said, pushing his palm higher up my leg and snaking my own hand over to his. "You've always been my god, Tristan Jameson. Sure have the body of one."

He stilled my fingers on their creep up to his crotch and looked at me sideways, "I think that's probably blasphemy."

"What? You're not serious." Again I wondered about Tristan's beliefs. I knew he attended church every Sunday with his family, but I had no idea what he actually thought about that. It wasn't like he ever gave me a rundown of the sermons, like he might retell the highlights from a baseball game I had missed. "Are you really that religious?"

He shrugged.

"Oh well, strike me down, God."

"Mekaela…"

"Now, please. Hit me with your lightning bolt for my terrible blasphemy!" I raised my arms up, stretching them across the expanse of the jeep's roof.

"That's Zeus."

"Huh?"

"Zeus throws lightning bolts."

"Oh. Same difference," I giggled. Tristan correcting me on the Classics was funny. But his expression was taught and I was probably being rude. "Sorry, I shouldn't have insulted your religion."

He smiled easily, "S'okay."

My insolence had no effect on his faith then. I'd have to ask him more about that later. "So, where are we headed?"

We were driving towards the interstate.

"Outta town." He gave me a wink and I knew he had something planned.

"Oooh, a surprise? The kind I like?" I rubbed my palms together in anticipation.

"You don't like any surprises."

"Good ones I do. Hey, that truck is totally in the middle of the road." I recognized the old red and white clunker heading our way, hair rising on my neck.

"Yeah, I noticed." Tristan flashed his headlights. "Hey, asshole, can't you tell there's two lanes?"

We had turned off the main valley road and were driving down a less-traveled offshoot that was one of Tristan's favorite shortcuts. There was plenty of room for two cars to pass each other, even though there were no traffic lines on the old dirt road. The truck was picking up speed, dust billowing up around it in a cloud.

"Tristan," my voice trembled with a rush of adrenaline, "I think they're playing Chicken."

"Well, I'm not." He slowed and moved far over to the right side of the road. "Maybe I should just pull over."

"No," I gasped, looking around wildly and seeing nothing for miles around but fields and pastures along the road, accented only by sparse telephone poles. There wasn't even a farmhouse or silo in view. The last thing I wanted was to be on a lonely road with the man I knew was in that red and white pick-up.

Tristan turned to me and his eyes went wide in alarm. "Damn it, Mekaela—your seat belt!"

I grabbed the buckle and hauled. My fist squeezed the door handle and my feet stomped the floorboards. Headlights flashed, horns wailed. I clamped my eyes shut.

The world stopped, a closed book.

part four:
gold mine

chapter thirty-three

A whistle pierced my ears. My brain was sliced in a thousand shards. Then silence. A hot bag hugged my cheek, pinned my head against something hard. I hissed as the pain started to seep from that needle of contact and around my skull, to my face. I raised one trembling fist and gingerly pushed at the smelly fabric, sought a clean breath. My mouth was plastered to my eyes somehow. No sight. No sound.

I spit out hair, fabric, and blood.

Then I felt a warm, strong hand grip mine.

Too strong. My fingers were sparrow bones in bobcat jaws.

The airbag started deflating. I marvelled at that tidbit, that I even recognized it as an airbag. When had I ever seen an airbag before?

Freed and able to move, I touched that spot on my head where I envisioned a target. I turned around and stared in wonder at the plastic seat belt harness next to the door, just above my headrest. It was cracked in two, metal innards visible.

Hand went to mouth. No teeth moved. But that irony taste. Did I bite my lip?

"Mekaela," bloomed into my consciousness. Like I had walked into a dark movie theater in the middle of the climactic scene. "Mekaela, are you alright?"

I twisted to a forward position and I looked at Tristan, dazed.

He was almost on top of me, one Nike between my thigh and the door, and the other between my ugly high heels. He gripped my shoulders, scrutinized my face.

I was so thankful he'd stopped brutalizing my hand.

"Mekaela, answer me. Now. Are you okay?"

Steel fingers tightened on my bones.

"Ow."

"Oh, thank god." He let go and slumped against the dash, the last of the airbag whining empty against his back. Over his shoulder I could see the hood of the jeep, obscenely crinkled around some sort of post. He followed my line of vision. "We hit a telephone pole."

"Oh…"

"Here." He took off his oxford shirt and held it up to my nose. "Pinch it at the top to stop the bleeding."

"Huh?"

"Your nose is bleeding, airbag musta hit ya good." He leaned forward to examine my face again. "Your eyes are dilated."

"What's that mean—"

"Are you dizzy?"

"Uh…a little, I think."

"Who are you?"

"Huh?"

"What's your name?"

"Meg Shannon."

"How old are you?"

"I'm eighteen."

"What year is this?"

"It's 2015. Tristan, please stop grilling me."

"You had me so scared. I saw you hit your head and—"

"Tha's wha you git, dumb bitch." A dirty finger jabbed through the open window and the smell of cheap whisky singed my nostrils. "No whore gonna take my goddamn money."

Tristan's worried frown morphed into the face of demon. In a flash, he cracked the ugly finger backwards.

"Argh! You motherfu—"

A fist in his teeth interrupted the scumbag's complaint. My door flew open as if its hinges had melted in the anger emanating from within the cab. Tristan was over my lap in a second, out the door, and ripping the limp airbag away before I understood what was happening.

I gaped at Terry Finley, crumpled on the ground beside the jeep. "Tristan…"

"Stay here." Tristan yanked the glove compartment open. It banged against my knee.

I didn't even feel it. "What…what are you…" I stuttered, shaken and reeling.

Without even fumbling, Tristan's hand locked on and emerged, holding a heavy, black, metal…gun.

A gun. A handgun. Jesus Christ.

I didn't know anything about guns but it looked like something powerful and dangerous and it looked like Tristan knew how to use it. I watched numbly as he hauled the degenerate to his feet, one hand fisted in a filthy T-shirt and the other holding the gun. The gun!

"No," I choked. It was all my shocked vocal chords could produce. I fumbled with my seat belt. I had to get out and stop whatever was about to happen.

Terry Finley landed on the hood of the jeep, the impact shaking the whole vehicle, the barrel of the weapon crammed under his eye.

"Wait!" He waved his hands in frenzy around his attacker's shoulders. "Wait wait wait wait wait!"

The attacker was my boyfriend. My Tristan.

A fingernail cracked back and broken plastic skinned my knuckle, but finally I got my seat belt unbuckled. "Wait…"

"Don't you ever talk to her like that again!" Tristan leaned his full weight into that proclamation, every ounce of his strength culminating in the black cylinder pressed against Finley's face. "Do you hear me? Never again!"

"Yes." The pathetic creature squirmed against the hood. "Yes yes yes…"

Now the voice I loved was so quiet and deadly I could barely understand him. "Never again or I'll fucking kill you, you hear me?" He turned the handle of the gun, twisting the barrel, and Finley held still as a corpse.

Every hair I owned pricked in alarm.

I had to stop it. For Tristan. For me. For Terry Finley, that bastard. I scrambled out of the jeep, caught my foot in the door, and went sprawling in the dust. My spine jarred into my skull and electrified a latent migraine. "Ugh—shit."

"Damnit," said the most beautiful voice in the world. As ugly as it had become with violence, it was laced with concern for me.

I looked up at my love from my place in the dirt.

He met my eyes and I saw his indecision.

"Mekaela, get back in the car."

"Please, Tristan."

"Why are you defending him?"

"I'm not."

"Get back in the fucking car."

I rose, but I was still unsteady. I inched toward him with my hand raised, head lowered. Peered from under my lashes. "Let's just calm down, okay?"

His whole body was tense, pulse visible in his neck. But he softened at my approach. "Get back in the car, Mekaela." And this time, his voice was kind.

"We's okay. It's fine. You just over actin' or …" Finley mumbled.

My heel hit hole in the ground and I stumbled.

Tristan grimaced. "No, fuck this." He reared back, the gun over his head.

"Tristan, don't!"

Finley whined. "Please—"

And then metal hit bony flesh. Once, twice. Finley melted against the hood in a puddle of filthy skin and greasy hair, held up only by Tristan's hip against his. Tristan moved back in disgust and Finley dropped like a sack of rotten potatoes.

chapter thirty-four

"Are you okay?" A gentle finger traced my jaw. "Just get back in the car, alright?" Tristan's voice was a lullaby.

I was so stunned I couldn't find my own. Or move an inch.

"Come here." His hands were as soft as his words. He reached under my shoulder blades and the backs of my knees, lifted me effortlessly. The hallucination of being lost in a cloud intensified. My vision spun. I felt the seat back—canvas and linoleum, squishy-stiff—underneath me. A feather kiss on my forehead. "I'll be right back. You're safe here, baby."

Baby.

My eyes fixed on him but he was looking past me, digging his cell phone out of a back pocket.

"Hey, it's me." I watched Tristan stroll away, calmly assessing the body puddled in the dirt and the friend hovering by the red and white pick-up truck. That guy didn't seem half the villain Terry Finley was. He was biting his nails, cuddling himself and rocking back and forth. Watching the horizon. He also seemed about half Finley's age and I wondered about their relationship. I had to know him somehow but recollection resisted names.

I couldn't take my eyes off the sunset either. It was otherworldly—rolling pink and orange clouds with blasts of white at the edges, the sky on fire. That was more comfortable than real life at the moment.

"Holy Mary."

I raked my fingers through my hair, wishing I were a smoker. A smoke made sense just then. Did Tristan just propose to me, shove a ring on my finger without an answer, then pistol whip some guy? The night seemed cooler than it was. I shuddered against the perceived cold and bent over to hold my aching forehead in my hands.

"No, she's fine I think. But I need to get her to the clinic...I don't think we need to go to Tenakho Falls, no....She might have a concussion... Yeah..."

Everyone was hushed but Tristan. He was all business. No anger or discomposure, just business.

"Nah, it's totaled. We'll need a ride there...Not an ambulance, no..."

He was matter of fact, devoid of emotion.

"I'd rather she not be here to witness that, actually…" Blue eyes slid my way, made contact. He smiled reassuringly and then moved out of earshot.

Witness? Was I a witness? To what I wasn't sure, but I was very sure I didn't want to *not* be a witness to whatever might happen next. Tristan's dad was the sheriff and as far as I knew, he was a much better guy than Tiger Mom. But she wasn't a guy. And how did a sheriff compare to a Bobcatt Queen anyway? And how did that mix with trailer trash like me and Terry Finley? Oh god, my head was going to explode. I wasn't making any sense and I knew it.

Tristan, finally off the phone, walked back to open the hatchback and rooted around for something in the compartment under the flooring. I closed my eyes and tried to remember happier times, imagining the blow-up mattress we usually stowed there.

"You."

Tristan's voice was so sharp I whipped my head up in response.

"Ouch."

But he wasn't talking to me. The bystander cringed and my shoulders relaxed.

"I want to talk to you. Stay there."

His tone made me look for the gun, but it was nowhere in sight. My discombobulated brain thought that was good.

"Here, keep this on your head." Tristan handed me what looked like the kind of instant ice pack you find in an expensive First Aid kit. I did as I was told with no complaint. The ice felt divine. I had the urge to nod off, but I didn't want to miss anything important. I made myself stay focused.

"You were just a passenger," Tristan was saying to Finley's friend. "You had nothing to do with this."

The guy shrugged. Oh, not a friend. Terry Finley was nothing to him either. "Yeah, sure. I'm good."

Tristan stopped inches from the guy and leaned in, his voice lowered. The two conspired for a couple minutes, Tristan doing most of the talking and the other guy bobbing his head in agreement.

"Help me get him in the cab," I heard somebody say, and watched them make Finley's clothes into an awkward stretcher. As far as I could see, the guy was a piece of dead meat. I gnawed on my fingernail and was greeted by nothing but nubs as usual.

"Shit. Is he dead?"

"Gi thu fukkoff me," the body said and began flailing as they propped him up in the passenger seat.

Tristan pulled a rag out of his back pocket, but he dropped it as soon as Finley grabbed for it. The desire to avoid touch was etched all over him. The friend seemed almost as repulsed, but helped Finley press the rag to his head wound. I couldn't help but feel sorry for the man bleeding, no matter how big of an asshole he had been to me. You just can't hold grudges like that and stay sane. Or kick someone when they're down.

"Hey." Tristan was suddenly close, face angelic once more. "Help's on the way, baby."

As if on cue, a far-off siren swelled. Cavalry was nigh.

chapter thirty-five

"You're one lucky lady. Good thing you had your seat belt on."

I caught the smirk on Tristan's face and rolled my eyes, then caught my breath at the pain that little move caused. "Yes, I know." I gripped my head and moaned.

"Don't worry, I think she'll start remembering to put it on now," he said to the nurse.

"Never ever forget your seat belt," she nodded, a grating nag counterpart not nearly as attractive. "It should be a habit."

"When will that Tylenol start kicking in?" I asked, accepting a fresh ice pack. The paper on the exam table crinkled under my butt as I readjusted myself to get comfortable. I hate doctors' offices. Too many questions and reproofs, very little substantive help, and lots of money I didn't have pissed into the wind.

The nurse crinkled her nose. Somebody must have told her that was a cute perplexed look once. "It's not already taking effect?"

I closed my eyes and sat still for a few minutes. Actually, my headache was ebbing, a mellow *zzzwwwrrr* of codeine buzzing the edges of pain.

"I guess it is," I blinked at my smug boyfriend, then whispered, "but lecturing brings it all right back."

He smirked, satisfaction wafting off of him. It was no secret that I would've been hurt a lot worse if I hadn't gotten my seat belt buckled before impact. Tristan was right and he knew it. So did I. As it was, the fact that I was caught in the act and leaning away from the headrest was the reason my head got battered. Tristan wasn't even bruised.

He watched the nurse hurry out of the room. "You should drink some more of that Sprite," he said, jerking his chin towards the paper cup in my hand.

I brought it to my lips, annoyed at the persistent tremble in my limbs. "I'm still all shaky, I hate it."

"You're probably just in a little bit of shock."

"You're not."

Tristan lounged against the counter top across from me, completely relaxed. Sexy. An arrogant half-smile lit up his features. "I'm used to violence."

The image of him with that gun sprang to mind. "What do you mean?"

He chuckled at my sudden alarm. "Football. Violent impact? That's why we wear pads and helmets and stuff."

"Oh. Right."

He cocked his head to the side. "What did you think I meant?"

"There she is," sang a perky voice from the hallway.

I looked up to see Tiger Mom striding into the room. "Oh no…"

Tristan looked stern.

I swallowed, tried for contrite.

"Oh, thank God you're alright," his mom said, grasping her chest with one hand and reaching for me with the other.

"Me?" I was sure she was talking about the Golden Boy.

But she was going in for a hug. With me. No. A kiss on the cheek? I feinted and we bumped heads. She deftly changed direction and air-kissed the side of my face, with a motherly squeeze on my opposite arm.

"How are you feeling, Meg Sweetheart?"

Holy crap, I'd just landed the Sweetheart surname. What planet was I on?

"She has a pretty bad headache. Probably a concussion," Tristan answered, and in explanation of my dumbfounded expression added, "and she's a little out of it."

Stephanie Jameson looked genuinely worried. "Is she?"

Tristan met her gaze with melodramatic concern. "Shock."

She played the perfect counterpoint, cocked her head and frowned. "Yes, of course…"

"She's doin' good, though."

"Have they given her anything?" Tiger Mom asked, and out of the corner of her mouth muttered, "You know I have some Demerol at home."

Demerol? Yes, please.

"They gave her some Tylenol 3 with codeine. Should be feelin' no pain pretty quick."

"Oh, that's good. I talked to Natalie and let her know I've got everything covered."

Natalie, my mother? How did she get my mother's phone number at work?

"Good. Thanks, Mom."

They went on talking as if I weren't there, and I was more than happy to let them. I needed a moment of silence to figure out why the hell Tristan's mother was being so nice to me.

"Brandon is already on his way back to Miami, so his room is all ready."

"Perfect, then I'll be right across the hall to keep an eye on her," Tristan said.

Tiger Mom went on, "Yes, and Amanda's at camp for another week, so she'll have some peace and quiet."

Wait a sec. Me? I would have peace and quiet? "Um, what's going on?"

"You're staying with us tonight, Meg Sweetheart," Tristan's mother cooed.

"I am?" Did my face show the confusion I felt?

"You need to be watched for twenty-four hours after a concussion, Mekaela," Tristan explained, firm and coddling at once. "And you can't be expected to watch Tessa and Charlie when you need to rest."

"Your mother's working tonight," added Tiger Mom. "But your sister, Piper, was very happy to help out."

Yeah, right. "Oh, okay." Not like I wasn't happy to be off the baby sitting hook.

"I can go pick up your overnight bag," Tristan offered.

Tiger Mom finished his sentence, "Once you're settled at our house."

My head was spinning. I had to wonder if that was part of the concussion thing or the mother-son tag-team nurturing thing, unfolding like a scary B-movie.

"Well, they're pretty much finished up here," Tiger Mom started.

"So, I'll go get the car," Tristan finished.

I wanted to scream, "Don't leave me alone in Oz with the Wicked Witch," to Tristan's back.

The Wicked Witch turned her gaze on me after he was gone and beamed me the loveliest smile I had ever seen on her face. She was actually very pretty without the habitual frown that I was used to. She sighed in contentment and gazed at me with...affection?

I nearly shouted, "What the hell is going on here, lady?"

But then three things happened. Stephanie Jameson sniffed, then she looked at my left hand, and then she wiped away a little tear streaming down her cheek.

I looked down.

Shit.

My answer twinkled up at me. I forgot to take off the damn engagement ring.

♠

My eyes popped open and clung to white space.

No beginning, no end.

Dots in every color of the rainbow punctured the white and started to swirl.

Ceiling.

But my ceiling at home wasn't white.

Or rainbow.

Where the hell was I? Fully awake, I rocketed to a seated position and cast around for familiarity.

Checkerboard curtains.

Marilyn Monroe poster.

Roll-top desk and swivel chair.

I touched my body and felt weird clothes. "Please. Life as I know it, come back to me." A residual sluggish feeling weighted me down, rawness on the edges barely blunting whatever lay beneath. Whatever had teeth. "Focus, Meg." I focused on…a buffalo china bowl…with a spoon. Macaroni and cheese.

"Macaroni and cheese is my favorite, the way my mom makes it."

"Oh, yes." I reached for the bowl with a flood of relief. "Tristan's house. Brandon's room." The bowl slipped and thudded to the floor, the spoon clattering against the ceramic dish.

"Mekaela?" Tristan stood in the doorway, his voice sleepy and his hair matted. Silhouetted disarray. "You okay?"

"How do you still form a six-pack three seconds after dream state?"

A hand clenched on the door jamb fell to caress his relaxing abdomen. He laughed softly, "Sorry, I was on code orange."

"I'm a bomb threat?"

He dropped his voice to a whisper, "Definitely." He stepped into the room and closed the door without a sound.

"Your bomb or mine?" I reached out in the darkness.

Hands slid past mine and around my back. "Both, probably."

His weight sunk the mattress. His chest pressed against mine. His fingers moved to the hem of my…what was I even wearing?

A nightgown?

Cotton.

Whose nightgown is this? "Wait a minute."

He settled his hips between my legs, arms surrounding me like a cocoon. "What?"

"I mean…someone might hear us."

"Who?"

"Her."

"So?"

"Oh really?" A marriage proposal was powerful stuff. I pushed at his chest feebly and giggled, "Come on, we're in your parents' house—"

"Stop it." In one fluid motion, both of my hands were locked together over my head. "I need to know you're mine."

"So serious—"

His lips stalled my protest.

I grinned, "Well now."

"Shh." He clutched my face and pressed his forehead against my temple. I lay still, acclimating to his change of mood while he caught his breath.

Was it the car accident? My refusal to answer? I was afraid to ask. The image of him with that gun flickered against my eyelids. *"I'm used to violence."*

He gripped my jaw with so much force it hurt, and his eyes were so close to mine I could hardly focus. He whispered, "I need you right now."

I nodded. "Okay."

chapter thirty-six

"I'm gonna miss you." I gazed at Tristan across my old Rabbit's tiny, cracked console. The jeep was still in the shop, but he insisted on driving.

Without looking at me, he said, "It's only a week."

That hurt.

He softened the blow by patting my thigh, but it was a little too brotherly for my liking. "I'll miss you, too."

Why did I feel like he wouldn't? Well, Cancun. He'd be crazy not to be excited about a fun-in-the-sun trip to paradise. I was sure he'd have a blast celebrating graduation with all of his friends. I tried to hide my scowl as a stray thought invaded my head: Ashley would be there, too.

"You'll call me, right?" I sounded so whiney I wished I could take the question back as soon as it left my lips.

"We all agreed on no cell phones," he said, matter of fact. As if he expected me to already know.

"What? Why?"

"It's like a pact."

"A pact?"

"Yeah."

We turned into the parking lot of Andrew Jackson High School, which was already well populated with cars and minivans, their doors and trunks opened. People unloaded luggage, parents made their last checks, siblings hugged and said goodbye. Kids from my class were walking towards a pair of Greyhound busses with duffel bags over their shoulders and wheeled suitcases bumping behind. Many of them were arm in arm. Jealousy roiled in my gut and I felt like kicking myself for refusing to go on the stupid senior trip. Again.

Since Tristan didn't seem inclined to elaborate on his last comment, I prodded, "So what's the pact?"

"You know, back to nature. No worries. Experience the good life."

"Like Cancun is so natural," I teased and reached over to tickle a rib.

He jerked to the side, away from my fingers. "Excuse me."

I frowned at him, taken aback. He'd been acting weird all morning. "Are you mad at me or something?"

He didn't answer me, but instead made a big show of concentrating on pulling into a parking spot perfectly straight. I kept watching him, waiting for a response, while he cranked the emergency brake and shut off the engine. He settled back against his seat and, still avoiding my eyes, pointed to my hand resting on my thigh.

"You know, you don't have to wear that."

I pulled my hand to my chest and twisted the engagement ring around my finger, protective all of a sudden. "Kinda weird to take it off now, especially after your mom saw it and all."

"She'll get over it."

"Get over what?"

His answer was to look out the driver side window.

He was acting so cold and I felt panic creeping up. "Look, Tristan. I don't like the feeling that decisions are being made for me is all. You're mad at me for that?"

I flinched when he met my gaze, his eyes hard.

"No. I'm mad at you because there's something you need to tell me."

"What?" I was totally confused. Was he trying to bully a "yes" to his proposal out of me? That wasn't his style.

After a few seconds of awkward silence, his eyebrows shot up. "I have to ask?"

"Again?"

A curt, humorless laugh. "No. Not that. I'm not asking that again."

Oh.

He watched me, waiting for me to catch on.

I was speechless.

"Did you kiss Ricky Mendez?"

All the air was sucked from my lungs and every nerve zinged to attention.

"Who told you that?" I managed to get out.

"Does it matter?"

And I knew. I knew it was that April girl. What, did Zach dump her and she decided to get back at the whole family or something? The blood rushed back into my face. That little bitch.

"Well. Did you?"

"Tristan…" I felt like I was in shock again, my mind blanking. "*He* kissed *me*."

"But you didn't push him away."

My thoughts raced, trying to recall how it all happened. "I…I didn't want to embarrass him."

"So you'd prefer to embarrass me."

"What? No. Why would that embarrass you?"

His scowl challenged my intelligence.

"Look, alright? He was drunk and being an idiot." How could I make Tristan understand that this conversation was madness? "He's my friend and he's had a crush on me for a long time. I didn't want to hurt him." Tristan's pained wince made the message clear: I was hurting *him* instead. I rushed on, "I didn't kiss him back! I broke it off right away, I swear."

Tristan stared at me. Even I heard the hollowness of my words. I sounded like such a liar. But I wasn't. I wasn't. He narrowed his eyes and I was stunned to see them starting to water.

"Honest! It was nothing, Tristan. Nothing. You're everything."

He shook his head and looked away again. My heart pounded so hard it hurt. The car was stifling with the engine off. I waited. Beads of sweat popped at my hairline.

"Mekaela…"

I held my breath.

When he didn't go on I whispered as gently as I could, "Yes?"

He dropped the car keys in my lap.

"You need to decide what you want."

He was already halfway out of the car before he finished that sentence. He flicked the seat forward, grabbed his duffel bag, and slammed the door.

I was alone. He strode across the parking lot.

"I want you," I said in a small voice, as he joined a group of jocks. I watched him as he boarded the bus.

He didn't look back.

chapter thirty-seven

Marvin Gaye crooned in my ear.
Get up, get up, get up, get up
Wake up, wake up, wake up, wake up
"Ugh..."
Ooh baby, I'm hot just like an oven
I need some lovin'
And baby, I can't hold it much longer
It's getting stronger and stronger
It was way too early to be awake on a Saturday. I am so not a morning person and Saturday was the one day that I had off.
And when I get that feeling
I want sexual healing
"Shit!"
That was Tristan's ring. I rocketed up, scrambled for my cell phone. My fantasy of Tristan racing home because he couldn't stand being apart for one more instant had come true. I found my phone and jabbed at the answer button.

I was breathless and sappy and I didn't care. "Hello?"

"Hey, Meg. Whatcha doin'?"

Liza's voice brought me back to reality. Tristan's house phone.

"Oh. Hey, Liza."

"Oh. Hey, Liza," she mocked. "You know T is in Mexico, right?"

I bit my lip. "Yes. I know."

"You weren't dreaming about him, were you? In leather or something weird? Cuz that's totally gross."

I couldn't help but laugh. I liked Liza, even in the morning. "No, unfortunately. I haven't mastered the art of lucid dreaming."

She made puking noises on the other end. "Well, get your ass out of bed."

How did she know I was still in bed? I looked at the clock and my anger resurfaced. It was only 8:30 a.m. On a Saturday. "Why?"

"Because we're taking you to breakfast."

"We?"

"Me and my mom."

I sat back on my haunches, shoulders slumped. "At Big Joe's?"

"Where else? The Kitchen, actually. New name, get with the friggin' picture already."

"Sorry."

"I know you don't work today, so what else have you got to do? Dream nasty dreams about T all day—ouch, Mom!"

"Well…" The fact was I had nothing to do all day. Everyone was home for once, even my mom. No baby sitting required. I probably *would* be daydreaming about Tristan all day, but not in the way Liza suspected. Our last conversation in the parking lot haunted me every free minute. In fact, a day with no distractions would be torturous.

"Well, what? Like you have a choice."

Liza was undoubtedly more persuasive than anyone I knew. "I mean…" How could I say it delicately? I would always love to hang out with her, but Tiger Mom?

Liza was almost as good at reading my mind as her brother was, though. "We have planning to do, you know? Big plans. Lots and lots of planning." And then she pitched her voice low, not really decreasing volume but comically whispering, "I'm sorry, but I'm acting under duress."

"Liza, you love weddings," I heard Tiger Mom complain.

Oh no. "Uh…wedding stuff already?" Jeez what was the rush?

"Well, if you guys are gonna bump uglies legally before school starts in the Fall—ouch! Mom, stop pinching me."

Oh yes, living together in sin was out of the question. "You can't seriously think a whole wedding can be planned before we leave for college?"

"My mother can do anything she puts her mind to, trust me."

I heard said mother cheering in the background like the Bobcatt Queen she still thought she was. Something like, "That's right, Mama Bear is on the job."

Mama Bear? Great.

They had no idea that I hadn't actually agreed to marriage. The image of Tristan getting out of the car and not looking back as he boarded that bus greeted me full force. I saw the anguish on his face when I admitted to kissing Ricky and I desperately wanted to erase that look from my memory.

I cracked my knuckles and scrubbed my scalp.

"Hello? Earth to Meg."

They had no idea that there might not actually be a wedding. Suddenly, there was nothing that I wanted more than to plan a wedding. Maybe that would make my hold on Tristan seem less slippery, as creepy as that would sound to admit out loud.

"Okay. I'll meet you."

"We'll come pick you up—"

"No!" The Rabbit, old and loud as it was, was at least less embarrassing than having guests at the Shannon Family Trailer. Stephanie Jameson, here? The smell of her freshly laundered sheets and lavender-scented candles clung to her wherever she went, but my house would douse that in seconds. "Let me just meet you guys, please?"

Liza couldn't care less. "Fine, but don't be late." She hung up without saying goodbye.

"Wait—"

I guess everyone else in Shirley County knew what time breakfast was served at Big Joe's. The Kitchen.

"Zip-a-Dee-Do-Dah. Guess I better get movin'."

♣

"So, have you thought about where you'd like to have the reception? Obviously, the ceremony will be held at St. James. Or—" Mama Bear's hand stopped stirring her coffee. She leaned in, eyes wide and blinking rapidly. "I'm sorry, that was pushy of me."

Liza fiddled with an empty sugar packet but remained neutral. Her mom glanced back and forth, pretending embarrassment. Her cheeks weren't even flushed.

"Um. No, I don't have any other plans for...for that." I had actually never been to church in my life. I scratched my neck, unwilling to just come out and say I had no religious inclinations.

Mama Bear's painted smile spread before she could stop it, then she jutted out a hand as if halting traffic. "I don't want to step on anyone's toes."

"You're not, don't worry." And you're not a bear, you're a tiger. "Mrs. Jameson, I would be honored to have the ceremony in your church."

"Thank you, Meg Sweetheart. And please, call me Stephanie."

"Oh. Okay." I was the one blushing. Could she hear my nicknames for her in my head? I added "brain raping" to my list of the tiger's skills. "Um, Stephanie."

I was all useless hands and darting eyes. It was more than weird to be treated kindly by Tristan's mother. The reason for her sudden change of heart was insulting, too. She was only tolerating me because I was going to marry Tristan (or, that's what she thought anyway). So, I was persona non grata before, but I was okay now, because I would be a part of her family? A part of her. It didn't really have anything to do with me as a person at all.

"St. James is absolutely wonderful for weddings. The stained glass, the velvet pews, the altar. You'll love it."

I nodded and glanced to Liza for a sense of normality.

"T will be tickled pink. Altars and incense and kneeling. So hot."

My blush deepened.

"Liza…" Tiger Mom warned over her coffee. "Enough with the sexual innuendos."

"I'm just saying he'll be so happy, Mom."

"Will he? Why?" Tristan rarely talked about church or religion. My guess was that he knew I would rather not talk about it, but I had always been curious what he really thought.

"T? His ears are probably red all the way in Mexico. He was an altar boy at St. James for like a million years."

"Really?"

"Yeah, he's the bestest Catholic boy ever. Pure angel, that one," Liza snickered.

Interesting.

"Oh, Liza. Stop it. Tristan is not here to defend himself," Tiger Mom said.

"He doesn't need to defend himself against me. I love T. So…the reception…"

Everyone was looking at me. "Reception?"

"Yeah, the after party?" said Liza, leaning forward with her elbows on the table. "The fun part of a wedding?"

"All parts of a wedding are lovely, Liza." Her mom glared at the elbows and Liza pulled them close to her sides.

"Well…" I trailed. "I haven't really thought about it."

But it was the first thing I dreaded since Tristan proposed. A reception would probably be expensive and from my limited knowledge, I believed the bride's family was supposed to pay for that. Some medieval dowry tradition or something. How could I break it to Stephanie Jameson that if my family had to bankroll the party, it wouldn't be the royal affair she was wetting her pants over.

"What about our place—with your rose garden, Mom?"

A break in the anxiety cloud. I could've kissed Liza. I blew out a breath so hard it moved Tiger Mom's hair-sprayed bangs. She pushed them back in place. I fingered my ring. But, did Tristan even want to marry me anymore? The lingering question made me sick. Our waiter appeared right on time and shoved a steaming plate under my nose. Grits, bacon and fried eggs, sunny-side up. I reached for my ice water in reaction.

"Thank you, Mary," Tiger Mom said sweetly.

"My pleasure ma'am. You ladies need anything else?"

A barf bag, please.

"No. Thank you, dear."

"Looks great," Liza said.

The tiger gazed at her cub, misty-eyed. "Oh, honey. I don't know. Do you really think my garden would be nice enough?"

"Huh? Yeah, why not?"

Liza didn't get it, but I did. Tiger Mom was fishing for a compliment and somebody better provide one quick. "Oh, Mrs. Jameson. Your garden would be perfect, it's absolutely beautiful."

She beamed at me across the table, "Is it?"

"I would love to have the reception there. It's gorgeous." And free.

Liza nodded, her mouth full of omelette.

"Well, sure," her mother giggled, glowing with pride. "If you really think so." She picked up her fork, then pawed me playfully, "And I told you to call me Stephanie."

"Stephanie, sorry."

A little smile played on her lips while she took a tiny bite of her pancake. "Maybe I could put in a trestle."

Liza winked at me and I almost choked on my eggs. She knew. She knew I couldn't afford a reception. That wink told me she may have even heard—or planned—the bed of roses on Homecoming night. I felt so naked I shifted my hips to make sure I had remembered to put on panties that morning. I glanced from the table for relief and my gaze landed on Ricky.

The opposite of relief.

He was across the dining room clearing a table, and he turned and caught my eye before I could look away, My blood ran cold. He smiled—or tried to—around a bruised lip.

What?

He lifted a tub full of dishes and made his way back to the kitchen.

What the hell?

My blood was rushing, my mind racing. Tristan hit him.

"So, have you?"

My attention snapped back to the breakfast table in front of me.

"Excuse me?" I tried to focus on Liza's frown. "Have I what?"

Stephanie Jameson was looking at me like I had a big bow tied to my head on Christmas morning. "Thought about what kind of dress you'd like to wear."

"Uh..." I tried to gather my thoughts around a pounding heart and shaking hands. "No."

"Oh, come on," Liza shoved my forearm, "Every girl has the picture in her head from when she was little."

"I don't." I knew that was rude, but I didn't care. Tristan hit him. He hit my friend.

"I always did, I'll admit it," Tiger Mom was saying.

Liza filled in for me, "Meg likes vintage."

"Is that so?"

"Yeah, remember the flapper dress? I only saw the picture of course, but T told me about it."

"Yes, I bet that made quite a splash at Homecoming." Tiger Mom smiled slyly and tickled my knee.

I swallowed the urge to tell her exactly what happened after that dance, and where.

Liza chuckled.

Her mom shushed her, a finger over her lips. "Do you like any particular style of vintage, Meg Sweetheart?"

"Well..." I looked from mother to daughter, forcing my insides to calm down. I just had to get through breakfast. Then I could go home to my hovel and pine for my boyfriend for the rest of the day. My jealous, violent, absent boyfriend.

Who was in Mexico with his ex-girlfriend.

Who was right to be mad.

The thought was like a wet blanket on my anger. I deflated like a popped balloon. "You know, anything authentic, I guess."

"Hmmm..." Her eyes twinkled and she stroked her chin, then looked at Liza in silent question.

Liza lifted a shoulder and nodded. "Hey, Meg. It's so freakin' hot outside, let's go swimming. Plus, you can check out the garden again. See where the trestle would go."

"Oh. I uh...didn't bring my suit."

"You can borrow one of mine," said Liza.

Not this again.

Her mom shook her head, "I think Meg might fit in one of Amanda's suits better, honey." She eyed my ample cleavage.

"Amanda has a huge ass, though, Mom. Meg's got a cute little butt."

"Well, we'll have to measure her anyway…"

Ricky moved around the tables next to us, gathering dishes and avoiding my eyes. I challenged the Fates to make my day any more hellish.

Liza smiled at me wickedly. "Cool, let's make a girl's day of it."

Tiger Mom's face lit up and she clapped her hands together. "Let's do. Uh, young man…" Ricky looked up and I stared at the table, inspected a fork. "…check, please."

chapter thirty-eight

"Get me a coke, will ya?"

"Okay." I closed the sliding door behind me, already shivering from the air-conditioning inside the house.

I shifted my towel from my waist to my shoulders and squinted. I had to pee, but it occurred to me that the only bathroom I had ever visited in the Jameson house was Tiger Mom's in the master suite. There had to be one close to Tristan's room. The living room was dim compared to the harsh summer sunlight outside, everything shades of gray. Gradually, furniture and bric-a-brac solidified and my vision focused on a large framed picture.

The photo was of me and Tristan. I stared at it, my mouth open wide enough to catch a fly. My heart in my throat, I walked over and plucked it off the bookshelf. It was a black and white photograph of us, unaware that we were watched. It was hard to tell the setting, cropped as close as it was, but we were gazing at each other like the only two people in the universe. Crazy in love.

"So it shows up on camera…"

I looked around. No picture of Ashley anywhere.

"Well, I'll be damned."

There was a tall wooden cabinet with glass doors on the other side of the room. Even in the dim light I could see the cabinet was full of guns. I crept toward it with morbid curiosity, like some fool rubbernecking at a passing car wreck. The image of Tristan with that handgun was still so vivid in my mind and I didn't know if I'd ever get it out. I shivered, even though my skin was actually warm enough by then. I mean, Terry Finley was an asshole, but pistol whipping? And the sheriff's son gets away with murder.

"Hey, did you get the cokes?"

I gasped and dropped my towel. "My god. Liza."

"What's wrong, guilty conscience?" She jerked her head towards the gun rack.

"No."

"That one's mine—Black Death." She tapped the glass near one of the weapons inside.

"You have a gun?"

"Of course. My dad's been taking us to the shooting range since we were little."

"Yeah, but…" I ogled the gun she claimed was hers, "…a sawed-off shotgun?"

"Well, if some creep is dumb enough to get that close to me," she chuckled. "I was never too good with a pistol. Maybe you will be, though."

"Me?"

"Daughter-in-laws have to train, too." She took a step back and sized me up, then examined my biceps. "Welcome to the family."

"Okay. I'm speechless."

"Oh come on, Meg. I wouldn't really use that thing, I wouldn't need to. Black Death would scare the shit out of anybody." She shook her head and turned towards the hallway. "You gotta protect yourself, you know. I have to pee."

"Are you kidding?" I called after her. "You're kidding, right? I can't tell…"

Her laughter died away.

Enough with the mixed signals, I'd have to pin her down and force her to be serious. Liza was the least violent person I knew. I couldn't even picture her holding a gun. What the heck was I getting into, agreeing to marry the Jameson's? Wait. I hadn't agreed to anything, yet. Why was I feeling so trapped?

"All done swimmin'?"

"Oh!" I clutched my chest, stalked from behind.

"Didn't mean to startle you. Good, I'm glad to get you alone for a minute, honey."

That sounded ominous. "Okay…"

"I want to show you something, without Liza there to comment," Tiger Mom said leaning in closer, "and influence." Then she erupted into a laugh that Liza was sure to hear.

I looked towards the hallway, hopeful for a rescue even though I knew it wasn't an option. Resigned, I followed Tiger Mom with leaden feet. When I realized we were about to enter the master bedroom, I panicked. Insane possibilities exploded in my mind, like her producing a condom wrapper from seven months ago. But she bypassed the bed and led me to a closet door.

"This is just an idea." She paused at the door handle. At first I thought she was building up dramatic suspense, but then she squeezed her eyes closed. She was nervous. She took a deep breath and pulled the door open to reveal the largest walk-in closet I'd ever seen.

I stood there, watching blankly, as she shoved clothes aside on a crammed hanging rack. There was another behind it, set deeper in the wall. I rolled my eyes at the obvious waste of wealth. No one needs that many dresses and sweaters and pants. I wondered where they got all their money. Being sheriff couldn't pay that well, could it?

Tiger Mom rifled through her wardrobe, humming to herself. Her clothes sure were pretty, though. Maybe I was just jealous they weren't mine. That thought was sobering. I'd never thought of myself as greedy before.

"There we go," she said with a grunt. She held up a heavy, zippered dress bag.

It was white and I was starting to catch on. I watched her lug it back to her king-sized bed, too stunned to offer help.

"Now, you will not hurt my feelings if it isn't your thing," she said, easing the zipper down.

I took a step toward the bed, then froze. Crammed a ruined nail in my mouth. What kind of wedding dress would she have worn twenty-five years ago? I pictured some pukey, puffy, white version of Ashley's homecoming dress. I wanted to squeeze my eyes shut as the bag split open, but I was so curious I couldn't look away.

"Okay, here it is." She stood back awkwardly, waving at the dress and quickly folding her arms over her chest. "When Liza said 'vintage,' I thought this might work. I had a theme wedding. It's a little silly maybe, but what smitten girl isn't a Jane Austin fan at that age?"

My jaw could've hit the floor and I wouldn't have noticed.

"Mrs. Jameson. It's…"

My fingers skimmed the soft, chiffon skirt. The heavy fabric revealed delicate satin folds under a central slit, all the way up to the empire waist-line. The corseted bosom was intricate lace, with a gossamer cowl and cap sleeves. I'd done enough sewing and read enough history to know the whole package was authentic. And expensive. I looked at her. Words failed.

"I forget the era, but that's vintage, right?" She bit her lip and I felt my chin tremble.

"Regency." I said, my voice catching on the last syllable. I cleared my throat. "The Regency Era."

"Oh, honey." Stephanie put her hand to her mouth, then went to zip the bag back up. "You won't hurt my feelings if you don't like it. I know it's old-fashioned—"

"I love it," I blurted so loudly she jumped. "Don't zip it back up, please. It's beautiful. I love it."

"You do?" Her eyebrows shot up and her shoulders sagged with relief. "Really?"

I could only nod, afraid my voice would crack again if I tried to speak.

She pushed the plastic back and fluffed the dress out into full view. "Your curly hair would make such perfect ringlets around your face, just like they used to wear back then. We could watch *Emma* or *Pride and Prejudice* to get the style just right."

I had seen both about a hundred times.

"Of course, we'd have to alter it some. You're taller than me but maybe we could add a lace hem at the bottom or something." She stepped back and admired the dress. She put her hands on her hips, grinning ear to ear. "It'll take some work. But if you want it, it's yours."

"Wait. You mean you're..." I was afraid to say it out loud. "You're giving this to me?"

"Well, of course."

"But I," I shook my head. "I'm not even your daughter." And the tears started flowing. "I don't deserve this, Mrs. Jameson."

"What?" She instantly produced tissues. "Of course you do, honey. What do you mean?"

"I...I..." God, I was blubbering. "I'm such a...such a..."

"Oh, Meg Sweetheart. Come here." She tugged my hand and I found myself sitting on her cushy bed, opposite the beautiful dress. On the fluffy down comforter—I deflowered her son in that bed.

A fresh torrent of tears spewed forth. "I'm such a creep," I said between sobs.

"Oh, honey. What are you saying?"

I cried into my wad of tissues and shook my head. Then she hugged me. And I let her. For several minutes.

"Meg," she said softly, "I know I've been hard on you. I know that."

I stared at my knees.

"And I'm very sorry for that, Meg."

I sniffled and stilled.

"I want you to know that I was really judging myself when I was judging you. I understand that now."

I closed my eyes and let a post-cry shudder take me.

"I don't know if you know this, but I was pregnant when I got married." She motioned to the gown wearily. "Hence the Empire waist-line theme party. We were trying to hide it. As if everyone didn't know." She gave a delicate little snort. "In Shirley County? Imagine. But, I was so ashamed."

I blew my nose. "That wasn't anything to be ashamed of."

She fell quiet. When I looked up I caught her studying the dress, her thoughts elsewhere "You're right you know? The thought of being ashamed of any of my children now is nothin' short of crazy."

"Super crazy," I agreed.

I was sure that we were both thinking of the same child. How could anyone be ashamed of Tristan?

"But I was only eighteen, just a stupid kid." She covered her face, embarrassed. "Don't take it the wrong way, all kids are stupid. The point is, I was brash and prideful and that's the reason I lost my own high school sweetheart."

I looked away.

"And don't get me wrong, honey. I am very happy with my life and I love my family more than life."

She stopped talking and watched me, eyes larger than I remembered them.

"But?"

"But if I'd known that I would never feel that way about another person again—the way I felt about Jamie." She shrugged and let her hands fall against her thighs with a defeated slap. "Well, I guess I would've fought a lot harder to keep him."

"Why are you telling me this?"

"Because that's the way you and Tristan feel about each other, Meg. It only happens once."

I looked at the dress. The ring. They weren't really mine. Brash and prideful sure summed it up.

"Of course I'm only supposing here," Tiger Mom went on. "I don't know your true feelings for my son. You and I have never really talked. I know. But Tristan has been very honest with me about his feelings for you. And well, the sun rises and sets in your eyes."

My eyes? My plain, brown eyes? What were those, compared to his crystal clear, Mentho-lyptus blue eyes, lined in thick black lashes like they're permanently covered in three coats of mascara? And the way the corners of his eyes crinkle when he smiles that beautiful, just-for-Mekaela smile. Nobody had called me Mekaela since he left and it was a painful void right in the center of me.

I finally looked up and realized she'd been watching me. "What?"
"Uh huh. I think I supposed right."

chapter thirty-nine

I checked myself in the bathroom mirror and snuck out the front door before Piper could see me wearing Tristan's shirt again. It swallowed me, but I didn't care. I wasn't ashamed to be wearing it again, just not in the mood for my sister's catty jokes.

"You look great in hunter green," I said to my reflection in the rear-view mirror, then backed the Rabbit into the dirt lane.

Maybe I was a little ashamed of the ploy I had to carry off to get the shirt. After lunch at the Jameson's, I *accidentally* got some ketchup on my own shirt, so I asked to borrow something to wear home. When I emerged from Tristan's room wearing one of his polo's, Liza and her mom stifled their smiles. I wondered if they knew I had snagged it from the hamper instead of from his closet. The problem was, after my second day wearing it, it didn't really smell much like him anymore.

By the time I passed through the entrance to Southern Cove I hated myself for being so sappy. Of course it was too late to go back and change shirts, so I had to keep it on. No choice. An embarrassed heat spread from ear to ear. I've always considered myself to be the unsappy type. I do love all those Jane Austin novels as much as Tiger Mom, but my favorite was the wheeling, dealing, and intrigue. Once it got to the lovey-dovey conclusion, I felt like the story was already over. I could do without the romance.

Usually.

I wished I had asked Tristan for some kind of trinket of his before he left. Something. It would've meant more if I didn't have to steal it, just like he had asked for something of mine before the lock-in and I gave him my ring. That was a rock in the pit of my stomach: he had not asked me for a little something before his trip to Mexico.

An image of Tristan and Ashley on a beach, sipping mocktails together.

"Ugh."

Cassie's ringtone broke into my unpleasant thoughts.

"Hey!"

"Why didn't you tell me you're getting married, you a-hole?"

"What?"

"I had to hear it from some lady named Stephanie Jameson, instead of my own freakin' cousin?"

That was out of line. How did Tiger Mom get Cassie's number? "Um, wait a minute. What did she say—"

"I'm asking the questions here," Cassie cut me off. She wasn't really angry—I could hear the smile in her voice. "This is Tristan's mother, right?"

I groaned. "Yes."

"So, my first question is how the hell you're gonna deal with that bossy bitch for your mother-in-law…"

"You make it sound so official."

"And my second question is when are we gonna get trashed for your bachelorette party…"

"That sounds a little better."

"And my third question is you're getting fucking married? Are you kidding me?"

I held the phone away from my ear. "Okay, I can explain."

"You better."

I pulled over to the shoulder of the road and turned off the engine. "Tristan did ask me to marry him, yes."

"Okay, when?"

"Almost a week ago—"

Cassie exhaled loudly, "Tch!"

"But, I didn't actually say yes, not yet. That's why I didn't call and tell you."

I shifted my phone from one ear to the other. Cassie could see straight through bullshit and I was giving her a load of it.

"So, why is this lady planning a wedding then?"

"We're planning it together."

"Oh, okay," she said in a high-pitched ditzy tone. "You're getting married at *her* church?"

"Tristan's church."

"Even though you don't believe in religion."

I watched the grubby roof of my car. "Yeah."

"And you're doing the reception in *her* rose garden?"

I could see Cassie ticking the list off on her fingers. "She told you that?"

"And you're wearing *her* dress. Whose wedding is this? I mean I can see why you wanna marry Tristan—god, he's a freakin' dream boat—but why is this lady calling all the shots?"

When she put it that way, it did sound pretty weird. "Why did she even call you?"

"She wants me to do your hair. The ringlet curls like they wear in *Emma*."

So, she was designing my hairstyle, too. "How did she even know I have a cousin with a salon? I mean, it was actually nice of her to include you."

"Meg! No it wasn't. It was creepy." She was shouting again, but I could tell she thought it was funny. "You know I'd be happy to do it, girl. All you had to do was ask. But I just wish *you* asked, not this lady."

"I'm sorry." I felt...squashed. "Listen, I have to get to work and I can't shift gears while I'm on the phone."

"Well, call me later. We have to talk about this, Miss I-Didn't-Actually-Say-Yes."

I rubbed my temples. "I know," I said, starting the car, "I'll call you, I promise."

"Alright, bye." And she hung up. Cassie never wasted words.

I pulled back onto the highway, glanced at the gas gauge and remembered that I needed to stop at the station first. My fingers fluttered against the steering wheel, wishing I had some music to get my mind off of that uncomfortable conversation. Cassie always knew how to hit the right nerve. The suffocation I felt at breakfast the other day came floating back like a black cloud. She was right. I was letting Tiger Mom control everything and I knew it. And the reason was that I didn't really want to get married. I could pretend with Tristan's mother, I could pretend with Liza, but I couldn't lie to myself. Or Cassie. What about when Tristan got home from Mexico? He could read my face like a book. But, if I didn't do this marriage thing, I might lose him.

I gripped the wheel harder as the hated image of Tristan catching Ashley's tear at the barbecue swam into my consciousness.

"I'm not a monster. I still care for her."

He had actually said it out loud. Maybe I had lost him already. What were they talking about in Mexico, right that minute? If she started crying again, would he wipe her tears away? He did before. She would marry him in a heartbeat, of course. Perhaps he missed her and all that blind devotion. If they were married, the abstinence issue wouldn't be a problem any longer, would it? Bile rose with that realization.

I banged the steering wheel with my fist and rammed the shifter into the next gear, shook my head to dispel the thought.

"Mekaela...You need to decide what you want."

He was so mad about Ricky. And what could I say to that? I was pretty damn mad at him, too. All the stupid fist fights over my honor aside, how dare he hit my friend? Ricky hadn't meant any harm and I didn't have a hell of a lot of friends. It wasn't just one more fight like all the rest—as if all the rest weren't bad enough. It felt like my life was being rearranged for me. I didn't want that. Or did I?

"Mekaela...You need to decide what you want."

I wanted Tristan, but I didn't want to lose myself in the bargain.

The gas station came into view and I smoothed my features. My sister, Jo, came walking out of the garage when the Rabbit's rattle sounded against the building. I was surprised, but relieved to see her. Jo was as normalizing as a guy and hated talking about emotions, boyfriends, and most especially weddings. I'd have hours of boring, thumb-twiddling time to think over all my problems at the library, so a couple minutes of normal conversation would be a blessing.

"Hey, I didn't know you were working today." I leaned my head out of the window, rolled the car to a stop next to one of the pumps. "I figured you were still asleep when I left the house."

"I wasn't scheduled, but they needed a hand. Manny picked me up early."

"Huh." Leave it to Jo to sneak out, quiet as a mouse without anyone even knowing she'd left. I hadn't thought to look for her that morning. Since Jo made more than enough money working at the garage to make up for it, she rarely ever had to baby sit our younger siblings anymore. Lucky devil.

She opened the fuel door, twisted off the cap, and jammed the gas nozzle into the Rabbit without a second thought. "Hey, I need to drive you to work so I can have the car today, okay?"

"Sure, whatever."

"You can find a ride home?"

"I guess."

The longer I stayed at the library, the less time I had to sit around the house bored as hell. With Tristan in Mexico and school out, all I did was work, sleep, and try to remember to eat. Liza went back to school for summer classes and Tiger Mom seemed to be getting things done without my input. I got out and leaned against the side of the car. My heart skipped a beat when Tristan's green Jeep Cherokee caught my eye. Like a moron, I looked around for him before I realized that the jeep must be parked at the garage to be repaired. Disappointment circled around my already dark mood.

"So, you guys are fixing Tristan's jeep, huh?" I asked, trying to sound nonchalant. I was dying for any piece of Tristan information, even if it was just technical blah-di-blah about engines or hoses or something.

Jo looked over her shoulder at the jeep and then gawked at me, the lunatic.

"What?"

"Are you joking, Meg? We're not fixing that."

"Why not?"

She laughed and scanned me head to toe. "They just sold it to us for parts. It's totaled."

"It is?" I wasn't exactly sure what that meant, but I didn't want Jo to know how clueless I was.

"Weren't you like *in* the car when it happened?"

"Yeah…" I murmured. I could only see the back end from where I stood, but it didn't look that bad. I left Jo pumping gas and walked across the parking lot for a better look. "I mean, I was pretty disoriented and we went to the clinic right after—"

The words dried up in my throat when the front of the jeep came into view. The whole front fender was smashed up towards the windshield, the metal a crinkled newspaper bow tie. The "knot" at the center was a perfect hollow half-cylinder, about two feet long. That must have been where we hit the telephone pole. I couldn't imagine what the engine looked like underneath.

"My god…" I made my way around to the passenger side window.

"There's blood inside," Jo said, like she was recounting a scene from a horror movie. "How'd that happen?"

Inside, the airbags laid against the dash like curtains, pooled on the floor in front of the seats. Dark reddish-brown encrusted the one on my side. "My nose was bleeding."

"Lucky you didn't break it."

I touched the tip gingerly, "Yeah."

"That guy wanted to kill you."

My hand shook as I felt the broken seat belt harness. "I didn't realize what a close call it was. No wonder Tristan was so mad."

Jo grunted. She took off her baseball cap, wiped the sweat off her forehead, then settled it back in place. "Surprised he didn't kill somebody."

"Actually…" I steeled myself, "he kind of…pistol whipped the guy."

"Really?" Her eyebrows shot up, delighted. "How many times he hit 'im?"

"I don't know. Twice?"

"Oh. That's not so bad."

"Jo, it's not funny."

"That guy needed his ass beat."

"Stop it. He probably ended up in the hospital."

"No he didn't," she said, mirth evaporating. "He ended up in jail, Meg."

"He did?"

"That was his third DUI, you idiot. He didn't even have a license anymore." Jo was watching me with her smart-people-are-so-dumb look. "Good thing Tristan kept him on the scene so he didn't take off again."

I stood up a little straighter. "Take off?"

"Didn't you hear about that kid who ended up at Tenakho Memorial—Chase Whatshisname?"

I didn't answer. She already knew I had no idea..

"Seriously, Meg. Your head is either in a book or up Tristan's ass all the time." She dodged my blow and clomped toward the garage. "I can't wait until you leave for college."

"Actually..."

She turned back, saw my hands twisted together. "What's your problem?"

"Tristan asked me to marry him." I recoiled, waiting for the harangue I deserved. Jo was always so practical and levelheaded—she'd never run off and marry someone right out of high school.

But she turned back towards the shop. "Whatever. Just don't ask me to wear a dress to some swanky shindig."

I followed her, totally confused. "You don't think that's crazy?"

"Why would it be crazy?" She pulled a towel out of her back pocket and threw it to me. "You're drooling just thinking about him."

"Jo..." Why did everyone assume I was always drooling over Tristan? I dropped the oily rag in the dirt. "What if I don't want to get married?"

"Then don't." She leaned in through a side door to the garage and yelled, "Hey, Manny! I'm gonna drop off my sister, be right back."

"'Kay." Manny kept his head under the hood of an old white Mustang and waved an arm, blackened to the top.

Jo pushed past me, "Come on, let's go. I only have like an hour for lunch."

"But," I whined, tripping along behind her. "I love him."

She grimaced, clearly grossed out. "So marry him." She already had the driver door open, ready to dodge the girly conversation.

I stopped on the passenger side of the Rabbit, threw up my hands, and glared at her over the roof. "What if I don't believe in marriage?"

"Then don't marry him."

She was being so thick skulled. Like it was that simple. "But everyone thinks I should, I'm sure. Like I should be jumping up and down to marry Tristan Jameson."

She finally stopped to look me full in the face, her eyes glinting. "Oh, that's rich. 'Cause you always do what everyone thinks you should." Without waiting for an answer, she slid into her seat.

chapter forty

"Zach, you don't read, do you?"

He swiveled around, guilty and baffled. A kid caught stealing something meant for grown ups. "Oh, uh...no."

"You know, you can just check anything out of the library for free." I pointed to the book he had stuffed under his jacket. "No heist necessary."

"I wasn't gonna swipe it," he whispered, eyes darting around the room. "I was just..."

I held out my hand and he offered it over, cheeks reddening.

"Oomph." It was a big one. I smirked, looked down to investigate my cousin's selection, and almost burst out laughing. "Poetry? You?"

He straightened his shoulders. "No, brainiac. It's not for me." He stalked off in a huff, leaving *Contemporary Love Poems* in my hands.

"Wait." I tucked the book under my arm and grabbed his T-shirt. "I'm sorry, I didn't mean to embarrass you."

"I'm not embarrassed."

"Please, Zach. I'm sorry."

He let his head fall back and exhaled loudly.

"Do you need my help with anything? It is my job."

Eyes narrowed, he considered me for a minute.

"Come on," I relaxed my face with an effort, "No more laughing, I promise."

"Alright, just keep your voice down, okay?"

I jerked my head towards one of the aisles and led him to privacy. There was a small wooden table and two chairs at the far end. I pulled out a chair and nodded towards the empty one, then sat and laid the poetry before me reverently. This was a big moment for a meathead like Zach.

"I actually know a lot about poetry, I'd love to help." I rested my chin on my knuckles and gazed up at him sweetly.

He collapsed into the opposite chair, then let it all out in one breath: "April wants me to read poetry to her and I have no idea what kind of thing girls like, okay?"

My back went ramrod straight. "I'm not helping you with that. Sorry."

"What? Why not?"

"Because your little girlfriend caused a big fight between me and Tristan. That's why."

"Whatever, she wouldn't do that."

"Oh, she would."

"She hardly knows Tristan. Or you." He grabbed the sleeve of Tristan's polo as I rose to go. "What are you talking about?"

I glared down at the offending hand and then at Zach's face. He looked constipated he was so off kilter—forehead all wrinkled and eyes too intense—so I decided to take it easy on him. Zach in love, what a novelty.

"Just tell me, Meg."

I removed his hand, looked around, then sat back down. "April hates me."

"Uh, no she doesn't."

I leaned across the table and hissed, "Then why would she run and tell Tristan that Ricky kissed me that night at the Mendez graduation party?"

Zach's confusion broke. He sat back and shook his head, "You, too huh?"

I narrowed my eyes. "You lost me."

"She was pissed at Ricky, not you. She's been smearing his name all over town." He chuckled at the thought, admiration glowing in his eyes.

"What? Why would she be pissed at Ricky?"

His face darkened. "Because he crammed his tongue down her throat and squeezed her tits, freakin' asshole."

I gasped. "Oh my god, when?"

"Uh, that night. After graduation. He was piss drunk, told her he was in love with her."

Humiliation rose hot and swift. There I was, thinking I was so special when Ricky was hitting on anyone with boobs. Honestly. April was just a little sophomore twit he barely knew and he was professing his love to her. "I don't believe it."

"Trust me, believe it. He admitted it after I punched his goddamn lights out."

"You were the one that punched him?"

Zach waved it away, "Don't worry, we made up. Bros before hoes."

Of course. Except he was sweating over finding just the right poetry for that particular hoe. Guys drive me insane. Ricky, that little creep. He made me feel so sorry for him that night. *You know I've always loved you. Don't make me look like an asshole here.* Did he actually think I was that easy?

My blood boiled with that thought. I should have punched his lying little mouth myself.

"Anyway, April doesn't hate you," Zach's strained whisper interrupted my thoughts. "You always think the worst about yourself, why do you do that?"

A large, warm hand covered mine. The ring pinched when he squeezed. I blinked down at it through a prickle of springing tears. "I don't know."

"Well, you shouldn't. You're awesome."

"Jeez. Thanks, Zach." I wiped an eye surreptitiously.

He cleared his throat and pulled his hand away. "Anyway...poetry," he said, like it was a death sentence.

"Right." He hadn't noticed the ring, and at that moment I was grateful for the male ability to ignore details. "I already have something in mind."

"Thank god."

"And don't feel weird about it." I tried to wink, but I probably just ended up blinking owlishly. "Tristan reads poetry to me, too."

♥

"And in payment for my help in this very important matter of proper courtship..."

Zach let his head loll in relief. "Anything, cuz. You saved my life."

I put his brand new library card on top of *Love Letters of Great Men, Volume 1* and pushed them both across the counter. "I need a ride home, can you come back at 5:00?"

"Yeah, no problem." He stuffed the card in his wallet and clutched the book to his chest. "I owe ya one," he whispered.

I wondered about his last visit to the library. The library card I had just made for him would probably still look crisp if I saw it in ten years.

"You know, you don't really have to whisper," I said under my hand, scrunching my shoulders and peering around. "There's nobody even here."

He flicked me a bird, then shouted from the doorway to make a point, "I'll pick you up later."

"Shhhh, not that loud."

The sunlight was so bright outside as he pushed through the exit that his curls gleamed. I could imagine how warm the sun would be on my face. My blood went cold, however, when Zach paused and held the door open to let Stephanie Jameson inside. I reminded myself that her presence no longer affected me like that, waved, and forced a smile as she approached.

She turned back and pretended to examine Zach from behind, even though he was already gone. "My, who was that?"

"Hi, Mrs. Jameson. That was my cousin, Zach Michaels."

"Ah, I didn't realize you two were related."

My jaw clenched protectively. "You know Zach?"

"Oh, just slightly." She giggled and flipped her hair. "The PTA president has to make sure she knows every kid at least a little."

"Uh huh." Zach likely never caught her attention at all. Until today.

She smiled wider than was necessary. "I heard him say, 'I'll pick you up later.' Where ya goin'?"

Oh, please. "I just don't have a car today, so he offered to drive me home." *Want to know what I'm having for dinner, too?*

"Is that so?" Her eyes twinkled.

My shoulders tensed. "Er. Yeah."

She stroked her chin and narrowed her eyes, "Transportation is a problem, isn't it?"

My ears pinked. "I get by."

"Uh-huh…"

"Oh good, you're here," my boss chirped behind me. "I'm starving. We goin' to Big Joe's, Steph?"

"Actually, let's go to my house." Stephanie looked at me and winked.

I froze.

What the heck was that? Did the whole family have the ability to rattle my brain with that little gesture? I nodded and agreed and assured until the two women finally left. Yes, I could handle the library by myself for an hour. No, I wasn't too hungry for lunch yet. Yes, I could wait. No, I didn't want Stephanie to pack a lunch for Aunt Meghan to bring me. I was so relieved once I was alone that I plopped in the office chair, pushed off the wall with both feet, and let it spin. I rested my head against the seat-back and gazed at the rotating ceiling for a good five minutes.

By that time, I knew Tiger Mom's plotting look. I had no idea what she was up to, but it must have had something to do with Zach since that seemed to set her off. I wondered whether she was already snooping around, maybe checking his driver license or something. Maybe she would call Cassie and pump her for information. She'd probably have a shit fit if she knew Zach would be taking me home on a motorcycle. Would I have to limit my joy rides if I were a Jameson? That thought finally made me uncomfortable enough to get up off my butt and get back to shelving books.

When Meghan got back from lunch, she had me clean up the ledgers and two hours flew blew in a flash. The Shirley County library system was still in the dark ages of technology—we literally used a rubber stamp on paper logs tucked in books, and collected dollar bills and coins for late fees. Everything was handwritten, so there was plenty of room for little addition and subtraction mistakes. Rarely were we out of the red anyway, but I loved ferreting out offending numerals and at least balancing the drawer. Anytime I get to do anything math related, I'm happy. Lately, it was the only way I could get my mind off of the tornado that had become my inner life.

Unfortunately, the *last* two hours were spent calling in fines on delinquent book borrowers. As much as I enjoy dialing numbers, cajoling, and being hung up on, the end of my shift meandered on at a slug's pace, leaving little tracks of unhappiness and regret all across the tri-county area. If I had known who would greet me at the end of the workday, though, I'd have happily made a few more calls to buy some time. I looked forward to nothing more than a hot shower and a microwave dinner, but my spirits plummeted when Tiger Mom walked in.

"Hey there, Meg Sweetheart. You ready to take off?" Her freshly applied, sparkly pink lip-gloss stretched across her face in cheerful command.

"Oh. Um…" I scanned the parking lot through the windows and saw Zach pulling out of the parking lot, his taillights glowing faintly. That butthead.

"I told him I needed a ride, too, but we couldn't all three fit on that motorcycle."

The way she said "motorcycle" made it sound like a sin, just as I knew she would. I pretended I hadn't heard her passive-aggressive reprimand. As I gathered my things and prepared myself for a chat-filled ride home, I realized she looked ready to pounce. That obscene smile never faltered. "Wait a minute. Did you just say you needed a ride home, too?"

"Yes siree bob."

"Is…is Meghan going to…"

"No, I'd like a ride home from you, please."

I was stumped. "Didn't I tell you I wouldn't have a car tonight?"

Against the laws of physics, her painted lips spread even wider. "You do now."

"Okay, you got me." I somehow returned her smile and calmed my building irritation. I just wanted to go home. Spare me the riddles.

"Oh, Meg," she giggled and grabbed my hand like a schoolgirl. "Just come outside and you'll see."

The warm, moist air felt good after a dried out day of air-conditioning and I sucked it in to brace myself for whatever lay in wait. As soon as we were in the parking lot, she let go and waved her arms wide.

"Ta-da!"

I looked around, still confused. Did she get Jo to let me use the car after all or something? "Uh…"

"What do you think, do you like it?"

"Like it?"

She jumped up and down, looking from me to a parked car I didn't recognize.

"I know Tristan likes Cherokees, but the Renegade has a better safety rating." She grabbed my upper arm and pumped it so hard I knew I'd have bruises later. "It's so cute, isn't it?"

"Oh!" Comprehension crystallized in front of my eyes as I stared at a shiny, new, red Jeep Renegade. "Wow. He'll love it. Yeah."

"Meg Sweetheart, it's for both of you," she said, her voice climbing an octave with the rush. "It's an early wedding present. I thought red might be a little more unisex."

I focused on the pink lipstick, struck dumb.

"Well, what do you think?"

"Me?" I stammered. "Present?"

"Yes! You. Of course, you. Both of you."

I looked at the car. Back at her. "You can't give me a car, Mrs. Jameson."

"I sure can and I just did." She put her hands on her hips, a crease forming between her brows. "You're gonna hurt my feelings in a minute."

"No! I don't mean it's not beautiful, Mrs. Jameson—"

"Stephanie."

"I'm sorry—Stephanie. I…I…it's just," I started, completely freaked out but sensing her rising temper. Shit, what could I say? She couldn't give me a car. It was absurd. "It's just such an expensive gift. My goodness. I could never repay you."

Her shoulders relaxed and she cocked her head. "Well, you don't repay gifts, honey."

I just stood there, still goggling.

"Look, you and Tristan will need a trustworthy vehicle. How are you going to get to Florida for school? On a Greyhound bus? The Cherokee was totaled and we got plenty back from the insurance policy."

"That's good, I guess. So, then it's Tristan's car."

She frowned. "If you're going to be married, dear, you're going to share a lot more than cars."

Oops. It was *dear*, now. Did she suspect my little white lie, my dirty secret? I had to get it together, pronto. "You're right. You're right. I'm sorry." *Yes, let's pretend there's going to be a wedding.* "This is new territory for me, and you're the expert."

"You're darn tootin'.". She shoved me playfully. "Twenty thousand years of marriage sure does make you an expert."

"Guess it does."

"Well, what are you waitin' for," she jingled the keys in front of my face, "gimme a ride Mrs. Tristan Jameson, to be."

I choked on that. I hate it when people call a man's wife Mrs. Insert Man's Name Here. So, not only is a woman supposed to lose her last name, but her entire identity, too? I accepted the keys and bit my tongue.

When we left the parking lot, I headed towards my own home. Tiger Mom stopped me right away. "No, no, no. You take me home. I have my own car, honey."

"Are you sure? Tristan won't be home until Saturday morning." In two days, sixteen hours and—I checked the clock—eight minutes. Approximately.

"Well, you can keep it at your place until you pick him up."

That was a surprise. Even I was worried about parking a brand new jeep in *my* neighborhood overnight. "Are you sure?"

"Sure, silly goose." I heard the strain in her voice. She was concerned, too. "Anyway, you can't go pick him up in that old clunker."

Watch it, lady. I turned the car around anyway and headed to her place, glad she didn't get to check out my hovel after all.

I tried to pay attention enough to respond with chatty fill-ins during the drive home from hell. I even let her comment slide about "needing a safe vehicle" when Tristan and I "start a family." My brain was still trying to comprehend the fact that I was the co-owner of a new car (a nice one), and that I was actually allowed to pick Tristan up from his trip by myself. Of course, Tiger Mom had found a way to insert herself into our reunion with the new jeep. Still, it was hard not to obsessively run the future moment over and over in my mind. Tristan coming home was a much prettier picture than the one his mother painted for me: wedding invitations, wedding dress alterations, wedding vows, wedding classes—we finally hit a conversational snag that tripped me up.

"Wait, what?"

"Wednesday night would be the best. I thought it would be easier if I just went ahead and scheduled them with Father Ringold."

"Wedding classes?"

Stephanie Jameson had the grace to look abashed. "Just two classes. Pre Cana is what it's called."

I fixed my dumbfounded stare straight ahead, but I couldn't hide the disdain in my voice. "I have to become Catholic?"

A sarcastic chortle on other side of the car. "I assure you, there's a lot more to 'becoming Catholic' than that, Meg Dear."

Dear, again. "Then what is it?"

"It's just a consultation."

"A consultation?" Flames buffeted my cheeks. I was so tired of not being good enough for people in this town. They'd just love me at Tristan's church. I couldn't wait to be under the microscope. Luckily, we were already on their street and I could get Tiger Mom out of the car before I lost it.

"All couples have to go through it, before being wed in the Church—whether you're Catholic or not."

I pulled up to their house, but didn't turn into the driveway. Shifting into park, I twisted to look at her, one elbow on the steering wheel. "But what exactly is 'it'?"

"Calm down," she patted my knee, "it's a good thing. Pre Cana is only to help prepare you for your life together. Make sure you're ready."

The irony was too much. I wasn't ready. All I could do was shake my head as she grabbed her purse.

"I'll bet some private time with Father Ringold would be a good thing, too."

That was her last slap before she hopped out, closed the door, and skipped up the driveway.

I sat there, stunned. Why did my new car feel more like a prison than a present? If it was mine, though, at least I could peel out. I hated myself for waiting until Tiger Mom was out of earshot to do so.

"Private time?" I said through gritted teeth. My tires squealed at every corner on the way out of Northern Estates. "Yes, I think I little private time would be great. How about right now, Father Ringold?"

chapter forty-one

St. James was the oldest church in Shirley County, built in the 1800's. I looked it up online right after "we" decided to hold the wedding there. I sat in the shady, tree-lined parking lot as the sun set and I couldn't help but admire the old building. It was mostly weathered stone and brick on the bottom, with whitewashed wood towards the steepled roof. It didn't look like a cathedral, but it was. What really set it apart from most of the churches in Shirley was all the stained glass. Wide panels of fragmented green, red, blue and yellow reached from ground to rooftop on either side of the front doors. I couldn't tell what the figures actually were from my distance, but the flickering light inside made them dance to the music seeping into the deepening night outside.

Shadows melted into gray and then black. The multicolored windows glowed brighter, and still I sat and waited. Church wasn't all a mystery to me—I remembered textbooks crammed with images of the virgin, the crucifixion, a million martyrs, famous altars, illuminated manuscripts. My notebooks were scrawled with all their names, dates, and purposes. So with the help of three years of Humanities in high school (plus chanting and organ music), I guessed that I had arrived during Vespers.

Waiting cooled my temper. I thought again of forgetting the whole thing and getting home to that hot shower I had been craving, but then the music stopped and the doors opened. Only a handful of people trickled out, mostly old folks. The majority of churchgoers in Shirley were Baptist and likely at some big Wednesday night warehouse church bash.

I shut the car door gently as I got out, afraid to make too much noise in the hush that had fallen. Incense tickled my nose as I approached the front doors.

"Mmmm. Neat."

It was actually kind of cool that Tristan attended St. James. It somehow seemed unique and special. His quiet confidence about religion matched perfectly with the atmosphere of his church. The doors were open wide and welcoming. I stepped inside, my sandals clicking on Mexican tiles.

"Evening," murmured an elderly woman walking stiffly towards the exit.

"Good evening." I went to hold the door for her, then remembered it was propped that way already.

"Oh, there's the fire," I whispered. There were candles behind the stained glass windows and I went to investigate. On either side of the doors, half a dozen small wooden tiers held white votive candles. Most of them were lit, only a few smoking.

"Huh." I wondered what each had been lit for. A prayer? A loved one? Praise?

"Meg Shannon."

His voice was so soft and kind that I didn't jump. I think I expected it.

"Hello. Father Ringold?"

"Lovely to finally meet you." He put out his hand and I accepted it. An impish thought of going on one knee to kiss his ring flitted through my mind, but he had a firm, solid grip and he pulled me to him in an embrace.

"Um. How did you know who I was?" My voice was muffled against his shoulder. He was a bear of a man, in total discrepancy to his almost melodic, rather high-pitched voice. The combination put me off my guard.

"Tristan has told me a lot about you." His rosy cheeks reminded me of Santa Claus.

"He has?"

"Oh yes, he's been quite loquacious."

"Er...I can't imagine what he would've told you." I cringed at the thought. "In confession or..."

The big man threw his head back in a belly laugh. "That's not what I meant, Meg."

I produced a nervous chuckle and tried to ignore the *bowl full of jelly* song in my head. "Well. Good."

"And confession is strictly confidential," he said, his voice singing with amusement. "We often talk outside of the booth, I've known Tristan since he was a baby."

"Really?" I pictured baby Tristan in a lacy white communion dress, Father Ringold sprinkling holy water on his head.

"I've been hoping to make your acquaintance for months, but I didn't want to just walk up and hug you on the street. Thought that might be a bit scary for you."

"Me, scared? Pshaw. I thought you said Tristan told you about me."

"Indeed he has, indeed he has." He nodded toward the candles. "I hope I haven't interrupted you."

I looked at the candles and back at him, alarmed. I wasn't supposed to be praying there, was I? "I was just thinking. Deep in thought, actually."

"Perfect for tonight."

"Is it?"

"Our Wednesday service is quite contemplative."

"What a coincidence," I turned back to the tiny fluttering flames. "I've got a lot to contemplate right now."

Father Ringold was quiet for a moment. "Yes, I know," he said so softly I barely heard him.

His expression was apologetic when I looked at him again. Did everyone know everything about me? I snapped, "Do you know I didn't actually say yes then?"

All the priest offered was a gentle smile. Sad, almost.

I knew that he knew, his expression said it all. There was no doubt Tristan had confessed *that*. And probably mentioned the rumors that haunted me wherever I went. A priest probably thought marriage was required, especially before sex, and that Tristan was rescuing me from my jaded past. All of a sudden wished I could leave, but Father Ringold was blocking the door. Trapped again, my heart was a panicked bird in it's cage.

He moved aside and sat on a nearby pew. "To be a little scared is completely natural, Meg. There are no judgements here."

That was the last thing I expected to hear. Wasn't that what church was for—judgments, commandments, guilt and all that?

"I'm not sure how much you've heard about me, Father. But Shirley County wouldn't be Shirley County without judgements. You know Tristan, but you don't know me."

His face was full of compassion when he said, "My love for you is as great as my love for Tristan. I know that."

I snorted. "How could that be? We just met."

"You are a unique human being, a gift from God. You are precious and priceless, as are we all."

Sounded like bologna to me. "Well, at least my price seems to be going up. Mrs. Jameson just bought me a car. Now, why does it feel like she's trying to buy *me*?"

"Does it?"

"Yes. It feels like she owns me now."

He held up his palms, "I can't speak to Stephanie's actions," then pinched the bridge of his nose. I wondered how many of Tiger Mom's cubs had gone to him with similar complaints through the years. "But what you and Tristan are offering each other cannot be bought or sold.

It's the most intimate connection two people can share, to bind their lives together."

"Bind my life? That's a little crazy isn't it? Sounds like something you'd do over a Ouija Board." I was trying to make a joke out of it, but neither of us laughed. "Sorry, I'm just a little freaked here."

"Why do you feel freaked?"

"Because I love him but I'm not ready for this and if I don't marry him he'll stop loving me." There, it was out. I watched my feet, begging him to say something and save me from the volcano my mouth had become.

"Have a little faith in Tristan."

I looked up. "Faith? Are you trying to convert me?"

He raised his hands in surrender, "You got me," then thrust them towards me as if I would handcuff him. He was hard to take seriously. And harder not to like.

"I'll let you off this time, I guess."

He stood, suddenly solemn. "May I show you something?"

"…I guess."

He motioned for me to follow him down the aisle and towards the altar.

I held back, glanced at the exit. "I'm not at all religious."

"Please." He extended his hand further.

"Why not," I groaned and fell in behind him. "I don't have to confess anything, do I?"

"No, Meg." When we reached the altar, he stepped behind it and started thumbing through a massive bible spread out on top. "I'd like for you to read something. Tristan told me you love to read."

"Yeah, not the bible."

"Think of it as poetry. I won't even name the verse, so it won't feel too religious for you."

"Ugh. Okay…" Figuring I was about to read about fire and brimstone and how I'd go to hell if I kept screwing my boyfriend without being married, I mounted the two steps and stood behind the altar.

He kept one hand covering the title of the verse, and pointed an index finger at a line of text. "Right here."

I cleared my throat and read aloud, "Love is patient, love is kind. It is not jealous, is not pompous, it is not inflated, it is not rude, it does not seek its own interests, it is not quick-tempered, it does not brood over injury, it does not rejoice over wrongdoing but rejoices with the truth. It bears all things, believes all things, hopes all things, endures all things." I looked up at Father Ringold, a weird tingle creeping up my spine.

"Keep going."

I finished, "Love never fails."

"And this is my favorite part," he said, moving his finger down a few lines.

My vision was wet and blurry, but I found the spot with my own finger and read, "So faith, hope, love remain, these three; but the greatest of these is love."

"Love, Meg."

I blinked at the darkened stained glass windows, the candles dancing in shadow on either side. "You think our love is that kind of love? Me and Tristan's?"

"My child," Father Ringold placed his hand over his heart in reverence, "that's the only kind of love there is."

chapter forty-two

I had only been parked for fifteen minutes, but I was already sweating. The jeep was running, the air-conditioner on. That was the only kind of cool I could claim, though. I glanced around the parking lot of Andrew Jackson High, begging everyone waiting there as well to ignore my presence. I had already been bombarded by three mothers, two dads, and one pimple-face pre-teen, each wanting to meet the shiny new red Jeep Renegade in Shirley.

Worse than the spectators: I wasn't entirely sure I would be welcomed in the pick-up parade when Tristan got off the bus. What if he hopped down those steps, chatting and laughing with his friends, and then his face fell when he saw me waiting there? What if he got off the bus, arm in arm with Ashley?

"No. Stop it, you idiot." I couldn't think that way. I reminded myself that I was better than that. Love is not jealous. Love does not brood over injury. Love never fails. As much as I hated it, that bible verse—or, my favorite parts anyway—had become a sort of personal mantra over the last two days. My life jacket on the Titanic. I was glad I didn't know the name of the verse, or I'd be an official bible beater.

Yet, I was beginning to suspect that I could be better than a person who worries and cries and gives herself an ulcer over what might or might not be. I deserved more than those poisonous thoughts eating away at my brain. Whether I ended up with Tristan or not, I would still be me. A unique human being, precious and priceless. Sure, it was a priest's line, but I liked it. Wherever you go, there you are. And I love who I am.

Tristan loved me—the real me—too. I hoped. Still.

On our first night together he'd said it: *"So beautiful. Deep down."*

I gnawed on a fingernail.

Okay, so it still mattered. I did care. I did know what I wanted, even if I sometimes had a hard time saying it when it mattered most. It would kill me if we broke up.

I switched on the satellite radio for distraction.

"You got me brainwashed
You got me so lost
You got me fucked up
Like you

You got me drugged up
You got me undone..."

Nope, that didn't help.

I switched it back off. I avoided eye contact with someone checking out the jeep. I flipped the visor down and checked my eye make-up. I fished around in my purse for gum. I didn't find any. I made a note on my cell phone to buy some gum.

Suddenly, someone crossed in front of me, waving and jogging in the other direction. A dirty silver bus was rolling through the parking lot.

"Thank god."

I frantically scanned the windows, but the tinting was too dark and the sunlight too glaring for me to make out anything inside. People got out of cars and followed the bus.

Eager beavers.

It would probably be a while until everyone unloaded, and Tristan could be the last person off. I wondered whether or not I should get out a book and wait in the car.

Screw that!

I knew what I wanted and everyone could know it. Tristan should know it. I left the door ajar, threw the keys in the seat and went for it. I was still running as the bus rolled to a stop. Up close, I could see faces in the windows. Laughing. I didn't care. Where was Tristan?

As soon as the bus settled, the doors slid open.

"...alright, alright, kid. Keep your shirt on," the driver was muttering.

Tristan shoved through.

"Tristan."

He was more beautiful than I remembered, unwashed and unshaven, his deeply tanned skin setting off his glowing blue eyes. Frustration drained from his face when those eyes found mine. A blinding smile.

"Mekaela."

I vaulted into his arms, and he was as solid as I remembered. Solid and real. "Oh my god, I missed you."

We melted into each other, hungry lips and greedy hands. I clawed his shoulders. His fingers were in my hair. My calf wrapped around his thigh. His hips strained against mine. A catcall sounded from the bus. He deepened the kiss and I reacted with similar force. Tongues twined and fingers bruised, and I couldn't care less.

"Don't ever leave me again."

"Never."

Full-on cheering erupted and I broke away to see our classmates pouring from the bus, flowing around us jeering. One of Tristan's friends shifted his duffel bag to whack him in the back as he passed. "Get a room, dude."

Tristan kept his eyes on me.

"All better now, bro?" A beefy hand clapped him on the shoulder and Will Bartlett ambled past.

"Yeah," Tristan murmured.

"Seriously, he was horrible all week, girlfriend," a female complained, hanging on Will's arm.

My mouth fell open. Shelly?

She turned back to smile at me. "Thank God you showed up to get him."

I raised an eyebrow at Tristan in question, but he looked like he was drugged. No answers there. And who in hell cared? I buried my head against his chest and breathed in deep. "I love you, Tristan."

"I love you, Mekaela."

A voice echoed in mocking falsetto, "I love you, Mekaela."

"Leave 'em alone, they're so sweet," a girl I didn't recognize said in passing.

Another chimed in, "Yeah, where's my ring, you asshole," and slapped a guy on the back of his head.

A cloud crossed over Tristan's features then. I hurried to make it disappear, rising on tiptoe to whisper in his ear, "Yes."

"What?"

"Yes, yes, yes!"

Suddenly, the breath was squeezed out of me and I was airborne, my feet dangling. He spun me in an arc, one sandal flying off.

"Yes?".

I nodded, my smile pinching and tears springing. "Yes."

He whirled me around again and I screamed and laughed like a kid, hair everywhere.

"She said yes!" he hollered and was answered with an ear-piercing whistle. "You make me the happiest person alive, baby."

"Uh-uh." I shook my head and pushed my crazy hair out of my face.

"That can't be, 'cause I'm the happiest person alive."

"You are?"

"I am now," I said and smothered him with another kiss.

I felt someone pound Tristan's back, "Seriously, dude. Room." Tristan flicked him off.

"He does have a point," he said between our mouths. "Let's get outta here."

"Actually, you're in for a surprise, my love."

♦

Tristan wasn't as surprised by the new jeep as I was. I supposed he was more used to getting expensive presents from pushy mothers. He merely lifted a shoulder at the color and mentioned how fast the purchase happened, then informed me that he would drive. The inevitable seat belt warning delivered, he wiggled his eyebrows over his sunglasses. "You really wanna get a room or just park in the closest shady spot?"

My belly tightened at the thought, but I had to shake my head no. "Neither, sorry."

"What?"

"We're expected home immediately after pick-up. Your mom's planning something," I twirled my finger in the air, "special."

He ripped off his shades and pitched his voice in annoyance, "You're kidding me."

"Nope."

"I've been jerkin' off for over a week, come on."

"Sorry." I threw my hands up. "Your mom'll be pissed as hell if we're late."

"Who cares?"

I exhaled sharply. "I care."

"Since when?"

"Look. I'd love to get it on, trust me. But your mother is expecting us." He let his head fall back against the headrest and groaned.

"Let's just get it over with." I faced forward and crossed my arms over my chest. How did his mother screw up our longed for reunion when she wasn't even present? I had my boyfriend back and right away I had to give him to her.

"Fine," Tristan snapped and started the engine.

"Fine."

As soon as we were on the road, his hand snuck over and squeezed my thigh. "Who are you and what did you do with Mekaela?"

I jerked my head around to deliver a nasty retort, but he was smiling too sweetly. I rolled my eyes, but couldn't help returning the affection.

"I really missed you," he said, his eyes crinkled at the corners the way I loved.

"I missed you, too." I leaned over and kissed his nose, then collapsed against the seat with his hand in both of mine. "So, tell me about Cancun."

The rest of the drive was relaxed, almost blissful, as Tristan told me stories about Mayan temples, zip line adventures, parasailing, and sunburns. He tactfully left out tales of drunken nights and hung over mornings, but I knew there had probably been plenty of those and I teased him about the holes in his report. He assured me there were enough chaperones to go around. I wasn't really concerned. I was just happy to gaze at his beautiful profile and listen. I pressed kisses into his hand and ran my fingers through his hair periodically. I must have looked like a lovesick puppy dog.

He grabbed my hand as it went to his hair yet again, kissed it, and held it against his chest. "So, what did I miss while I was gone?"

"Nothing, believe me."

"I doubt that. You musta taken at least a few showers while I was gone, gotten undressed once or twice."

I giggled, "You creep."

"All the excitement I need. I definitely missed out."

"Oh yeah, being measured for a wedding dress and talking to priests is so exciting."

"That stuff already?" His forehead furrowed in concern.

"That stuff already."

"Ouch. Like…a lot of that stuff?"

I chuckled and patted his thigh. "You'll see."

When we pulled into his driveway, there were balloons tied to the mailbox. "Welcome home," Tristan read under his breath. He glanced at me, then away, anxiety etched all over him. "You hate this shit, I'm sorry."

"It's fine," I lied, fluffing my hair in the rearview mirror.

He pursed his lips.

"Really." I nodded towards the front door, at plenty of bleached blonde curls and pink. Lots of pink. "Here she comes."

"So she does."

Tiger Mom was on us in seconds. "Tristan, you're home," she said, but it was muffled through the glass.

"You're supposed to protect me from all this," he muttered, then opened his door. "Mom, hey."

"Et tu, Brute," I said. "You have no idea."

Plastering on my best fake smile, I prepared to enter another uncomfortable Jameson party. My charade vanished on the threshold when I saw my mom's car parked down the street. "Oh, shit."

Tristan looked back, but could only mutely question my sudden dread through his mother's constant stream of chatter.

I shook my head. *It's fine.*

But it wasn't. I hadn't even mentioned Tristan's proposal to my mom yet, and apparently she had to hear it through the grapevine. The Stephanie Jameson grapevine. I was in for it, no doubt about it.

"You'll have to upload all your cellphone shots so I can print them out and make a photo album of the trip," Tiger Mom was saying.

"Sure, Mom. I will."

I fell in behind Tristan as we entered the main room, hoping to make myself invisible while I cased the place. My littlest sister Tessa was gazing up at Amanda and one of her friends, gossiping off to the side. They were ignoring her and she was modeling their stances and expressions with chilling accuracy. Charlie was intently coloring at the dining room table, his short legs swinging underneath in the tall chair. Tristan's brother Brandon was observing over his shoulder, just as quietly. Jo was stuffing her face at a buffet table by the back door. No Piper. That didn't bode well; I hadn't mentioned the wedding to Piper either and she had drawn herself in wedding dresses since she was able to hold a crayon.

And then I locked eyes with my mom. She was talking to Tristan's dad, her face an emotionless mask. Her eyes slid away from mine without a hint of recognition. "Double shit."

Tristan found my hand. "Hey Mom, let me go put my bag down—"

"There he is," Sheriff Jameson bellowed, ambling over with his arms outspread.

My mom slipped away.

"Tistan!" Tessa shouted, then amended her joy when she caught Amanda's scowl.

"Yay, you're back," Amanda said with an ironic half-smile.

Her fair-haired friend blushed from head to toe, wiggled her fingers. "Hi, Tristan."

"Hey, Dad." Tristan held on to my hand while he accepted several hearty thumps on his back. "I feel like I kinda need to change clothes real fast," he said, scrubbing his chin, "and maybe wash up some. Mekaela, come with me."

"Oh, no you don't." Tiger Mom tugged on my other hand. "I need Meg to help me in the kitchen."

Great. Of all times to achieve the much sought after status of kitchen assistant. I looked at Tristan helplessly. His grip tightened and a muscle in his jaw popped.

"You go get washed up," his mother tickled a rib and he jerked away, dropped my hand, "you're stinky." She wrinkled her nose at me and giggled.

What could I do but reciprocate? My stomach felt so queasy I thought I might need a bathroom. I was an automaton, trying to just get through the moment. Tristan's face darkened and he stalked down the hallway to his bedroom without another word.

"Shoo," Tiger Mom said to his back. "Okay, all the food is already made. I just need your help assembling, Meg Sweetheart. Amanda is terrible at that."

I waved at Charlie as she hauled me past him, off to the kitchen. No sign of my mom.

"I like to lay down a blanket of lettuce—make sure you use the greenest, prettiest pieces—under the sandwiches…"

Tiger Mom pointed to sliver platters, tubs of prepared finger foods, cheeses, fruits, dips, and doilies, sweetly commanding and correcting. I monitored the party over the bar dividing the kitchen and living room while I worked. Tristan appeared to be deep in conversation with his dad and Jo, but I wasn't fooled. His arms were crossed over his chest, tense, and he was nodding in the way I knew meant he wasn't hearing a word. His eyes searched for mine and when they found me, he smiled. My pulse rocketed and my thighs went up in flames. Could anyone else feel that electricity between us? It was like a physical thing.

"Oh, those need to be soaked in the lemon water first, honey."

"Huh? Oh, I'm sorry."

"So they don't turn brown." Tiger Mom scooped up the apple slices I had arranged on some lettuce and tossed them in a bowl next to the sink. "Just for a sec, so they stay crisp."

"Okay…" When I looked again, Tristan was gone.

"I'll be right back, you just finish that last apple. I need to get something from the garage. Don't forget the fruit dip," she called over her shoulder as she bustled out.

I let my shoulders slump and allowed myself a slow, steadying breath.

"Hey." A deep whisper tickled my ear and an arm encircled my waist.

I gasped and then chuckled, leaned back into Tristan's embrace. He hadn't washed up after all and I was glad. "You know, you shouldn't scare a girl wielding a chef's knife."

"You're sexy with an apron on."

"Gross. Your mom insisted."

"It's hot. I keep imagining you in nothing but the apron."

"Really? That's kinda kinky."

"Mmmm," he nuzzled my ear.

"Have you seen *my* mom? Is she still here?" I was nervous that she hadn't come back to the kitchen to help, too.

"Let's stop thinking about our moms." He trailed kisses down my neck. "I wish—"

"Oh, you two," Tiger Mom's falsetto tore through my libido.

I stiffened and pushed Tristan's hands away. "Sorry."

"Lovebirds," she clucked and aimed a wooden spoon at Tristan's rear-end. "Out, Mister Man."

"Come on, Mom. Get Amanda to help you." He looked to me for aid, but I was keeping mum. I pursed my lips and shook my head so only he could see and he narrowed his eyes at me. "Where's Liza?"

"She couldn't make it. Now, go."

Tristan put his hands on his hips and widened his stance, as if he were ready to argue. I gritted my teeth and glared. *Don't rock the boat.*

"Fine." He slouched back into the living room.

By the time we cleared all the empty appetizer plates from the table and replaced them with main course platters, my stomach was really beginning to growl. Another cursory search for my mom made my insides turn liquid again, though, and I winced as Jo stuffed a whole mini quiche into her mouth.

"Where's Piper?" I asked, afraid of the answer.

"She's super pissed at you," Jo said around her food. "Doubt she'll talk to you for a while."

I groaned. "Really?"

"Lucky you."

"Why didn't you mention it to her? Or mom?"

Jo's blank expression told me she hadn't given my possible engagement another thought after I had first mentioned it at the garage. "Why didn't *you?*"

"Well." That was tough to answer, even to myself. "Have you seen Mom?"

Jo dove into the cucumber and rye sandwiches. "Think she went outside to smoke a cigarette with Brandon."

"Good, at least we can do this outside." I drew in a deep breath and turned towards the sliding glass door that led to the back yard. "Might as well get it over with."

"Get what over with?"

"Oh, Jo…"

The afternoon had turned sticky and oppressive, stepping outside as refreshing as stepping into a sauna. The pool deck was bleached in glaring sunlight and pain shot to the back of my skull as I peered around.

"I need to go make a phone call. Excuse me," said a masculine voice behind me.

I turned around to see them sitting in the shade of an awning.

"Sure, go ahead. Thanks for the conversation," my mom said to Brandon, shading her eyes as he stood to go.

"Hello, Meg. Good to see you again." He squeezed my shoulder as he walked past.

I stood sweating and shifting, noonday sun beating down on the top of my head.

"I'm not sure if I can explain how I feel right now, Mekaela."

My mom hadn't called me that since I was seven-years-old, when she caught me dancing in a bucket of motor oil in my new cowboy boots.

"Mom, I'm so sorry."

"Sorry for what?" Her voice was deceptively quiet. "Sorry for not bothering to tell me you're getting married, or sorry for throwing your life away just when it's about to take off?"

I watched my toes, wriggling in my sandals. "I'm not throwing my life—"

"Married at eighteen-years-old. Is that really the best you can do?"

"No—"

"And what do you think comes next, huh? Haven't you done enough baby sitting? Haven't you learned anything from my mistakes?"

I finally met her gaze and it was blazing. It took all the heat out of my response, "Just because I'm married doesn't mean I'll be a baby factory."

She snorted derisively at my lack of conviction and I glanced away. "I thought I taught you to shoot for the stars, not the altar. Looks like you're falling short of one and stumbling towards the other."

"I'm still going to college. We both are."

"Only one person can climb a ladder at a time, Mekaela."

I twisted my fingers together. It felt stupid to say, but I was going to say it anyway: "Maybe Tristan will keep the ladder steady for me."

She was silent for a beat. "And that's what you need now? I raised you to be independent."

I looked at her. "Independence can be pretty lonely, Mom. Tristan isn't what I need, he's who I deserve."

Seconds ticked by while we stared at each other. I jumped at an apologetic knock on the glass and turned to see Tristan's questioning frown at the door. I nodded and he eased it open to lean his head out.

"Sorry to interrupt, ladies."

"It's okay." I could've fallen on my knees in gratitude for the interruption.

"There's uh…some cake my mom wants us to cut. A wedding cake sample or something…" he trailed off.

My mom was already gathering her purse. "Well, I'll leave you to it."

She left by the back gate.

chapter forty-three

I was pacing. My stockings were so silky that my satin shoes kept slipping off, regardless of the elastic strap.

I was melting. Cassie had caked on way too much makeup, insisting that my skin should look as flawless as porcelain in the professional photos that I'll show my grandchildren.

I was cussing. Liza still hadn't gotten back with the champagne I requested hours ago. Tiger Mom had left some cooling on ice in the bridal suite, but it was non-alcoholic. What was the point in that?

I was stooping. The "bridal suite" at St. James was little more than an outhouse at the back of the property. An outhouse for short people. It might have been quaint in a cooler season, but August turned the badly insulated, poorly air-conditioned little cabin into a hellhole.

I looked out the window in search of Liza once again, wondering whether the bride was supposed to feel honored or sequestered.

Not that I minded exile. I had Cassie policing the pathway to my steamy prison, ensuring that no one bothered me for at least half an hour. I couldn't take it after a drunken Father Ringold had barged in and seen me practically naked, the flower girl accidentally popped off one of my dress buttons, Tiger Mom replaced my bacon croissant with a dry bagel, and Piper started crying for the fourth time that morning. When my mom handed me a blue, lace handkerchief from her own wedding I nearly burst into tears myself. Then Cassie screamed at me for daring to smudge my eye make-up.

It was understood that the bride needed a moment to reflect on the blessed occasion. Alone.

Actually, I was about to have a panic attack.

There was a light knock on the door.

"What?"

Liza wouldn't have knocked. I had just seen Cassie standing guard outside. Who slipped by?

The door creaked open, just a crack, and my favorite voice whispered, "Mekaela…"

"Tristan?" I hurried over to the door to hold it closed. "You're not supposed to see me before the wedding. Everyone will freak out. It's bad luck."

"Gimme a break, Mekaela. You don't really believe that, do you?"

I dropped my hands, considering for a minute. "No."

"Then open up."

"Oh, fine." Who cared, I just wanted to see him. It felt like years since I had, with all the parties, showers, dinners and rehearsals going on. I could've sworn Tiger Mom put all her effort into keeping us apart for the last month. The woman had to own a crystal ball or a voodoo doll of me or something. "Come on in."

"Actually, I'm gettin' you," he grabbed my wrist and tugged as soon as the door was open, "the hell outta here."

I stumbled onto the soft grass and blinked up at him in the sunlight. "Huh?"

"I just want my girlfriend back." He planted a swift kiss on my glossy lips, then locked his fingers with mine. "Let's go."

"Tristan, are you insane? We've got about a hundred people waiting in that church to see us married." I leaned my weight the other way.

"Do I have to throw you over my shoulder? Because I will." His eyes glittered with excitement, his smile mischievous.

I gawked at him. "You wouldn't dare."

"I would."

Yes! My heart hammered. I made a few hesitant steps in his direction. "Where are we going?"

"See that limo over there?" He nodded towards a white stretch limousine, partially hidden across a small field in the opposite direction from the church. He picked up his pace and tightened his grip on my hand.

"Wait! Tristan, wait," I hissed.

He kept moving but looked over his shoulder, shook his head in exasperation. "Come on, Mekaela. Come with me, please. Forget all this crap. We don't need it. We never did."

"Just stop." I planted my feet and he finally did.

"Please. This isn't you, and I want you back." He took my face in his hands. "I love you, Mekaela."

"I love you, too. I just need to take off these damn shoes."

His pained frown split into a gorgeous smile. His home run smile.

I ripped off the prissy slippers and tossed them over my shoulder. "Okay, let's go."

Hands clenched together, we hauled ass across the field. My stockings ran and my hair tumbled out of the bobby pins.

"Hey," Cassie called behind us. "What are you doing?"

Tristan and I locked eyes.

"Go! Go, go, go," I screeched, laughing wildly. I clutched at a stitch in my side and slowed.

"Come here." Tristan scooped me up and dashed the last few yards to the limo with me bouncing against his chest.

A tall, dark-skinned man as big as a bouncer opened the door and waved us in like a traffic cop.

"Barney!" I squealed. "It's you!"

"Can you believe it?" Tristan panted. "I knew it was fate when I saw him."

Both of us dissolved into hilarity as we tumbled inside the cabin and Barney slammed the door behind us. We started rolling within seconds and I fell back against the floor, tears streaming down my cheeks.

"God, that was a rush," I shouted, still catching my breath through relentless laughter.

"There you are." Tristan planted a wet, sloppy kiss on my mouth. "There's my Mekaela. Welcome back, beautiful."

He crawled to the bench and tapped on the divider window.

The window slid down, motor whirring. "Where to, sir?"

Sir, indeed. "I love you, Barney," I called from the floor.

Tristan flashed his annoyance. "Hey, now."

"Oh, be quiet." I slapped his cute little butt. "Yes, where to, sir?"

He raised an eyebrow, "You're the only one who knows the way, baby."

"Oh, that's right," I breathed and pressed my fingers to my lips. "Ingenious."

Our honeymoon suite was the one thing I insisted on planning, and I hadn't divulged the location even to Tristan. It was the one thing I could control, and the one place I wanted to be on my wedding night. There was a swanky lodge across the gorge, about twenty minutes south of Shirley Valley. It was called The Meadows. That place was a legendary lap of luxury when I was a kid. Rich people lounged there and were catered to like royalty. I imagined it to be enchanted by fairies when I was little because of the infamous and endless gardens surrounding the resort.

When I looked into it, it was much less expensive than I thought it would be. Since I wasn't really paying for much of the actual wedding (the one perk of having your wedding planned by a control freak mother-in-law), I was able to save up enough for the honeymoon suite in a couple of months. I kept the destination a complete secret, scared to death that if I didn't, Tiger Mom might just show up there for breakfast the next morning.

Since we didn't plan on a honeymoon vacation more involved than driving to Florida and stopping at some beach motel along the way, Tristan and I were already packed and ready for school. I had driven the jeep to The Meadows the previous evening—loaded to the hilt and towing a trailer packed with graduation gifts, wedding gifts, two wardrobes and all our college supplies—and then I caught a cab home. It was expensive, but my secret remained safe. The perfect getaway.

"So…where to, ma'am?" Tristan teased.

"If I told you, I'd have to kill you." I pointed to the seats on the far side of the cabin.

Tristan crawled on all fours, then collapsed on the opposite bench. He put his feet up on the sideboard and plugged his ears, while I whispered our destination to Barney. Barney grunted and nodded, then I turned back to my outrageously sexy boyfriend. Boyfriend. I loved the word. His feet were perched right next to the neck of a bottle, sticking out of an ice bucket.

"My goodness, is that my champagne? How did she know?"

Tristan cocked his head and let a lazy smile spread across his lips. "Liza strikes again."

♠

"Hurry up, room service stops running soon and I'm starving."

Tristan's voice echoed in the enormous bathroom, "Just order whatever."

"Not for our non-honeymoon dinner, no way." I closed the door on billowing steam and padded through the suite. I knew what I craved next, and I wasn't just hungry for food.

I slid open the patio door and stepped onto cool, smooth cobblestones. We had a private alcove that looked out over the gardens, complete with two chairs and a table you might find in the White Rabbit's house in Alice in Wonderland. Hanging plants, flowers in urns, and vines climbing trestles were everywhere. I was dying to check it out since we arrived but we were busy making up for lost time, consummating our non-marriage.

"So cute," I said, sitting down on a white wrought iron stool. "Maybe we can have dinner out here."

It was so secluded. So quiet. So exactly as I hoped it would be. We'd kept our cellphones off and the "Do Not Disturb" tag on all day.

"Feels like we're the only two people in the world." I admired my surroundings, completely contented. Then I saw the stars. "Except for you, Sagittarius."

I wandered into a tiny meadow gazing upwards. The grass tickled my feet, nighttime cool but not yet dewy. Eucalyptus wafted out of our suite and Tristan's arms slipped around me. "You found the robes, too."

"Cozy, huh?" I pointed to the sky, "The Archer."

"That a constellation," he murmured against the back of my neck.

"Uh huh. Some legends say that Sagittarius was placed in the heavens to guide the Argonauts in their travels. It's perfect."

"How so?"

"Because look at what we have ahead of us." I snuggled in closer to him, pulled his arms around tighter. "I'll miss the stars."

"I'll find you some more."

"New stars?" I glanced back, an eyebrow raised.

"Trust me."

Trust. I did trust him. Faith, hope, and love. I had all of those, too.

I breathed in the rich fragrance of the gardens I had always wanted to see, felt the warmth of the man I hadn't believed I could truly have. I knew the future would be just as challenging as the past—what was high school bullshit compared the real world? But I was ready for it. Somehow more whole than I was before.

"*ReeeORK!*"

We froze. Tristan held still as a statue and I held my breath.

"*ReeeORK. ReeORK. ReeeORK!*"

Then we looked at each other and laughed. We were quiet for long enough that the frogs had started singing.

"Frogs. There must be a pond out there."

"Shhh," I whispered. "I like the frog song."

"Really? Wanna dance, then?"

"Oh, I like it. Our non-wedding song."

"Yeah." He held his left hand up for me to accept as I turned around to face him. "Will you honor me with the first dance?"

"Only if I can have the last one, too."

"That's a promise."

The light of the stars glinted off his dark hair, his face in shadow as I looked up at him and ran my hands around his neck. I gasped as a meteor arced behind Tristan's head. I almost made a wish, like I always have whenever I see a shooting star. I started to out of habit. But just at that moment, I couldn't think of a single thing I wanted that I didn't already have.

epilogue

I watched Tristan stroll into the gas station for a snack. Would I ever get tired of that view? On impulse, I rolled down the window and whistled like a horny construction worker. He stopped, looked over his shoulder and winked.

"Oh, that did it," I laughed. "We're definitely gonna have to make it an early night now."

"Good, my ass is sore."

"Still looks fabulous. Get me some beef jerky."

"And?"

"And a Coke."

He turned fully towards me, one foot on the curb and one hand on the door, poised to enter. "And?"

I knew he was demanding the magic word. Utter bullshit, but he was so cute. "And I'll give you a big kiss when you come back."

He let his head drop in disappointment, but his shoulders shook in a laugh.

"Please," I supplied dutifully.

"I love you, Mekaela," he murmured and went inside.

"I love you, too. And I'll kiss your ass later, if it's sore!" I rolled up the window and settled into my seat, content.

Then my lower back pinched and I shifted to one side.

And my left butt cheek prickled, so I leaned the other way.

"Guess I've been sitting on my ass pretty long, too."

I decided to get out of the car for a minute and let blood flow a little better. We'd already made it over the Florida border, after driving all day. I was pushing to make the entire trip without stopping—everything on the way just looked too boring for a non-honeymoon stop and Savannah would've added an hour to our trip—but Tristan rarely let me take a turn at the wheel.

"I still say we coulda done it," I put both feet on solid earth and stretched like a cat, "if someone wasn't a macho shmuck." I found his gaze through the store window and grinned. He held up a handful of beef jerky sticks and a Coke at the register, fluorescent lights inside glaring against deepening dusk. I blew him a kiss.

Truth was, I loved his macho shmuckery and it *was* a thirteen-hour drive. Wondering at how a person could be so tired, just sitting all day, I turned back to my beloved new car to do some more sitting.

Then frowned.

I'd stuffed my pillow into the crack between my seat and the side of the car, and it had fallen out onto the ground. I guessed stuff must've shifted around in the back or something. I picked it up and dusted it off, sure to position the gas station tainted side away from where my face would lay, then hopped back in and closed the door. The cab felt unnaturally quiet after the buzzing highway sounds outside. My senses were heightened, almost like someone was watching me. Like someone was there with me.

"Hey."

"Oh god!" I clutched at my chest, heart hammering.

Tristan's eyebrows knitted and he pushed a lollypop from one corner of his mouth to the other with his tongue. "Don't worry, they even had Cherry Coke." He handed over the ice-cold, sweating bottle through the driver side window, purple sweetness tainting his lips.

"Thanks. Sorry, you just startled me."

"Didn't think I'd be back?" The jeep rocked with his weight as he got in, set a plastic bag in my lap, and pulled his seat belt across his chest. "So, the guy in there said that there's a really nice Hampton Inn just up the road. Like twenty minutes."

I attacked the loot like a raccoon. No, a bear. A black bear. I let the memory of our camping trip trickle through me and peeled open my meal. "Well, someplace with room service would be better. I'm starving."

"He said you can get awesome pizza delivered."

"Exactly what I meant, of course."

Tristan rested a hand on my thigh as he maneuvered through the parking lot, breeze from his open window ruffling his hair. "That's my girl."

I snorted. "Princess."

"Exactly what I meant." The air stilled at a stop sign and he leaned over with his eyes half-mast. "Hey, what happened to that kiss?"

♣

There it was. Hair. Blonde. A blonde fucking braid. I glared into the back of the jeep in disbelief.

"What the hell are *you* doing here?"

I grabbed the braid and pulled.

"Ow!"

"Get out of my car, you little demon."

"Let go of my hair," came a whine, muffled under cardboard moving boxes.

"Out! Now!"

"I can't crawl out if you don't let go of my hair."

That made sense.

I flung the braid and stood back, hands on hips. To my utter horror, Zach's girlfriend April came worming out. I shook my head and watched, as boxes and clothes shifted and swayed on top of her. She probably could've used some help but I wasn't about to offer any.

"I knew I smelled some kind of crappy fruity shampoo," I muttered. It had been an annoying itch at the back of my mind, barely there but now crystallized in front of me.

April at least looked ashamed, as she set her sneakers on the pavement and straightened to stand. "I'm sorry. I just knew you'd never go for it."

"Go for what? Aiding a minor in running away from home? No, I wouldn't have gone for that."

Her eyes went round and she spread her fingers wide, "No, no, no." Her hands fluttered in a panic and she looked around, blinking under the harsh lights in the Hampton Inn parking lot. "I'm not running away, I swear."

"What, then?" A glance in the direction of the hotel lobby showed no sign of Tristan yet. I'd had enough of my family embarrassing me for a lifetime. Zach was going to pay. "You better explain before Tristan gets back."

She folded her arms over her chest and turned her face away, chin jutted in defiance.

"Okay, then." I stalked to the front of the car. "Not that I can't understand wanting to get out of Shirley, but not like this, honey."

April tripped over my heels. "That's not what this is about, I swear."

"Oh yeah?" I grabbed my cellphone off of the console. "I'm calling your parents. What's your number?"

She scowled at me, indignant. "I'm not giving you their number."

"Fine. I'll call Zach. He'll come pick your ass up right now. I don't care if he has to drive all night."

"That won't work either." Her pout turned into a smirk.

I narrowed my eyes and punched in my cousin's number. "The hell it won't." I put the phone to my ear and glared at her.

A mean smile spread across her features when the tinny sound of a cellphone ring erupted from her back pocket. She held up Zach's phone and tipped it side to side. "If I don't get to Zach within the next twenty-four hours, he's dead."

Blood drained from my face when I recognized the emotion behind April's mask of pretended indifference. Fear.

from the author

Want to know more about what Zach and April are up to? The two of them star in my flash fiction serial, Gaslight. Read the story on my blog for free at http://sarahwathen.com/gaslight/ and look for the graphic novel in 2017!

While you're there, check out my contact page for links to all my social media outlets. I love connecting with readers!

Read on, for a Gaslight excerpt...

gaslight

April sucked in her breath as a hand slipped around her belly under the covers. She felt his nose between her shoulder blades, hot breath seeping through her cotton nightgown. So his head was under the blanket, thank god. Whoever he was…

Light burst crimson across her eyelids. Kitchen smells and lived-in aftershave wafted into her bedroom on a gentle hallway breeze. She heard her father's impatient sigh, felt his gaze on her like a slap. She held her breath to keep from heaving, but there was nothing she could do about her racing pulse.

Please just go. Nothing to see here, Dad. Just g—

She felt a stiffness poking into the back of her thigh, and the warm body spooned around her went to stone.

"April?" her dad whispered.

Corpses never laid so still.

Until a thumb stroked the skin around her bellybutton. And stone melted by degrees. April's heart was a jack hammer—there was no way her dad couldn't hear it. A feather caress against her back.

Curls.

A calf hooked around her foot.

He's tall.

"Damn brats." Dad's voice was already trailing down the hallway. "Gotta get up at freakin' six-o'clock…"

A hand brushed past her breast and up to her face, a tender stroke on her cheek.

Zach. My god, it's Zach.

If she just turned her head a fraction, her lips would touch his thumb.

"Zaaaaach…" came her brother's whisper from the window, a sound she relished and abhorred. "Come on, dude. Let's go."

Bedsprings creaked and her body fell back against the sudden declivity behind her. Then the mattress sprung flat again as Zach's body left hers.

"Alright, I'm coming," he whispered to the open air outside. April lay like a dead fish as lips pressed against her cheek. "Bye."

www.ingramcontent.com/pod-product-compliance
Lightning Source LLC
Chambersburg PA
CBHW072131250626
47159CB00007B/2647